A TALE OF THREE CITIES

Elana Gomel

A TALE OF THREE CITIES

Elana Gomel

PROLOGUE

The sky is starless, but they are sitting in a pool of pale, anemic light. From the porch she can see the garden where jagged branches like spikes of barbed wire jut into the dead air, black on black. There is a pitcher and two glasses on the table but when she tries to pour some lemonade the liquid runs heavy and viscous. A song is playing somewhere in the depths of the house, a scratchy, tinny sound: "Dark summer days/sweet summer nights."

Her companion smiles at her with the right side of his face. The left corner of his mouth where flesh still clings to the bone curves down in disapproval.

She stares at her hands. They are marble white, the skin taut like virgin paper. Touching her cheek, she slides her fingers toward the place where she thinks her mouth should be.

The voice keeps repeating the same phrase and she thinks: **The needle is in the groove.**

What is a needle? What is a groove?

She drops her hand, not having found anything.

Her companion stirs by her side, and the pale light flares in the sky, and a wave of emotion surges through her. She cannot give it a name.

"*There are no nights anymore,*" he says.

But there will be, she thinks.

The song sputters into discordant notes and she wills it to continue but it does not.

Not yet.

Another flare in the sky and she thinks: **The sea is coming.**

"*It won't reach us here,*" he says, *and she suddenly knows the name of the emotion that pours into her emptiness like water into a broken cup.*

Hatred.

"*Sweet summer days/dark summer nights,*" *the song erupts again, the scratchy baritone defying the silence.*

It is a gramophone, *she realizes.* **It is a needle in the groove.**

It has started again.

"*These are the people,*" *says her companion, and beyond the tangle of the dead garden she glimpses a dusty road and people walking by: women carrying bundles and silent babies; men, their shoulders bent, and their faces hidden, balancing flotsam of lost lives on their backs; ragged children; cripples in carts pushed by other cripples.*

There cannot be any people! Where did they come from?

The people are not alone. There is a skulking fox creeping in the wake of the procession, and a wounded hare, leaping behind, and an asthmatic bobcat, its torn hide dripping dark blood into the dust.

No!

"*Not many,*" *says her companion.* "*Not many at all. But enough. Perhaps.*"

Where are they going?

"*There is a City,*" he says. "*If they reach it, they will be safe.*"

They will never be safe, *she thinks*, **they will never be safe from me**.

PART ONE

THE SLAUGHTERED ONES

CHAPTER 1. THE BODY ON THE HILL

The phone call came close to midnight. Mara Raven was awake. She seldom went to bed before dawn, preferring to wander around her large, empty apartment, hoping against hope to hear a knock at the door and see Ronald standing there. In the year since her husband went missing, she had become an insomniac. It was beginning to interfere with her dreamfishing.

The harsh ringing of the phone yanked her from her reverie.

She knew who was calling, of course. Her mentor. Her benefactor. Her only friend. Which was the reason she stared at the shrilling apparatus with a mixture of apprehension and reluctance. But there was no avoiding Mr. Seal when he wanted Mara. She grasped the handset, accidentally knocking the ornate bronze machine off its stand.

It clattered to the ground and went silent. Cursing, Mara put it back and replaced the handset. Since Mr. Seal had installed this newfangled device in her apartment, she had used it only twice, and always for communication with him. Mara was a loner by nature, and it was not easy being a loner in a City that was bursting at the seams as the growing population huddled together, close to the Temple of the Ancestors, for companionship and protection.

The phone squealed again. Mara picked up the handset and spoke into it.

"Good evening, Mr. Seal."

"I'm sorry to disturb you so late, Mara." His soft voice poured like soothing oil over her irritation.

"What is it this time?"

"Murder, of course."

Of course. He would not waste her Power on anything less than that.

"But the chief constable said he did not want me to consult on violent crimes anymore."

Mara was not privy to the endless jockeying for positions in the Temple and the Animal House, though, unlike most people in First City, she was insulated from the fallout of power shifts by her husband's money. But she knew that the chief constable was less than enthusiastic about employing a woman.

"We have a new chief constable."

"Really?"

Another shake-up in the Animal House? Well, if it allowed her to do what she wanted to do, which was dreamfishing, she was on board with it.

"What's the new constable's name?" she asked.

"Adrian Jay-Mole."

Despite the seriousness of the situation, Mara snickered. Double names, indicating two totems, were uncommon and either a mark of distinction or a vulgar heresy, depending on who you asked.

"That's some combination!"

"Sky and earth; good for a constabulary man, don't you think? Anyway, he is more ... open-minded than his predecessor. And this is a shocking case!"

"Who is the victim?"

"A woman."

A domestic? Mara hoped it did not have an obvious solution. Complicated cases allowed her to dive deeper into the dream-sea. Except, of course, the one complicated case that she needed to solve above all else and that the dream-sea refused to help her with. Her husband's disappearance.

"There are some unusual features," Mr. Seal said, as if reading her mind. "The body is outside, for one. Close to the Temple."

That was interesting. Most bodies discovered in the streets were likely to be thrown off the vertical slums of the Lonelyhearts district, where constables seldom went. The Temple precinct, on the other hand, was regularly patrolled.

"On the Hill?"

"Yes."

The Hill was the only elevation on the endless Plains of the North Continent. It was so steep that pilgrims used to huff and puff on the climb, trying to get to the Temple and pay obeisance to the Ancestors. Nowadays, with cars, it was easier to do, but cars were expensive, and few people owned one. Mara could afford a private car if she wanted to, but it never crossed her mind. After graduating from high school, she had never gone to the Temple either. Mara considered herself an unbeliever. A Humanist.

"I am sending a car for you," Mr. Seal said. "How quickly can you get ready?"

"I am decent," Mara said. "Except the makeup, of course, but this is optional, isn't it?"

"Mara, my dear ..."

"All right," Mara said. "Ten minutes."

"Of course."

Ten minutes later, Mara was putting on her deerskin moccasins in the hallway when she heard the concierge's heavy tread on the stairs. In this short time, she had managed to pin up her ash-blond hair, apply a layer of foundation to her pale skin, and add some lipstick. She glanced at the picture of Ronald to see if he approved.

During their brief marriage, he had often asked her to wear makeup because all the ladies of his social circle did. Mara hated doing it but complied, as she complied with everything else the love of her life had asked of her. She did try to explain to him her objections.

"They say we need to cover up our naked skin because it is an affront to our totems, our animal Ancestors, right?"

"That's what the Guardians say."

"But it makes no sense. The Ancestors are a metaphor. A story. A legend."

"I know you think so, sweetie, but a lot of people believe otherwise. What's the point of offending them?"

"But both men and women are supposed to cover their naked faces but actually, only women wear makeup. How is it fair?"

"Men paint Ancestors' sigils on their faces."

"When was the last time you saw one? Nobody does it anymore."

"Social rules are important, Mara."

Mara wrenched her mind away from replaying a conversation with her husband. No matter how much she yearned to hear his voice echo in her memory, she had to focus on the here and now.

The concierge knocked on the door. Mara's apartment building was located in the most exclusive area of First City. The concierge was supposed to keep away suburban riffraff who would try to grab at least one night in the City center by bedding down in accessible doorways. In practice, she was a gossipy and harmless older woman whose totem of the Squirrel made her better suited for finding bargains in the market than for guard duty.

Mara opened the door and saw Betty Squirrel in the company of a slim, dark-haired young man.

"Detective Hart at your service, ma'am," he said. "The car is outside."

As Mara stepped out, he flinched away from her. Really? She had no interest in men other than Ronald, but she knew she was attractive. Then she realized that he was looking at her moccasins and remembered his name. *Hart* meant that his totem was Deer, and her shoes were made of deerskin, which he would be forbidden to touch.

Mara's lips curled in disgust. Being a Humanist, she despised believers who accepted the *Book of the Remnant* as the literal truth. She had never read it from beginning to end, skipping the obligatory religious classes in school, but she knew it was nonsense. During the Dark Years, long before she was born, religious wars had almost torn First City apart. Only when the depleted population realized they had nowhere else to go was the civil order restored, and the slow process of secularization began. The story told in the *Book of the Remnant* was so convoluted and unbelievable that only idiots could take it seriously. The Rebellion that supposedly separated humanity from its benevolent animal Ancestors; the permanently shut gate to the Ancestors' Abode; and the Slaughtered Ones, victims of humanity's wickedness! Preposterous!

It was raining again. It had been raining for the last twenty days. Rain in the First City came in many forms: hard icy curtain rods descending from the flat sky and relentlessly beating the exhausted earth into submission; endless monotonous drops falling from the incontinent clouds; gentle drizzle floating in gray air, so saturated with moisture that it seemed as cozy as a feather pillow; harsh brassy sparkle on the dancing water, when the sun suddenly flashed through the rifts in the piled-up thunderheads. Since the end of summer, the rain had run the gamut of all these and more until tired and dispirited, it settled into the routine of the leaden sky, leaden water, and leaden mood.

The car was at the curb, its engine idling, the chauffeur dozing off. Mara was impressed by the barely leashed strength of the throbbing machine. Technology was power, and unlike her own Power, it was freely available to all—or at least, to all who could pay for it. There were hundreds of cars in First City. As far as Mara knew, she was the only dreamfisher alive today.

The streets of the First City were deserted at this hour, the occasional insomniac's window like a single pip on the black domino tiles of the high-rises. They cut through Victory Boulevard, where the old gas streetlamps surrounded by misty haloes were outshone by the new neon signs. One of them, the image of a Lion selling home insurance, hissed and winked, crippled by the black star of a stone-throw.

The Hill loomed ahead, a darker shadow against the background of the Plains, a crouching shape in the middle of unrelieved flatness, as if the land arched its back, trying to shake off the invading humans.

The car chugged upward. The Temple was hidden by the shoulder of the Hill. The windshield was a blank expanse of wet darkness until they rounded a bend, and she was blinded by electric glare. The car stopped, and they exited. Mara followed Detective Hart on a rain-slicked path that was broken into slivers of light by the high-voltage lamps perched among the tangle of hawthorn bushes in the clearing ahead.

In the clearing, a huddle of figures, all holding umbrellas, stood by a dark shape.

Mara felt a stirring of excitement.

Mr. Seal broke away from the knot of people, his lardy face striped by the chiaroscuro of shadows. He gripped her arm and propelled her toward the body.

The woman was stretched on her back in a puddle of water. She was young, glittering with expensive makeup: crushed sapphire on her eyelids and liquid crimson on her lips, smeared by the rain. Wearing a long leather coat, she was one of the City's pampered elite: devout enough to obey the ritual injunction to hide the shame of her naked human skin under paint; secular enough to dress in animal products. Even though her marriage to

Ronald had made her part of this elite, Mara felt nothing but contempt for them.

A man kneeling by the body got up and brushed his knees.

"Dead at least three hours," he declared. "A single stab wound to the heart. Will tell you more when I get her on the table."

"Is the weapon here?" A voice spoke from the group of constabulary clustered around the body.

"We need a fingertip search. Impossible to say with all that water around."

All that water around? Yes, even with the rain, there is too much water!

As Mara's eyes adjusted to the electric glare, she saw that the bushes fringing the clearing had been beaten into the ground, lying in sodden heaps. The turf was so saturated with water that her feet were sinking into the ground. The woman's hair floated in the puddle that framed her head like a halo. It was as if the endless drizzle of the last week had been concentrated into a single powerful blast of water that had spent itself in this one spot.

"Take her away!" another voice said.

"Wait, please," intervened Mr. Seal. "Mrs. Raven is here. She would like to examine the body *in situ*. It might help her with her research."

Mara, who doubted that *research* was a proper word to describe the exercise of her Power, stepped forward. Conscious of the officers' skeptical gazes, she knelt beside the corpse. She would hardly confess it even to herself, but she was disappointed by how little the body had been changed by death. In her first case, the corpse had been that of a man savagely cut with a butcher's knife, exposing the fascinating landscape of organs, muscle, and bone. But this sodden woman was just that: a sodden woman. She even looked a bit waterlogged as if her flesh had soaked up excessive moisture.

She took the unresisting hand and realized it was noticeably warmer than the surrounding puddle. Mara frowned, looked up, seeking the forensic examiner to ask him about the rate of post-mortem cooling-off.

Her fingers released the woman's wrist—and remained stuck to the body.

The bloated flesh clung to Mara's hand. The corpse's face suddenly puffed up, distorting into a grotesque toadstool. The body swelled like a bladder being pumped with liquid. The buttons of her leather coat popped open, and flesh squeezed through, breasts tearing the underclothes with a smacking sound.

Mara jumped up. She was buffeted by the panicking men, some of whom tried to back off and others crowding close, trying to get a look.

The body shuddered, as if trying to come back to life. But it was only the blind, mindless, ferocious pressure of the flood, seeking an outlet, and eventually, the skin and muscles could take it no more.

The corpse burst with an obscene, wet sound, and a steaming rivulet gushed out from the fissure. A hot stream lapped at Mara's moccasins, soaking them through, and flowed over the already swampy clearing.

"Run!" somebody screamed. Mr. Seal grasped her hand and pulled her along.

People were rushing into the darkness, slipping, falling to their knees, and crawling in the dirty water, grasping at the clumps of grass that were torn out of their hands by the growing flood as it rolled downhill, toward the streets of First City.

CHAPTER 2. THE BOOK OF THE REMNANT

"*And the four of them stood at the gate. And one had stripes like cinders and ashes. And one had a face like a leper. And one had a body that crushed rocks and made the earth bleed as it crawled. And of the last one nothing can be said because its claws tore off the skins of the living and made it a garment thereof.*"

Mrs. Louisa Ferret closed the worn volume. Reading the *Book of the Remnant* sent a shiver down her spine, and yet she could not stop herself from doing it. Not that she had anything better to do on those lonely nights when her memories and the hum of the City outside were her only companions.

She glanced at the two pictures on her dresser. The portrait of her late husband had been done by a self-taught dabbler who had spent his entire stock of craftsmanship on rendering the deceased man's totem—Lizard. In comparison with its lovingly detailed scales, Andrew Lizard's face was a generic blur. Not that Louisa needed the painting; she remembered her late husband very well. He had been a kind and gentle man, and if his wages were not enough to lift them out of suburban poverty, he more than made up for it by being such a good father to their only daughter. Louisa's eyes flickered to the second picture—an expensive silver print done later by the most expensive photographer in First City. Mara's strikingly regular features stood out against the strange background of blurred shadows that was way too artistic for Louisa's taste, her unsmiling lips and her wide eyes confronting her mother with an unspoken and obscure accusation.

Ronald had paid for this portrait, as he had paid for everything else. Louisa sighed. She had been in awe of her rich son-in-law; so much so that she had forgiven Mara for the unusual step of adopting his totem instead of the one she inherited from Louisa. Each citizen in First City owed allegiance to one of the Ancestors, and though lines of descent had become hopelessly tangled, one's family name was an indicator to what totem animal one was supposed to pray, provided one prayed at all. Mara never had. Now Louisa blamed herself for not inculcating faith in her only child. Would it have been better for Mara to have something to fall back on after the mysterious disaster of her husband's going missing? But on the other hand, it was not like Mara was devoid of support. Even if their relationship was not what Louisa hoped for, Mara had Mr. Seal. And she had her Power, even though ...

As usual, when she thought about what Mara called *dream-fishing*, Louisa felt her mind shy away from the abyss of the unknown like a timid little animal flinching away from a fire. No, the *Book of the Remnant* was better, and even if she did not quite understand it herself, there was a panoply of the Guardians at the Temple to explain it all.

She picked it up again, intent on squeezing the last drop of consolation from her flagging belief. She opened it at the beginning and let her eyes follow the groove of the familiar story, even as unwanted questions kept churning in her head.

The Book claimed that once upon a time, humans had lived happily side by side with their animal totems in the Abode of the Ancestors. And then the Rebellion happened, during which the Four leaders of the Ancestors, the Tiger, the Lion, the Seal, and the Bear, were killed. Henceforth they were known as the Slaughtered Ones.

But why? Louisa's lips moved as she whispered the worn-out words to herself, trying to fix them in her mind as the truth and yet hearing the annoying small whisper of doubt.

If humans were so happy, why did they rebel? How was the ancient sin of killing the Four supposed to be expiated, so that humanity could pass through the sealed gate to the Abode and return to their animal bliss? And who was the Revealer, a messenger from the Abode, who would show up to open the gate?

The gate itself was the worst of the enigmas that the Book planted in Louisa's mind as a sort of mental itch, whose scratching only exacerbated her blasphemous doubts. Louisa was a practical person. In the City that its inhabitants could not leave, space was all people could think about. If you were rich, you lived close to the center marked by the Animal House and the Temple, the centers of secular and spiritual power. If you were of "strained circumstances," as Louisa and her husband had been, you found a place in the sprawling suburbia. And if you were poor, you moved to the outskirts where the City met the countryside, there to fall prey to mysterious and disfiguring diseases.

But where was the gate to the Abode of the Ancestors? Louisa had heard in the Temple that the gate was a metaphor for "condition of being." She did not understand it and suspected that the Guardian who preached that sermon did not understand it either.

Louisa closed the book. Better to think of practical matters than torture herself with useless metaphysical speculations! Gate or no gate, neither she nor Mara had to worry about location anymore, thanks to Ronald's generosity. Mara lived in the Ravens' posh apartment close to the Animal House; Louisa's more modest dwelling was still within the best urban zone.

But what would happen if Ronald remained missing?

Fretting was exhausting. Louisa glanced in distaste at the

rain-slicked window. The weather was unbelievable; she could not remember anything like this unceasing downpour in her entire life.

She put the black volume back on her bedside table. Better minds than hers could solve the riddle of First City's history. And perhaps Mara was right, and the *Book of the Remnant* was nothing but a fanciful tale; the totems—mere names that people adopted to designate family relations; the gate a metaphor for death; and the Slaughtered Ones—bugaboos with which the Temple tried to hold on to its vanishing power as people became more secular.

But if so, what was there to keep one from despair? Was that rain plopping on the glass and empty room all there was to life? Was her husband simply gone as if he had never existed? Was the rift between her and her daughter a random misfortune, no more significant than a stubbed toe or a broken finger? Was she, Louisa Ferret, an aging woman, quietly sliding into decrepitude?

Wasn't even the cryptic horror of the *Book of the Remnant* preferable to emptiness?

Louisa turned off the light and told herself she would phone Mara tomorrow.

CHAPTER 3. THE FUR GUARDIAN

"I t's not the first case," said Mr. Seal. "There have been others in which corpses of murder victims exploded or were used as conduits for floods."

He was seated on the sofa, his back ramrod straight. Mara nestled in the armchair close to the fireplace, wrapped in her thickest robe, her hair still wet and her skin tingling after she had scrubbed herself raw in the bathroom. The blinds were down to keep out the grungy light, but she could hear the plopping of raindrops on the pavement.

She wanted another cup of coffee but Mr. Seal, with avuncular sternness, prohibited too much stimulant and forced oversweet cocoa upon her instead.

"Who were the other ones?"

Mr. Seal hesitated.

"Perhaps another time ..." he said. "You're still upset after last night, my dear, and no wonder. I blame myself for bringing you there."

"But ..." Mara started to protest but let it go. There was no use arguing with Mr. Seal when he decided to be protective of her.

They fell silent, Mr. Seal watching her as he always did. He probably thought she was not aware of his constant scrutiny.

"Just tell me where the other cases were," she finally said.

"Lonelyhearts."

Perhaps this was why he did not want to take her there. The Lonelyhearts district was a slum: dilapidated dwellings like swallows' nests haphazardly piled on giant multilevel platforms that had been erected in the vain hope of easing intercity congestion.

Mara rubbed her temples. Mr. Seal's hand hovered in the air as if he wanted to touch her.

"You should go to bed," he insisted.

"No. Not until I can swim."

"Can't you now?"

"No."

"Why not?"

"I don't know. I need something more."

Mr. Seal's hand dropped back in his lap. It occurred to Mara that his hands were quite beautiful. The rest of him filled her with vague unease, though if asked whether he was a handsome man she would probably say yes. He was tall, solidly built, with regular, if bland, features and short, slick hair the color of wet sand. Of course, he was old. Certainly forty, maybe more. She was not sure; had never asked about his age.

His surname indicated an aristocratic origin; only those born within the ring of old mansions surrounding the Animal House had Seal, Lion, or Tiger as their totems. But he never talked about his family, and she never asked. Maintaining a proper distance was important. She was the student; he was the teacher. Both of them preferred it that way.

Her phone rang.

She jumped up and contemplated the machine with awe. The second call in twenty-four hours!

She gingerly lifted the handset.

"It's for you!" she told Mr. Seal.

"For me?"

"Yes. The chief constable."

Mr. Seal took over, leaving Mara to wonder how the chief constable knew where to find him.

Mr. Seal's side of the conversation consisted of polite noises but when he put the handset down there was some color in his sallow cheeks.

"I must go," he said. "The chief constable has a visitor. He wants me to be present at their meeting."

"Who?" Mara asked.

Mr. Seal hesitated.

"The Fur Guardian."

Mara's eyes opened wide. There were three Chief Guardians in the Temple, supposedly overseeing the three orders of totem animals: Fur, Fish, and Fowl. Meeting one of them in person was unheard of for ordinary citizens.

"What does he want?"

"Well, I would say an unnatural flood directed through a corpse so close to the Temple somewhat impinges upon his official duties, don't you think?"

Mr. Seal rarely employed sarcasm in his dealings with her. It ought to have made Mara cringe. Instead, it spurred her into action.

This is what I need!

Where the dream-sea was concerned, she was fearless.

"I'm coming with you," she said. "If the constabulary wants my help, I must be present at every stage of the investigation. You know that dreamfishing is not some stupid clairvoyance. I need hard facts. I never know what will turn out to be the bait."

"But Mara," objected Mr. Seal, "the Guardian may not like it. They denounce all Powers except their own."

"So, tell them I'm your secretary," snapped Mara. "I know the Temple does not like women who refuse to cover their faces with paint or have a career. Well, too bad, but we are living in a new age. Women have rights, we vote, and the Temple cannot tell us what to do! Now give me five minutes to get dressed."

She stormed into her bedroom, slammed the door, and dragged out a theologically acceptable cotton dress and jacket. Despite her outburst, Mara realized it would not be prudent to offend the Fur Guardian by wearing animal fibers. She plastered her face with a heavy dun foundation of the kind favored by old women mumbling prayers to stuffed animals in the dingy temples that smelled of mothballs and incense.

They did not talk during the ride, each of them alone with his or her thoughts inside the boxlike car. Feverish from lack of sleep, Mara felt herself slip into a familiar trough of depression from which only the dream-sea could rescue her. But now, in the everyday dampness of First City, on the rain-glistening street flanked by crumbling brick tenements awaiting the wrecking ball to make room for newer, taller, and equally dingy buildings that would house the burgeoning population, the dream-sea felt unreal. Ronald was gone and he would never come back. And she would never know what happened and would spend her life grieving and slowly succumbing to daily grind, growing old and common like her mother ...

The car rounded the corner, and she was jolted out of her melancholy by the sight of the Animal House and its stone fauna climbing up the walls, clinging to the spouts, crouching on the eaves. A whiff of autumnal rot touched her memory. It had been a wet autumn day when her mother had brought her, a poor suburban girl, into the heart of the City to show her how the rich lived and ruled. And since then, they became inseparable in her memory: the shaggy-dog odor of wet leaves; her mother's then-strong hand in hers; and her own determination to come back one day and never leave.

And here she was.

On top of the six-story gray pile, above the architrave, loomed four huge sculptures representing the four Slaughtered

Ones: the Lion, the Tiger, the Seal, and the Bear. Mara had always been fascinated by these awesome and terrible images but now her eyes were drawn to lesser sculptures: foxes, weasels, deer, and in particular, to the large stone ravens perched on the roof corners. Ronald had been proud of his family name. And she had been so happy to exchange her own plebeian Ferret, which reminded her of her mother, for his aristocratic and rare Raven.

"People used to come here looking for their totems," Mr. Seal said. "There is a belief that every Ancestor whose name exists in the City is represented by a statue on the Animal House. But it's not true, even though its owner wanted to make it true."

"Its owner? The government, you mean?"

"No, the House was built by a private citizen and only later sold to the government. A rich and eccentric merchant. And it's not as old as people believe. Some say it has stood here since the Rebellion but in reality, it's only two hundred years old."

"It's old enough for me," said Mara. "Was this guy mad?"

"No, just devout."

"It's the same thing," said Mara, earning a dirty look from their driver.

Mr. Seal smiled.

The Animal House was the official seat of the secular government of First City. It was surrounded by the sprawl of faceless brick buildings housing the ever-swelling bureaucracy. When Ronald came here on business, he would not take Mara with him, so she was not sure where the headquarters of the constabulary were located.

The cab turned the corner and rolled into a side courtyard, the squat brown buildings of the compound huddling together under the lowering sky. Mr. Seal dismissed the driver, and they walked into a cavernous hall. A constable on duty led them to the second-floor office where the chief constable, a hulking man who looked nothing like either of his totem animals, stood to greet them. The second person in the office remained seated. If it was a person.

Mara tried not to stare. She had never seen any of the three Chief Guardians from close up. As a child, she had been taken to some religious festivals by her parents but since her father's death in a fishing accident, she refused to go. She seldom looked closely, even at minor Guardians who led religious processions in the streets, averting her eyes with a mixture of disdain and fear. But now there was no backing off. The Guardian was so close she could smell the strange musky odor of his mangy pelt.

The Temple surgeons who had transformed the man into a simulacrum of an animal totem were skilled: the scars, if any, were lost in the rugose hanging jowls that framed the shallow muzzle into which his nose and mouth had been fused. His face was free of the brindled fur that covered the rest of his body. The fur looked dirty and unkempt, with balding patches or perhaps areas where the transplant had failed. The brown-and-white matted coat also covered the top of his head. His arthritic fingers ended in dark claws. On the middle finger of the left hand the claw was missing, and the fingertip was raw and sore. Mara risked one glance below the Guardian's waist, saw a pathetic dangling thing that the fur failed to cover, and blushed under her layer of makeup. She noticed that the chief constable had put a carelessly drawn Jay sigil on his face as a conciliatory gesture toward his guest. Mr. Seal had not bothered.

The chief constable motioned them to the stuffed armchairs arranged around a fashionable copper table of the kind used in expensive coffeehouses and advertised as being produced on the South Continent. The Guardian seemed unfazed by this dubious Humanist furniture, lolling in the armchair and sipping—to Mara's surprise and envy—from a tiny coffee cup. Mr. Seal and she were not offered drinks.

The Guardian spoke first. His clipped upper-class accent was more unnerving than the animal growl she half expected.

"We have a serious situation here. So serious that I'm willing to go along with this ... shall we say, unorthodox procedure."

"If I may be so bold to suggest—" began Mr. Seal, only to be interrupted by the chief constable.

"You don't have all the information, Jeremy. Let me bring you up to date."

Mara was surprised to hear her mentor addressed by his first name, so infrequently did he use it. He was always Mr. Seal to her.

"There is a conspiracy in the City. An underground terrorist organization. It is small, we believe, but growing, feeding on popular discontent. I don't need to tell you that there is a lot of grumbling in Lonelyhearts."

"Not unjustified," the Fur Guardian interjected. "Maybe the secular rule is not as good as the City was promised."

The chief constable winced but plowed on.

"This organization killed the woman on the Hill. We have identified her, by the way, as Mrs. Elvira Sparrow, a rich socialite."

"Why?" Mara asked.

"As a sacrifice to open the gate to the Abode of the Ancestors."

"A sacrifice?"

"They call themselves the Army of the Revealer," the chief constable said.

The Revealer! Mara frowned, trying to remember what that meant. Oh yes, wasn't there some nonsense in the *Book of the Remnant* about a messenger from the Abode of the Ancestors who would open the gate to that nonexistent place?

"This organization," the Guardian chimed in, "is as much a menace to the Temple as it is to civil order. They are murderers. Heretics."

Mara's head spun.

"So, what do they want?" she asked, addressing Adrian Jay-

Mole. She sensed that he liked her. She felt a wave of disapproval radiating from Mr. Seal but decided to disregard it. He was the one who always pushed her to develop her Power; so why was he so uneasy now? As for the Fur Guardian, she simply did not know what to make of this silver-tongued man who had mutilated himself to look like an animal. But it was he who replied to her query.

"They want to bring back the Ancestors."

"Isn't this what you want?"

The Fur Guardian bared his pointed teeth in what was intended as a smile.

"I see that we need to do more to improve religious instruction in schools. No, madam. We believe that the Ancestors, our totems whose names we bear and who we worship, will indeed one day Return and take us back to their Abode. One day they shall walk the streets of First City. But before that, the Revealer shall appear and open the gate to the Adobe. It is a blasphemy to try to hasten his arrival. And an even worse blasphemy is to try to open the gate ourselves. And I suspect this is exactly what this conspiracy is trying to achieve."

"I always thought that the gate to the Abode of the Ancestors was a metaphor," Mara said.

"It is not a metaphor," the Fur Guardian said. "It's the barrier that separates us from the Abode of the Ancestors."

Mara felt like she was going insane, as if the Guardian's religious madness was contagious. She could not, would not, accept the *Book of the Remnant* as anything more than a myth!

"Are you saying it's a physical barrier?" she finally asked, trying to keep skepticism out of her voice. "Where is it?"

"Nobody knows," the Fur Guardian replied. "Our world is simple, madam. Two continents, North and South. The human City, the only place where human life and civilization are possible. But Temple teachings tell us that what we see is only a thin layer of appearances over a deeper reality, a disguise, an illusion.

The gate may not be an actual place, but it is an interface between this deeper reality and our world."

"What does it have to do with this secret organization?"

"We rebelled and killed the leaders of the Ancestors, the Slaughtered Ones," the Fur Guardian explained. "The Ancestors expelled us from their Abode and closed the gate. Until the Revealer comes, it should remain closed. But now you have conspirators who are trying to break it down. They claim they are acting for the Revealer, but in fact, they are dangerous heretics."

Jay-Mole intervened.

"It doesn't matter! Do you think the conspirators give a hoot for theology? They are nihilists, pure and simple. Hungry for power. They want the City, and they don't care if they end up with a pile of rubble. We already had the Dark Years when anarchy ruled. We can't go back to that time!"

Mr. Seal, quiet until now, finally entered the conversation.

"Perhaps we should go back to the facts of the situation," he purred. "We have the murdered woman on the Hill. Mrs. Raven can help to apprehend her killer or killers."

"My predecessor tried to explain your abilities," the chief constable said, "but I am not sure I understand. Is it some kind of divination?"

"It is a Power," Mr. Seal said. "The most unusual and potent Power. Mrs. Raven goes into a realm beyond the visible one to find answers to her questions."

For some reason, Mara felt irritated by her mentor's bluster on her behalf.

"It does not always work," she mumbled.

Why was she self-sabotaging? Normally, she was extremely proud of dreamfishing. Beyond her love for Ronald, it was the one thing that gave her life meaning. Her bond with Mr. Seal was based on his trust in her Power and his training in how to use it. But now she felt unsettled. The presence of the Fur Guardian did something to her, though, perversely, she also liked him. If only she could close her eyes, listen to his human voice, blank out the sight of his animal body ... Then, perhaps, she could tell him that while she had confidence in her Power, she also knew how capricious and cruel the dream-sea could be.

"I congratulate you on your modesty, madam," the Fur Guardian said. "Humans are tainted creatures, flawed and imperfect. But if you have the Power to solve this crime, perhaps you're less flawed than the rest of us."

"We believe that finding out the identities of the killers will lead us to the head of the Army of the Revealer," the chief constable said. "To the person who these lunatics believe *is* the Revealer."

Mara blinked. The image of the body discarded on the Hill like so much trash haunted her. That woman, with her expensive makeup, so cruelly mutilated ... What was her name? The chief constable mentioned it. Sparrow? Her totem was a tiny chirpy bird. It did not protect her. Totems never did, and yet people believed in them. Mutilated themselves for their sake like the Fur Guardian had done. Killed for their sake ...

"I will find out who did it," she said. "I will find out who killed Elvira Sparrow."

CHAPTER 4. DREAMFISHING

Mara went through her apartment pulling down the blinds and turning off the electric lights. She held a candle inserted into a red flower-shaped holder, and the warm glow seemed to melt into the flesh of her fingers and run up her arm like a drowsy potion.

When she had discovered her Power at the onset of puberty, she had thought it was a symptom of insanity, and being secretive and proud, she had decided not to tell anybody, to bear her sickness in dignified silence. Fortunately, her father once brought home an old book picked up at a jumble sale. The book described Powers of divination, listing dreamfishing as one of them. It reassured her that she was not alone in her madness, which she had come to cherish already. Not less importantly, it gave her a name for her condition. And once a thing is named, it is tamed, as an old Lonelyhearts' saying went. Still, the name was ironic, considering that it was her father who delighted in fishing, and she was indifferent to it. Fishing was his undoing: His boat overturned, and he drowned, fueling the malicious satisfaction of their devout neighbors who looked askance at the wanton killing of any animal, even as mindless as fish. Mara and her mother had been left alone and impoverished until Mr. Seal appeared, having heard of a teenager who dreamed strange dreams. Then a couple years later, he had introduced her to a young, rich friend, Ronald Raven ...

Mara lay on her bed and stared at the candle until her vision was filled with a swirling storm of glitter, and out of it emerged a swarm of purple and green luminescent rings that swam, wove, and danced around. They were her guides and friends who would open the portals of the dream-sea for her. She called them Light Puppies. A puppy was an old name for a wolf cub, her father had once told her, and for some reason, she liked the sound of it, even though there was no resemblance between a frisky four-legged creature and these phantoms of light.

"Light Puppies, Light Puppies," she whispered, "guide me and preserve me from the creatures of the deep. Help me find the answer."

And as she was drifting away, she kept repeating her query.

Who killed Elvira Sparrow?

The last thing she saw before sleep took her was the dead woman's brightly painted, dead face.

~

She finds herself on the beach, having passed through a confused zone of faint sounds and shadowy images.

The beach is always the same; it is the sea that varies. A wide strip of white sand backed by dark green thorny bushes, the beach is curving away sharply, closed off by piles of black rock, in the fissures of which live large crabs and centipedes.

She thinks that this must be a small island. Sometimes—but not today—there are other islands visible in the distance.

The sea is friendly today, a deep, glassy green glistening like watered silk. The sky is pale gray, shading into whiteness at the horizon. The quality of light hints at early morning or late afternoon, but it does not mean anything. There are no times of day in the dream-sea. There is no sun or moon. It is never totally dark, but she cannot see where the light comes from.

She pauses at the sea margin, letting wavelets lick her toes. The sea is warm. Occasionally she has to dive into icy coldness or boiling heat.

Taking a tentative step, she feels the water caress her feet, reach up with silky tongues, and climb her legs like mercury.

The water reaches her thighs and flows inside. As always, there is a sharp moment of pain, or maybe pleasure. Such distinctions are not for the dream-sea.

She draws the water into her lungs. It tastes of mint.

The visibility is good, but the seabed is empty: just the corrugated white sand and a couple of translucent bottom-feeders with long, coiling antennae. They are always present, occasionally gathering in swarming schools, but they bear no messages for her. Sometimes she wonders if they are meant for other fishers. Are there other fishers? She has never met one.

Something appears ahead, a slim rock, pierced and fretted with holes like stone lace. She swims closer and sees a large blue eye peering at her through one of the holes.

The eye is shaped like a human eye but it is the size of a football.

The creature moves away from the shelter of the rock and faces her. It is a dreamfish, but one unlike any Mara has seen. Its long, sinuous body is scaleless, pinkish, and soft like a baby's bottom. The single eye is set at the end of a weaving stalk anchored in a bulbous protrusion. There is no mouth.

Mara approaches, hoping the fish won't swim away. She needs a bait.

She cannot prepare the bait in advance because she does not know what it is: Part of her mind clacks open like a secret locker and releases the object that will bind a dreamfish to her will. She has no control over her actions, and she never tells Mr. Seal how helpless she really is, how much surrender is involved in her Power.

She swims almost nose-to-nose with the fish and still her hand is empty. The fish waits patiently and then suddenly turns around and streaks away. The eye hoisted on the end of the erect stalk looks back at Mara.

Mara gives chase. The water caresses her body like a silk-gloved hand as she flies over the white-sand bottom. Things are appearing below: scarlet cabbages the size of a house; rocks covered with thick, waving tentacles of lilac and rose; round, dark holes from which eyeless faces with pouting red mouths pop out and disappear. A giant worm, its head a bunch of parrot-colored feathers, rises up in her path like a question mark and subsides again. For a while she swims over a flat patch of brownish tissue that heaves and wrinkles as if in distress.

The fish speeds on and her hands are still empty.

The bottom suddenly falls away. Mara and the fish shoot over the lip of the chasm into an empty space illuminated with a distant glow from the darkness below. There is a scatter of winking golden lights and Mara feels giddy, as if the sea and the sky have flipped around.

Something shifts inside her. The bait materializes in her hand. She feels relief, like expelling a breath held in for too long.

The fish slows down.

Mara brandishes the bait. It is the dead woman's arm in its black leather sleeve, trailing tendrils of dissolving blood.

The fish approaches reluctantly, its flexible body weaving from side to side, its single eye popping, shiny with a mixture of desire and resignation. Mara laughs. She knows that this is the right bait; the ugly creature cannot escape! The fish surges forward. In one desperate blink the eye takes in the bait, swallows it whole, so that it fills the iris and then falls into the black tunnel of the pupil, gradually diminishing as it penetrates the fish's inner core. Mara grabs the fish, squeezes it hard, its body warm like a man's, and the two of them shoot through the aquamarine water and into the milky whiteness above the emerald sea. With one powerful jerk Mara tears the fish apart and a hot fountain of blood bathes her from head to toe.

Her bloodstained fingers close around her clue.

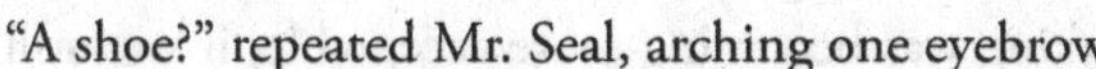

"A shoe?" repeated Mr. Seal, arching one eyebrow.

"Soft leather," mumbled Mara. "Flat sole. Left foot."

She was seated in Mr. Seal's study. She had phoned him in the morning, cranky after four hours of sleep. Her scribbled report was woefully short. He had insisted on seeing her. She was unwilling to let him come to her place and took a cab to his instead. Now he was walking her through the details of the dreamfishing for the second time.

"What footwear did she have?" she asked.

"Mrs. Sparrow? Pumps, I think. High-heeled."

Mara shrugged.

"It'll be relevant," she said. "The dream-sea is never wrong."

"If asked the right question ..." Mr. Seal suggested.

Mara rolled her eyes.

"I did. I asked who killed Elvira Sparrow."

"Perhaps if you were a little bolder in your questioning ..."

Mara pretended she did not hear. Mr. Seal had been dropping hints about her "exercising her Power to the full" for the last couple of months. She did not know what he meant, and more importantly, she did not want to know.

After Ronald's disappearance, she plunged into the dream-sea repeatedly, desperate to find out what had happened to her husband. Every attempt was futile. The last time, Light Puppies barred her way. Somehow, she knew that if she persevered, she could be barred forever. And this could not be allowed to happen. Better losing the love of her life than the dream-sea. The realization made her feel cold and disloyal, but she could not argue with the certainty of her being.

"I need more coffee," she said.

"Mara ..."

"This fishing has taken a lot out of me. I'm hardly awake."

Sighing, Mr. Seal went to the kitchen and cooked a single cup in the prohibitively expensive bronze cezve Mara had bought on the black market, loading it with sugar, which she hated. While coffee-drinking was becoming more acceptable, it was still regarded as an expensive vice, which did not stop the proliferation of coffee shops all around the City and the explosive growth of plantations on the South Continent.

"So you say that the fish looked at you. But you said before that creatures in the dream-sea don't normally react to you unless they attack. Why was this time different?"

"I have no idea. Maybe it recognized me."

"What do you mean?" Mr. Seal asked.

"I don't know." Mara pressed her fists to her aching forehead. "Oh yes, there was something else. I saw lights in the abyss, like the lights of the City seen from the Hill."

Mr. Seal blinked.

"Did you try to get down to it?"

"No!"

The idea frightened her, but she did not know why. Suddenly Mara was seized with an irresistible desire to be alone.

"I have to go," she said. "I'm not feeling well."

Mr. Seal helped her into her raincoat with old-fashioned courtesy. Mara felt guilty about disappointing him and tried to come up with a neutral parting remark: something to defuse the emotional charge that had recently begun to gather around their every discussion of the dream-sea like a premonition of a thunderstorm.

"The Fur Guardian ..." she said.

"What about him?"

"He was such a gentleman."

"He *is* a gentleman. I know him."

"Then why those horrible grafts? I know, this is a stupid question; people who believe in the Ancestors will tell you it's to bring us closer to them, blah-blah. But I mean, if you want to look like a b ... an animal, what's the point of behaving like a human? He doesn't even wear clothes, for crying out loud!"

"Well," Mr. Seal said, "do you know how Guardians are made?"

"Surgery?"

"Tissue grafts. The higher they rise in the Temple hierarchy, the more grafts they accept. They have the best-trained surgeons. It requires great skill to fuse a human body with animal tissue. The Temple surgeons are all Guardians themselves."

"Where is it done?"

"There are special hospitals. In suburbia mostly."

"But what for?"

"Grafts give you Powers. Not like your Power, which is unique, but others. Seeing what is unseen; hearing voices of the past; understanding animals. The devout folk only talk of the Return of the Ancestors, but the Temple hierarchy is trying to make it happen. No matter how much the Fur Guardian denied it, they are looking for a way to open the gate."

CHAPTER 5. BUNNY

Mara decided to walk back home. Pulling her hood over her head, she set off. It was raining, of course; not that she expected anything else. It seemed to have rained nonstop during the thirteen months since Ronald's disappearance. When she looked back at that time it seemed to blur into one dirty gray strip, like those long smudges left on whitewashed asylum walls by dragging hands or drooping heads.

She hoped a walk would calm her but instead, she felt a mounting restlessness as the streets of First City, so familiar they became invisible, slipped by: an endless procession of damp apartment blocks, the newer ones built of mud-colored concrete with ugly raw angles, the older brick ones hunkering down, their rusty balcony grills bared like a skull's smile. The streets were crowded: They always were, except late at night, as humanity tried to fit itself into the bursting-at-the-seams garment of its City. She rubbed shoulders with small-time clerks out to lunch, pale and unhealthy from days spent in dusty municipal offices; with women in shapeless raincoats burdened by shopping bags and children; with schoolboys and schoolgirls in sad, worn uniforms. She cared for none of them and yet she craved their company.

Mara decided to take a new route, realizing that she had always walked the same way home from Mr. Seal's. This was a schoolgirl's habit, and she was not a schoolgirl anymore. She reminded herself that she was almost twenty-two. For some reason, this thought frightened her.

She turned the corner and found herself in the older and more prosperous part of the City, among substantial stone town houses. Many of them were separated from the sidewalk by the pits where stairs led down to the servants' basement. Occasionally a detail would catch her eye: a molded medallion set into the wall with the owner's blurred totem animal; a red door in a water-stained façade; a bow window with a tattered doll propped against the glass. This was the kind of area where Ronald and she might have lived but he had preferred a newer building, even though it was further away from the Animal House. She remembered that his younger brother had a place nearby, but she had not talked to any member of Ronald's family for months. They did not like her, and the feeling was mutual.

In the City, the rich and the poor lived cheek-by-jowl out of necessity. The prosperous area ended abruptly. She went through a maze of rubbish-strewn alleys where leaning wooden-frame houses almost met above her head. Wet laundry, hanging from a rope strung between two balconies in the vain hope of sunlight, slapped her face.

Something nagged at her, a forgotten memory of something important, but she could not grasp what it was. She saw a plaque with the name of the street.

"*The Way of the Four.*"

She stared at it, feeling cold and shivery.

A cab navigated the street, splashing her as it moved through the puddles. Mara knew from history books that before she was born, horses had been the main means of transportation in the

City, as they still were in the farmlands abutting the suburbia. She could hardly imagine it. Horses, like cows and sheep, were not totem animals and so could be worked to death or killed for humanity's benefit. Theoretically, Mara was in favor of this; being a Humanist, she was even in favor of the occasional hunting of deer and foxes, which was where her expensive moccasins and fur coats came from. But the idea of generations of animals routinely sacrificed to move loads of wood or grain from place to place made her queasy. She was glad that human engineering had put an end to this practice or at least removed it from visibility.

She took an alley that she thought would bring her back to the center. A large building across the road drew her attention. It was L-shaped, with stucco walls and a sloping red-tile roof.

The building was abandoned, slowly going to ruin. Some of the windows were broken and piles of garbage rotted in the courtyard. There were few such properties in the City, where prices of real estate went only up. She realized that somehow, she had gotten lost. A headache was slowly building up, as if the sight of the dilapidated building or the entire depressing area were radiating their sickness upon her.

She kept on walking until she came upon a tiny park, one of those misbegotten places that the Animal House had stuck throughout the City in an effort to demonstrate to the taxpayers that it was making good use of their money. It was hardly more than a mound of rotting grass crowned with a plaster statue of the Bear and surrounded by benches.

Mara sat, breathing deep, trying to expel the hard nugget of pain lodged between her brows.

Somebody was staring at her; she could feel it. She looked up: There was a man on the bench opposite.

He got up, walked around the mound, and sat beside her, prompting her to shrink away.

"Sorry," he said. His vowels were broad and slurred. "I could not help noticing you. I know everyone who comes here and it's nice to see a new face."

He was old enough to be reassuring, with a long face, elaborately folded and creased as if life had treated him like a piece of origami. His clothes were shabby but carefully mended.

He was poor like Mara had been. It made her feel ashamed of her first reaction of fear and distrust.

"I'm lost," she said. "I'm not sure where I am. I wanted to take a walk but somehow, I wandered off and found myself here."

"The City has led you here for a reason. You'll find out why."

"What do you mean?"

"The City knows what it does," the man said. "I've never set foot outside. People go to the countryside, but the City was good enough for the Ancestors and it's good enough for me. And as for the South Continent ... forget it. What is there? Dust, sand, emptiness."

"They say there are marvelous things there," objected Mara. "Beautiful beaches, rocky deserts. This is where coffee comes from."

"But no people," said the man. "What's the use of so much land if there are no people?"

"I heard talk about founding a permanent settlement there."

The man laughed.

"What else will they come up with? People cannot live outside the City, every child knows it! I'm George Hare, by the way. Friends call me Bunny."

"Mara Raven," said Mara, shaking hands. Bunny's fingers were calloused.

"Beautiful name. As beautiful as its owner. Hope you don't mind my saying so, miss. I have a daughter your age."

"What does she do?"

"Works in a sewing factory. She and her fellow are putting money aside to buy a house when they get married. I also have a son, a bit older."

"And your wife?"

"She's dead. Has been dead for seven years. It's only Jamie, and Jenny and me now."

They sat for a while in companionable silence. Mara was beginning to relax. She realized that she had been starving for human interaction. Apart from Mr. Seal, whom had she seen in the last week? She had few friends, and none close. And she had not spoken to her mother in ages. Mara felt a prick of guilt.

"I worked my whole life as a mechanic," said Bunny. "Hard work, especially when they started coming up with those newfangled inventions: motorcars, wireless radios, chill-boxes ... I kept up with the times, didn't go under like many of my buddies. Built a nice house, had a nice family. But Bella is dead, Jenny's leaving ... And I ask myself: What is it all for?"

Mara looked at him sharply.

"What do you mean?" she asked. "You said yourself: You had a good life. Isn't it enough?"

"It's not enough for a man," he said, emphasizing his words by stabbing the air with his finger. "Work, and work, and then you drop dead. There's got to be something else. Take the City; why would it be here, if it wasn't built for us?"

"The City is here because men have built it."

"Men?" Bunny's eyebrows shot up, almost disappearing in the complex arrangements of skinfolds on his balding forehead. "No, miss, men could not have built it. Look how it leads you, how it protects you, how ... how it talks to you."

"Talks?"

"Sure. Sometimes I lie at night and hear the hum of the City and then I feel like they're talking to me."

"Who are they?" asked Mara, irritated at the turn of the conversation, her mellow mood gone.

"Who? Well, the Temple people would say the Ancestors. I have never been much of a Temple man myself. When I was young, we used to go to those Workers' Debate Societies. You probably never heard of them."

"Yes, I did. Charles Finch used to lecture there."

Charles Finch was a famous scholar of the previous generation and Mara's personal hero. Unfortunately, he never mentioned the dream-sea in his controversial books and articles.

"Can't say I remember him. Anyhow, we used to be pretty freethinking and freespeaking in those times. There were some who said the Ancestors were just a legend."

"Aren't they?"

"No. Perhaps those Temple people go too far; I can't say I approve of all this Guardian stuff. They don't look like Ancestors to me; just freaks if you pardon the expression. But I know the Ancestors are for real."

"How can you know such a thing?" Mara exclaimed, trying to tamp down her unreasonable anger.

He is an old guy, uneducated and poor.

He is a fanatic. That conspiracy the Fur Guardian talked about ... the Army of the Revealer ... what if he is part of it?

Conspiracy of faith.

"I told you; they're talking to me," Bunny went on, oblivious of Mara's reaction. "Not what you'd call real talk but ... Calling, more like it. And it's not just me; a lot of people have heard it. Look, I'll show you something."

Gingerly, Bunny unbuttoned his coat and drew out a rag-wrapped bundle. He shook it out. Inside was what appeared to be a doll. But when he offered it to Mara, she saw that it was made of brown plush and represented an animal, even though it was upright, with straight arms and legs like a man. Its flat face was covered by a flap of gauze. When she lifted it, she saw that the face was made of lighter fabric and decorated with two black button eyes and an embroidered, smiling mouth.

"Good, isn't it?" said Bunny, misunderstanding Mara's disgusted expression. "My Jenny made it for me. She's good with the needle. But I had to explain it to her many times until she got it right. Some of the women in her factory saw it and are making one for themselves."

"What is it?" asked Mara. "It has a veil like the Bear. But ..."

"It *is* the Bear. A real one. Look at that thing." Bunny gestured toward the white, hulking bulk of the Bear statue that decorated the park. With its humped back, powerful shoulders, huge claws, and veiled countenance, the statue was meant to convey a sense of power and menace. "How can it be one of the Slaughtered Ones? They're good to us. They love us."

"Really?" Mara asked. "After what we did to them?"

"They've forgiven us," said Bunny with conviction. "We're their children. You ask any parent: Won't you forgive your child even if he turns obstreperous? Many a time my Jenny was insubordinate, rude even, and so what? I don't love her any less. And Jamie too."

The pinprick of guilt Mara had felt at the realization that she had neglected her mother grew into actual pain, blending with her burgeoning headache. There had always been something off between her mother, Louisa Ferret, and herself. The problem was that she could never attribute this sense of wrongness to any actual misdeeds on her mother's part. It was as if there was some shadow between them, and neither knew what it was.

But Mara prided herself on being conscientious—a substitute for being good. She did not believe herself to be a good person. Different from everybody she knew, she sometimes suspected that the name for this difference was *evil*.

I cannot control my being. But I can control my actions.

She would give her mother a call as soon as she got back home.

Meanwhile, Bunny wrapped the small Bear in the rag and tenderly replaced it under the coat.

The Four Slaughtered Ones, the Seal, the Lion, the Tiger, and the Bear, were the leaders of the totemic Ancestors. During the human Rebellion that led to the expulsion from the Abode of the Ancestors, they were killed. Nevertheless, they were still worshipped, in some reincarnated form perhaps, though Mara had no desire to delve deep into the theology of their dubious existence. She knew that of the Four, the Bear was considered to be the most mysterious, powerful, and in some undefined way, dangerous. That was why its face was covered with the veil. People regarded the Bear with awe, and nobody had it as their totem. Bunny making the Bear into a cuddly, benevolent toy struck her as dangerously misguided.

"I have to go," she said, standing. "Thanks for your company."

Bunny beamed at her.

"My pleasure. Why don't you come here again? It's a nice, quiet place. I'm here every day."

"Perhaps," Mara said with no intention of doing so. She turned to walk away but then remembered something.

"Do you know," she asked, "what that building is? The big one with the red roof?"

"That?" said Bunny. "That's an old hospital. I forgot how it's called. But it's empty now."

"What kind of hospital?"

"I don't know. It belonged to the Temple. In the old times, there were always Guardians in the courtyard. We kids used to go there and gawk at them."

She walked home, feeling her muscles sing with a surge of energy. It was a good feeling, and her headache faded. But the elation of physical activity dissipated when she entered her apartment: dark, silent, and cavernous like any place left on its own for too long.

After Ronald's disappearance, she had resisted when her mother suggested she should stay with her for a while. Mara had stood her ground and won her right to the echoing silence, to the clothes strewn on the floor, and books left open on the kitchen table. Even her friends, such as they were, seldom set foot in Mrs. Raven's expensive apartment, left in her possession after the disappearance of her husband. That was the only thing she knew with certainty was hers.

For her daily expenses, she drew from the bank account set up for her allowance. Everything else she left with the family's solicitors, who were not inclined to consult her. She had asked Mr. Seal's opinion about the disposition of Ronald's fortune, but he was confident that Ronald was alive and that a reunion was imminent.

He's more optimistic than me.

Her depression eluded her analysis like a ball of mercury. Yes, her husband was missing but he had been missing for the last thirteen months. She was young, attractive, and independent. And most importantly, she had the dream-sea. She repeated it to herself as a litany: She had the dream-sea.

But what if the dream-sea refused to have her?

She felt a moment of panic and almost ran into the bedroom to throw herself into the bed, call upon the Light Puppies ...

Mara forced herself to breathe. Mr. Seal had taught her proper discipline. She could not go into the dream-sea every night, uncontrollably, the way she had as a teenager. It would drive her mad.

What if I'm already mad? What if I have always been mad?

She realized she was hungry. Ronald and she had employed a cook, but she fired her when it became clear the master was not coming home anytime soon.

Mara walked through the dining room into the kitchen. The polished oak of the table reflected the crystal and bronze of the chandelier; the gold-framed portraits of Ronald's family looked at her accusingly, each topped with a gilded effigy of a raven. She liked none of the furnishings but was not sufficiently motivated to redecorate the apartment to her own taste.

The ultramodern kitchen was better. Mara regarded the chill-box with satisfaction: It was her choice, purchased at her insistence (though Ronald had been eager to comply, believing his wife was finally taking interest in housekeeping). But it was the technology that fascinated her. She loved the chrome fittings and the bracing breath of cold in her face.

Inside the box was only some wilted lettuce and a piece of dispirited blue cheese. At least she had coffee. Even though it was prohibitively expensive, Ronald had kept a decent supply at home and she had quickly become addicted. Coffee was imported from the South Continent and, in addition to its other virtues, had an aura of the forbidden because it was cultivated by indentured workers living far from the City. To Mara's mind, it indicated that the idea that humans *had* to live in the City was superstitious nonsense.

Mara cooked her thick, gritty coffee on the gas stove in the kitchen. Bearing the coffee cup on a tray, Mara went back into the living room, picking up a book from the floor where it lay like a squashed multi-winged moth. It was an old romance given to her by Mr. Seal. She was not sure why he wanted her to read this trash. Starting at random, she found the hero riding on some parlous errand. The language was stilted. This was one of those books written half a century ago when the Dark Years had suddenly become fashionable. The prosperous society titillated itself with tales of mighty heroes and doomed lovers set in the time of pestilence and anarchy. In these tales, as opposed to the dismal historical reality of rack and ruin, the Dark Years' City was decked out with fanciful towers and splendid temples. Even the Plains were represented as a playground of adventure rather than the featureless wasteland that they were in reality.

Mara wrinkled her nose at the book's improbabilities and scoffed at its monarchic sentiment. In the checkered history of First City, periods of more or less constitutional monarchy, in which the rulers were appointed by the three Supreme Guardians, were interspersed with intervals of anarchy, leading all the way back to the mythical Rebellion. The opponents of the present system, in which James Otter had been elected the first-ever president and the monarchy had been officially abolished, liked to argue that the City was heading toward another breakdown. Mara believed that the victory of democracy was irrevocable. But what if the doomsayers were right?

Mara's eyes followed the lines on the page as the protagonist and his love interest met in a carefully tended park, which, she was pretty sure, did not exist in the ruined City of the Dark Years. But there were parks now, and her mind wandered back to the moment, three years ago, when she and Mr. Seal walked under the spring-blooming trees along the Bird River, and Mr. Seal stopped when a man walked toward them and said: "Fancy meeting you here! Mara, let me introduce you to a friend of mine, Ronald Raven. Ronald, this is Mara, my student."

The day was a kaleidoscope of vivid colors in her memory: the gold and azure of the sunny sky; the pink of cherry blossoms; the emerald glow of new leaves. Had there ever been another spring like that in the City? Sunlight fell across Ronald's face in a broad band. She remembered thinking how handsome he was. She had never had a boyfriend before Ronald, though it was not for lack of male attention. Her beauty, which she coldly acknowledged, seemed an imposition, as if it belonged to somebody else. But now, for once, she was glad of her porcelain skin and blue-green-gray eyes whose color shifted with her mood. Even her thick ash-blond hair, which some people mistook for premature gray, shone like silver in the spring sunlight. Wasn't it as romantic a meeting as anything in this stupid book?

Instead of answering her own question, she threw the book against the wall and went back to the kitchen for more coffee. She did not want to think about Ronald now. Thirteen months of obsession were enough. She needed a respite.

The book snapped shut; the next chapter titled "The Tale of the Four" disappearing from view.

CHAPTER 6. EDNA LYNX

Mirrors and crystal chandeliers and dark wood and wherever Mara looked, she could see her reflections multiplying into infinity, the dove-gray flow of her long dress bracketed by the black silhouettes of her companions. In evening clothes, Detective Hart looked dashing and Mr. Seal looked paternal and the other patrons of the Waterlily restaurant, mostly couples, must have wondered about the configuration of their relationship.

That Mr. Seal had arranged for a meatless restaurant was understandable in view of the current climate of opinion. But the Waterlily served dairy, and when Mara ordered fried goat cheese, she caught Detective Hart's grimace. She liked him less as her attraction to him grew. She had been in Mr. Seal's sexless company for too long; the mere presence of a good-looking young man with dark hair, blue eyes, and a dazzling smile sent her pulse racing. But she found his manner arrogant and his fastidiousness ridiculous.

"So what do you have on Mrs. Sparrow?" Mara asked, stubbornly returning to the case after the conversation had wandered from the unheard-of bad weather to the president's possible resignation in the wake of the latest setback in the Animal House. She felt that Detective Hart was not taking her seriously.

"Elvira Sparrow," said Hart with a shrug. "Thirty years old. Married Julian Sparrow, a wealthy banker-merchant who was twelve years her senior, when she was twenty. No children. All the usual: charities, expensive shopping, wild parties, a string of lovers. The husband seems to be upset, though. Perhaps he thinks it's bad publicity to have his wife murdered. Rather tabloid stuff."

"What was she doing on the Hill in the middle of the night?"

"Went to meet another lover, I suppose."

"Do you know who he is?"

Hart sighed.

"Look, Mrs. Raven, we treat this as a terrorist attack. Terrorists don't handpick their victims. We don't have the time to go through Elvira Sparrow's extensive list of affairs."

"Aren't you too hard on her?" Mara asked. "She's been murdered and mutilated. You can't have it both ways: to call her an accidental victim and to come down on her lifestyle!"

An uncomfortable pause ensued, broken by Mr. Seal.

"I agree," he said. "We cannot blame the poor woman. But Detective Hart is right too, Mara. We have to focus on the broader picture."

"As far as I can see," Mara said, "the broader picture consists in the fact that some people are so sick they want again to be servants of the beasts."

She tried to make Hart angry by uttering the b-word but succeeded only in making him look disgusted.

"Not all worship of the Ancestors leads to terrorism," he said. "We owe them a debt of gratitude."

"Do we?" persevered Mara, emboldened by the growing wine-buzz in her head. "What was the Rebellion supposed to be about if not human emancipation? I don't believe in the *Book of the Remnant* anyway. But if it's true, why would anybody want to go back to the time when humans were enslaved by animals?"

"It's a distortion of theology ..." Hart began, but Mr. Seal, his eyes darting from his face to Mara's and back again, intervened.

"The Army of the Revealer claims that when we lived in the Abode of the Ancestors, we were not slaves but happy and innocent children of our totems."

"Why do they call themselves the Army of the Revealer?" Mara asked. "Who is this Revealer, anyway?"

"This is to indicate their belief that the Revealer will come soon and our sin against the Four Slaughtered Ones will be forgiven," Mr. Seal explained.

Mara shrugged. The Army? The Dark Years had lots of self-styled armies killing each other over a trashy alley or an empty barn as they fought to gain control of First City. Surely, no more armies were wanted or needed! And as for the Revealer—whoever this mythical figure was supposed to be—Mara could not understand why he was needed to expiate the supposed sin of the death of the Four. Even if humanity had killed its benefactors millennia ago, so what? How could you feel guilty about something that happened in the past and in which you had no part?

"Even in the *Book of the Remnant*, the Bear, the Tiger, the Lion, and the Seal are not portrayed as sympathetic characters," she said. "And if these people are trying to open the gate, they are insane. It was locked for a reason."

She was mortified to realize that she had acknowledged the veracity of the *Book of the Remnant*, which she believed was no more than a collection of bad poetry and dark fairy tales to scare children with.

"They want to break out of the City," Mr. Seal said. "It is ... cramped."

"The City is enough for me," Mara responded. "I don't want the nightmares that lie beyond."

"Nightmares, or dreams," Mr. Seal replied.

Was he about to discuss dreamfishing in the presence of Detective Hart? Mara would never forgive him if he did. She was proud of her Power but also ashamed of it. Dreamfishing was private and intimate, not to be flaunted to a supercilious stranger.

Fortunately, Mr. Seal seemed to have read her mind because he deftly shifted the conversation back to politics. But it did not help to restore the friendly atmosphere. Mara felt that Hart was arrogant and prejudiced, while he undoubtedly felt that she was abrasive, not to mention too much of a Humanist. Flushed but not tipsy anymore, she fell into sulky silence and was relieved when they finished dessert and rose to leave. Mr. Seal offered to accompany her home, but she insisted on taking a cab alone. Prompted by an obscure impulse, she told the driver to drop her off by the Animal House. It was not raining for a change. She stood looking up at the tense, dark shape looming in the burnt-orange sky, a bunch of stone muscles, as if all the separate carved animals melted into one giant, misshapen body without head or limbs. There were few lights in the windows: The House clerks and officials had mostly gone home.

Skirting the overflowing puddles, she walked down the empty street. Undefined sadness pressed upon her, a feeling of impending doom and of inchoate guilt, as if she had failed somebody and could not remember who.

Or perhaps it was simpler than she pretended it to be. Ronald was still missing. Mr. Seal insisted that her Power could find him. She knew it could not; that for some reason, the dream-sea would not allow her to ask personal questions or she would be barred from it forever. She could go dreamfishing for the name of Elvira Sparrow's killer but not for the whereabouts of her husband. But Mr. Seal refused to believe it and pressured her to try harder, making her feel guilty and angry; compliant and rebellious by turns. Now rebelliousness seemed to be on the ascendant, eating into the link between her mentor and herself like slow acid.

Mara lifted her face, and a gust of wind threw rain into her eyes. Through the blur of water, she could make out the platforms of Lonelyhearts like tremendous kitchen shelves, each level heaped with what appeared to be broken crockery but was in fact wooden huts and tin shacks climbing over each other and sliding down in a chaos of stench, filth, illegal electric wiring, and cooking fires. Some of those shimmered like glowworms in the dark, almost pretty from a distance. Even though the Animal House and Lonelyhearts were parts of First City and the distance between them could be walked in several hours, they seemed to belong to different worlds.

She rounded the corner and stopped at the open door of a temple spilling amber light onto the pavement. She knew that the temple was there but had never been inside.

She peered in. The interior was lit by heavily scented candles that made her eyes water. There were vases filled with chrysanthemums, asters, and bunches of reeds. Animal paintings and masks hung on the yellow-and-red walls. Most of them seemed to Mara cheap and tawdry as if picked at a flea market. On the altar stood the centerpiece, a stuffed lynx, arching its back. Its glass eyes glinted yellow in the candlelight. The altar was separated from the pews by a carved rail and there was a figure leaning on it. Mara made to leave but the person turned around and Mara saw it was a young girl. Curious, Mara walked forward and stood beside her.

The girl was dressed in a lettuce-green pantsuit. Mara had tried the new fashion of ladies' trousers once, but Ronald had objected, finding it too provocative. She wished he could see how virginal and unattractive—like an ill-fitting armor—the outfit looked on the girl's scrawny figure. Her face was scrubbed and her nose challengingly shiny. It made Mara, who was wearing the bare minimum of makeup, feel a sort of kinship. The girl apparently felt the same way because her eyes lingered on Mara's face.

"I often come here at night," she said, surprising Mara by her cut-glass posh accent. "It's peaceful. I feel I can really communicate with them."

"Them?"

The girl nodded at the stuffed lynx.

"The Ancestors," she said.

"Is it your totem animal?"

"Yes. I am Edna Lynx."

She offered her hand to Mara who shook it lightly. It was clammy like a wilted flower stalk.

"Mara Ferret," she said. She did not know why she used her maiden name, but it was a fortuitous slip because Edna's eyes lit up.

"Ferrets and lynxes are related," she said, "so we are almost like sisters. This is my only totem-temple in the City. Most temples are dedicated to the Slaughtered Ones but it's not fair. All living beings are our Ancestors, all deserve worship."

"True," agreed Mara, not sure whether this was theologically correct but deciding to go along. "But there are so many. I don't even know if there is a totem-temple for Ferret."

"Sure," said Edna. "On Potters' Street, not far from Queensgate."

The more they interacted, the more Mara disliked Edna with her plain face, her upper-class accent, and her unconscious aura of superiority. The Edna Lynxes of the world had made her life miserable during her marriage by their well-bred snubs of Ronald Raven's odd suburban bride. But something kept her talking. Her mind filled with thoughts about the Army of the Revealer, she was curious about the psychology of a privileged young woman spending nights in solitary devotion in a tacky street temple.

Edna seemed to have taken to Mara and was clearly in a conversational mood, prattling on.

"The Temple lackeys would tell you we only have to worship the Bear, the Tiger, the Lion, and the Seal because we are guilty of their murder, but it's not true. The Ancestors love us. They want our love, not our punishment."

"I thought you were devout," Mara said.

"I am. But not in the Temple Way. We have our own group. We are different. We read the *Book of the Remnant* and understand it as it is meant to be understood. We call ourselves the Army of the Revealer."

Mara started.

"What?" Edna turned to her.

"No, nothing. But ... why are you praying, then?"

"We pray to the Ancestors. But they don't need fancy decorations or ugly Guardians. Every patch of grass is their sanctuary."

"Not going to the Temple, then?"

"The Temple sold out. They only want our money. They have distorted the teaching of the Book. Look at how they insist on women wearing makeup! This"—she touched her unadorned face—"is what they condemn because it's naked. But it's natural. We're naked animals, like the Ancestors were furred or feathered. So we're proud of our natural faces. There is no shame in it, no matter what corrupt Temple lackeys say!"

"So, you want to restore the true faith?"

"Yes. And more than that, we want to escape from our prison. To leave behind this packed stinking City. To unlock the gate."

Mara thought furiously.

"I've never been religious," she said. "My family ... well, they're Humanists. Kind of. But ever since my bereavement I felt the need to ... you know, talk to somebody. Try to understand why it happened to me."

"Your bereavement?"

"My husband died a year ago."

She felt a fearful finality as if saying it in this way would sway the balance of uncertainty and make Ronald truly and irrevocably dead.

Edna's eyes glittered.

"Your husband died? I'm so sorry! But you're so young, I wouldn't think you were married."

Mara smiled; she knew that Edna would fall for a sob story. She steered the girl into the pews.

"Let's sit, all right? I've been out on a date, the first time since … My mother's friend arranged it, wanted to introduce me to a 'suitable' young man. I hated it but I could not refuse. It was a disaster, of course. How could I, after Ronald …"

They sat together in the pews, Edna's bony knee almost touching Mara. From close up, she was even less attractive: stringy, mousy hair and small, blinking eyes with sparse lashes.

"How did your husband die?" she asked. "Sorry, maybe I shouldn't have asked …"

"No, it's fine. It's a relief to talk about it. We were married less than a year. A fairy-tale romance, everybody said, and it was …" Mara felt her throat constrict with pain and was pleased with the effect it had on Edna who lapped up every word. "One day Ronald went to the office. Except usually he had a car come up for him but on that day the chauffeur was sick, and Ronald gave him a day off. So he called a cab. The constabulary later interviewed the driver, and he said Ronald had asked to be let off on Victory Boulevard, a couple of blocks away from his office. He wanted to take a walk, he said. Well, he never arrived at the office. His secretary phoned me later, several times, but I was out. I went shopping and then met a friend for lunch and she and I went to the promenade. It was such a beautiful day …"

Edna patted her arm. Mara hoped she did not feel her involuntary twitch.

"Well, I came back home rather late and expected him to be in. He was not, so I called the office and they said he was not in the whole day. So, I called the constabulary."

In fact, she did not. She called Mr. Seal first. He came over and suggested she go into the dream-sea to find out what happened. She tried. The dream-sea spewed her out.

"The constabulary came and interrogated me. I think they suspected I had done away with him somehow and hidden the body in the apartment. They searched everything."

"How awful!" exclaimed Edna.

"He was listed as a missing person. The file was kept open, they said; they 'pursued all lines of inquiry.' But I heard nothing for a long time."

"Did you consult a Temple seer?" Edna asked. "I'm against the Temple officialdom; they are collaborators with the Animal House ... But some of their seers are good."

"No. See, Edna, my husband was against the whole thing."

"Of course, of course. We've been poisoned by lies for so long. My parents keep nagging at me to wear makeup. The Temple is only good for keeping the status quo. And when something terrible strikes, like it struck you, people are left in the lurch. So did you find out what happened to him?"

"Six months ago they found a body floating in the Bird River. It was in the water for so long ... Anyway, I was not allowed to see it and even his brother could not identify him with any certainty. But they found a monogrammed handkerchief in his pocket. I embroidered it myself, a gift for his birthday ... We managed to keep it out of the newspapers and had a quiet funeral."

This was only a little bending of the truth. A body had been found in the river, so bloated that it did not look human anymore (she had insisted on seeing it against the hysterical objections of her mother and had stared at it, unmoved, for a long time). But there had been no handkerchief, nor had she ever held a needle in her hand except to use as a toothpick. Ronald was still officially listed as a missing person.

"You poor thing!" exclaimed Edna. Mara sighed.

"So you see," she said in a tremulous voice (*Don't overdo it*, she warned herself). "I ask myself, why did it happen to me? I look for answers but there is nobody to talk to. And the Temple ... it's all pomp and outdated ceremonies, and I was taught as a child to laugh at all this."

Edna stared hard at her for a moment and then squeezed her hand as if she had reached a decision.

"I think I can help you," she said. "Let's meet here tomorrow and I'll introduce you to some people who could give you answers."

CHAPTER 7. BIRDS OF PREY

A single Light Puppy hovers before her, its colors sickly and dim. Slowly it lengthens like a caterpillar, stretching itself out, remolding itself into the light-limned outline of a wolf cub.

She is staring at it in consternation. She never thought they could imprison themselves in an animal shape.

A baby is crying. A shrill, insistent, terrible keening.

A wolf is howling, as if its hide is being lacerated with metal-tipped whips.

She is peering into the darkness populated by these sounds, by the screaming of many voices and trampling of many feet. The darkness is not the mere absence of light. It is a black curtain stitched roughly from patches of cloth. Running her hands over it, she realizes those are clothes: torn-up pieces of dresses, suits, and coats sewn together by a blind seamstress, stitched by the incessant murmur of fear and grief.

A greenish snout pokes at the darkness in front of her and it parts, letting in the feverish light of the dream-sea.

She steps through. The flat, four-legged outline of the Light Puppy tries to follow her, but it fades in the flood of the red, angry light streaming from the sky-dome. Walking away on the maroon sand, she *seems to be heavier than usual, leaving deep footprints that are slowly filling with blood.*

On the margin of the sea, red foam is licking her naked feet. Under the brassy sky, the sea is dirty brown, with flashes of red when the sluggish waves break the wrinkled crust that forms on the surface like milk-skin.

She dips her toe in the blood-warm water. A stinking vapor touches her face.

A soft yelping sound behind her and she turns around heavily, her body strangely distended.

The Light Puppy is dragging itself along the beach, the storm-cloud light eating holes in its insubstantial body. Only the single curving line of its head manages to reach her and its flat jaws tug feebly on her ankle, trying to prevent her from going in.

The surface of the sea suddenly domes up as if a giant dreamfish is about to surface. Her dreamfish, the one that ...

Mara sat up in bed, her nightgown soaked with sweat, hugging herself so tightly that her nails dug into her flesh. After a while, she got up, moving like an old woman, and went to the window.

It was raining, of course, and the lights of First City shone murkily in the wet darkness. The grandfather clock in the corner showed four in the morning.

She lay back in bed but did not sleep again, waiting for the familiar sounds of the City waking up. Only when she heard the first cab splash through the puddles did she allow herself to doze off.

This had been the first time in seven years that she had gone to the dream-sea involuntarily.

~

They were to meet at five, before the evening worship at the Lynx temple. Just before they parted, Edna began to have second thoughts: She grew evasive, hinted at some unspecified difficulties, and made Mara promise several times she would tell nobody. Mara swore up and down that she would be circumspect. This was her opportunity to prove to Mr. Seal (not to mention Detective Hart) that she was more than a hysterical woman with a strange Power. If Edna could lead her to the Army of the Revealer, there was nothing Mara would not do to pursue this lead—in the real world, for a change, not in the dream-sea.

There was a whole empty day to get through before the meeting. Mara took a bath, got dressed, and was about to go out for breakfast when the phone rang. She had not spoken to her mother in two weeks despite her resolution to call or drop by for a visit. For some reason, Mara felt it must be her and was tempted not to pick it up. But curiosity won; she lifted the receiver and heard Mr. Seal's voice.

It affected her strangely. Overlaid with phantom rustles, it sounded both alien and familiar, as if it were a voice from the distant past. He asked her how she was feeling.

"I'm fine," she said. "I'm going out to grab some coffee."

"Stimulants are not good for your Power."

"I still need coffee in the morning. And it's not like I'm going dreamfishing tonight."

"What Detective Hart said—"

"Detective Hart said nothing important," interrupted Mara. "Detective Hart is a pompous ass."

A pause and then Mr. Seal said:

"I thought you liked him."

"Liked him? He was barely civil to me. The constabulary must be hard-pressed for manpower if they accept religious freaks like him!"

"He's competent enough," said Mr. Seal. "I thought with the new information he provided you could go into the sea again."

"Hardly 'new information!' No, I don't feel prepared. Remember how I used to go there every night and what it did to me? You taught me to control it. I don't think it's healthy for me to go more than once a week."

"Of course," said Mr. Seal, "your well-being is paramount. But let's meet anyway. There are things to discuss."

"Sure," said Mara. "Tomorrow?"

Mr. Seal hesitated as if he would prefer sooner but agreed to go out for dinner tomorrow.

Did he try to set me up with Detective Hart? This was absurd; he kept telling her that Ronald would be back. But had there not been a change in his voice when he asked whether she liked Detective Hart?

And she lied to him by omission. She did not tell him about her involuntary sojourn in the dream-sea.

Well, maybe it's time to keep some things to myself. I don't need a mentor anymore, do I?

~

She stood on the Lynx temple porch in the drizzle, having already been inside for more than twenty minutes. The sky was the color of smoky rose. Failure sat like bitter lemon in her mouth. Edna did not come.

She was about to walk away but then decided to take one last look in the temple. She was surprised to see some lit candles around the altar that had not been there before. She squinted into the murk when a hand touched her shoulder. She whirled around, stifling a cry.

Edna, in her lettuce-colored pantsuit, put a finger to her lips and led Mara outside.

"Let's go," she said. "I don't like the local Guardian. He's a snitch."

"Was it him inside?"

"Yes."

Edna hurried forward, casting nervous glances around. Mara

almost had to run to keep up with her. Not sure how to dress for undercover work, she had selected a heavy olive-green gabardine skirt and a black belted coat with wide lapels. Her boots were made of artificial rubber and squealed unpleasantly. She had agonized over makeup but finally put on some drab green eye shadow and pale lip gloss in order not to stand out in the streets.

Edna trudged on, unwilling to answer questions, and Mara was wary of pressuring her. They moved through a maze of side streets and blind alleys, dismal backyards with broken swings and trash barrels, and a pitiful square of foul, wet sand in the middle for stunted children to play in. An occasional heap of rags in the arched doorway would fall apart to reveal a drunk inside, like a moth in a cocoon.

They suddenly emerged into an open space. Mara gasped. Across the road stretched a low L-shaped building, whose roof looked almost black. The abandoned hospital!

"You know this place?" Edna asked.

"No," said Mara. "I passed here before, that's all."

With her eyes darting in all directions, Edna grasped Mara's hand and dragged her into the hospital through the splintered and unlocked front door.

The entrance hallway was dank and dark, the smell of wet blankets and mice overlaid with a sweetish odor like the attar of roses. When her eyes adjusted, Mara realized that some light was seeping through a doorway at the opposite end where somebody stood, watching them.

A man ushered them into a room that appeared to have been a doctor's office. A white examination table with one broken leg was pushed to the wall and set with several candles in tin holders that provided the only illumination. No electricity.

There were five people in the room including the man by the door who followed them in. Three men, two women, not counting Edna and Mara. One of the men sat cross-legged on the filthy floor, the rest on rickety stools and sagging couches.

Mara scanned their faces, apprehensive. Suddenly undercover work no longer seemed such a good idea. Still, the presence of Edna and the two other women gave her some reassurance.

A beer-bellied man with a neatly trimmed beard and round black eyes sprawled on a couch. Edna introduced him as Mr. Muskrat.

The two women who sat on the stools like a pair of scrawny birds were sisters, Viola and Carla Marmot. Viola was a thin, dyed blonde whose skin seemed to hang loose on her emaciated body. She wore no makeup but was decked out with numerous bracelets and necklaces, cheap imitation stones sparkling in the candlelight. Her younger sister Carla dressed plainly, and her broad face was marred by acne, but she nevertheless had a raw attractiveness Mara found off-putting.

The man sitting on the floor barely glanced up. He had a beautiful profile with a slightly domed forehead, chiseled nose, and firm chin. But in full view his face disintegrated into a jumble of mismatched features, one eye slightly lower than the other as if the two sides of it had been carelessly glued together. His name was George Buzzard.

And finally, the last man, the one by the door, was called Thomas Hawk. Bird names were rare (this was why Ronald was so proud of his) and to find a Raven, a Buzzard, and a Hawk in the same room was quite a coincidence, provided, of course, that the names were real, which Mara doubted. But whoever he was, Thomas Hawk was the one who turned this ragtag collection of strangers into a purposeful meeting. He was young, perhaps Mara's age or slightly older, with preppy charm and a well-scrubbed face, dressed in expensively understated clothes. He had one of those mellifluous voices that dominate every conversation because people want to listen to them, no matter what they say. He smiled and seemed pleased to see Mara.

The way they greeted Edna indicated that her position in the group's pecking order was not particularly high. With the exception of Carla Marmot, who gave her a hug, everybody else muttered or nodded in her direction. She dropped to the edge of the couch, straight as a ramrod. Mara remained standing, feeling vulnerable in the crossfire of so many eyes. It was Thomas Hawk who, with a smile and a kind word, motioned her to a chair in the corner where she sat, considerably relieved.

She did not expect them to plunge straight into conspiratorial talk but even so, she was surprised by the innocuous nature of the meeting. It began with a prayer to the Ancestors. Next, Viola Marmot talked about her recent experiences of communion with her totem. This involved eating nothing but uncooked greens (which, Mara thought, accounted for her famished appearance) and meditating on the goodness of nature.

When Viola was done, Mara thought, *Now they will get down to business*, and was discomfited when Thomas Hawk addressed her.

"We have a guest with us tonight," he announced in his beautiful voice. "Will our new friend tell us about herself?"

Feeling everybody's eyes focus on her again, Mara blushed and hated herself for it.

"Wel-l-" she stammered, "there isn't much to tell. My name is Mara Ferret. I live uptown, not far from the Animal House, and I met Edna yesterday in the Lynx temple in my neighborhood. We started talking and she told me … told me about you, that you meet and discuss … well, spiritual matters. And I'm interested in those."

"Didn't you suffer an unfortunate bereavement recently?" Hawk inquired.

"Yes." Mara looked down, hoping that Edna had not checked her story. "My husband. Disappeared more than a year ago; the body found in the Bird River six months later."

"Did he jump in and drown?" a rough, deep voice asked. This was George Buzzard who had not opened his mouth before.

"I don't know," Mara said.

"How so?" George insisted. "No letter, no debt, no mistress?"

"Nothing like this," retorted Mara with mounting color in her cheeks.

"George, please!" Hawk interfered. And to Mara: "What a terrible tragedy! Were the constabulary helpful?"

Mara shrugged. "Not really. They couldn't even tell whether he'd been murdered. The coroner gave the verdict of death by misadventure."

Carla Marmot, silent until then, suddenly gave a low chuckle.

"Death by misadventure!" she repeated as if amused. "What fools! There is no such thing as misadventure!"

"No?" Mara asked. "Why not?"

"Everything that happens," Carla said, "happens because it is meant to. There are no accidents. If we don't see the pattern, it is because our eyes are blinded to reality. We're prisoners of the great delusion."

"This is our punishment," chimed in Edna, who seemed to have become calmer since Thomas Hawk took over the handling of Mara.

"So," Mara addressed both women, "it must be part of the pattern that I'm here tonight?"

Edna blinked, and Carla said nothing, as if unwilling to countenance such a direct application of her belief. Hawk intervened once more.

"What do you want, Mara?" he asked. "What are you looking for? I hope you don't mind my calling you Mara. We're all brothers and sisters here."

What do you want? For a moment, Mara was taken aback because the question had a kind of directness that ill fit her role of a spy. What do you want? *I want to find Ronald, I want, I want* ... and a sudden surge of vertigo, like a splash of dark water somewhere inside her mind.

"I want to understand," she said.

Nobody said anything but she was aware of a sudden relaxation of the tension in the room as if somehow, she had hit the right answer. Hawk nodded.

"Yes," he said. "This is what we all want. To understand our world. To understand the City. To know why we are here. But understanding is not enough, Mara. To understand and to act—this is true wisdom."

The atmosphere lightened. People stirred, changed positions, and Carla brought out a plate of bland oatmeal cookies and a pitcher of herbal infusion. Mara accepted a cookie and found herself accosted by Hawk. He smelled of freshly cut grass and lemon flowers. She remembered the fashionable cologne from the parties she had attended as Ronald's wife. She also remembered its prohibitive cost.

"Your face is familiar," he said. "I'm sure I've met you somewhere."

Mara looked at him skeptically. This was the oldest pickup line in the book, but she did not think Hawk was interested in consoling the tragic widow.

"Where could we possibly have met?" she asked.

"A Raccoon's party?" he suggested.

The Raccoon family were well-established bankers. Mara and Ronald had attended their famous parties a couple of times.

"Perhaps," she said. "But I'm not sure ..."

"Raven and Co!" he exclaimed. "Was that your husband?"

Mara sighed. Her cover was blown—not that it had been much of a cover to begin with.

"Yes," she said. "Ferret is my birth totem, but I adopted his after we got married. Ronald Raven was my husband. He managed the family company. Now his younger brother Philip does it."

He nodded and smiled. But Mara decided it would be best not to enlighten him about the fact that Ronald was only missing, not declared dead, and that she had no influence upon the company's affairs.

"So, Mara," he said with a familiarity she found grating, "you are a seeker of truth, aren't you?"

"I suppose," said Mara.

"We've been fed lies and distortions throughout our lives," he continued. "The Humanist establishment has grabbed the power in the City and is leading it toward perdition. If they have their way, we'll be nothing but a bunch of mindless prisoners content with our lot, rotting in jail and calling it home."

"What do you mean by jail?"

"The City!" suddenly cried the hitherto silent and self-effacing Mr. Muskrat. "It is a prison, a horrible dungeon, and we eat, drink, and make merry, and our enemies look at us and laugh!"

Tiny globules of spittle flew out of his mouth. It was so unexpected that Mara dropped her cookie. George Buzzard laughed.

"Some eat and some starve, Ratty, old pal!" he cried. "The Humanists make sure the goodies go to their friends in the Temple! The Ancestors left us a whole world and people in Lonelyhearts live on top of each other because there isn't enough room for them in the City!"

Mara focused on him, finding his rage easier to take than the uncompromising flame of faith that glowed in Mr. Muskrat's glassy eyes.

"I think it's a disgrace, Mr. Buzzard," she said. "But what do you think should be done about it?"

He shrugged, looking away.

"Lonelyhearts is of no importance," Viola Marmot declared. "We need a new heaven and a new earth, not just a new government."

Clearly, she was surrounded by dangerous fanatics. What would they do if they found out she had a Power? Even though her Power was not transferrable, they might try to take advantage of her in some crazy way. She would not mention the dream-sea to them.

"You confuse our friend," Thomas Hawk said. "She does not know what you're talking about. Do you, Mara?"

She shook her head.

"Well," he continued, "without getting too specific, suffice it to say that we believe that the prophecies of the *Book of the Remnant* are coming to be fulfilled soon. The gates are about to open. Then we'll come face to face with the Ancestors and our ancient sin toward them will be expiated."

"What will happen to First City?" asked Mara.

"It'll be destroyed," Hawk said without hesitation. "It'll be leveled to the ground and a new City will be built. Where First City is low and creeping in the humility of our guilt, the new City will rise to the sky. Where First City is flooded by the tears of Nature, the new City will be always dry and warmed by the sun. Where First City is sad and lonely, the new City will be bustling with life."

Mara had pegged Hawk as a rich playboy playing at being a revolutionary but he sounded sincere. It made her even more apprehensive.

He is not only a clever manipulator; he really believes in this rigmarole.

Just like Hart.

How many of them are in the City?

"However," continued Hawk, "there are powerful people in the City who are trying to prevent us from fulfilling our destiny. The elites. The Humanists and their Temple lackeys. All they want is to preserve the status quo. They're willing to let humanity rot in the City, stained with the blood of the Ancestors, cut off from the Abode of the Ancestors."

"What is the Abode?" Mara cried, exasperated. She was done with this theological doublespeak.

Hawk blinked, as if unsure what to say, but it was Viola who answered.

"It is another City."

"And where is it? The South Continent?"

"No," Viola said with forceful conviction that contrasted with her previous meanderings. "It is in the spiritual world. We have been barred from it by our sin, but when the Ancestors Return, the gate will be opened and we will be welcomed back."

"What is the sin? The Rebellion?" Mara pressed.

Hawk produced a slim black volume with an embossed cover. He opened it in the middle and began reading:

"And there were animals and men and machines, all scattered and blackened by fire. And the stones were covered with sores, and the walls shook with ague. And the blood spilt cried from the streets, and the earth would not accept it and spewed it forth. And the blood spilt cried from the sea and the sea would not accept it and vomited it out. And the blood spilt cried into the air and the air would not accept it and drew away."

"Stop!" Mara cried. "This is horrible!"

Hawk started.

"This is what we did to the Four," Edna said. "This is what we did to those who succored us. Now you see, Mara, the sin we have to expiate. And the Humanists tell us that men can live for pleasure, eating and drinking, selling and buying, and think nothing of our guilt!"

"It's not just guilt," Hawk said. "You see, Mara, it does not mean we have to waste our lives in self-torture like the Repentant did during the Dark Years. The Guardians would love it if we did nothing but cried over our crime, acquiesced in our imprisonment, and paid the Temple tithes. No, the new age is dawning, the age of forgiveness and reconciliation, when the prison gates will be opened and we will march forth to meet the Ancestors."

"How?" Mara asked. "Isn't it true that nobody knows where the gate is?"

"Maybe," Hawk said. "But maybe we know how to make new gates."

Suddenly, George Buzzard laughed.

"All it takes is a corpse! Plenty of those in Lonelyhearts. And then we are going to call up such a flood that the old gate will creak, and squeak, and break!"

A flood.

Dirty water. A bloated corpse.

Elvira Sparrow!

"Shut up!" Hawk yelled.

Buzzard spun on his heels, glowering at the younger man. The air between them grew charged with tension. Carla Marmot reached out and put a hand on Buzzard's forearm. He shook her off without even glancing in her direction and strode out of the room. Hawk bit his lip and then smiled sweetly at Mara.

"Well," he said, "we have disagreements like everybody else. But we all work for the common goal. George is a little ... unstable."

"How dare you!" Carla cried and, extricating herself from her sister's restraining hands, rushed out to follow George. After that, the meeting wound down. Edna and Viola whispered to each other, and Muskrat stared into the distance.

Mara decided it was time to go. Murmuring apologies, she made her way to the door only to be intercepted by Hawk.

"You mustn't go out alone," he said. "There are rats in the hallway. Let me escort you."

He deftly led her through the smelly darkness of the hallway and paused outside.

"I am sorry about this altercation," he said. "George has a passionate nature, which is not always nice. But he is a seeker of truth, as we all are."

"It does not matter," said Mara. "I've learnt a lot."

"Does it mean we're going to have the pleasure of your company again soon?" Hawk asked. In the damp glow of street-lights his smooth face sprouted grotesque protuberances and deep pits, bleeding slicks of shadows.

"Yes," said Mara.

"Very well," he said. "I'll inform you of the next meeting. Perhaps we could also meet, just the two of us, for a private talk. I hope I don't sound like a snob, but it's clear that you and I have more in common than, say, you and poor Viola."

"What about Edna?" asked Mara.

Hawk smiled.

"Ah, yes! Edna's family has old money and a lot of connections in the Animal House. But she is a little ... obsessed with her guilt over the Slaughtered Ones. I mean, it's important to be aware of humanity's crime but too much brooding plays straight into the hands of the Humanists and their Temple lackeys. This is why a thousand years were wasted in inner squabbles and futile repentance. We want something more."

"Who are 'we'?" asked Mara. "The Army of the Revealer? And who is the Revealer, anyway?"

Hawk's shadow-ringed eyes gleamed at her.

"'We' are those who want out of the prison," he said. "And nobody knows who the Revealer is. He is the one who will finally open the gate. But before it happens, there is work to do. So, may I have your phone number? You do have a phone, don't you?"

Mara nodded and mechanically dictated her number, which he wrote down on his shirt-cuff with a slim golden pen.

"I'll call you," he said. "I have a sense, Mara, that you're destined to go far."

CHAPTER 8. THE TORNADO

She could not sleep. Faces floated in the darkness—Hawk, Buzzard, the Marmot sisters—and she saw, with a painful clarity, feathers and fur, a sharp beak, an unblinking bird's eye ...

I don't even believe in the Ancestors! she reasoned. But something inside refused to listen. A heavy presence stirred in the depths of her mind, poked its snout out of the darkness, and wallowed in its dank lair. *I should go into the dream-sea; I could outswim her.* The strangeness of this thought convinced her that she was finally falling asleep, drifting into the comfort of oblivion.

There was a loud bump outside and Mara sat up in bed, dry-eyed and wide awake.

Midnight again; irrationally she thought that Mr. Seal would call, telling her that a body was found on the Hill.

It had already happened, she reminded herself. But the sense of déjà vu persisted.

She waited; the phone did not ring.

But something was strange and after a while she realized what it was. The persistent, stealthy splashing of rain had stopped; the first time in weeks.

Mara padded to the window and drew the curtain aside. A squall shook drops from the naked branches of the tree below. The street was deserted. In the eerie silence, Mara heard the soughing of the wind and the perpetual murmur of the City.

The moment of silence stretched. And then an echoing crash, so powerful that the windowpanes rattled and the floor under her feet trembled, rolled across the City.

Mara cowered, hiding her face from a shower of broken glass. But the window held as the night was roiled by a swirling darkness above the rooftops, a churning blue-black cloud against which the silhouette of the Lonelyhearts' platforms stood out in deeper black like an insect's spidery legs. The cloud heaved and another gust of wind bent the trees below. Then the cloud parted and exuded a vapory proboscis, a twisting column that danced and whipped around in the sudden hush. The column was outlined in running golden sparks that coalesced into thin lines of fire.

The tornado kissed the upper platform of the Lonelyhearts and the whole ungainly construction started collapsing, slowly at first and with gentle grace, and then gathering momentum, shedding tatters of impromptu dwellings and dots of flying bodies. Licks of golden fire blossomed in its wake but were doused by the heavy rain that suddenly pounded again upon the City.

Mara cried out but did not hear herself—only the crash of the ruined world outside.

~

"Mara," Mr. Seal said, "a woman was killed yesterday."

He had knocked on her door early in the morning. The phone lines were down, and he could not wait. So he walked to her apartment, oblivious of the commotion and chaos in the streets, the constables blocking Victory Boulevard trying to contain the heaving human sea as rumors went flying and emergency crews tried to clean up the mess of construction materials and mangled flesh that used to be Lonelyhearts. He did not care about any of this—only about Mara and her response.

She let him in. Her hair was tangled, and her robe was carelessly tied. He averted his eyes from the pale triangle of bare flesh at the neckline.

But now he was watching her, as he always did. She seemed upset but he could not gauge her reaction any further. It was as if the transparency of her mind was slowly darkening with some unknown sediment, becoming opaque to him. And this could not be allowed, of course.

She was staring out the window, leaning against the sill, her back to him. This, too, was new and concerning. Since she was a child, her face would always be turned to him, her teacher, following him like a sunflower follows the sun.

The rain was intensifying. Lines of water crossed the gray cityscape like bars.

Mr. Seal coughed.

"Mara?"

She looked at him.

"How many were killed in Lonelyhearts?" she asked.

"The official estimate is two hundred. In reality, of course, it is much higher."

Mara laughed, a strange dry cackle that scraped Mr. Seal's raw nerves.

"Did you read the *Book of the Remnant?*" she asked.

Mr. Seal blinked. "Of course."

Mara picked up a book that he had not seen in her home before.

"Listen," she said. "*And the four of them stood at the gate. And one had stripes like cinders and ashes. And one had a face like a leper. And one had a body that crushed rocks and made the earth bleed as it crawled. And of the last one nothing can be said because its claws tore off the skins of the living and made it a garment thereof.*"

Mr. Seal nodded.

"The Four," he said. "The Slaughtered Ones."

Mara put the book aside, as if it were made of glass. She seemed deep in thought. And tired. And on edge. He felt as if he were drowning in trying to guess her mood.

Her eyes, with their ever-shifting colors, were circled in black.

She has the dream-sea. I have her eyes.

But now her eyes told him nothing.

"Do they know how the tornado was made?" she asked. "It's not a natural disaster, is it?"

"The Animal House has not issued the official bulletin yet but …"

"Don't give me this bullshit!"

Mr. Seal was shocked, both by her tone and her use of profanity. She had never talked to him this way before.

"A Power was employed," he said. "They don't know how. Too many bodies."

"But you said that another woman was killed?" she asked. "One of the victims?"

"No, these are still being identified. This one was found in a different area. It seemed that somebody tried to repeat Elvira Sparrow's gambit."

"What do you mean?"

"Elvira's body was used to call up a flood, as we both saw. This body was used for a similar purpose. It was slit from the sternum to the pubes, and there was some water around. A copycat murder, perhaps. Or somebody who knew how to open the gate but did not have the Power to control it."

"How to open the gate," Mara repeated. "It is to kill somebody, right? This is the way to open the gate into the Abode."

Mr. Seal nodded.

"How long have you known that?" Mara asked. "Why didn't you tell me before?"

"I only realized it recently," Mr. Seal replied. It was a lie, but he thought Mara would not spot it in the confusion of the moment.

Mara frowned, tapped her narrow foot on the floor. Her ash-blond locks, uncombed and unpinned, fell like a veil around her face. She swept them away. Her every movement seemed to him more real than the faded living room around them and the washed-away cityscape outside, as if the fabric of everyday strained and tore under the weight of who she was.

"I tried to go into the dream-sea last night," she said.

Mr. Seal frowned. She normally told him in advance. Before her marriage, she would sometimes ask him to sit beside her as her eyes were closing and a waxen immobility spread over her features. Unfortunately, that idiot Ronald put an end to it.

"Why?"

"To find out the origin of the tornado."

"Did it work?"

"No. I stopped halfway. When I saw the Light Puppies ... they seemed agitated. Jumpy. And I realized I could not go in. I had too much on my head. Fear, confusion, uncertainty. I would contaminate the sea because there is no difference between thought and action there. Feelings become monsters. I withdrew. It was hard. Like making love and pulling away in the middle."

Mr. Seal's lips twitched.

"How could you possibly contaminate the dream-sea?"

"You told me that the dream-sea is humanity's outflow of the imagination. That everything we dream about, long for, love, and fear exists there. I was reading the *Book of the Remnant* as bait because these terrorists, the Army of the Revealer, believe in it. But then I thought about that passage. These things, the Four, must be in the dream-sea too ... What if I go there and bring them back?"

Mr. Seal did what he had not done for years and grasped Mara's hand.

"Mara," he said, "this is exactly what you have to do, because the dream-sea is also the place of memories. That is where the past of humanity is hidden. And this past is linked to the Four. What you just read ... it's only one aspect of human history. Other parts of the Book paint quite a different picture. You know, there is that image of Paradise, where men and their totems are one, and we are released from the burden of guilt and fear. But whatever it is, we have to know who we are and where we came from."

"Why?" asked Mara. Mr. Seal frowned.

"The City." He made an expansive gesture. "It's so small. So cramped."

"We can build it bigger."

"So? We would still be tied to it. Humans cannot live far from the City. There is a reason why convicts are sent to work in the farmlands, the worse the crime the further from First City. And as for the South Continent and the coffee plantations ... indentured workers there tend not to come back. No, there is only one way out for humanity. Through the gate that was slammed behind our backs. Through the dream-sea."

"Escape into the dream-sea? You have no idea what you are talking about. It is a place of dreams. Of nightmares. Nobody can live there."

He was shocked by the cold vehemence in her voice. Was it really his Mara speaking? Yes, *his* Mara, even though she could never be his in the way vulgar crowds understood it.

"How can you say this, Mara? You, of all people? The City is a nightmare from which we are trying to awaken!"

She looked at him with such a steely glint in her blue-gray-green eyes that he shuddered.

"What happens to my body when I go into the dream-sea?" she asked.

He averted his eyes.

"Well, nothing. I mean ... you're asleep but your mind goes there ..."

"If my body remains in the City, then the City is real."

"And the dream-sea is what? A fairy tale?" Mr. Seal was beginning to lose his temper.

She picked up the *Book of the Remnant*.

"It's like this book," she said. "Words are powerful; they can make you laugh or cry. But they can't heal a wound or fill your stomach or raise you from the dead."

"You are wrong. Words can make you kill. What's more powerful than that? Whoever killed Elvira Sparrow read the Book and decided to act. When they used a Power on the corpse, what came through? Water, Mara. Water."

"So?"

"The dream-sea flowed through the portal of the body into our world. You think bodies are real and dreams are insubstantial? Just the opposite. We are made from the stuff of the dream-sea. It is the City that is a dream and a delusion."

"You talk like them!" she snapped.

"Like whom?"

Mara turned away, sulking. Mr. Seal longed to touch her and forced himself not to.

"Perhaps I haven't been quite honest with you, my dear," he said. "I taught you that the dream-sea is a spiritual realm that pools all of our fears and desires. This is what I believed when we met. But over time, I have come to believe ... to suspect ... that it is more than that. And I didn't want to tell you of my suspicions, partly for your sake. I thought you might be afraid to dive into it if you were convinced of its materiality."

Mara laughed, a dry rattle that seemed older than her and scraped against his nerves like an echo of some forgotten scream.

"Nothing would stop me," she said, "even if every dreamfish I met took a bite out of me. It's like food, or drink, or sex. I've got to go, no matter what."

He winced at her language but persevered.

"Anyway, my research and your reports have convinced me otherwise. Yes, your body remains here—but perhaps it is our bodies that are a mirage, imposed as punishment or dreamed up in remorse, who knows. And our real selves, the essence of what we are, they have come from the dream-sea. Perhaps each of us has a counterpart in the dream-sea, not necessarily in the shape of a human being but … well, I don't know what. Something else."

"A fish?" asked Mara.

He stumbled. She was clearly mad, and he had never seen her like this. It made him tremble. Her eyes cut into him like knives, mocking, cruel, shifty eyes, whose color suddenly spun away from him in a rainbow of morbid hues: the blue of ice, the gray of thunderclouds, and the green of bile. *It's not Mara*, he thought with awe, *it's* …

She dropped her gaze, and she was his Mara again.

"I'm sorry," she said, and he rejoiced, finally hearing the familiar submission in her voice. "I'm being a pest, I know. But I can't believe it."

"Think, Mara! How come you find answers to your questions in the dream-sea? Why does it respond to you?"

"Because every thought that somebody in the City thinks is reflected there."

"Then why is it so difficult to believe that our personalities are also reflected there? Our selves, our souls? And then the next step: What if it's we who are the reflections, and the originals are in the dream-sea? After all, the gate is supposed to separate our world, our City, from some dangerous realm. The Temple people call it the Abode of the Ancestors, but they don't know what it is. I believe this realm is the dream-sea."

"What about the real world? This world?"

"No, Mara, this world is not the real world, the ingenuous

theories of Charles Finch notwithstanding. It is a delusion and a snare. The real world is out there, in the dream-sea. That is where we came from, that is where we have to return."

"I don't want to hear this!" Mara said.

He felt his control of her slipping. There was nothing to do but to retreat, apologize, and regroup.

A truce was restored but it was a brittle one. Mara complained of a headache and begged off their dinner engagement. Mr. Seal, with some effort returning to his avuncular persona, fussed over her and insisted she take some herbal pills and go to bed. He was about to leave but she stopped him at the door.

"You said that the woman was identified, right? The one who was murdered? What was her name?"

Mr. Seal wrinkled his forehead.

"A rather common name. Marmot, I think. Yes, Carla Marmot."

Seeing the expression on Mara's face, he frowned.

"Did you know her?"

"No. When can I see the body?"

"The body was removed and forensics searched the crime scene. In any case, there are bigger things to fish for in the dream-sea than another murder clue. The tornado was created by exercise of a great Power. People must have been killed to unleash it, more than that woman, I believe. But because there are so many bodies and they have been mutilated by the collapse, we can't tell accidental victims from deliberate sacrifices. Jay-Mole will contact me when they sort it out, and then you and I can start working on it."

"You and I?" Mara said, lifting an eyebrow. Mr. Seal did not respond.

"What was that place where she was found?"

Mr. Seal's lips thinned.

"An abandoned hospital, slated for demolition. It belonged to the Temple," he said in a distant voice. "It had some official name, but everybody called it the Hospital of Transformation. It was there that Guardians were made. Children were brought in, some as young as two or three, and operated upon—purified as they called it—and then over several years, sometimes as long as ten, grafts were made to give them Powers. Depending on the child's resilience the number and complexity of grafts were increased until they hit the limit, and the body began rejecting them. The limit was individual: Some children could accept a lot of grafts, some only few. There was no way to predict it before-hand, or so they said. There were rumors, of course, that it depended on the child's and its family's piety or more reasonably, on age and sex."

"Are there many female Guardians?"

"Almost as many as males. But after a certain stage, sex no longer matters."

"Why was the hospital abandoned?"

Mr. Seal put on his hat, a round felt thing with a soft crown and a black ribbon. Its shadow crossed his pale, waxy face.

"There was a scandal," he said. "Something to do with an improperly done surgery. A child who had undergone the prelim-inary stages of purification but rejected all grafts. There was the threat of a lawsuit, and the hospital was henceforth seen as unlucky. It's all superstition, of course, but the Temple thought it prudent to shut it down. Anyway, there are newer hospitals in the suburbia, and they work better."

CHAPTER 9. THE WIDOWER

The door clicked behind his retreating back, the latch falling into place. Mara padded back into the living room, shivering from the dampness and the cold. Carla Marmot. The thick purple lips, the gray cardigan around the round shoulders, and the scars of acne on the broad cheekbones. The woman had been alive yesterday and now she was a gutted corpse in the chill-box of the constabulary morgue.

The thought meant nothing. Mara wanted to feel pity or horror but all she could muster was distant curiosity.

Since her involuntary swim in the dream-sea, she had felt as though she was not completely alone. A heavy presence sat at the back of her mind, something inchoate and shaggy like a pile of unclean fur, smothering her thoughts and feelings with its deadly weight.

Was Mr. Seal right? Had she picked up something in the dream-sea, something that had crossed over riding piggyback upon her innermost self? A monster ...

I can't think like this or I will never go into the dream-sea again.

The horror of being locked up in the world of mud, rain, and irrelevance whipped her into action. She could find the murderer of Carla Marmot by herself! She did not need Mr. Seal's permission! And she certainly did not need the condescension of Chief Constable Jay-Mole and Detective Hart! She had her own leads to pursue!

Mara rushed into the bedroom, upended the shoulder bag she had carried yesterday, and clawed among odds and ends for a note with Thomas Hawk's phone number, only to remember that while she had given him hers, it had not occurred to her to ask for his. Self-respecting women did not ask for gentlemen's phone numbers.

Whispering the filthiest words she knew, which were not many, Mara kicked the stand with the phone on it. A slim green volume slid from the shelf and landed on the carpet. Mara picked it up. It was the phone book that Ronald had proudly purchased when the phone was installed. She had never made any use of it before. It was arranged alphabetically, and she was surprised at the number of phone subscribers in First City. The technological revolution was proceeding apace. However, while there were several Hawks—not too many compared with far more common Hares and Harts—there was no entry for Thomas Hawk. Of course. This could not have been his real name. She checked for Buzzard. There was only one Buzzard family, Mr. Jonathan Titmouse-Buzzard and his daughter Maud. George did not look like a man with a permanent address, let alone a phone subscription.

Discouraged, she sprawled on the floor, desultorily leafing through the phone book. The inhabitants of the First City passed before her eyes: the Badgers and the Boars; the Thrushes and the Toads; the Squirrels and the ... She stopped. Black on white, the names leaped at her from the page. Julian and Elvira Sparrow followed by a short number. She stared at it as if hypnotized, then stretched her hand to the phone and dialed.

"Hello?" said a deep male voice.

"Mr. Sparrow?" asked Mara. "Husband of the late Elvira Sparrow?"

"Yes," responded the man. "Who is it?"

"My name is Mara Raven. I am a consultant with the constabulary team that investigates your wife's death. I would appreciate it if you could spare some time for me."

"But your people already talked to me. Detective ... whatever his name ..."

"Detective Hart?"

"Yes."

"But I'm not the constabulary. As I said, I'm an independent consultant. It might be important."

"Consultant?" the voice repeated. "Oh well, why not. We're closed today in any case, my office, I mean. Do you know where I live?"

"No."

"Birch Avenue 5. Can you be here in an hour?"

"Yes," assured Mara, and put down the receiver. She discovered that her palms were sweaty, but she felt exuberant. The heavy watcher in her mind was gone.

As she went outside, the gale slammed into her, throwing a handful of broken rain over her black cashmere coat. Her carefully arranged hair fluttered loose. She hailed a cab and gave the driver the address. Birch Avenue was one of the fancy, exclusive communities where the rich planted trees and flowers around their homes to create an illusion of nature, while clawing their way ever closer to the rough triangle of the heart of First City marked by the Animal House, the Temple, and the Hill.

Why would anybody try to pretend they lived in the countryside? The countryside fed the City, but its inhabitants were rumored to live short and sickly lives, plagued by a variety of strange maladies. Nobody knew exactly how far from the heart of the City was too far for comfort, but the elite did not take any chances. First City had grown slowly over the centuries, spreading over the flat Plains, draining the marshes, felling the sparse woods, and tilling the grasslands. Superstition and fear of disease drew waves of returnees back to its core, creating the congestion of Lonelyhearts, while hunger drove the poor out into the country where they farmed and traded. Harried by its inexorable and unknown rulers, humanity advanced and retreated like the waves on the dream-sea's beach.

Mara's family had been one of the decent poor, clinging with their fingertips to the genteel "strained circumstances." They had lived far from the center but not quite on the slummy growth-edge of First City. Until she met Ronald, her whole being had been focused upon two things: the dream-sea and the City center. Even when regarding her gift as a kind of madness, part of her had been convinced that the way to the heart of the City led through the dream-sea. This conviction had been vindicated when she had met Mr. Seal and then Ronald. And now Mara was alone, ensconced in a damp, sad huddle of rooms that would appear to her childhood eyes as an impossible luxury. Were all fulfilled wishes that disappointing?

She finally realized that the driver was talking to her.

"Sorry, what did you say?"

"We have to take the long road. Some streets are flooded. Gutters overflowing, sewers blocked up. This damn rain!"

He was a small man with protruding front teeth and a moth-eaten moustache.

"It's a crazy weather, isn't it?" she responded with forced conviviality.

"It's a sign," said the driver. "The Ancestors are coming back!"

Another one, thought Mara disgustedly, and pretended to be engrossed in repairing her makeup. The cab drove through streets she did not recognize, and she had a moment of irrational panic:

Perhaps they were not in the City at all; perhaps it was another City, unfamiliar and hostile. She shook her head to dispel this delusion and concentrated on her reflection in the compact mirror. But instead of anchoring her back in reality, her own pale face with its severely perfect features and large blue-green-gray eyes under the incongruously dark eyebrows appeared to her alien, as if it did not belong to her. Was it why Guardians insisted on makeup, so that people would not suddenly encounter the nakedness of their borrowed faces?

Mara licked her lips that she had tinted with carmine gloss for decency's sake. In their natural state, they were barely darker than her paper-white skin. She suddenly remembered how her mother had urged her to stay in the sun when she was a child, "to get some color in your cheeks." She had not seen her mother for almost as long as she had not seen the sun in the permanently clouded sky of First City. A stab of guilt made her resolve to call Louisa Ferret later.

Handing the fare to the driver, Mara glanced at the small plaque with his name. It was Jeremiah B. Rat.

The street was unnervingly empty: The town houses were set too far apart, surrounded by indecently large gardens. The gate to Number 5 was open and a paved walk, slick with rain and fringed by herbaceous borders looking as if they were about to sprout seaweed, led to a modern villa built of brown brick, with a white pediment and white-mullioned windows. There was a black wreath hanging on the door.

A substantial maid opened the door. A dry mouse paw lay almost horizontally on the black-clad shelf of her chest, a totem amulet.

The maid escorted Mara to the living room, which was a strange mixture of ultramodern functional furniture—all chrome fittings and straight lines—and frilly feminine ornaments. The room looked like the result of a truce that was satisfactory to neither side. On the mantelpiece stood a large studio photograph in a plain frame, tied with a black ribbon. A plump girl wearing a ball gown, blond curls tumbling down her naked shoulders. Mara narrowed her eyes and saw the insipid face transform itself into a swelling, bursting mask under the relentless beat of spotlight-silvered rain.

"Elvira, my wife," said a voice behind her back.

"I know," said Mara, still hypnotized by the pathetic self-confidence of this debutante smile, cradled within the loop of the mourning ribbon. "But it must have been taken some years ago."

"She is twenty here. Soon after our wedding."

Mara finally turned around and started, not too obviously, she hoped. She had pictured Julian Sparrow as a sugar daddy, an aging moneymaker who had bought himself a young wife, now either relieved at the death of the woman who had become an embarrassment or upset at the loss of his acquisition. But the man who shook her hand and motioned her to sit was neither old nor fussy. In fact, he was striking: trim and fit, not tall but with the broad shoulders and tapering waist of an athlete. His angular face had a bird-of-prey quality about it, resembling an eagle or perhaps a kite but hardly a sparrow. Mara thought that he and his late wife were, like Mara herself, people whose totems did not fit their personalities. She had no connection to the Ferret and was glad to get rid of her mother's totem by adopting Ronald's instead. And Elvira's style of beauty was swanlike, if one wanted to be charitable, or gooselike, if one didn't, but with nothing of the chirpiness of a tiny street bird.

"You're not what I imagined a constabulary consultant to be," Julian Sparrow said, echoing her thoughts.

"I've worked with the constabulary on several cases already," Mara responded.

"Oh, I did not mean to doubt your competence," replied Mr. Sparrow. He had beautiful eyes, dark green and wide set, though they betrayed his age by the crow's feet that deepened when he smiled. His skin was white, delicate like a woman's and slightly crumpled; his hair fine and black, with just a sprinkling of gray at the temples.

"I would gladly employ a fortune-teller or even a Temple seer if I believed they could shed any light on my Elvira's death," he continued. "With the recent upheavals I suspect the constabulary gives low priority to one killing, no matter how atrocious. I will offer a reward, of course. The b ... the monster who has done what he has done to her must be caught."

Mara noted with pleasure that Julian Sparrow was about to use the b-word, a sign of a freethinker and a Humanist.

"The constabulary gives priority to your wife's murder, Mr. Sparrow," she said. "It is a terrorist attack, after all."

The moment she said it, she knew she had made a mistake. Julian's eyes widened.

"A terrorist attack? Nobody told me this! They said that Elvira was caught by some maniac, some perverse beast, and ... and killed and mutilated ..."

His voice shook and for the first time Mara saw a flicker of real feeling, more indignation than grief. Suddenly she realized what had happened. Unwilling to concede that a Power was employed to turn Elvira's body into the focus of a flood, the constabulary had told Julian Sparrow that the injuries had been inflicted prior to death. Mara could not imagine any weapon capable of doing what had been done to Elvira's body but perhaps the constabulary morticians had been at work on it before they showed it to the grieving husband. She was filled with anger at this cruel charade.

"There is still no confirmation," she said. "It's a working hypothesis. But if you ask me, Mr. Sparrow, yes, I believe that your wife was a victim of religious fanatics."

~

They were drinking verbena tea from tiny porcelain cups with gilded rims, having been served by the amulet-bearing maid whose pursed lips sufficiently indicated what she thought of this frivolity in the house of grief. Mara noted that though the maid was dressed in mourning, the widower was not.

"Tell me about your wife, Mr. Sparrow," she said.

Julian Sparrow mused. "What can I say? I married her when she was very young, very naive. She was still young when she died, and still naive, I'm afraid, even though she would consider herself a woman of the world."

"Was she clever?" asked Mara.

Julian Sparrow looked at her and smiled.

"Not what you would call clever, perhaps," he said. "But she was good-hearted, generous, and impulsive. Nothing dull about her."

He did not seem grief-stricken; in fact, there was a neutral quality in his voice when he was talking about his wife as if she were merely an acquaintance. His attention seemed to be focused on Mara, but she realized he was one of those rare people who give even casual interlocutors the impression of deep and undivided interest.

"Did you love her?" Mara blurted.

He's too slick, she told herself, *better he be offended so he might betray himself.* But he did not seem to be offended; in fact, he smiled again.

"You do come straight to the point, don't you? Well, no, I didn't. Not in the last years of our marriage. I was older than her. I fell in love violently with a pretty young girl and then coasted out of love, so to speak, slowly and painlessly. But I tried to give her what she wanted, and she tried to reciprocate, poor dear."

"And what did she want?"

"Money, to spend on gewgaws and pretty clothes. Attention. Security."

And what do you want? She wanted to ask. But he forestalled her.

"Now, confession for confession. What about you, Miss Raven? Or is it Mrs. Raven?"

She had her wedding ring on, but it was not obvious as such. Ronald and she had exchanged custom-made bands, ruby-studded wreaths of gold roses. After his disappearance, she started wearing hers on the right hand because of a superstition that the right direction is where the missing are found.

"Mrs. Raven."

"What does your husband think of your work with the constabulary? Is he a constable, too?"

Mara flushed; she hated not being taken seriously.

"My husband is an entry in the constabulary blotter," she said. "He disappeared more than a year ago."

Julian Sparrow spilled his tea and burst into apologies, but Mara saw that his impersonal attentiveness had given way to a more specific interest in her. Pressing her advantage, she went back to the subject of Elvira Sparrow.

"Your wife was perhaps a random victim; this is what some of my colleagues think. But she was found on the Hill at night. Was she the type to wander alone?"

"Absolutely not. She would not even join me on my excursions into the countryside. And she was not athletic. How did she get to the Hill?"

Mara bit her lip; she had not thought of asking Detective Hart or Mr. Seal about it.

"We're looking into it," she said.

"Perhaps ..." he started, then stopped.

"What?"

"No, nothing. But could she have been killed somewhere else and brought to the Hill?"

"Then whoever brought her must have carried the body up the Hill or driven there. But even if he had a car, the body was found in a clearing some distance away from the road, so he would have had to carry it through the bushes."

"Didn't they find footprints?"

"There was flooding," said Mara. "Part of the topsoil was washed away."

She hoped he would not inquire where the flood originated, and he did not. He was frowning and playing with his teaspoon. Mara watched the dainty movements of his fingers.

"Was it possible that your wife was lured to the Hill?" she asked. "Went there to meet somebody?"

He shrugged.

"Unlikely but possible."

"Was she devout?"

"Devout? Elvira? No. If you're thinking about some crazy Ancestral ritual, forget it. The only way she could be lured to a place like that was if she went to meet a lover."

Seeing Mara's shocked face, he laughed.

"You asked whether I loved my wife and I answered. Part of our arrangement was that we gave each other freedom. Don't misunderstand me; I was fond of her. Perhaps almost in a parental fashion. We have no children and I felt responsible for her. But I was not jealous, if this is what you want to ask. Why should I be? I told you, we were both free."

"So why not divorce?" asked Mara. "It's easier now than it used to be."

"It's still inconvenient and expensive. And what for? Neither of us wanted to remarry and the arrangement suited us fine."

Mara thought, *And then you could easily dump any woman who got too close.* But what did Elvira really think about it?

"So did you know if she had a lover?"

He shrugged.

"I assume she had. Poor Elvira was romantic as a schoolgirl and pined without excitement in her life. But I don't know who he was. The last affair I knew about ended some time ago."

"Who was the man?"

"One Thomas Rabbit, an up-and-coming young functionary in the Animal House. But he treated Elvira badly. Ditched her when she became an encumbrance to his career."

"And she told you about this?" asked Mara.

"She was heartbroken and cried on my shoulder. She always did."

Mara supposed she should feel scandalized but instead she was amused and titillated. Her own marriage appeared dull and old-fashioned in comparison. And Ronald and she were younger than Mr. and Mrs. Sparrow!

Which reminded her that she and poor Elvira did have something in common: Both took the names of their husbands' totem animals, which was uncommon. She wanted to ask Julian about it but there was something else more urgent she wanted to know.

"Have you ever heard the name of Thomas Hawk, Mr. Sparrow?"

"No. Should I have?"

"George Buzzard?"

"No. I've never met anybody named Buzzard. Do they still exist?"

"Buzzards? In the South Continent, I think. Did they ever live on the Plains?"

"At the time of the Ancestors. That's the idea, isn't it? That every creature whose name we own lived here in First City under the benevolent tutelage of the Four."

He was speaking lightly and with an undercurrent of irony.

"I don't believe it," said Mara. "Do you?"

Their eyes met.

"No," he said. "I don't believe it either."

CHAPTER 10. THE ATTACK

Mara stood at the entrance to her apartment building, looking up into the piled-up clouds, heavy and reddish against the night sky like drying puddles of blood. For a change, there was no rain, only a brisk chilly wind that had torn irregular gaps in the clouds, sent them scudding across the huge emptiness above the Plains, and allowed the anemic crescent of the moon to peep suspiciously down upon the City.

Mara was seeking out the stars, but they were hardly visible, a handful of shimmering points of light. The pollution in the City was getting worse each day, so that even the protracted rain had not managed to clear the atmosphere completely. This, of course, was one of the main grievances of the devout: that having killed the Ancestors and enslaved lesser creatures, man was now destroying Nature wholesale.

But Mara was thinking about the enormous empty spaces outside the tiny human stronghold, for large as the City had grown, it still covered only part of the Great Plains, and beyond the Plains were mountains, and hills, and valleys, and then the endless ocean, and scattered islands, and the scorched deserts and peculiar rock formations of the South Continent, and then the ocean again. And no human presence beyond First City and its growing girdle of fields and agricultural settlements. She thought about the City as it would be seen from above, by a hawk or a raven or a buzzard: a glowing mass of light, almost solid at its core but thinning out at the circumference, disintegrating into handfuls of embers scattered here and there. And then a solitary defiant light in some outlying cabin, a hermit poring over the *Book of the Remnant* or a madman seeking solitude—she had heard about such people. Perhaps a tiny brave gleam as a lonely ship plied the dark waters on its way to the South Continent. And then nothing. Miles and miles of darkness, damp woods with their shivering, miserable inhabitants whose dim brains would never teach them the use of fire; silent hillsides, gorse and heather beaten into the mud, late flowers rotting, scree and bare rock and dying insects and hibernating snakes ... And no mind to understand it all, no voice to speak, no hand to touch. She was filled with vast and inchoate pity toward the dumb creation without man. And then she pitied man too, but in a detached way, as if she herself was not only an observer, a cold and hollow presence, trying to fill itself with alien emotions.

Mara shivered. It was moments like these that made her fear madness. From long practice she knew action of any kind was the only countermeasure to distract herself from her intrusive thoughts. And today she had action, more than she expected. Fumbling in her purse for the front-door key (it was so late that the concierge would be asleep already) she let her mind drift back to Julian Sparrow.

Their conversation prolonging, neither willing to say good-bye, he had finally asked her to have dinner with him. It was irregular but Mara did not care. He took her to an expensive restaurant that served meat. Since Ronald's disappearance Mara had not been out to places like this; an occasional dinner with Mr. Seal tended to be in scholarly clubs with starched tablecloths and elderly waiters in frock coats. But she felt at home as they entered the glitter of the restaurant and she saw the sleek women in daring sleeveless dresses, their faces almost bare, and the men in white, silver, and powder-blue suits. The place smelled of perfume, sweat, and roasted meat, and the unnaturally bright flowers in chrome vases were made of paper. The rain was still falling outside but this was a place for humanity.

Julian was well known here. Some women looked at her curiously; she suspected that it was not only because of her conservative clothes but because they had some sort of relationship with her companion.

It is not like Ronald, she told herself. When her husband courted her, she was tossed around by the waves of emotion so strong that she did not even try to control them. She let herself go, plummeting to the depths of despair when he failed to call and instantly being lifted into ecstasy when she heard his voice. She had no hopes, no plans; she thought of nothing except seeing him again. She barely knew who she was. This state of self-forgetfulness only started to dissipate after their wedding, and she felt a stab of regret when she first realized Ronald's presence was no longer capable of obliterating space and time.

But Julian Sparrow ... She could see what was happening; she had felt a similar stirring in the presence of Detective Hart, only to have it squashed by his fanatical arrogance. Julian Sparrow was handsome, sophisticated, and intelligent. He was also older than she, which meant he was at a disadvantage in the game of attraction. Or thought that he was. She was not going to fall in love with him. She loved her husband. But her husband was missing and meanwhile, she was entitled to a life of her own. Real life, not the vivid hallucinations of the dream-sea.

They talked about the dream-sea too. He asked, "What kind of consultation do you do?"

Mara considered giving an evasive answer but suddenly felt tired of circumspection.

"I have a gift," she said. "A Power."

He raised his delicately arched eyebrows.

"But you are not Temple-affiliated, are you?"

"It has nothing to do with the Temple," Mara responded. "It's a talent, one of those that seem to have been much more widespread in the old times. It is listed in several books of divination."

"What is it?"

"It's called dreamfishing."

Plainly, he had never heard of it, which was not surprising, but he was interested, so Mara continued:

"There is a theory that all dreams come from the same source. This source has been called the dream-sea. I have the ability to access it. Once there, I may look for answers to specific questions. It's not easy and the answers are never straightforward ... but that's what it is."

It'd been a long time since she had had to explain her Power to an outsider and she felt defensive, but Julian Sparrow appeared to be fascinated.

"You mean, you go to this place, this dream-sea, every night?"

"Not really. I used to when I was a teenager and did not know how to control my dreaming. It would leave me exhausted, unable to get up. My parents became concerned; they thought I was sick or crazy. Fortunately, they got in touch with a man, a scientist, who knew what was happening, and he trained me, taught me how to enter the dream-sea only when I wanted to, how to ask specific questions and to hunt for answers."

"But what is it like, this dream-sea?"

"It's beautiful," she said.

"As beautiful as the real sea? The one beyond the Plains?"

"More so. I saw the pictures, read books by explorers. I used to think that maybe my dream-sea was a real place, somewhere in the world, and I could go there. But it seems very different. The way they describe it, the real sea is gray and cold, empty shingle beaches, sharp rocks, little life, some lichens and weeds on the shore. The dream-sea is lush and there are ... there are some amazing creatures in it."

"But is it a real place," he insisted, "or an illusion?"

"What's real?" she asked.

At this point a waiter brought her main course, a lamb casserole with peas and carrots. She put a piece of chewy meat into her mouth with the brief thrill of an expensive indulgence. She hardly bothered to cook for herself and certainly not meat. Julian was having veal cutlets and eating them with no fuss.

"I wanted to be an explorer when I was a boy," he said. "Of course, my father objected and being his only son, I had to comply and take over the business. I had never heard about the dream-sea, or I would have been tempted to try to develop this ability you have."

Mara shook her head.

"It cannot be developed. It's inborn."

She knew it well, having repeatedly tried to teach Mr. Seal to accompany her and failing. He had been sorely disappointed; she had been secretly relieved. She wanted the dream-sea for herself.

"So," he said, "you travel there in your dreams for pleasure. But you also do the constabulary's commissions and are paid for them. Aren't you lucky."

"Well," said Mara, "the wages are more of an ideal than reality. The bureaucracy cannot decide what budget allocation can pay for dreams. But yes, I suppose I'm lucky."

"Are you going to ask the dream-sea who killed Elvira?"

"It's not that simple. I have to have clues. The dream-sea responds to my state of mind, my emotions, even to my health. The times when I was sick and went inside, the sea reacted violently. The water was the color of blood. And sometimes it would cure me, and sometimes it would make it worse. So now I only go there when I'm healthy and balanced in body and mind. Also, I have to be clear what I am asking: The sea can be obscure in its answers and even mischievous."

"Strange. You talk of it sometimes as if it were a place, and sometimes as if it were a living being. Which one is it?"

Mara frowned; nobody, not even Mr. Seal, had ever asked that.

"It is a place," she said. "I don't know where it exists, but I know it exists outside of my mind. There is also an intelligence there. Or perhaps more than one. And these ... entities talk to me. Some of them. And some ..."

She shook her head, frustrated.

"I don't know how to say it," she cried. "It's so different from First City! It's a different place and a different me."

Julian smiled.

"I would like to get to know the First City Mara better, for starters. And the dream-sea Mara too, eventually."

This was a promise and standing in the pool of thick shadows in front of her building, still fumbling in her purse for the key, she smiled at the thought of what it implied. He had wanted to see her home, but she refused, feeling more than a little drunk and afraid to spoil the perfect balance of their date. She had taken a cab instead.

Finally, her fingers clutched the key. And at the same instance, she felt a presence behind her and before she turned, the world dissolved in blinding light and then went black.

～

Her face is pressed against the sand; sand crunchy in her mouth, salty and hot like pork rinds; sand tickling her nose, separate grains crawling on her forehead. Her back feels as if somebody is holding a torch close to her skin.

She flops over and cries, clapping her hands over her eyes. Even through the intertwined fingers she can feel the pitiless golden glare drilling into her brain. Her body is bathed in sweat that glues patches of sand over her nakedness.

Her lids seem to be welded together. She pries them open with her fingers and risks another glance into the sky. The dizzying dome overhead is uniformly yellow, shining and hot like a shield of beaten gold, shading away to bronze over the horizon. It looks as if the sun has been stretched like putty, smeared over the heavens.

She clambers to her feet and looks down at herself. Her thighs are dark with caked blood. She sways, falls to her knees, and crawls toward the sea. It is still and glaring, a polished copper sheet under the sky of bronze and gold. It magnifies the heat, giving off no hint of freshness.

The sand heaves under her. Something bright shoots out like an arrow of gold, difficult to see against the background. A slim yellow snake traces an arc in the incandescent air and dives back into the sand.

The margin of the sea is close, but its unnatural stillness terrifies her. She imagines it boiling with suppressed fury, so that the moment she touches it, it will lash back at her, uncoil like the snake, and squash her with its immeasurable might.

Another movement. Something large crawls across her path, something orange and scarlet. It is a centipede as big as Mara, its segmented body giving off a sharp odor like a squashed bedbug. Its innumerable paddle-shaped legs pass close to Mara's face. An almost invisible tendril trails slime across her cheek.

She runs headlong into the sea, splashing gold. It is like running into a pool of acid. The hot, angry water washes over Mara's body with an audible hiss. But after the first shock the pain subsides. The water does not cool her but rather inures her to the heat so that the combined glare of the sea and the sky does not hurt anymore. Her skin burns as it is licked clean by the astringent sea; the blood on her thighs dissolves and gingerly touching herself, she discovers the skin clear and unblemished.

"Thank you," she whispers.

Something shifts at the corner of her eye, a dark shadow against the golden light. She lifts her head. A small island pops out from the water, not far from the shore, a jutting, irregular rock, its tip crowned by a single giant tree bearing clusters of eyes. Another one appears beside it, lower, its shape like a crouching animal, but also with an eye-festooned tree. And then another and another. Mara's island is being circled by sentinels.

"What do you want?" she cries.

~

"Mara?"

Something cool touched her forehead.

Mara opened her eyes. Her mother's face swam into focus, its wrinkles and faded blue eyes as familiar as the back of her own hand. Now it crumpled, preparatory to tears.

"You're awake? Praise the Ancestors!"

The thoughtless piety—for her mother was a Humanist by default, having been reared in more liberal times—irritated Mara and nipped in the bud any softer emotions. She pushed away the restraining hand and sat up. She was in her own bed at home. The sky outside the window was gray with daylight.

"What happened?"

"The concierge phoned me. She was awakened by the pounding on the door and when she went out, she found you on the doorstep, unconscious. I've been here since midnight."

Mara tried to take stock. Her temples throbbed, there was a foul taste in her mouth, and she was sore between the legs but when she touched the back of her head there was no bump. She remembered the presence behind her.

"Was I raped?"

Her mother's eyes opened wide in horror.

"Mara, please!"

"Please what? I want to know what happened to me. Did you call a doctor? Was I examined?"

"No, I mean ... there was no need. Mr. Seal said ..."

"What Mr. Seal? Did you call him instead of a doctor and the constabulary? Where is he?"

Her mother nodded in the direction of the living room. Mara sighed. Her mother's attitude to Mr. Seal was predictable: She needed a male presence to give stability to the lives of her daughter and herself. Once it had been Mara's father, then Ronald, and now Mr. Seal. Mara was convinced that her mother nursed a secret hope that she would marry Mr. Seal after a decent period of mourning.

"Did he examine me?"

"Of course not," said her mother. "I undressed you and your clothes had not been interfered with."

This was reassuring. And yet Mara remembered the unexpected sojourn at the dream-sea and the blood on her thighs. And she did feel sore.

"You said somebody pounded on the front door. Who was it?"

"The concierge does not know. By the time she got there, you were alone, lying on the doorstep. She brought you in and phoned me straight away."

Mara swung her legs over the edge of the bed and stood disregarding her mother's protests. She walked into the bathroom, and locking the door pulled off the nightgown that her mother had dressed her in.

There were no bruises or abrasions on her body and when, gritting her teeth, she examined her genitals with a hand mirror, there were no signs of violence or sex. And yet she felt violated deep inside, deeper than her vagina, as if somebody had roughly touched those parts of her that were not meant to be seen or handled: her uterus, her liver, or her heart.

She filled the tub and lay in the hot water until it was only tepid. Her mother knocked on the door, but Mara told her she would come out in her own good time and if Mr. Seal wanted to go home, he was free to do so.

Trudging into the kitchen in her robe, she heard voices from the living room and realized Mr. Seal was still there, talking to her mother. She roughly pulled the door of the chill-box, took out a couple of eggs and some cheese, and busied herself with making breakfast, daring her mother to pop in. But Mrs. Ferret, familiar with her daughter's temper, prudently stayed in the living room.

Mara felt both famished and nauseous. She devoured a plateful of scrambled eggs and drank a mug of herbal tea. It filled her stomach but failed to settle it. Finally, she decided that facing her mentor was unavoidable. Pulling her robe tighter around her, she marched into the living room. He turned sharply when she walked in and she saw something in his face that was both unexpected and vaguely alarming, a kind of hunger. He came up to her and squeezed her hands.

"Tell me what happened!"

The long habit of obedience kicked in and she told him almost everything. But she did not mention that she had been to the dream-sea. Since she learned to call up Light Puppies, such spontaneous visits became rare. But this time she had felt rudely pushed onto the golden beach. Or had she been perhaps pulled in?

"This Julian Sparrow," Mr. Seal asked, "could he have followed you?"

"What?" Mara looked at him with amazement. "You think he attacked me? Why would he?"

"He's a suspect in his wife's death."

"No, he's not!" Mara exploded. "He has no connection to your putative conspiracy. He's not a believer."

"Most murders occur in the family."

"You can't have it both ways! Either Elvira Sparrow was a chance victim of the Army of the Revealer, or her husband dispatched her, which I see no earthly reason for him to do. In any case, I can't imagine him employing a Power to turn his wife's body into a flood!"

Mr. Seal peered at her.

"You like him," he asked, "don't you?"

"Yes, I do!" Mara said. "And I don't for a moment believe he hit me on the head and left me lying on the doorstep."

"All right, but if not him, who? A vagabond? It's not impossible. There has been an epidemic of muggings, robberies, and even … assaults on women. How could you have been so reckless, Mara, to walk home alone at such an hour?"

"My mother says I wasn't raped," said Mara, watching his reaction, and she was not disappointed: There was a flicker of anger in his eyes, and his answer came as quick as a whiplash:

"Would you like to have been?"

She expected something like this but nevertheless was as shocked as a child who discovers her parents having sex. Mr. Seal's shoulders slumped.

"I'm sorry, Mara," he mumbled. "This was uncalled for. I'm concerned for you."

"I understand," she said. And she did, only too well.

"Could this attack have been linked to the Sparrow investigation?" she asked after a pause, trying to maintain the semblance of normality. For herself, she decided it had something to do with Edna's group. But she never told Mr. Seal about it and did not intend to. She wanted to pursue this line of investigation on her own, without involving the constabulary. She was pretty sure that Mr. Seal would instantly inform the chief constable and perhaps the Fur Guardian, and then the investigation would be out of her hands, and she would be sidelined.

She would not be surprised by any kind of violence from George Buzzard—she was sure he killed Carla Marmot. Nor would she find it improbable that he found out where she lived. But what did he try to achieve by attacking her? Did he try to kill her and fail? Not likely. Did he try to scare her? Send a message? What message?

"The only people who know about your involvement in the investigation are the chief constable, the Fur Guardian, Detective Hart, and me," Mr. Seal said. "Surely you're not suggesting that one of us has betrayed you to the terrorists?"

Mara said nothing.

"In any case," continued Mr. Seal, "we ought to take precautions. Perhaps a bodyguard ..."

"No!" cried Mara.

"But ..." he began.

A strange grumbling sound came from the outside, so low that it reverberated in their bones. They rushed to the window, joined by the agitated Mrs. Ferret, and looked out. For a moment, all seemed normal, the midmorning street outside as drab as a dishrag. Only the rain had stopped.

Something small and dark went by the window, so quickly that Mara did not make it out. A hailstone? It seemed too big, too irregular.

Another hailstone-thing and then another. They pounded the pavement but with no sharp cracking sound of hail. Instead, the noise that came faintly from behind the closed window was wet and plopping.

"Look!" Mrs. Ferret cried.

Below the pavement was turning red.

A man popped out from a doorway across the street and stood staring into the sky, his mouth hanging open. A small scurrying shape clawed at his scalp, another one clung to his coat, yet another clambered up his sleeve. The man, finally jolted out of his shock, windmilled his arms, batting at the falling shapes, trying to shake off the crawling population of his body. Even through the double-glazed window they could hear his screams.

It was raining mice.

Flinging away the accumulating weight of rodents, the man ran back into the house. Mrs. Ferret blubbered. Mara stared.

It stopped as suddenly as it started. The street was covered by tiny bodies that exploded, strewing their innards all over the asphalt. The later arrivals that had landed on their fellows and survived nosed among the bloody fur in the gutters.

Mrs. Ferret made a gagging sound. Mr. Seal turned away; his plump hand pressed to his lips.

Mara kept staring, trying to decipher the calligraphy of blood.

CHAPTER 11. BLACK FLOWERS

"They had cleaned up all the main streets," Mrs. Ferret said, more for the sake of having a one-sided conversation than reporting news that Mara was aware of. The latest issue of the *Voice of the City* was spread on the breakfast table; in the living room, the usually silent wireless was droning unceasingly. Mara's mother abandoned her previous distrust of this newfangled invention and became an avid listener. She had her own device at home but for now, she was staying with her daughter.

Mara was not happy about this arrangement, but she did not have the heart to send her mother back to her home through chaotic streets infested with rotting mice and fear. Louisa Ferret was alone and lonely, even though her new home (paid for with Ronald's money) was more centrally located than the poor suburban apartment she shared with her daughter when Mara was growing up. Mara did not love her mother but since she had no actual complaint against her to justify her coldness, she periodically tried to be a better daughter. She did not know why it seemed important to her to present the dutiful façade, but it did. For herself, she had long ago resolved never to have children.

It was different with Mr. Seal. Something shifted in their

mentor-student relationship, something so weighty and yet so elusive that Mara avoided dwelling on it or trying to give it a name. She had icily told him that she would like to rest and that she would inform Detective Hart of the attack herself when, and if, it became necessary. She was practically showing him the door as she would have never dared to do even a month ago. Mr. Seal must have realized what was happening because he did not object. He silently picked up his hat and walked out. If he expected to guilt Mara into feeling remorse, he miscalculated. She felt only relief when he was gone.

And now, Mara was slumped over her breakfast. There was no particular ache she could pinpoint but her guts felt raw as if they had become too large for her body and were rubbing against each other. She refused to read the newspaper, but the drone of the wireless was becoming unendurable.

"The Fish Guardian says—" Mrs. Ferret continued.

"I'm going out, Mama," Mara declared.

"You're sick!" Mrs. Ferret squealed.

"No, I'm not!" Mara snapped back. "I have things to do!"

In fact, she had nothing to do but as she was getting dressed an idea formed. She decided to go back to the Lynx temple where she had first met Edna. Perhaps she would meet her again. Or perhaps she could talk to the local Guardian who Edna had called "a snitch" to find out more. But as she was putting her coat on, the phone rang in the bedroom. She rushed in to forestall her mother, picked up the receiver, and felt a pleasant warmth spread through her body as Julian's voice said, "Hello."

They chatted for a couple of minutes. He wanted to know how she felt. She said she was fine, saying nothing about the attack, of course. They made appropriate noises about the mice rain.

"Do you think it's the end of the world?" he asked.

"Yes," she said, and his brief silence indicated he realized she meant it.

"So would you like to escape from the City with me?" he finally asked.

"What?"

"A day trip. I often drive into the countryside."

"Drive?"

"Yes. I have my own car. Didn't I tell you?"

He hadn't. Private cars were rare because of the prohibitive expense of upkeep and fuel. The rich used cabs, the middle class —train and trolleys; the poor walked. In the countryside, some still relied on horses.

"It's a terrible waste of money, and I cannot really afford it. But do you remember, I told you about my childhood desire to be an explorer?"

"Yes, I remember."

"Well, in default of mapping out the South Continent, I travel all over the countryside. I have discovered some amazing places. Abandoned villages, old houses, caves."

"Really?" Mara felt a stirring of interest. "But don't you need quality roads for a car? I thought many places outside the City only had mud-tracks."

"Not true. There are some old, paved roads. Really old; perhaps even ..."

He did not complete the sentence, but it pricked her interest even further. Was he really about to say "before the Rebellion"? The common assumption was that there was nothing built or made before the Rebellion because, before that mythical event, humans had lived in the Abode of the Ancestors.

"Would you like to see?"

"Yes."

"How about if I meet you in half an hour? Where do you live?"

Mara gave him her address and told him to wait in the car. She had no desire to fend off her mother's onslaught of questions.

Outside, the sky was the color of weak tea, and the rain-laden air had a sharp smell, like a fire drenched with a bucketful of water. Underlying the grayness of the autumn day was a jaundice of the universe giving a yellowish tinge to the sky, houses, and people's faces.

The car was idling at the curb and Julian got out when she approached. He was wearing a thick sports coat and smelled of nettles and pine: some expensive aftershave, no doubt. Mara approved; she liked strong perfumes and after Ronald's disappearance, never again wore the flowery scents he preferred. The one she had on now was made of bitter almond with an undercurrent of heady musk.

They drove through the crowded streets, the first pedestrian rush of the morning petering out. Mara scanned the faces, looking for signs of tension and anxiety and finding plenty. Julian entertained her with a whimsical account of his earlier encounter with a disheveled procession chanting "We want the Ancestors!" They had banged on Julian's car at the red light, but to his luck a stray raccoon crossed the street and the enthusiastic devotees ran in pursuit of the hapless creature that, with no awareness of its own spiritual significance, sought panicky retreat in the nearest alley. Mara's lips curled contemptuously.

"They will destroy the City," she said.

"Don't you give them more importance than they are worth?"

"Where do you think the rain of mice came from?"

"I don't see the connection."

"It's not a natural event."

"I can't imagine anybody in the Temple having that kind of Power."

"Maybe not in the Temple. But what about the people who caused a flood to issue from your wife's dead body?"

The car screeched as he hit the brakes.

"What do you mean?"

Mara told him. If he was the murderer, she was not telling him anything new. And if he was innocent, then he deserved to know how his wife died.

She watched his face as she spoke, but it was unreadable.

"Why wasn't I told?"

"I don't know. But I think you have the right to know."

"Damn I do! I thought Elvira had been tortured. But do you understand what that means?"

"That it was a terrorist act perpetrated by the Army ... by religious fanatics; that your wife was a random victim; that the aim was to send a message to the Temple; and that the same people who killed her will not rest until they have destroyed the whole City."

"But the murder and the ... the flood did not coincide in time, did they?"

"No. Elvira had been dead for at least two or three hours when I arrived on the scene."

"So how do you know that the murder and the desecration of the corpse were perpetrated by the same person?"

"I don't know," she said. "I assumed they were. What would be the reason to believe they were not?"

"The best reason in the world. Whoever employed a Power to call up a flood through my wife's body must have been present at the scene when it happened."

"What?!"

"Don't you know that? You have a Power. Can you transfer it to somebody else?"

"No."

"A Power cannot be employed at a distance. Can you ride a bicycle sitting in an armchair? Who else was there with you?"

"Plenty of people, but all of them from the constabulary."

"So? If there is a religious conspiracy, it stands to reason the constabulary would be involved."

"How do you know that?" Mara asked. "How come you're such an authority on Powers? I thought you had no love for the Temple freaks."

"I don't. But I read about Powers."

"Why?"

"Why? You have your dream-sea to escape to but we ordinary mortals don't. It's easy for you to look down at the fools who march and wave banners and scream for the Ancestors to come back and lead us away from here. But have you ever considered what it is like to be condemned to prison without knowing your crime?"

"Prison? It's our City, our home!"

"No, it's not. It wasn't built by us. We're chained to it. We're orphans in this world, Mara. Don't you know it, don't you feel it? Yes, I despise the Guardians who turn themselves into beasts, and the silly old women who spend their lives atoning for the sins they've not committed, and the mindless grass-eaters, and the fashionable penitents, the whole lot of them! But there is something, Mara. There must be something beyond what we see, what we know! I would gladly give all my money to know what it is."

"And would you kill for it?" Mara asked.

He turned the ignition, and the car took off with a wet screech.

"No," he said. "I have a philistine's prejudice against murder."

They drove in silence, lost in a maze of squalid alleys with garbage lying in huge mounds, and dilapidated huts festooned with garlands of paper flowers, and laundry rotting in the ruined courtyards. They turned a corner and the street opened into a huge gray emptiness. Mara gasped.

Julian pulled up and they both walked to the edge of the devastation. The ground dipped and below was a wasteland of ruins: bricks and boards and plaster mixed with mud into a gray-brown paste, beams poking up into the sky at sharp angles like broken bones, flattened tin huts and empty doorframes, gaping in mute screams. Some rags were draped over an overturned, splintered chair, by accident or design she could not tell. At the edge of the wasteland somebody had left a pathetic bunch of flowers, beaten into the earth by the incessant rain.

"Lonelyhearts," she whispered.

"Yes."

"Why aren't they working, clearing away the ruins?"

"Today is a Temple holiday, remember?"

"But there might still be survivors trapped there!"

"The Temple officials declared there are none. They are going to wait four days and then conduct a purification ceremony. Only after this will the Animal House send work crews to clear the site."

Mara opened her mouth to voice her indignation, but she was suddenly pierced by a sickening jolt of pain that came from her lower belly. The world seemed to shift and wobble. Julian caught her arm.

"Are you unwell?"

"I'm fine," she said, but it was a lie. Even though the pain and the heaving subsided, she suddenly caught a glimpse of a tiny pale hand clutching at the rusty edge of an iron sheet in the field of devastation. And though the rest of the body was buried under the rubble, she seemed to be able to see through the metal sheets and broken bricks and locate the pulpy mass the hand was attached to. She saw more and more bodies as if the ruins of Lonelyhearts were fading, becoming transparent, and only corpses remained: a man impaled by a broken bedstead; a woman flattened under a collapsed wall. Mara squeezed her eyes shut and when she opened them, the vision was gone.

She did not know where they were but Julian drove confidently, as if he had navigated those mean streets many times. She was surprised to see that the area of the slums did not signify the outer limits of the City. On the contrary, once they passed through a ring of garbage mountains, houses held together by graffiti, and naked toddlers splashing in rainbow puddles, the landscape started improving. It was also changing. The streets were wider and cleaner now but poorly paved, whole stretches of nothing but mud and gravel. The houses were small, white-washed affairs, surrounded by orchards and vegetable gardens, separated from each other by peeling fences or tangles of chicken wire. A couple of times Julian had to slow down as a rooster followed by a procession of hens majestically crossed the road. When Mara saw the tall trees with thin silver bark shading the rain-beaten track ahead and a white rabbit hopping along the grass verge, she knew they were in the country.

She had never been here. Having grown up in suburbia, the countryside had been the dreaded abyss into which she and her mother would plummet if they lost the little money they had. The direction of her dreams had always been inward, toward the heart of the City. She was shocked to see that, at least outwardly, the farming folk had better living conditions than the urban poor.

Julian seemed to read her mind.

"It's not too bad," he said. "At least if you don't look too closely. Lots of sickness here."

"So, is it true that there are diseases in the countryside?"

"It's true. But don't worry, you need to stay a couple of years to be affected."

"I am not worried about myself," Mara said, and she was not. Instead, she was perturbed by the realization that she did not know enough about the geography of the City. She had been escaping into the dream-sea from the humdrum reality of every-day, but now it turned out that everyday held unanswered questions and mysteries that were weaving around her like a net of slimy seaweeds, trapping her in the gray zone between two worlds, neither of them her own.

The car glided forward. Mara studied Julian's hands on the steering wheel and thought that she would like to learn to drive.

But Elvira was on her mind, and she finally asked a question she had forgotten to ask before.

"What was your wife's totem animal before she got married? I may need to know it in the dream-sea."

Julian pushed on some pedal and the car leaped through a puddle, splashing the windows with dirty water.

"Sparrow," he said. "It is her original totem. I took her name when we got married, not the other way round."

Mara was flabbergasted. She had never heard of any man doing this. It was on the tip of her tongue to ask what *his* totem animal had been when a hunched shape suddenly darted into the street in front of the car that slewed and screeched as Julian fought to gain control of the shuddering metal. Mara was thrown forward but restrained by the seat belt that Julian had made her put on, despite her protests that it was unnecessary. Now she was profoundly grateful.

The car finally stopped with its blunt nose stuck into the grassy verge. A stream of curses followed as Julian rolled down the window and yelled at the man who stood next to a small house staring at them with one round eye, as yellow and glistening as an eye of a carp. The other eye was covered by incrustations of inflamed flesh. The man's mouth was also round and lipless, and small, pointed teeth chewed at his chin as he listened to Julian's colorful descriptions of his Ancestors with the attention of a toddler learning that words had meaning. A stocky woman came out of the house and pulled the man inside. He obeyed meekly, his splayed, almost fused, feet making splashing noises in the puddles.

"I'm sorry," Julian said. "Please forgive my language. You expect to deal with stupid pedestrians in the City, but here?"

"I've heard worse," Mara said, which was a lie. "But this man ... what was wrong with him?"

"Countryside sickness. One of many. Again, I'm sorry. This is not the adventure I envisioned. Do you want to go back?"

"No, not at all. Let's explore."

They drove on the now-deserted road, and Mara was thinking furiously.

"Do you know of Charles Finch's theories?" she asked.

Finch who had died some years ago was a darling of Humanist intellectuals, and an object of scorn and vituperation from the Temple.

"Yes," Julian responded. "He believes that humans evolved from animals naturally, perhaps on the South Continent, and then migrated here, settled on the Plains. There were never any Ancestors, it's just a legend."

"Do you think he is right?" Mara asked.

She expected him to say yes. And then it would be yet another way to differentiate between him and Ronald, who had no interest in human origins but who insisted on his wife's parroting whatever platitudes were common among the elite at any given time because it was good for his business. But Julian hesitated for such a long time that Mara's heart sank.

"I want to believe it," he said, finally. "I certainly don't take the *Book of the Remnant* literally or pray to the Slaughtered Ones. But look at where we are. You would expect First City to have a boundary of some kind, but it doesn't. It peters out, and then the countryside begins. And all those villages run into each other. A field here or there, a cluster of homes ... It is as if the human population spread out from the City center in waves, populating the country on an ad hoc basis, settling where the land was good or there was a source of water. And then successive waves pushed the envelope a little further. But humans need food first. They would start by settling in small villages, growing crops, and only later, with better technology and increasing numbers, start building a City. Not the other way round."

"No!" Mara exclaimed. "Humans need cities. This is what makes us human!"

Julian glanced at her, surprised by her vehemence.

"Is there a City in the dream-sea?" he asked.

Mara started, remembering Mr. Seal asking the same question.

"Yes," she said, even though she did not know where her sudden certainty came from. "I haven't dived into it yet, but I will. I will."

The road narrowed to a gravelly rut between the banks of sodden grass and thorny bushes. There were no more houses in sight. The car was making alarming noises but steadily chugging along. A splatter of rain landed on the windshield.

The lane wound between high hedges but suddenly the landscape flattened out into a vast field covered by brown rain-rotted stubble and bounded by the charcoal fringe of the naked woods. And in the middle of it ...

Mara had never seen any building that so palpably gave off an aura of age. The oldest structures in First City—the Temple and the Animal House—seemed young by comparison.

Julian stopped the car, and they got out. Mara's boots sank into the liquid mud, but she paid no attention, spellbound by the sight. Broken circular walls rose up from the accumulation of humus and rocks, composed of giant uneven stones larded with thick layers of mortar. There was something crude and primeval about the stonework. The rough surface was mottled with yellow and brown lichen.

Mara rushed forward, clambered up the heaps of debris, and pushed her palms flat against the wet stone. Mute shock surged through her body, insidious and penetrating.

Julian followed her but did not touch the wall. They stood side by side, contemplating the ruins. They appeared to be remnants of several towers closely grouped together. The highest wall was a little above Mara's head. But there were nettle-covered hammocks nearby, created, Mara thought, by the collapsed stonework. There was no saying how tall the towers had originally been.

"I want to show you something else," said Julian. "Follow me carefully; it's easy to break a leg here."

They rounded the tower, Mara's boots slipping into the crevices. On the other side the wall was only half Mara's height and the circular space inside the tower was visible. It was covered with short, silky grass, lush and green in striking opposition to the stubble outside. Here and there the grass was dotted with large velvet-black flowers, shaped like double butterflies. The moisture-laden air was thick with a pungent perfume, like wet iron and sweet blood mixed together. Mara inhaled it greedily.

"What are they called?" she asked. "I have never seen flowers like these."

Julian shrugged.

"I don't think they grow anywhere else. When I first came here, it was midsummer, and you could not see the grass for the blooms. The stink was so bad I thought there was a dead body inside. But when I tried to ask around, nobody knew anything. It's like this place does not exist."

Mara's fingers tightened on the stones.

"There are more islands of these flowers inside the other towers," he went on. "I thought about bringing a natural historian here. I know a man who was Charles Finch's last student. But there is something about this place that gives me the creeps. And at the same time, I want to keep it to myself. You're the first person I brought to see it."

Mara suddenly vaulted over the low wall and landed on the juicy turf.

"What are you doing?" exclaimed Julian.

Mara knelt and started digging with her bare hands in the squishy, oily earth. She loosened up the bulbous root of one of the black flowers and gently tugged on the stalk until the plant popped free. Its hairy stem dangled a fist-sized reddish mass that pulsated feebly but rhythmically. The mass was lobed and veined, with two short, hollow tubes protruding from its upper part.

"What is this?" Julian cried in disgust.

"It is a heart," Mara answered. "A human heart."

"Let go of it!"

Mara contemplated the pulpy root for a while and then cupped it in her palm and squeezed. Red juice squirted out and the thick black petals of the flower folded like a dying butterfly's wings. She let the plant drop and vaulted back.

"Let's go home."

They drove back in silence. It was only when they were entering the City center that Julian finally shattered it with a question:

"You said you had never seen these flowers before. How did you know to dig for the root? How did you know it was a human heart?"

Mara sighed. "I did not know. But when I saw them ... it was like I had to do it. And yes, it was a human heart."

"But it was beating!" Julian exclaimed. Mara shrugged.

He bit his lip as they navigated the darkening streets.

"Could it be you saw flowers like these in your dream-sea?"

"Perhaps. I don't remember."

She saw he was looking at her hands, still stained with the juice of the black flower. The thick liquid had dried into flaky maroon ribbons. She knew it was blood. She should have cleaned it up but for some reason, she was not bothered by it.

He flicked his eyes away, not before she read a shadow of dread in them. She wanted to say something, to break this horror-filled moment between them, but she could not. Something large and unwieldy was stirring inside her, squeezing her heart and darkening her vision.

Julian was pulling over to the curb in front of her house. He opened a door for her and perfunctorily offered his arm.

"You should rest," he said.

She nodded and watched his car speed away. The day trip had not been a success.

CHAPTER 12. GEORGE

As Mara was climbing the stairs to her apartment, a man was kneeling in a squalid room on the outskirts of First City. The room was in a two-story building whose upper floor had caved in, leaving only an arched window with shattered glass standing. Through a similar window, partly masked by the rotted shutters, the man had seen a solitary car pass by, an unusual sight in the slums. The people in the car, a well-dressed man and woman, had not seen him, of course, which was all to the good, considering his occupation right now. He was meticulously working at the dead body in front of him with a handsaw.

He was not good at it. He knew little of anatomy and sawed in wrong places, cutting through the flesh instead of carving the joints. His saw was blunted. His clothes were stiff with coagulated blood. The smell in the room was intolerable. The pale naked heap in front of him did not look human anymore; it was an unwieldy, slack thing, a botched job, to be thrown away in disgust.

But the man was stubborn. It was not his first job of the kind, but he'd had limited success so far and he was determined to do it right. Swearing, sweating, his dark curls glued to his domed forehead by mixed blood and perspiration, he kept on sawing. Only twice did he express his frustration by kicking the inert thing. Once he had to stop to relieve himself in the corner. There were brown smears on his face that could not quite mask its attractiveness, evident especially when the man was seen in profile.

At some point, he was so tired he had to sit, drink some cheap wine from a bottle he had in his knapsack, and eat an eggplant sandwich. Because of the smell, he had no appetite, but he had to keep up his strength for this task and for the tasks ahead. A huge bluebottle buzzed into the room, despite the rainy chill outside, and the man sighed in frustration. Flies, like everything living, were holy but he would prefer to do his job undisturbed.

But it was the fly that pointed the way to him. It alighted on the thing's sternum, which was largely free of lacerations, since he had concentrated on dismembering the body by cutting off the limbs first. He had been told that to fashion even a modest gate, he should have four large exits (corresponding to the Four) and that the easiest way to do it would be to chop off the limbs at the juncture with the trunk (since his notion of anatomy was based on pornographic pictures whose models appeared boneless, he had not realized what a tricky proposition this would be). Of course, some people, not even mentioning the Revealer, were so gifted that one modest exit was enough but George Buzzard (whose real name was Jamie Hare, the only son of George Hare also known as Bunny) had to work hard to develop his latent Power. So be it! He was not afraid of work! His old man, a silly bugger though he was, had taught Jamie one unforgettable lesson: Hard work will get you through.

Now, grasping his handsaw with renewed determination, he suddenly saw the bluebottle crawling over the thing's puny chest, and had an inspiration. Wasn't he told that Powers were inextricably linked to the body? And if so, didn't it stand to reason that the more important a body part, the greater its latent store of Power? Arms and legs may be important but if he, Jamie, was asked to choose between his arm and his dick, what would he choose? Now, the thing did not have a dick, having been a female, and Jamie (or rather George Buzzard, as he preferred to think of himself) was too squeamish to go *there*. However, it did have a heart and while one could live even without a dick (not much of a life, of course), one could not live without a heart. Therefore ...

Flexing his sticky fingers, he jabbed at the body's sternum with the handsaw. It slid off but the second try was more successful and soon a ragged hole appeared below the breastbone. Huffing and puffing, George reached inside, feeling slimy things slither against his hand. Grimacing in disgust, he groped for something the size and shape of his fist, caught it, and pulled.

He was not sure that he had got the right thing—this veined, lobed, reddish object like a chunk of butcher's meat. The thought was so disquieting that he almost dropped it. But suddenly the object fluttered in his hand, contracted, and relaxed and with his heart beating wildly, George watched the dead heart in his hands begin to beat and bleed.

It bled profusely, dark venous blood at the beginning, but soon the liquid that ran down his arm and splattered onto the filthy floor lightened to bright red and then to pink and then to rose and finally a growing stream of water cascaded down, drenching his stiff clothes and washing off the bloodstains, dissolving the filth and leaving a track of gleaming wood where it snaked across the floorboards.

Success! George was so exhilarated he let out a triumphant whoop, unmindful of his soaked clothes. Water drizzled upon his face, and he tasted it: salty.

The stream was lapping at the warped door and George thought he should go out, carrying the heart as a sign of the coming victory. He should show it to the hungry, apathetic, despairing denizens of the slums whose cause he was championing, even though they had so far treated him with no greater respect than they gave to any petty criminal. But the heart was proving hard to control: It was beating irregularly, spurting great globules of water that drenched him from head to toe and then growing heavy and flaccid again. Perhaps he should try to experiment more, develop his latent Power, even though that prick Thomas Hawk claimed he had none. He would show him, and the whole damn crew of stuck-up aristocrats, as he had already shown that stupid bitch, Carla. Too bad that hadn't worked out. But this subject—she was a lucky hit, a small-time whore who had asked for more than was her due—and yet such Power, even in her filthy flesh!

The heart suddenly spasmed so strongly that it flopped out of his hands and fell to the floor. There it lay, heavy and immobile. The stream dwindled to a trickle and then disappeared altogether. George swore in frustration. Was this all? Just some water? True, it was more than in his last experiment but even so ... Who wanted more water when the City was all but drowned by the fucking rain? They told him the flood was a sign of the opening of the gates, a little spillage from the Abode. But if this was all that the Abode had, why bother?

He kicked the heart in frustration. His shoe sank in and remained there, the organ like a wad of clay stuck to it. Crying out in disgust, George tried to shake it off. The heart contracted once again, squeezing his foot painfully, and then started to grow.

His mouth falling open, George observed the livid lump of muscle twitch and shoot out innumerable tendrils that crept up his leg, enclosing it in a loose mesh of scarlet and blue. Yelling, he hacked with the saw at the tendrils, but they were as tough as wire and he only managed to cut himself. Something nudged at his balls and with horror he saw a veined leaf the color of meat unfolding at his crotch. The thing that crawled up his body was as warm as blood, and it smelled of the whore's cheap perfume and cheaper sex. The disgust that overwhelmed him was so total that it blanked out the last vestiges of rationality. Crying out, he blundered toward the door but slipped upon the wet floor and landed with a splash in one of the puddles left over from the aborted flood. The salty water that flowed into his mouth strangely calmed him. He lay unresisting as the flesh-plant grew all over his body, its sap like blood, its leaves as tender as skin, caressing his nakedness as it insinuated itself under his torn clothes. When it reached his face, a shoot like a small tongue parted his lips and slipped inside. And as soft velvety darkness flooded his eyes, George had an epiphany: He remembered his sister Jenny's pet hamster and how he had despised the small, furry, smelly thing, revolted by its excremental pellets, its stupidity, its beady eyes. This hamster, he realized, was the whore and now ... But what now he could not think because his time had run out as a noiseless dark explosion turned his brain to mush. A velvety black flower shaped like a double butterfly erupted out of George's shattered head and swayed in the dank air, seen by nobody. The flower bloomed for an hour and then withered, folded in upon itself, and dissolved in the salty puddles that lapped at the two equally mutilated corpses lying on the floor in a run-down shack on the outskirts of First City.

CHAPTER 13. DR. BLACKBIRD

Mara leaned against the creaking stair rail. This was an old building, one of those places with stained glass rosettes set into skylights. The stairs were covered by brown carpet and stank of mice.

Her hair was wet. She shook it out and gathered it with an ornate enameled clip in red and black. The poverty of her upbringing had left its indelible mark on her. Her husband gave her gold and diamonds; she bought all her favorite jewelry in flea markets. Now, with Rondal gone, she reverted back to wearing cheap trinkets and simple clothes instead of the elaborate wardrobe of her married life.

She was dawdling, putting off her appointment with the doctor. It took her some time to find a female gynecologist. Women had been practicing medicine for the last fifty years, but male physicians still outnumbered female ones five to one. However, she had been determined not to appeal to her own GP bequeathed to her by Ronald, a kindly old man who looked through her as if she were invisible. Finally, the phone book—Mara was beginning to feel it was an invention greater than the telephone itself—had given her the name and address of Dr. Anna Blackbird, obstetrician, gynecologist, and licensed midwife.

Taking a deep breath, Mara marched to the door on the next landing, which had a white plaque with the doctor's name and qualifications on it, and pressed the electric bell. The door was opened by a maternal-looking receptionist who ushered Mara into the empty waiting room. Mara leafed through an old issue of the *Ladies' Home Journal* and acquainted herself with a recipe for spinach-stuffed potatoes. Finally, the door to the inner sanctum opened and a heavily pregnant girl who looked about sixteen walked out. Mara looked at her wobbly belly and shuddered.

Dr. Blackbird was different from Mara's image of a female physician. True, she had large, round glasses and a severe bun of sleek black hair, but she was quite young—perhaps five or six years older than Mara herself—and attractive, despite looking undernourished. Mara could not decide whether she inspired confidence or apprehension.

"How can I help you, Mrs. Raven?" she asked in a pleasantly neutral voice that somehow reassured Mara that the doctor had more to offer than the sisterhood of their sex.

"I'm afraid I'm pregnant," blurted Mara.

The doctor nodded and wrote something on a large, lined card.

"Has there been a delay in your monthly function?"

"It's too early to tell."

"I see. And when was the last time you had sexual congress, Mrs. Raven?"

"Thirteen months ago."

Dr. Blackbird put her pen aside, pushed her spectacles up her nose, and stared at Mara.

"I'm sorry," said Mara, flustered. "Let me explain."

She told the doctor about the assault and about the strange malaise that had been plaguing her ever since, manifesting itself in nausea, headaches, and an occasional blackout. She refrained from mentioning that all these symptoms were secondary to her deep and irrational conviction that something malevolent was growing inside her. Dr. Blackbird nodded and frowned intermittently.

"I see," she repeated as Mara finished her recital. "So, you don't remember anything about the assault?"

"No."

"But your mother tells you that there were no signs of rape?"

"That's what she says."

"Don't you believe her?"

"I can't imagine she would lie about something like this," Mara said. "On the other hand, she might want to spare me the shock and the indignity if she thinks she can get away with it. After all, we did not inform the constabulary and the assailant will probably never be caught."

"I see," said Dr. Blackbird, making Mara wish she would change the refrain. "I have to examine you, Mrs. Raven. Would you please go into the cubicle, remove your underwear, and lie on the chair?"

The examination that followed was as intrusive as Mara had expected it to be but less humiliating. Dr. Blackbird treated her with a brisk impersonal familiarity that made Mara bless her decision to seek a female physician. As Mara was dressing, Dr. Blackbird washed her hands at the sink, a puzzled frown on her face.

"I don't think you're pregnant, Mrs. Raven," she said when they returned to the consulting room. "It's early, of course, since the assault happened according to your account four days ago, but I can see no signs of forced penetration, no abrasions, or lacerations. It is more likely that you suffered a mild concussion when you were knocked on the head. This would explain nausea and blackouts. However ..." She hesitated.

"Yes?"

"There are some indications of a problem," said the doctor. "I don't want to alarm you, Mrs. Raven, but it would be better perhaps if you consulted a different specialist."

"Are you saying I have a tumor?"

Dr. Blackbird looked her straight in the eye, as if energized by the bluntness of the question.

"It is possible," she said, "but it might be something else. In the last year or so I have witnessed an array of strange cases. There is nothing like them in medical literature. There is something peculiar afoot affecting people's bodies in various ways."

"Women's bodies?"

"Not only, though I deal with women mostly. Did you see the girl who was here before you?"

"Yes. She's far too young to be pregnant."

"Quite so, and she's unmarried. But the point is, though I try to reassure her, I'm pretty sure that her baby is not human."

"An animal?"

"Perhaps. She believes that it's an Ancestor reborn. She claims the father is a Guardian but knowing how they're made, I doubt it."

"How are the Guardians made?" asked Mara.

"Why do you want to know?"

"Because I've never been told. One of the things that I—we —have never been told."

"True enough. I cannot enlighten you, really. It's Temple medicine, not taught in secular medical schools. All I know is that it involves extensive surgery of a kind that my colleagues or I would never be able to perform because in our hands it would result in a shock to the patient's system and they would die. There are many cases in which such surgery might have saved lives, but it is never done outside the Temple hospitals. It also involves grafts of animal tissue which all secular medical authorities flatly claim to be impossible."

"But they are done!"

"Precisely."

"Why?" cried Mara. "Even if one swallows the entire spiel about the Ancestors, and how animals are our wronged brothers and sisters, and how First City is a prison and we are locked up to atone for the murder of the Slaughtered Ones ... even if one believes all this nonsense, why tamper with human bodies? Pain, mutilation, self-torture to make yourself look like an animal? Animals are comfortable in their bodies. Why can't we be?"

Dr. Blackbird took off her glasses and put them back on.

"Do you know what happens to people who stay outside the City for long?" she asked. "Farmers in outlying communities, exiled criminals, and nowadays, workers in the South Continent?"

"They get sick, right?"

"Yes. And their sickness is nothing like what we see here in the City. Some of them become so distorted that they are said to resemble Guardians. This is all very hush-hush, you understand? The Animal House and the Temple have many secrets. But the authorities seem to have lost control of what is happening in the City. These terrorist attacks ..."

"The Army of the Revealer," Mara muttered.

"What's that?"

Mara clammed up. She liked Dr. Blackbird, but her natural distrust made her unwilling to confide in her. And wouldn't she be putting her at risk if she said too much?

"So, you can't tell me what's wrong with me?" she asked instead.

"Possibly, nothing. You look healthy enough, Mrs. Raven. But your body is ... changing. I can't tell you more than that because I don't know what it is. I think a big change is coming to all of us. And it's coming to you."

"Could this change still be pregnancy?"

"Unlikely but possible."

"If it is," Mara said, "can you take care of it?"

Dr. Blackbird's thin lips twitched.

"What you are suggesting, Mrs. Raven," she said, "is illegal. Not to mention immoral, at least according to some folks."

"You don't believe it is," Mara said, "do you?"

Dr. Blackbird repeated her glasses-on-and-off gesture.

"You may not need anything like this," she said. "I cannot determine whether you are pregnant, and I think it is unlikely. But if you are, and it is the result of a rape ... well, come back to me."

She was walking in the vertical cylinder of water created by the overflow from her umbrella, feeling as isolated as if she were on the South Continent. The hum of the City barely penetrated her watery cocoon. Occasionally a splash of light from an approaching car danced in her field of vision, broken into an irregular weave of light filaments by the rain.

The curtain of water suddenly parted, her umbrella snagging on another one, and she found herself face to face with a man in the tenuous privacy of their joint dry spot. It was Mr. Seal.

"Mara!" He caught her wrist and pulled her toward him. "How fortunate! I've been looking for you!"

She wrenched herself free. She was exhausted, and all she wanted was to be alone in the echoing stillness of her apartment. Her mother had finally left, with many complaints, both vocal and silent, leaving Mara in possession of her solitude.

And yet she could not bring herself to walk away from him yet.

He led her, unresisting, to the nearest coffee shop, a spot of brightness in the streaming murk of the night rain, with red flower-shaped lanterns and a couple of solitary customers idling over expensive cups of the exotic brew.

"You're soaked," he said. "Hot milk?"

"I'm not a child," she replied. "Coffee."

A pretty waitress with a mass of blond curls and a strangely shaped pendant brought them their orders: tea and a carrot cake for Mr. Seal, coffee for Mara. The pendant, she realized, was the symbol of the Humanist Party engraved on a pewter disk: two sticklike human figures holding hands. Mara was glad to see it so challengingly displayed between the young woman's bouncing breasts.

Mr. Seal looked haggard. His restless eyes bore into Mara, but his gaze was losing its power over her.

"Are you well, Mara?" he asked. "You look strained, my dear."

Mara considered telling him about her visit to Dr. Blackbird, to see his reaction, but decided against it. She was too tired for an emotional roller coaster.

"You haven't been to the dream-sea recently." It wasn't a question.

"No, and I'm not going to."

It was a lie, but she did not want to tell him what she decided to go there for.

"Trying to muzzle your Power won't do you any good."

"My Power is useless. I could not solve Elvira Sparrow's murder. I could not find my own husband, and now he is dead. I have finally accepted it. Ronald is dead. It's time to move on."

"Ronald is not dead," Mr. Seal said.

"You've been telling me this all along, but I don't need to be hushed up by false hope like a child by a pacifier. If Ronald were in First City, he would've been found by now. So, he is dead, buried somewhere on the Plains."

Mr. Seal sighed and steepled his fingers in a gesture as familiar to Mara as her own.

"I saw Ronald the day before he disappeared," he said in a voice so soft that Mara had to lean in to hear him. *Soft and rotten,* she thought.

"What? Why didn't you tell me?"

"I did not think it was important. Ronald was constantly

abuzz with new business ventures, as we both know. And after he went missing, I expected you to break through the barrier that prevented you from finding the answer in the dream-sea."

Mara gulped down her treacle-like coffee and its bitterness coated her mouth like betrayal.

"What did he say?"

"He said that he had found a way to open the gate, and he was going to try it out before telling you. That is why I have been so insistent that the key to finding him lies in the dream-sea."

"Gate? What gate? Ronald was not into the cult of the Ancestors. He was not even interested in the dream-sea."

"Of course, he was," Mr. Seal said. "Why do you think—"

He stopped. But Mara finished the sentence for him.

"'Why do you think he married you?'" she said. "This is what you were going to say, weren't you? You set me up, didn't you? You set me up with him to sell my Power to the highest bidder. But what was his interest in it? Ronald was only interested in money. Did he expect to open up a subsidiary of Raven and Co in the Abode of the Ancestors? And you? Why didn't you marry me if you wanted it so much? Why didn't you try to get into my panties when I was sweet sixteen? I would have let you, you know? I was stupid enough at that time. And then you could pump me for information, of course—and I could not refuse!"

"Mara!" cried Mr. Seal in anguish, but instead of pity or remorse, she felt a vast, shaggy presence soaked in rust and blood stir inside, trying to get through the insubstantial cover of her skin and reach for him.

Mara could not allow it to happen. She rushed out, overturning her chair that clattered onto the floor.

CHAPTER 14. THE SHOE

Mara lifted herself off the floor of the bedroom. She was not sure how she had ended up there. Her entire body hurt. She staggered to the bathroom and was violently sick.

Wiping her mouth, she remembered what Dr. Blackbird had said.

Something is changing ...

Was she sick? Was she pregnant?

She focused on her body because it kept her mind off her confrontation with Mr. Seal. She could not let herself think about him. Or about Ronald. Even thinking her husband's name sent a wave of shivers through her.

She touched her forehead as her mother had always done to gauge whether little Mara was feverish. This gesture brought about a flicker of guilt, but she could not face Louisa Ferret's solicitude. She had to be alone and take care of herself. She had to be her own mother.

When Mara had a cold, Louisa would fetch a lemony-honey powder from the apothecary, dissolve it in hot water, and give it to her to drink. It had always been comforting in a deeply satisfying kind of way. Mara decided to get to the nearest apothecary and get the powder. One glance outside confirmed that the rain had dwindled to a dispirited drizzle, which qualified as good weather. She put on a belted green jacket and woolen skirt and went to the hallway closet to fetch her shoes. It would be almost dry enough to wear her favorite deerskin moccasins.

She pulled them out of the closet and stared at them in shock. The soft leather was puckered and warped, studded with boils of discoloration. One shoe gaped obscenely where the top had come off the sole.

Of course! She had worn them when she knelt by Elvira's dead body as it was being torn apart by a Power, made into the fleshy gateway for a flood. The moccasins were ruined, soaked and blistered by corpse fluids.

Compared to all her recent losses, the ruination of expensive shoes was less than nothing. She could afford another pair. And yet something about these moccasins made of the skin of a totem animal, the brave challenge they posed to the Temple orthodoxy, brought a lump to her throat. She remembered the last time she had worn them. She remembered the way Detective Hart flinched ...

She sat on the floor of the hallway for a long time, her fingers digging into the tough leather as if trying to shred it. Then she got up and went to the phone.

She dialed the constabulary headquarters. A young woman answered, sounding as breathless as a long-distance runner.

"I want to speak to Detective Hart," she said. "Tell him it's Mara Raven."

"Detective Hart is off duty today."

"I want his home phone number and address."

"I told you, he is off duty. He needs rest. We all do. Do you know what's happening? And who are you, anyway?"

"Listen," Mara said through clenched teeth, "I must speak to him urgently. I have important information. He knows who I am. I need his home address—now! Either give it to me or put me through to the chief constable and kiss your job goodbye."

The woman squawked indignantly and then rapidly dictated the address and slammed the phone down.

The address was not far from Mara's house. The woman had not given her a phone number; perhaps he did not have one. She decided to walk.

Shivering in her padded jacket, she trudged through the puddles. The rain increased once again, lashing her bare head and soaking her hair, plastering it to her head.

How natural was that rain? First City was always chilly in the fall, but Mara could not remember a wet season that went on for so long without a respite.

Soon she found herself in the City's walled shopping district, Queensgate. This was where the cobbled streets and flower baskets still recalled the atmosphere of the pretechnological age; where tiny shrines, often stuck in the middle of the narrow sidewalk with delicate animal figurines and offerings of flowers, evoked a gentler Ancestors worship; where old-style tearooms innocently mixed fruitcakes and ham pies on their menus. But it was also the place where the first department store, the Badger Brothers Consortium, had opened its doors to the public twenty years ago. Ronald had insisted she do her shopping there and she reluctantly obeyed, even though she disliked its obsequious staff and its atmosphere of mixed snobbery and crassness.

There were people going in and out of eateries and pubs: office workers on their lunch break and here and there a gaggle of middle-class housewives seeking a shadow of normalcy in their favorite tearoom. But the crowd was thin and anxious, eerily silent. As she passed one of the street shrines, Mara saw that it was packed with offerings, not just flowers but candles, bags of coins, even clothes. A roll of fabric lay soaked and unraveled in a puddle.

She slowed in front of the Badger Brothers Consortium, an

ornate building with plaster garlands around the display windows, through which Mara could see its empty halls. She looked up and started. On the cornice above the entrance used to be a small statue of the founders' totem animal, a Badger. But now it had been removed and a devotional effigy of the Bear stood there instead, the powerful humped back and oversized claws stained with red, and the obligatory veil represented by a blank surface in front of a barrel-shaped head.

The Bear was the most powerful and feared of the four Slaughtered Ones. Mara only dimly remembered her devotional instructions in school, but she knew that the Bear was supposed to mete out retribution and revenge. The Bear was so feared that its countenance was always hidden by a veil. Mara shivered, remembering the recently read passage in the *Book of the Remnant*: "*And of the last one nothing can be said because its claws tore off the skins of the living and made it a garment thereof.*"

The Bear was also the one Ancestor nobody claimed as their totem animal. There was a powerful Lion family in the City. Mara knew of a smattering of Tigers, though they seemed to have dwindled. In fact, Ronald's mother was a Tiger, though he had taken his father's totem as was customary. Mara had taken her mother's before her marriage to Ronald. And of course, Mr. Seal was a daily reminder that the Seal still had his clan. But she had never heard of anybody named Bear, and for the first time, she wondered why. And another question came up instantly. The Bear was seldom referred to by any pronoun. While the Lion, the Tiger, and the Seal were all envisioned as male, the Bear's gender was ambiguous. He? It? Perhaps even she?

Mara decided she had no time for theological ruminations. But as opposed to the Mara of several months ago, she could no longer tell herself that theology did not matter because it was a bunch of silly superstitions.

When superstitions cause a rain of mice, they cease being silly.

Hart lived in a small, detached house squeezed between two apartment blocks. Mara could not believe that his constable's salary was enough to pay for the luxury of a single dwelling. Either Constable Hart was independently wealthy, or he had other sources of income besides the official ones.

The front of the house had a bow window like a goggle-eye above the peeling door. Mara knocked. The only response was silence. She tried the handle, and the door swung open.

It smelled wet and stale inside, the mingled odors of moldy bread, rain, incense, and rot. And there was something else: a sweet, nauseating undertone that made the hairs on her arms stand on end.

The dim hallway was lined with closed doors. At the entrance was a broken ceramic umbrella stand and a pile of raincoats tossed haphazardly on the floor.

She opened the door that led to the living room. The room had no furniture in it, at least none for human use. Detective Hart's devotion bordered on eccentricity, the fact either unknown to his superiors or overlooked. The floor was strewn with straw mats, each bearing a plate with an offering of soft overripe fruit: black-spotted apples and brown pears. A large altar with icons of the Four dominated the room. The icons were garishly painted, set in crystal-studded frames, and looked new.

The next door led to the kitchen. Here the origin of the rotting smell became clear. Smashed crockery lay like hailstones all over the floor, melting into the puddles of greasy liquid consisting of the sauces, oils, and condiments from Hart's well-stocked vegetarian pantry. The chill-box gaped open, and its vegetable contents were dumped onto the counter. All the drawers had been pulled out and the cutlery lay in silvery heaps.

Mara picked up a kitchen knife from the counter and went down the hall.

She found Detective Hart in the bedroom. It had also been ransacked but somehow half-heartedly compared to the fury that had descended upon the kitchen. The doors of the wardrobe hung open and clothes had been scattered about. But it was the modest, narrow bed pushed to the wall that dominated the room. The bedclothes, she was sure, had always been neat and white but now were brown and crusty with dried blood. Hart was lying across the bed, his head thrown back, one arm hanging down. His shirt was painted by a huge splotch of brown surrounding a singed hole. A small black contraption lay on the floor and his sausage-like fingers, bloated with incipient rot, seemed to strain toward the gun.

She knew what an appropriate reaction should be. She should shriek. Or maybe scream. She went through a list of emotions in her head, lifting each one of them like a pebble on the beach, weighing it, and dropping it. She felt nothing.

Mara touched the dead flesh that was cold and moist but soft. Rigor mortis had come and gone, and Detective Hart was about to be subsumed into the same indifferent cycle of growth and decay as the rotting food on his kitchen floor.

She looked around. A pair of Detective Hart's rubber shoes stood beside a chest of drawers. She stared at them, a smile crinkling her lips and staying there, never reaching her eyes. After picking up the gun, she exited the dead man's house.

When she trudged up the stairs to her apartment, she was weary and chilled to the bone. Inside it was dark and cold; the central heating was on the brink. She sat down and cried. Her guts churned, her body ached, and the restless heaving at the core of her being went on and on, mindless and implacable, not painful but as unstoppable as the onset of decay in a corpse. She stumbled into the bathroom, peeled off her wet woolens, filled the tub with steaming-hot water, and poured half a bottle of rose essence into it. When she lowered herself into the fragrant warmth, it brought momentary relief. No matter how she scoured herself, she still felt unclean. Getting out of the tub, she wavered and clutched the edge of the basin. Her mouth filled with sourness, and she vomited black bile.

Wrapped in a wet towel, she went to the bedroom and crawled under the blanket. She nested in bed, trying to control the violent shivers that racked her.

Mara closed her eyes and willed the familiar purple and green luminescent circles. When they finally appeared, they looked thin and undernourished, as if they were sick.

They barred her way, joining like interlocking rings.

"Light Puppies, Light Puppies," she subvocalized, "let me through!"

They remained immobile, a web of hostile light. She knew from long experience that she could not ask anything for herself; could not beg the dream-sea to deliver her from the strange malaise that took root in her. She had tried in the distant past to ask how she and her mother could escape their grinding poverty. Once she had tried to inquire how to make Ronald love her. And of course, she had repeatedly attempted to find his whereabouts since his disappearance. In each case, Light Puppies would not let her pass to the shore. She could only swim in the dream-sea when she had a query about a crime.

"Who killed Detective Hart?" she asked.

The web of purple-and-green light (*The colors of rot*, she suddenly realized) parted as she dove into the dream-sea, her mind firmly on the black gun, now resting under her knickers in the drawer.

CHAPTER 15. THE WOMAN WHO WOULD NOT BE MOTHER

The sea is dark, blue and violet as if bruised, and throwing the torn lace of whitecaps onto the churned sand. The sky is lowering and steel gray: There seems to be no reprieve from the ghastly weather of First City even here. There are clouds scudding across the face of something that is not the sun; something like a pewter-colored dome giving off a dull, soulless light. Tiny bare islands stick out from the sickly water.

She drags herself to the waterline. She has to drag herself because she cannot walk. Her belly is grotesquely swollen, swaying from side to side like a pouch. The rest of her is one dull ache, varied by sharper flashes of pain from her tender breasts, the nipples oozing blood. Her joints creak obscenely.

The water is icy cold, but she would go in anyway, except that the hissing waves are dangling something black and hairy like a giant scalp being washed in the surf. The black tendrils spread along the margins of the sea as far as she can see.

Mara is seized by revulsion. She wants to throw up but cannot; her stomach is squashed by the weight in her womb.

Slowly, the black tendrils gather themselves into a tangled mound protruding above the water. Something heaves and bubbles in the shallows. A crab the size of a plate scuttles by Mara, then another and another. There is an exodus of crabs and other creatures, hairy centipedes and something that looks like a drowned rat with patchy fur but is alive and prancing on thin legs.

The sea suddenly erupts some distance away from the shore. A wave crashes onto one of the tiny islands and when it recedes, there is something pinkish and alive, crawling over the rock. Is it another giant crab somehow robbed of its armor? A congregation of worms? A naked turtle?

It is a hand.

The fingers, each the size of Mara's body, grip the rock and she can see glimmers of dull light in their nails. The black, hairy mound in the water heaves and pushes up higher as if a head is mushrooming from the sediment on the bottom. And the other islands are also astir with restless movements. One is covered with folds and swirls of parchment-like skin; on the other, raw purplish guts slowly weave together; the third, higher than the rest, has a waterfall that gushes blood instead of water.

It is her baby. Both inside and outside of her, trying to be born. Trying to shed the thin membrane that is keeping it—her—imprisoned.

The membrane that is Mara.

She waddles into the polluted water and dives with her eyes shut. Coarse hair brushes her cheeks and her guts clench with a humiliating pain like the onset of diarrhea, but she swims on. And quite suddenly she is in clean water.

She opens her eyes. She is suspended in the soothing gray, empty space, some seaweed floating nearby and a couple of translucent bottom-feeders. She looks down. The ridged expanse of white sand and then nothingness, as the seabed falls away into a darkening abyss. She recognizes the place. This is where she had hunted the one-eyed dreamfish.

She suddenly feels at peace. Her distended belly still hangs on her like an old sack but the alien intruder inside is stilled. Slowly she swims forward. And sure enough, she can see the twinkling lights below, in cool blue darkness. She can discern the grid of streets and squares outlined in shimmering dots.

She wants to dive deeper and explore but something gently butts her on the shoulder. She turns around and feels a silly grin spreading across her face. It is a tiny transparent mermaid, no bigger than Mara's forearm, but perfectly proportioned, with perky breasts and hair like spun glass. She can see her pulsating heart like a living jewel within the jellyfish's torso. Such mermaids had been her constant playmates at the beginning of her dreamfishing, but it had been a long time since she saw one.

The mermaid swims ahead and Mara follows, marveling at the creature's purposeful movements: Normally, they are as stupid as goldfish, though more playful. But intelligence in the dream-sea is mercurial.

Soon they are surrounded by a school of tiny mermaids, all identical, their faces doll-like, their bodies subtly lit from the inside like so many glass lanterns. They swim up to the surface. They are far from the shore, in the midst of the expanse of gray water, gently shading off into violet and lilac. The sky is tarnished silver. In front of them an island hunches up. The mermaids urge her on to the crescent of a white beach.

The mermaids gesture toward the beach and much as she is loath to leave the silky warmth of the water, she obeys and clambers onto the sand. It is getting dark, and the mermaids glitter in the surf like a handful of stars. There is a dark shape waiting for her in the shelter of the trees and she hesitates, but the shape walks toward her, and she realizes it is a land version of the mermaid, though larger, almost as big as a human being. The mermaid has a pair of legs that look more like overgrown flippers, and she waddles as she moves, but somehow, she manages to do it with dignity. When the mermaid motions to Mara to lie on the sand under the overhanging trees, she obeys. She is glad to lie down because the weight inside is choking her.

The land mermaid examines her protruding belly. Her fingers are like glass but warm and firm. Her touch seems to have eased the pressure. Mara looks into her face, but it is as expressionless as that of a fish. The land mermaid turns away from her and emits a jingling sound. Several others emerge from the trees, all glowing with different colors, pink, aquamarine, lemon, and red. As they approach, she sees that they are also different in body shapes. One, shedding a deep incarnadine glow, folds itself on the sand beside Mara. Its nether parts are almost human, slender legs and well-shaped thighs, but its upper part resembles a giant swordfish. It aims its jagged bony saw at Mara's belly. Mara cries out and tries to roll away, but the other land mermaids pull her down and keep her pinned to the sand. Mara screws her eyes shut and then the bony saw pierces her stomach. She feels a warm gush of blood over her legs and then her flesh parting as the saw widens the gap. She can feel all these things but there is no pain. Absurdly, she imagines herself as a can being opened.

There is a wrenching tug, and she screams. And then there is a feeble whining sound. She opens her eyes and sees another one of the land mermaids holding up a dripping object that twitches and convulses. It is flabby and yellow, dusted with a sprinkling of dark fur. Its face is covered by a flap of skin.

The mermaid walks to the water margin and pitches the mewling thing into the sea.

Mara steals a glance at her belly. The wound has closed, and the pale scar is fading.

The land mermaids help her to her feet and nudge her toward the sea where their tiny sisters still swarm in a cloud of twinkling, multi-colored lights.

"Thank you," she whispers, looking at the alien faces that regard her with no expression.

She heads for the water margin, but one mermaid stops her and hands her something. She stares at the object, and her head is filled with the white noise of outrage.

After throwing the thing aside, she dives into the warm water and glimpses glowing dots scattered on the bottom of the abyss like the lights of a hidden City.

The uneven patter of rain woke her. Rain was by now the default setting for the First City weather, but there was something strange about the sound as it roared with the strength of a storm and then abruptly softened into a gentle purr.

Mara switched on the bedside lamp and was surprised to see it was almost eight in the morning. The sky should be pearling by now, but it was still dark outside.

In the bathroom, she stripped naked and regarded herself in the mirror. There was no scar on her smooth stomach. But she felt blissfully empty. Purified of anything but her anger, which she held close as if it were a blade.

The idea of bearing a child always filled her with dread. She had never been one of those girls who peered into baby carriages and rocked dolls to sleep. It helped that she was an only daughter of an only daughter. She never had to explain or justify her revulsion. As for her mother, Louisa's devotion to her child was so absolute that she accepted Mara's lack of maternal inclinations as she accepted her every other peculiarity.

But now, looking at her body with the scratchy, dry eyes that seemed to be filled with the dust of dead centuries, Mara questioned everything she knew about herself. Her beauty, which she had always taken for granted, now seemed grotesque. That skin, so pale that sunlight refused to linger on it. Those long, supple limbs, almost spidery in their pliancy. That thick, wavy hair, the color of ash, like the billows left on the site of a house fire. And that white face with its regular features like a death mask, the blue-green-gray eyes glittering with a glassy sheen. Mara shuddered and shook her hair forward to cover her face like a veil.

How could anybody fall in love with her? How could Ronald ...

Except that Ronald had never been in love with her.

She realized that she had accepted Mr. Seal's revelation with the relief of a patient having their gnawing apprehension of a deadly disease confirmed. She had known it for a long time even if she had refused to admit it to herself. Her husband, her Prince Charming who had lifted her out of poverty and installed her in the palace of her dreams in the heart of the City, had never loved her. He had married her for her Power.

Mara examined her heart and found it empty and still. The realization did not hurt. Her love for Ronald, the love that had filled her for the brief duration of her marriage, was dead. It lay inside her like a dead fetus and needed to be expelled before it rotted and poisoned her.

She thought about Julian Sparrow. At least, it brought up a tiny spark of some undefined emotion in the cold wasteland that her mind seemed to have become.

But before talking to him again, she needed to deal with her assailant.

Mara shivered and realized she had been standing before the mirror for a long time. She gave herself one last distasteful glance when she saw a slow rivulet of blood on her inner thigh. Dr. Blackbird would be happy; her "monthly functions" were back on track.

Did it mean that she had actually been pregnant? Mara tried to pinpoint what had been revealed to her in the dream-sea, but as usual, the language of dreams and archetypes resisted translation into uncouth human speech. Her question had been answered. But perhaps it had been a wrong question.

Could she go back and ask again? No. For some reason, the dream-sea could not abide blood on her. The first time she got her period at the age of thirteen, she ended up in the dream-sea and had to swim through the choking, lashing, carmine-colored sludge that coated her mouth with the taste of rust and salt. Even a scratch would make the sea angry.

Mara got her pads and twisted the tap to wash up. It gave a hoarse choking sound and dripped some rusty drops. Mara swore. While electricity blackouts were becoming commonplace, this was something new and unexpected: The one thing that First City had in abundance was water. As if to confirm this, the patter of rain rose to a deafening drumbeat on the roof of her apartment building.

The tap cleared its throat and coughed out a clot of viscous substance that spread scarlet in the basin. Mara rushed back to the bedroom and wrenched the window open. It was still dark but for the wet glow of streetlamps in the haloes of falling drops. The haloes were red. She stretched her hand out into the rain. It came back splattered with rubies.

Mara closed the window, wiped her hand on a towel, threw it into the laundry basket, and turned on the wireless. Soft music was playing. It was almost nine, time for a daily news bulletin. The music played on.

She cleaned up the best she could and huddled in the armchair, bundled up in a thick robe. The monotonous sound of the rain hammered on her ears. Lulled into half sleep, she became aware of the rushing of water close by. She ran into the bathroom, where the overflowing basin splashed clear puddles onto the tiled floor. Mara closed the faucet and went to look out the window again. The anemic dawn was finally breaking, the sky gray and sullen. It was still drizzling.

CHAPTER 16. THE NEW RAIN

In the predawn darkness a woman was trudging determinedly through the empty streets, the chilly reflections of the street-lights shivering in the puddles. Her thin cotton dress was damp, but she did not feel cold. Strange; she had always been delicate. Though she refused to wear animal fibers, she always put on layers to warm up her thin blood.

But not today. Today she wanted as little covering as possible. The City, the hated brooding presence, hunched up in the dark like a man, its breath stinking of oil fumes, its eyes lewd and unblinking, its spatula-like fingers reaching for her. But she was untouchable. It seemed to her that her body, which she used to hate for its scrawny forearms, its drooping buttocks, its flat chest, was now floating away from her like a balloon and she was filled with nostalgia for the discarded flesh. But only for a moment, as she stumbled, stubbed her toe, and felt nothing. The body was falling off of her like a prisoner's dirty smock. The prison gates were opening.

She passed a small temple and paused to whisper a brief prayer and to light a candle in the iron holder on the porch. She did not want to go in, even for a communion with her namesake.

Soon she would join the wild creatures, untainted by humanity, and she would talk to the Lynx as an equal. Or rather, she would *be* the Lynx, freed forever from the tangle of pain and self-awareness, of incomprehension and rejection, and the innumerable petty distractions of the human condition.

Leaving the temple, she thought briefly of a tall blond girl with shifty eyes she had met here, the strange girl who claimed to be a widow. There was something both off-putting and compelling about her, and later she could see the men in the group drooling when she walked in. Hawk had grilled her about their meeting, and she had told him to go to hell. It was this confrontation that had crystallized her decision to make the sacrifice now, without waiting for the cowards at the top to give a go-ahead. But now, warmed by the glow of the Ancestors' Abode, which was so close that she could practically see its sunny emerald fields and leafy woods, she thought of the girl with gentleness and forgiveness and hoped to see her again as a friendly black bird, happy and free, when their human forms would finally be discarded, and their true essence would shine.

The strange numbness, which she knew to be the gift of the Ancestors who were waiting for her to make the atonement and join them, was spreading through her body, and at some point, she realized she could no longer feel the handle of the knife stuck in her belt. She frantically groped for it and was relieved to touch the familiar wooden handle, polished by months of solitary devotion. At first, she shrank from the idea of sacrifice. She had always been sickly, afraid of pain, and her hatred for her body coexisted with strange solicitude. Her vegetarianism began as a health measure against the headaches and nausea, which doctors refused to take seriously. To fight her fear of the knife, she had made it her companion, stropping, and then gently caressing the gleaming edge, polishing the handle, sleeping with it under her pillow. And for all that she distrusted man-made things, the knife had become her friend. She sometimes thought she detected in it echoes of her own desire: the longing of the iron to go back into the ore, of the wood to be reabsorbed into the tree.

She rounded the corner. At this early hour, the City was empty of human presence, and she thought: *This is how it must have been when it had been ruled by the Four, and its buildings grew like flowers; and its streets flowed like creeks.* But the harsh electric light gave a lie to the sweet illusion; it was obviously a human invention. And then she saw her goal ahead, the dark shape of the Animal House, the statues poised as if awaiting her arrival. Only a wide expanse of pavement separated her from it, the distance that she could cross in a couple of minutes, an interval of time consumed by stray thoughts or everyday concerns. But now it was the length of her life.

She stepped onto the cobblestones and felt relaxation and the flowing away of something, as if she was already bleeding. It was out of her hands. It was beginning and she could do nothing to stop or change it. And with this realization came the blessing of calm.

She walked across the empty square, alone and yet not alone, because the Four watched and welcomed her. There were lights in many windows already; the early officials were at work or perhaps some committee that had been burning midnight oil. She had chosen this time deliberately: The Animal House was patrolled by uniformed constables during the hours of its official activity. She knew there would be enough people there even early in the morning, but the security would be lax. Not that it mattered; she was not concerned with individuals. First City was to be returned to its rightful owners; the animals caged in human farms and in human bodies were to be set free; and she would be the one to have started it.

She was almost at the entrance, the heavy door slightly ajar and light spilling from the foyer where a guard was dozing, when a shadow crossed her path. A man almost collided with her. With a disagreeable sinking sensation, she confronted him. He was young and handsome, with the kind of face that would have made her cringe once but should be powerless to move her now. Except that it was not.

"Excuse me, miss. Are you looking for something? May I help you?"

She knew she should fib him off; find a plausible reason for wanting to get into the Animal House, but she realized she could not speak. Her throat clenched. She felt as incapable of human words as if she were with the Ancestors already.

She saw his eyes widen with suspicion as he stepped back, his hand dropping to his pocket. He must be a plainclothesman, she thought, probably armed, and in any case, he could easily overpower her.

It was shame that released her from paralysis. Edna drew her knife from its hiding place, plunged it below the breastbone, and pulled it down, eviscerating herself. She felt no pain; nothing but the heavy resistance of the flesh as it strained against the steel, the body trying to heal itself even as it was dying. Warm wetness streamed down her legs, and she felt dreadfully embarrassed but then realized with relief that it was blood. She reached for her Power but could not find it and only as she toppled over and saw the dark streams rise in twisted columns into the sky she knew it had not failed her. But it had abandoned her, she realized, as her eyes dimmed, and now it was doing its work with indifference ... The impossible unfairness of it all struck her even as the rain of blood splashed upon her upturned face. And as the constable vomited upon his shoes, the heavy scarlet rivulets ran down the Animal House's windows, interrupting the filibuster inside.

After breakfast, Mara wandered aimlessly from room to room. Drumming her fingertips on the weeping windowpane, she observed for a while the building across the road: a squat four-story mansion that had been subdivided into apartments for rent, its blue walls and stocky white columns faded to the colors of old laundry. A lacy curtain twitched in one window, as if an invisible observer was surreptitiously returning her gaze. There were people behind each one of these windows, people like her: women who could have been her friends, men who could have been her lovers, children who could have been hers. Why did she feel so alone, so disconnected from everybody else, so weary and yet so contemptuous, yearning not for human contact but for her need for such a contact?

She started when the doorbell rang. It was the concierge (Mara in vain tried to recall her name) who had received some fresh eggs from a cousin in the countryside and was offering them for sale to the tenants. Mara thanked the woman, handed her the money, and got the eggs, which the concierge put for her in a sort of funnel made out of a newspaper.

"Is it from today?" Mara asked.

"Yes. I can't read this stuff, ma'am, swear to the Ancestors! Just got one look at the horror near the Animal House and wanted to throw up. And little children can see it too, ma'am. Kids who know nothing of the world and should know nothing, if you know what I mean ..."

"What horror?" Mara asked. "No, wait a second. Give me the whole newspaper. I have some wrapping paper, take it instead."

Mara flattened out the crumpled newspaper on the kitchen table. The headline shouted: *Terrorist Attack at the Animal House!!!* She scanned the news, tried to make out the blurred photographs. The text was singularly incoherent and there was only an oblique reference to the rain of blood as "an unusual meteorological phenomenon that accompanied the attack." The name leaped out at her. The terrorist was identified: a young woman of a good family, Edna Lynx.

Julian Sparrow slipped out of the bed and padded into the bathroom, trying not to disturb the woman whose even breathing had been the steady accompaniment to his nightmares. She turned to her side and threw her arm across the empty space where he had been. He could see the waterfall of her blond hair spilling down the side of the bed but in the chilly dawn light it looked bone white.

When he came back, she was sitting upright and rubbing her eyes. He stopped and looked at her, marveling with a strange detachment that she could possibly want him. Laura Lion, wealthy, young, aristocratic, and beautiful, could have any man. He suspected she chose him because she did not need to hide her razor-sharp intelligence when they were together. And the fact that they were distant relations gave a cozy intimacy to their affair.

But it was coming to an end; he could feel the emotional charge running out as inevitably as the sand in an hourglass. He was not angry; in fact, he felt a gratitude that was beginning to outweigh the waning desire. She had been with him on the night Elvira died. She had provided his alibi. But more importantly, he had not been alone while his wife was being killed.

"Bad dreams?" she asked.

Her voice was the one feature of hers that was not perfect. It was too high-pitched, occasionally producing the same shuddery feeling as the screech of a wet finger on glass.

"Yeah." He came over and hugged her, feeling the small, rosy nipples of her high breasts harden against his chest and the corresponding stirring in his groin. It was amazing how persistent the body was, how determined to squeeze every ounce of pleasure out of its daily functioning, how brave in defying the inevitable. He looked down with gentle and resigned affection at his own nudity, the muscles still well defined but the skin beginning to loosen and sag. Their caresses soon petered out and they lay together in companionable embrace, listening to the tattoo of droplets on the wet branches of the garden outside.

"Is it always the same?" she asked.

"Mostly. Sometimes I don't remember but I wake up and know I've dreamt about it again."

"The end of the world?"

"No. This is what they talk about nowadays. The Return of the Ancestors. But in my dreams, it's more ... intimate."

"I thought this was what it was all about."

"No, no. I have no fear ... The Ancestors won't come back and if the City is destroyed, we'll have only ourselves to blame. But my dreams ... I feel pity. Sometimes I wake up with tears in my eyes. Such horrors and yet I feel only pity."

"Perhaps this is what is frightening you. That you feel no fear."

"I'm not afraid of the sight of blood. Never was. But I don't like it. I brawled in school, of course. But I taught myself to fight well, so I did not have to hurt people. I don't like the sight of all the mess we're hiding inside exposed to the light of day. I never wanted children because of this. I imagined a child forcing its way through a tunnel of blood ..."

"But Elvira wanted children."

"No, she did not."

"Yes, she did. This is about her, isn't it? You're still blaming yourself."

"No, I'm not. Oh well, maybe. What right did I have to keep her chained to me? I thought I was giving her a good life, protecting her from her own silliness. She would be my child if she could not be my lover. But maybe this was what she wanted, heartbreak, and excitement, and an unhappy marriage and ungrateful children who would hurt her and whom she would adore. What right did I have to take it away from her?"

"Tell me about your dream."

"You don't like hearing about Elvira. Are you jealous?"

"Huh?"

"Right. Well, my dream. I walk through an empty field, only it's not soil. It's covered with some sort of gray substance like asphalt only it's smooth. And it stretches as far as the eye can see. There is nothing else, just this gray surface, and on the horizon some slender structures, like pylons, and they sort of shimmer."

"Is there the sun in the sky?"

"No, it's overcast. Funny, you ask. The air is polluted and there is a burnt smell to it. Do other people ever dream of smells?"

"Sometimes."

"Anyway, as I walk, I stumble, and I see that it's a child's shoe. And there is another lying nearby. A small shoe, yellow with a red pompon. But I think, how can I stumble on an empty child's shoe and then I see it's not empty. It has been severed with the foot in. The stump is bleeding."

"Bad."

"Yes, and it gets worse. The field, it's strewn with clothes and pieces of luggage. I see one large suitcase, open. It's jammed with clothes. There are some papers, torn and smudged. And there is a baby among the clothes, naked, with a handkerchief sticking from his mouth. He has suffocated."

"And this is when you wake?"

"Not always. Last night, I did. But sometimes I don't and then it goes on and becomes so much worse ..."

"You can talk to me about it."

"No, I can't. It is not real to you because you're so young and beautiful you think you're immortal. And I wish you were, Laura. I wish you were. But you're not."

"Aren't there some flowers in it?"

"Yes. Black flowers that grow out of death."

"This is why you were so spooked by what that woman did. What was her name?"

"Mara, Mara Raven. Yes, it was like something out of my

nightmare. I convinced myself that I began dreaming of the flowers only after I had discovered the enclosures of black orchids in the countryside ruins. But this is not true. I had seen them before. When she pulled up that flower and I saw a pulsating human heart at the tip of it, I almost passed out."

"Are you sure this is what it was?"

"No. I went back afterwards and dug up another orchid. It had a large tuberous root, true, but nothing like a human heart."

"So, it was a hallucination."

"But she saw it too! She knew what it was!"

"Are you going to see her again?"

Julian rolled over and faced Laura, his hand teasing her nipple, another cupping her smooth buttock.

"I don't think I can," he said. "I'm afraid of her."

Julian paused at the exit from the alley that led to the large square in front of the Animal House. It had taken him an hour to park his car, and he regretted the vanity that had made him drive instead of getting a cab. On the other hand, a cab would have been as hopelessly snarled in the atrocious traffic as his own Model 5, and at least some pedestrians reluctantly stepped to the sides at the sight of his Humanist tech. Money and status still mattered in First City. He wondered for how long.

The square would normally be deserted in the middle of the day, but now it was swarming with uniformed constables and crisscrossed with useless crime tape. Julian was not sure that they would let him through.

Dawdling in indecision, he let his gaze slide up the hulking gray façade, disregarding the frozen multitude of totem animals that covered it like swollen ivy. Hares and lizards; moles and snakes; ravens and gazelles ... They neither frightened nor attracted him. But he seldom let his eyes linger on the four oversized statues that crowned the architrave. Today, though, he could not help himself. His eyes traveled to the Four Slaughtered Ones and remained snagged there.

The Seal was a giant shapeless bulk, distended and bulging, as if rotting from within and pumped up with the gases of decay. Its tapering upper part reared into the air, sluglike. The tiny hands—or were they flippers?—seemed squashed by the weight of creased flesh. And there was no visible head. The body came almost to a point at which it was surmounted by a disproportionately tiny face perched at a wrong angle, like a hat. The face was human but blank and drooling.

The Lion was a mass of painfully straining muscles, a flayed image of frustrated strength, its clawed feet digging into the tiles of the roof, every convolution of its sinuous body screaming its rage. As opposed to the Seal, its most prominent feature was its huge face. Surrounded by a streaming mane, it was a face fretted and eaten by leprosy: a flat, squashed nose with gaping nostrils, thin lips stretched over broken fangs, empty eyes staring into the night as if their lids were cut off. Julian shivered and bit his lips. The Lion was his totem. He had given it up when he changed his name to Sparrow. But was it so easy to get rid of your deity?

The Tiger was an articulated four-legged skeleton, whose tail wormed its way in and around its barrel-like rib cage. But its abdomen was a sagging sack, filled—according to the legend—with live coals and ashes, for there was an undying flame within the Tiger that burnt it to madness unless it was fed with precious offerings and human lives. Its head was the most animal-like of the Four: an elongated, empty-eyed skull, its maw gaping as if choking on its own all-consuming appetite.

And finally, the Bear who according to the *Book of the Remnant* was the leader of the Four. Julian's eyes stung as he forced himself to look at the naked, crouching mass. An animal is never naked, and if the Bear appeared as such, it was only because it was indeed on the opposite side of the scale from the Tiger: the most humanlike of the Four and the most repulsive. It looked like a deformed baby, unfinished and soft, its lumpy upper limbs desultorily appearing to grow both fingers and claws, the folds of its bare flesh seeming to hesitate whether to form human pectorals or to cover themselves with a pelt. Its face would be intolerable to see, were it visible. It was not. It was veiled by a piece of stone drapery, masterfully rendered by an ancient sculptor. But Julian knew it was not supposed to be drapery. It was supposed to be flayed human skin.

He shook himself off as if waking from a nightmare and tried to make his way through the crush of constables whose sporadic attempts to enforce order only generated more chaos. Julian was stopped by a couple of uniforms who intermittently yelled at him and at each other. But he could not even muster any outrage at their stupidity because in their sweaty faces he saw the same emotion that bubbled inside him: fear.

The man he was about to meet suddenly came out of the impressive entryway, looking around in helpless confusion at the melee of constabulary, protesters, and visitors. Fortunately, Julian saw him and waved his arms in the air, trying to attract his attention.

"Thomas!" he yelled. "Thomas Hawk!"

CHAPTER 17. THE STUDENT AND THE TEACHER

Jeremy Seal was walking back home in the cobalt-colored twilight, the one moment of a rainy day between the gray and the black when everything turned rich blue, and the drab cityscape became alluring and mysterious. He had trained himself not to look at the City, to regard it only as a tedious background to the game he was playing. Still, the blue light made him sentimental.

Shaking the moisture off his substantial woolen overcoat (no ridiculous cotton rags for him, no reverence for bleating sheep and cud-chewing cows) as he walked up the stairs to his third-floor apartment, he thought of Mara. This hour, melancholy and dangerous, always made him think of her. In fact, almost everything made him think of her, contrary and random things: snow and sun, flowers and ruins, leather-bound freethinking tomes that he collected and an occasional pornographic chapbook that he would peruse avidly and burn or throw away. He was proud of his willpower; after their quarrel, which he had faced with both delight and consternation, he had not run back to her, had not called to offer explanations and excuses. He had set a deadline for himself: If she did not call in two days, he would go and see her.

Every minute stuck to him as if made of viscous tar. He consoled himself with the thought that it was inconceivable he would have to wait two days. She would come to him before his self-imposed deadline.

He jiggled the key in the lock, but it would not turn. The door was unlocked, even though he knew he had locked it since he always did. He hesitated but then pushed it and walked in.

His apartment had no hallway; the front door faced the huge floor-to-ceiling double-glazed window that let in the lights of the City. Guests often found the room uncomfortably exposed, but he enjoyed the sense of power it gave him. He could look down at the faceless multitudes in the streets without being seen.

The overhead light was not on, but he could see the silhouette in the armchair dragged into the middle of the room. As always, his heart leaped when he recognized the familiar outline of her head against the glitter of the streetlights.

"Mara," he whispered. "Why are you sitting in the dark, my dear?"

His eyes never leaving her, he pushed the switch. She did not stir when the harsh electric light came on, only her pupils narrowing. She was sitting primly, like a schoolgirl, the knees pressed together, one hand lying on the armrest. The second hand firmly grasped a small, oily-black gun that pointed straight at Mr. Seal's midriff.

"Sit there," she said.

There was a chair thoughtfully placed near the door, facing her. Moving cautiously, he sidled up to it and lowered himself onto the seat. The gun followed his movements, never wavering, and so did her eyes, as cold and distant as always. Gray and green and blue, the shifting colors of the sea.

"There is no need for this, Mara," he said.

She shrugged.

"I need some answers. And I don't have the time to play games. A gun is a great way to simplify matters."

"Could you shoot me?"

"I know how to aim and pull the trigger. If I do it several times and quickly enough, chances are I'll kill or wound you."

"But *could* you do it?" he insisted.

She looked at him with the same heartbreaking, impenetrable eyes.

He sighed and looked at his hands folded in his lap, heavy masculine hands, their backs dusted with sandy hair.

"I'll tell you anything you want to know," he said. "I was going to anyway."

"Who killed Detective Hart?" she asked.

"I did."

"Why?"

"For what he did to you."

"He raped me, didn't he?"

"Nobody raped you, Mara."

"Then what did he do?"

"Something incredibly stupid. He tried to implant a Guardian graft in you. Fortunately, it did not take. You are like me. Impenetrable. He told me about it, that idiot!"

She blinked, her forehead creasing.

"What? How did he do it?"

"There was no indignity involved. When you passed out from a blow to the head, he slipped a piece of tissue down your throat. It was supposed to take root and spread. But your body rejected it."

He almost expected her to gag or at least cry out but except for the blanching of her lips, she showed no reaction. The gun never wavered in her hand.

She could really shoot me!

He still refused to believe it.

"How do you know it did not take?" she asked in the same dead monotone that sounded like a malicious parody of the voice he had heard almost every day and every night in his dreams for the last eight years.

"You would know if it did. Your body would start changing. By now it would have shown these changes."

She licked her lips, and he saw a hint of uncertainty. But he was sure of what he said. One of his spies had followed her to that disgusting female doctor. If Mara was worried about a potential sexual assault, she was not undergoing a wrenching transition into Guardianship.

"Why would he do such a thing?"

"Because he was an idiot. And impatient. And crude. It is never done to adults anyway. But you don't need to think about him, Mara. He is gone. I cleaned up the mess he made."

"Not all of his mess, surely. He killed Elvira Sparrow."

Mr. Seal started.

"Don't try to lie to me," Mara said, shocking him again with the casual cruelty in her voice. "I know he did."

"How?"

"The dream-sea, of course. I should have known it weeks ago, only I was too stupid to understand what it was telling me. Remember the shoe I pulled out of that fish? It was a deerskin moccasin. When I first met Hart, I was wearing deerskin shoes, and he cringed away from me because of his totem. I went into the sea to ask for the name of Elvira's murderer, and it gave it to me, loud and clear!"

"What else did you ask?" Mr. Seal whispered.

"I am not going to tell you. I am not going to tell you anything anymore. You have lied to me all those years. You sold me to your buddy, Ronald Raven. You let it slip he was only interested in my Power, so it was not hard to figure out the rest. Why did you do that? For what? What was your gain in this scheme? When you first showed up in our house like the Savior Wolf in the fairy tale of the Red-Haired Girl, I was infinitely grateful. You showed me that I was not insane or sick or weird. I had a gift, a Power! I could use it to help people and to make money. My mother adored you. And I had a crush on you like the brainless teenager that I was! You could have married me yourself! Why did you involve Ronald?"

"Who do you think I am?" Mr. Seal felt a familiar emotion welling up; the emotion that had never shown its ugly face in his dealings with Mara before.

Anger.

"I am not Ronald's puppet master. He fell in love with you. He proposed. You accepted. Yes, he knew about your Power. I had told him before you two met. But you were in love with him too, Mara. So, don't blame me for your own choices!"

"But you still won't answer my question," Mara responded. "Why didn't you marry me yourself?"

Mr. Seal stared at her for a long time. Then he sighed.

"I suppose it's inevitable," he said. "Let me show you something. Please don't shoot."

In the enormous foyer of the Animal House, the chaos continued. The gray walls hewn of the same solemn granite that faced the imposing façade were plastered with handwritten and crudely printed notes. The curving staircase that led to the offices and conference rooms and continued beyond, to the top-story official quarters of the president, currently occupied by James Otter who was nowhere to be seen, was thronged with harried officials. The newly installed elevator emitted alarming clanking noises as it strained to carry loads of people up and down.

But Thomas Hawk was in his milieu as he navigated the knots of bureaucrats, dispensing a smile here, a hello there. Julian Sparrow followed in his wake, content to let him take the lead. His eyes flickered to random faces as he passed them, trying to read the future in the hieroglyphs of shock and anxiety.

Finally, they made their way to Hawk's office, which, while small and not on one of the prestigious upper floors, was at least reasonably quiet. Hawk closed the door and motioned Julian to take a seat. They stared at each other warily.

Julian and Thomas knew each other from moving in the same rarefied social circles: the secular elite of First City. They had never been friends, but Julian had been in the boarding school with Thomas's uncle, and so when he needed a contact in the Animal House, his thoughts immediately turned to the up-and-coming young undersecretary for public safety.

"So, how can I help you, Mr. Lion?" Thomas asked.

Julian winced.

"It's not my name anymore," he said. "Just call me Julian."

"Yes, I've heard about it. You changed your totem, right? May I ask why? It's not commonly done."

"I got married," Julian replied, which was not the whole truth but as much as this smooth talker deserved. "And this is what I need to talk to you about. My wife was murdered, and the investigation stalled."

"This is hardly surprising in the light of the current events. The constabulary is stretched to the limits dealing with ... well, everything that is happening."

"You mean the conspiracy to bring about the Return of the Ancestors?" Julian asked. He was used to negotiating with rich and entitled people, and Thomas struck him as somebody who would run circles around you if you tried to be circumspect but would wilt under direct questioning. He was right; Thomas fidgeted and looked away.

"How do you know about it?" he asked.

Julian laughed.

"Everybody does. What do you think, people are blind? Tornadoes, rains of mice and blood ... The Temple is thronged with worshippers for the first time in ages, so I heard."

"So you know why we cannot allocate sufficient resources to solve your wife's murder."

"Bullshit! I know what happened to my wife's body. Her murder is part of the conspiracy."

"Who told you?" Thomas Hawk was now spooked.

"Never mind." Julian was pressing his advantage. "It is in your best interests to solve Elvira's murder as soon as possible. I am here to help. I want to offer a large reward for any tip that helps find the killer. The reward is to be split evenly between the tipster and the secretariat of public safety."

Hawk cleared his throat.

"How large?"

"Fifteen thousand florins."

Hawk raised an eyebrow.

"It is ... large indeed."

"And for that," Julian insisted, pressing his advantage, "I want you to deploy unorthodox methods."

"What do you mean?"

"I know you have ... consultants on the payroll. Consultants who employ Powers."

He expected Hawk to query him again on how he knew that and had a plausible deflection ready. He was in control now, having offered Hawk what amounted to a bribe and seeing his tacit acceptance. But for once, Thomas Hawk did not react as predicted.

He looked aside and licked his dry lips.

"Do you have business interests in the South Continent, Julian?" he asked.

Thrown off, Julian paused before responding.

"Yes, I do. My firm has recently invested in a new coffee plantation. But what has it got to do with my wife's murder? Rest assured, I have enough funds to underwrite my promise of reward."

For the first time, Thomas Hawk looked him straight in the

eyes, and Julian saw a web of burst blood vessels surrounding his yellowish pupils.

"I don't want your money," he said. "I want a passage on one of your ships. I want out of First City."

~

He rose and unbuttoned his shirt. He took it off and folded it neatly on the floor. Then he unbuckled his belt and pulled down his pants.

He was standing naked in front of Mara, her gaze sliding off his perfect porcelain nudity like water off an oilskin. His body repelled all prurience because there was nothing to see. Under the pale skin his muscles rolled in gentle undulations, from the broad chest unmarked by nipples down to the blank triangular space at the juncture of his legs.

He let Mara look her fill and then dressed with the same unhurried dignity.

"The Temple's botched job," he said. "I was meant to be a Guardian. My parents dedicated me in the cradle. They were poor and devout. Besides, they had four other sons."

The story he had told her floated up in her mind.

"Is it ..." she began to ask and had to stop and swallow because her throat was so dry. "You told me about the Hospital of Transformation. Were you that child? The one whose surgery they botched?"

"Yes. The hospital closed because of my case."

"Why did they do it? Even the Fur Guardian, I saw, he had ... had genitals."

"Largely nonfunctional. But the Temple techniques are constantly refined."

Mara had the strangest impression that his body was looking at her through the fabric of his suit but like a blind man through his spectacles, straining to see and not able to.

"Why did the grafts fail?"

"Nobody knows. They went a bit further with me than is customary. You see, there is a theory that in order for a Power to manifest in a person, they need to be cleansed from all human impurities. Humans have naked skin. Humans walk upright. And humans are obsessed with sex, unlike animals who mate for procreation. All these things have to be eliminated before we become as our totems and acquire their Power."

"What Power?" Mara asked, feeling faintly sick.

"There is only one. The Temple talks about Powers of divination and even Powers of mechanical ingenuity but this is all nonsense. A smoke screen. The only Power everybody wants is the Power to unlock the gate that keeps us in the prison City. The Power you have, Mara."

CHAPTER 18. THE REVEALER

Mara stumbled back home through the slippery dark streets, still clutching the gun. Seal's gun or at least, the gun he had used to shoot Detective Hart. The thought of it brought another wave of nausea.

She remembered the clue that the dream-sea provided when she asked who killed William Hart. The object that the land mermaid handed her.

A seal. One of those used to stamp official documents in the Animal House.

The dream-sea was fond of puns. A seal—Seal. Deerskin—Hart.

She was glad Hart was dead. But the thought that Mr. Seal had killed him to avenge her—if this, in fact, was the reason—only made it worse. Her mentor, her teacher, her friend.

A murderer.

She went over their conversation in her head again and again, as if she could find something else there that would exonerate him or at least provide a better explanation than the revolting madness he had offered her in the same soft voice and with the same soft smile that used to be her emotional anchor in the days following Ronald's disappearance. But the more she dug into his words, the more she felt like she was scrabbling in a grave full of rotting flesh.

"I was destined for great things," he said. "So, they did a thorough job, cleansing my body. However, once they tried to graft animal tissue, it failed to take. My body rejected everything. So, there was nothing to do but to pay me a handsome compensation, reimburse my family, give me a good private education, and hush the whole thing up. They were decent; I have an independent income till the day I die. They've even given me a new name as part of the severance package, an aristocratic name."

"This is why ..."

"Yes, this is why I'm legally Mr. Seal. They did not risk much. Obviously, I cannot pass it on to my descendants."

"How old were you when it happened?"

"Ten. So it's not like I can be tormented by memories of the pleasures I've lost."

The fact that he was castrated meant little to Mara. She pitied him, but the sight of his sexless body, while shocking, changed nothing in the balance of their relationship. The crush she had had on him when she was a teenager was an embarrassing memory. At one time, she had been grateful that he never took advantage of her. Now this reason for gratitude was gone, together with the rest.

But was it possible that he was, somehow, in love with her despite the futility of such an obsession? It dawned on Mara that love came in more hues than she had realized, some darker than the others.

But even obsession would be preferable to the madness that oozed from what he had said next.

"First City is a prison. The gate to escape it to freedom has been locked. You are the only one who has the Power to unlock it, Mara. What Hart did was not only outrageous but stupid. You don't need any animal grafts to acquire the Power. You already have it."

"The Temple teaches that beyond the gate lies the Abode of the Ancestors. I have no idea where it is."

"Of course, you do. You have been to the Abode many times. And you can lead the rest of us there. The dream-sea is what the Temple people call the Abode of the Ancestors."

"Only the Revealer can lead humanity back to the Abode! Isn't it the teaching?"

"You are the Revealer, Mara."

The man who called himself Thomas Hawk (though his real name was Thomas Rabbit) fidgeted with his coffee cup as he waited for his handler from the Temple Security Office.

The day, raw and blustery, was slowly dying beyond the dirty window of the inconspicuous café where the few patrons gazed dully at the pages of the *Voice of the City*. The wireless droned on about the latest terrorist alert, or was it a flood warning? Hawk shivered in his elegant double-breasted suit and for the umpteenth time wished to be somewhere else.

That arrogant prick Julian Sparrow was his last card. He had been astonished by Hawk's request or pretended to be. Hawk could not believe the supposedly shrewd banker was so clueless. He suspected Sparrow had already secured a nice warm cabin on a cargo ship plying the route between the North and South Continents and probably had a new mansion built somewhere near a coffee plantation. The South Continent had unlimited land and one could live in as big a house as one wished. Thomas, squeezed into a tiny though prestigious apartment within walking distance of the Animal House, found it hard to imagine.

"This can be arranged," Julian had said, "but aren't you afraid of the diseases? The South is as far from the City as you can get."

"I don't believe the diseases are real," Thomas had said. "It's a rumor by the Temple to keep us confined."

In truth, he was not sure. The rumor had been too persistent, and though he had never ventured far from the heart of First City, some of his friends went on joyrides into the countryside and came back with hair-raising stories of crippled, lame, and disfigured farmers.

But Thomas did not care. He would brave the hazy dangers of the South Continent if it meant escaping from the web that he had foolishly entangled himself in. At first, acting as a double agent for the Temple Security, which was separate from the secular constabulary and theoretically dealt with religious matters only, had been a blast. It padded his bank account, which his meager official salary was unable to keep in the black. It gave him a dizzying sense of power and self-importance, which his mind-numbing job, signing endless paperwork, failed to provide. And it appealed to what he believed was his adventurous nature.

Now he knew better. After the fake secret cell that he had been so proud of creating and managing had gone so disastrously off the rails, he longed for a return to his safe days of routine and boredom. He longed for it so much that he even considered praying to his totem. Rabbits were good at escaping danger, weren't they? And hawks could see far ahead, though strictly speaking, he had no business adopting somebody else's totem. Wasn't it some kind of infraction? Thomas, who could preach at great length about the Return of the Ancestors to his glazed-eyed followers, did not believe a word of the *Book of the Remnant* himself. Though with everything that was happening, he was beginning to reconsider.

The man who lowered himself into the armchair beside him had an uncannily soft walk despite his considerable bulk. Hawk was so lost in his own misery that he did not even notice him entering the café.

"You're late," he said, going on the offensive.

His handler did not react. He did not look well. His graying hair was rumpled, his cheeks pale and greasy.

"Did you talk to the woman?" he asked.

"What woman?"

"You know. What's her name? Viola Marmot."

"She knows nothing. She saw Mara at the meeting and that was that. It was Edna who introduced her."

"And Edna gutted herself at the doorstep of your office. You let your followers run wild."

"I did what I was supposed to do!" Hawk struck back. Unfortunately, the effect was spoiled by his voice rising into an indignant whine. "You wanted to flush out discontents, heretics, potential terrorists. I gave you a bunch of them. Why weren't they arrested before the whole thing got out of hand?"

"These people are nothing. Small fry. A couple of hysterical housewives and a thug or two. Lonelyhearts was leveled. It was not done by your pathetic crew. The conspiracy is greater than what you offered us so far."

Hawk swallowed a couple of times and reached for his coffee cup, which was, unfortunately, empty. He had inhaled the thick brew when he came in and now there was nothing left to help his flagging courage.

"I did what I could," he said. "I want out."

His handler looked at him with those glassy, impenetrable eyes of his that always made him shiver. Hawk suddenly noticed that there was very little white surrounding the darkness of the bulging irises.

"You can be out when you find Mara Raven," the handler said. "If you try something stupid before that, your file will be on the desk of the chief constable tomorrow."

Thomas pretended to be indignant but in fact, he was relieved. It was better than he had expected. He had an ace up his sleeve—Mara's phone number, which she had given him at their one and only meeting. He would start there.

"Why is she so important?"

"It does not matter."

"That chit of a girl!" said Hawk. "Who would have thought. There was so much talk when Raven married her. She's not bad looking but there is something strange about her. Something … almost repulsive."

"Shut up!" said his handler. "We have to find her. And as soon as possible. That's all you have to know."

"She has a Power, doesn't she?"

"Yes, she does. More than anybody else. But she can't use it against individuals in the City, so your hide is safe."

"So why wasn't she taken to the Temple, made into a Guardian?"

"Among other reasons," said his handler, "because her Power was discovered when she was almost fourteen and it's too late for grafts. Also, Mr. Rabbit, we don't kidnap children. She was the only child of secular parents who would as soon have thought of dedicating her to the Temple as of offering each other to some maniac with a passion for anatomical experimentation."

"Now look!" cried Hawk. "William Hart was your man, and I did not 'offer' Elvira to him!"

"No, you dumped her upon him when you tired of her, knowing perfectly well that the silly goose would fall for him and that he would have no interest in her apart from his mad scheme of calling up the Ancestors by staging a public ceremony of a gate-opening on the holy site of the Hill."

"I did not know he would use her for this!"

"Doesn't matter. It was a stupid and reckless thing to do, and his next step was even worse. Fortunately, he was neutralized before he could do more harm."

"Did you do it yourself?" asked Hawk.

"What kind of question is this?" His handler appeared shocked. "Of course not. It was a constabulary job. They take care of their turncoats."

"Anyway," said Hawk after a pause, "none of my people have any idea where she is."

"How about that George Buzzard? He's a dangerous man but he has contacts in the slums."

"George disappeared," said Hawk. "I suspect he's dead."

"You didn't tell me that!" His handler bent forward. "Did he try something stupid?"

"He used to talk a lot about developing his latent Power," said Hawk. "He believed that everybody had a Power, and that the elite kept this knowledge from the common man. He was a democrat."

"A fool, more likely," said his handler with contempt. "He got it all backwards. Every *body* can be used by those with a Power."

"What do you mean?"

"Human bodies are keys to the gate that leads to the Abode. They can be turned by violence, but only people who have a Power can do it. And only few do. Developing his latent Power, indeed! He probably went out and killed somebody and then was shocked that the Ancestors did not appear!"

"But isn't it true," persisted Hawk, "that things are changing? When I grew up, Powers belonged to the Temple and the Guardians. My old man did not even believe they existed! My mother thought they were a gift of grace. And now, about anybody can poke at the gate by spilling blood."

"This is why we need to contain it!" His handler leaned forward, the armchair creaking as he shifted. "The Temple knows more than your so-called 'elected president' does. Every half-sane person should support what we are doing. We understand what might happen if the gate is opened. What we have seen so far is nothing. The people in Lonelyhearts, the flood on the Hill ... This is the beginning. Much worse things are coming."

"But why?" Hawk insisted, offended by his handler's offhand reference to himself as "half sane." Strangely enough, even though he disliked and feared the man, he was very sensitive to his opinion of himself. "What is changing?"

"Why? Because the Revealer is here, this is why."

Hawk opened his mouth and closed it again, at a loss as to how to react. He did not believe in the Revealer. In his previous conversations with the man sitting in front of him he took it for granted that he was a rational skeptic like himself, doing his job for the Temple because it was his job. Nothing in his previous assignments, which focused on tracking down fanatics, fundamentalists, and assorted loose cannons, had changed his mind. To be confronted with the fact that the man genuinely believed in the rigmarole of the Return of the Ancestors was creepy.

"But ... isn't it what the Temple always wanted?" he asked. "The Return?"

The man stared at him, and Hawk suddenly realized that his protruding eyes did not look human at all.

"None of your business," he said. "Find Mara Raven, and this will be your last job."

Hawk looked at the empty coffee cup on the table, its bottom encrusted with muddy grounds, at the damp napkin, and the glazed sugar pot. These objects suddenly appeared infinitely precious in their solid ordinariness.

"I'll do all I can," he said, and rose, hoping that was the end of the interview. His handler nodded, lost in his thoughts.

When Hawk finally left, his handler, deputy chief of the Temple Security Bureau, Jeremy Seal, sighed and sank deeper into the armchair.

He despised the little dickhead. Hawk, or rather Rabbit (and nothing characterized the man better than the contrast between his real and assumed names), was a mindless bureaucrat. In the past, people like him had run the City. Hell, they had also run the Temple.

But the tide was turning. What Jeremy Seal had hoped for, studied for, worked for, betrayed for, was coming to pass. The whole tiresome machinery of living was being dismantled. The puerility of ambition, the hopelessness of aging, the frustration of his deformity, were about to be swept aside in the one glorious moment of revelation, in which the gate would be opened, and he would finally see what lay beyond. The gray City, so familiar he did not notice it anymore, would be forgotten like an old school lesson. He knew with the assuredness that transcended reason that the Return of the Ancestors could no longer be postponed or averted. This knowledge came to him in the dreams he could not remember. It permeated his body, that flaccid thing that he normally regarded only as a necessary evil. It put fever into his sluggish blood and spring into his heavy gait.

And yet at this moment, with revelation so close, he could not think of the opening of the gate or the Ancestors. He could think only of Mara.

She had disappeared after their last disastrous conversation. He still could not believe he had mishandled it so badly. It hurt to think about it, and yet he could not help it, going over each word spoken, each painful truth revealed, like a man with an irresistible itch digging into his own bloodied skin in the vain attempt to scratch it away.

When he had finally followed her, shaking off his stupor of shock, she was nowhere to be seen. Initially he had not been worried. He knew how small her social circle was, having worked tirelessly to keep it that way for years. He checked with the concierge of her apartment building who confirmed that Mrs. Raven had not been in. He called her mother but Louisa Ferret, used to her daughter's brooding moods, was not particularly concerned about her absence. Still, he ordered her house to be under surveillance. He even inquired with Ronald Raven's surviving family, which consisted of his younger brother, who hated Mara when Ronald introduced her as his fiancée and had not changed his feelings in the years that followed.

The worst thing was that Mr. Seal's intuition was betraying

him. Since he met Mara eight years ago, he had developed an unerring awareness of her moods and whereabouts. Their relationship had at all times been a model of propriety. It could not have been otherwise. But he knew that she had fallen in love with Ronald before she knew it herself (on that night he had tried to get drunk and ended up throwing up and then walking endlessly through the wet streets of First City). He knew when she was in the dream-sea, lying sleepless in his bed, consumed by a different but equally painful kind of jealousy. But now he could not even imagine where she could be hiding.

Could she be dead? This was something he refused even to contemplate, but emotions aside, he reasoned that the gathering strength of the phenomena that his Bureau classified as "the signs of the Return" testified to her being alive. With the Revealer gone, the process would stop.

Had she crossed into the Abode of the Ancestors, having finally entered the dream-sea in the body? But for that to be done, the gate that had been locked since the Rebellion would have had to be breached. And this had not happened, occasional cracks created by violated bodies notwithstanding. The prison City still stood. And the gate, woven of the minds and bodies of all the people who lived in First City and believed in its reality, was still locked.

A waiter approached him.

"We are closing, sir."

Mr. Seal rose to his feet and exited into the wet night.

CHAPTER 19. THE SECOND CITY

Swimming furiously, she plunges into the depths. The water is muddy and polluted; fine grains of silt burn her eyes. Drawing the dirty water into her lungs is like breathing smoke.

But it's not only silt and sand; though visibility is poor, she can discern broken pieces of wood lazily gyrating around her, chipped bricks and dressed stone, sharp slivers of metal.

She has never seen anything like this before in the dream-sea, which is alive in its every part. Everything in the dream-sea is alive, from Light Puppies to dreamfish to the swaying multicolored corals on the softly breathing sand bottom. But this urban debris is dead.

She is too angry to pause and reconsider her precipitous dive. She plummets down like a stone, butted by floating cornices and window frames, scratched by door handles, and scored by shards of glass. She is going down, down, down, toward the distant lights of another City. First City's underwater twin.

Her memories of the beach are hazy: She knows she was there, but was the sea welcoming or sulky?

Never mind! She is the mistress of the dream-sea, not its servant! It can no longer stop her from finding out the truth.

Something makes her pause. She looks up, squinting through the layers of debris. Something sparkles there, a momentary flash of purple and green.

"Light Puppies?" she whispers.

A Puppy is descending toward her, a luminous double ring of lilac and emerald. But its bright colors are dimmed by the filth in the water, and the flotsam and jetsam flock around it like sharks drawn by the smell of blood. A jagged self-propelling piece of board jabs it. A sharp splinter of glass sadistically draws its edge along the Puppy's inner ring, releasing a cloud of sparkling green blood. A chest of drawers snaps at it with its multiple hungry mouths.

Should she go and help her friend? No! It would stop her. It would prevent her from discovering her destiny.

It would not let her see the Ruler of this underwater City, of which First City, almost drowned in rain, is but a pale copy.

She turns around and with powerful angry strokes propels herself downward. Without a pause, she catches a floating table leg and snaps it in two.

Visibility improves; the water lightens and the lights of the second City below twinkle in the grayish mist like inverted stars. Her speed increases: She is a comet falling into the City, blinded by her own momentum.

The silky gray light around her is getting stronger, as if the hidden moon in the depths is waxing to illuminate her approach.

And then she is standing in the street, looking around. It is both like and unlike First City. It is underwater, of course, so paradoxically, it looks less drowned than First City with its overflowing gullets and flooded sidewalks. A school of rainbow fish is darting among the trees planted along the sidewalk like colorful birds. The trees are leafless but garlands of seaweed draped around their branches make up for this. But apart from this, the buildings marshaled along the wide sidewalk are much more ornate than the utilitarian architecture of First City. Apart from the Animal House and the Temple, most houses in First City are simple receptacles for as many living souls as they can possibly contain. But these buildings are true architectural marvels. They are elaborately decorated, with molded cornices, friezes, pilasters, railed balconets, statues, and caryatids. She does not know how she knows the names of these bewildering decorations, but she can name each one of them. Above the peaked roofs, she glimpses the tops of several towers, so slender and graceful they seem to be made of stone lace.

There are no people in the street. The windows are blind; the elaborate bronze doors of the front entrances are locked.

She begins to walk toward the nearest intersection. It is strange to walk in the dream-sea: Her feet barely touch the pavement and occasionally she hovers above the surface.

Suddenly, she sees a small figure rush across the street ahead of her and disappear into an alley.

This is no dreamfish! Though it was too quick for her to get a proper look, its movements are not the fluid, languid undulations of mermaids, dreamfish, or bottom-dwellers. That was a human being. A child!

She rushes to the alley, but the water grows cold and heavy. She struggles to draw it into her lungs, and when she does, she begins to choke. Is she to drown in the dream-sea? The idea is so outlandish that she stops and tries to persuade herself that it is not happening.

But it is. The water is pressing down on her, as ineluctable and indifferent as the tornado that devastated Lonelyhearts. She is becoming aware that the dream-sea is so much larger than her. Her playground, her refuge, her escape from the doldrums of everyday; it is no longer hers. She is a visitor here. An unwanted and reluctantly tolerated guest.

Struggling to breathe, burdened by this realization as much as she is pressed down by the immense weight of water above her, she struggles to follow the child.

The alley dead-ends in a spiky gate made of rusty iron rails and crowned with tangles of sharp wire. She feels revulsion rise in her, so powerful that she is afraid she will be sick. The gate is open a tiny crack. The child—if it was a child—must have snuck through.

A smudge of maroon floats in the water above the gate, a lazy, undulating cloud, sending tendrils and shoots toward her. She can taste the salty, hungry tang of it.

She wants to run away. But something stronger than horror and revulsion propels her forward.

She pushes the gate, and it gives.

Beyond it is a landscape unlike anything she has ever encountered in the dream-sea. A barren expanse of sand and gravel that used to be a park of sorts because she can see the bare skeletons of trees stuck here and there among the maze of paths, as if to mask the real nature of this place. But the trees are dead, reduced to rotting trunks colonized by drab sea worms.

Among the trees are cages.

They are large and sturdy, made of heavy metal bars. Some have metallic mesh instead of bars as if whatever was contained inside could not be allowed to reach out. Beyond the bars and railings, the concrete or stone floors are littered with some unidentifiable debris: overturned basins, torn mats, broken chains.

The door to each cage is wide open, swaying in the currents of the dream-sea. The cages are empty.

She passes them, following the tang of blood dissolving in the water like sugar in hot tea. But she can still taste its appalling sweetness and it leads her on, unerringly, toward her goal.

The small body lies on the path, crumpled and pathetic. She barely spares it a glance, enough to ascertain that it is indeed a child, a boy perhaps five or six years old. His throat is torn but the heart is no longer pumping, so the blood is seeping through the wound, dissolving in a cloud above him.

She steps over the body.

Behind it is another cage. This one is locked. Its occupant, too big and heavy for the tiny enclosure, stirs at her approach.

She wants to turn around and run away, but she cannot. Involuntarily, her arm is stretching toward the cage, her fingers tensed, as if ready to break iron.

But as she touches the lock, the cage door swings open.

Mara sat at the kitchen table, staring into the wet dawn reluctantly breaking above the roofs of the apartment blocks across the road.

Julian's "Good morning" reached her as if across a vast distance. She mouthed something in return as he busied himself making coffee in a small bronze cezve and warming slices of bread in a pan. This finally broke her stupor. She had never seen a man make breakfast. Certainly, Ronald would have never demeaned himself by such a womanly activity.

"Did you sleep well?" he asked. He was wearing a fancy velvet robe. Mara twitched, adjusting the robe that hung off her shoulders but barely covered her knees. Elvira's expansive clothes did not fit her own slimmer and taller frame.

"Not really," she muttered, watching as he poured coffee into a tiny cup and offered it to her. The bitter taste on her tongue was pure bliss.

Julian poured his coffee and offered her toast and jam. They sat at the kitchen table in a strange parody of domesticity.

When she had run out of Mr. Seal's apartment, a tempest of fear, anger, and indignation filling her head, one thought had managed to penetrate the white noise of her emotions.

She could not go back to her own place.

Mr. Seal had a key. But even if she changed the lock, what good would it do? He could bribe the concierge. He could probably break down the door. If he really believed she was the Revealer, he was clearly insane. And this insanity that must have festered inside him since their first meeting all those years ago made him capable of anything.

So, where could she hide from him?

Mara thought about her mother. But as ambivalent as she was

about their relationship, she could not bring a murderer into her mother's house. If Mr. Seal did not find her at home, Louisa's would be the first place he would check. Louisa would not be able to lie convincingly, but she could tell the truth—that she did not know where her daughter was—and be spared.

Mara went through the list of people she knew and realized, with deepening horror, that there was not a single person who would offer her shelter. She had no real friends, barely any acquaintances. For ages she thought about her solitude with pride. She was special, unique. She did not need vulgar friends because she had her Power, her husband, and her mentor.

Now her husband and her mentor turned out to be traitors. As for her Power, it made her a target, prey. The dream-sea could not shelter her physical body. And the body was all she was. Standing in the rain, wet and cold and hungry, she realized that she was no better than the huddled masses of Lonelyhearts she used to despise. She was like them: a shivering animal, in need of a burrow to hide from predators.

At the end, she walked. When she knocked on the door, she was so drenched that water sloshed in her shoes and her hair was plastered to her scalp. Julian did not seem to recognize her at first. When he did, he ushered her in, gave her a glass of wheat brandy that burnt her throat and warmed her belly, and took her to a room upstairs.

"Make yourself comfortable. All the clothes are clean. We will talk in the morning," he told her, and shut the door.

Waking from her stupor, Mara looked around. The windows were covered with wine-colored velvet drapes. The dresser was groaning under gewgaws and sets of makeup. Every spare surface was covered with antimacassars, runners, and embroidered cloths. There was a large icon of the Four on the night table.

The bed was made with more pillows and throws than Mara had ever seen outside a department store. And the large wardrobe held rows and rows of frilly dresses, boned corsets, blouses, and skirts. A separate compartment displayed flower-and ribbon-decorated hats that most women had given up wearing because of the incessant rain.

Mara felt queasy about wearing a dead woman's clothes but, cold and miserable as she was, she had to. Her teeth were chattering, and she knew she risked pneumonia. She took off her soaked dress and petticoat and put on the thickest and plainest robe she could find among this rainbow riot of expensive fabrics. It did not fit but this did not matter. What mattered was that the robe had a pocket. Mara put the gun she had taken from Hart's house there.

She washed up in the en-suite bathroom and considered the neatly made bed that looked as if nobody had slept in it for ages. That made sense since the owner of these silk pillows and tasseled blankets was dead. But where was the widower sleeping? Did he fix a temporary bedroom somewhere else?

But then it occurred to Mara that there was no way Julian would have ever slept in this cluttered nest. Mr. and Mrs. Sparrow must have had separate bedrooms.

Now, reluctantly chewing a piece of toast, she hardly dared to look at Julian. When she did, she was surprised that despite his casual attire, he did not look different from his regular self. Ronald had often been disheveled and grumpy in the morning. Julian's black hair was neatly combed; he was clean-shaven and smelled of his nettle-and-pine cologne. She did not know whether it was done for her benefit or was a habit. In any case, it made her aware of her tangled hair and scrubbed face.

He did not pressure her; instead telling her the news. There had been an assassination attempt on Claire Mink, the undersecretary for labor. A man got close to her car and slit his throat. Something like a tentacle emerged from the wound and smashed up the car. Witnesses blabbed about black flowers on the site, but nobody was clear about what it meant. There was nothing but blood, bodies, and twisted metal when the constable arrived.

"They identified the assailant. One Bennie Muskrat," Julian said.

Mara remembered Mr. Muskrat at the meeting of their conspiratorial cell. How many of them were still alive? Carla Marmot killed, Edna Lynx a suicide and a terrorist, and now Muskrat. She doubted George Buzzard was around, remembering the pure light of madness in his narrow eyes. That left Hawk of whatever his real totem was. So much for the Army of the Revealer!

Her Army.

She realized that Julian was looking at her. She swallowed.

"I know who killed your wife," she said.

His face froze.

"His name was William Hart. He was a constable."

"Was?"

"He is dead."

"How?"

"He was murdered."

"Who did it?"

She told him everything.

CHAPTER 20. THE LIONS

At some point, it got cold in the kitchen, and he motioned her to follow him to the sitting room where he made a fire. Mara's gaze was drawn to the two big portraits above the fireplace. They were paintings, not silver prints that were all the rage today. A man and a woman; he in a dark frock coat, she in a short dress that was fashionable several decades ago, in a more liberal and Humanist time. The man's angular face had a single totem sigil on his cheek, but it was so stylized, Mara could not tell what it was. The woman had bobbed hair and such bright makeup that it dazzled even through the muted palette of the painter.

"My parents," Julian said. "Deceased."

Mara came closer, as the woman's face looked faintly familiar. She saw the names on the plaques screwed into the gold frames: *Martin Lion* and *Rose Lion*.

"They were third cousins," Julian said. "The family tries to keep its assets together."

"Rose Lion! I read about her. She was a famed beauty; she introduced rainbow eye shadows! But wait! If they are your parents, you are ..."

"Yes. My original totem is Lion. I took Elvira's when we married. To be frank, that was one reason why I married her. Sparrow is as far from Lion as can be."

"You did not want to be associated with one of the Four, did you?" Mara asked.

Julian smiled.

"No. Neither do you, right?"

"I'm not ..." She stopped.

"It was common knowledge in the business community," Julian said, "that your husband's money came from his mother, who was a Tiger. His father may have been a Raven, but he conveniently ran away when his kids were young and was not heard from again."

"Tiger, Lion, Seal. Three of the Four. The Slaughtered Ones."

"*And of the last one nothing can be said because her claws tore off the skins of the living and made it a garment thereof,*" Julian quoted.

"Her?" Mara repeated.

"Yes. The Bear is female. You have not read the *Book of the Remnant*, have you?"

"I couldn't. I tried but ... I couldn't. It made me sick. I don't know why. I scoffed at it when I was younger, of course."

"We all did," Julian said. "My mother ... you are right, she was a famed beauty and a fashionista. She would show me all those crinkly dresses, and bottles of new perfumes, and makeup palettes of wonderful colors. Her room always smelled nice, like apples and cinnamon. She did not believe in the Ancestors, and when I asked her about our totem, she laughed and told me it was nothing but silly superstition. The City was our home. Animals were our dumb cousins, and had to be treated decently, but they were not our totemic prototypes. And there were no divine Four, locked up in the Abode of the Ancestors and waiting for the gate to be opened, so they could come in and lead us away. And there was no Revealer who would open the gate and expiate our sin of rebellion against the Slaughtered Ones. Except now there is."

"Don't say it!" Mara cried. "Seal is insane. It's horrible that I looked up to a madman all these years, but his delusions have nothing to do with me! I'm no Revealer."

Julian's smile did not reach his eyes, which deepened to dark jade as he looked at Mara.

"But you have a Power." This was not a question.

"Yes, but it is only the Power of entering the common realm of dreams that we all share."

"But isn't this realm the Abode of the Ancestors?" Julian persisted.

Mara was silent.

"Isn't it?"

"Mr. Seal believes so," she whispered.

"And do you?"

"I did not in the past. Now ... yes, maybe. But I meet no totem animals there. And certainly, no Slaughtered Ones. Anyway, they should be dead, right? Lion, Tiger, Seal, and Bear. They should all be dead!"

The crooked smile on Julian's face remained in place as if he had forgotten it was there, but there was no mirth in his voice as he started talking, so low that Mara had to lean in to hear.

"I started reading the *Book of the Remnant* after Elvira got into religion, started going to the Temple. At first, it was so I could argue with her, bring her back to rationality. Then ... It started making sense. The same kind of sense you get in dreams. See, it indicated that nothing really dies in the Abode of the Ancestors. Death only rules our world."

"The real world, you mean."

"No. The book insisted that our world is an insubstantial creation, smoke on the water of what you call the dream-sea. And we are ... I don't know. Smudged copies of lost originals?"

"Stop!" Mara cried, jumping to her feet.

Julian put a hand on her forearm, and Mara felt a sharp jolt as if his fingers were naked electric wires. She sat down.

"I am not saying I believe it. I am saying this is what *they* believe. Those people you call the Army of the Revealer. The ones who are after you to unlock the gate."

"I don't know how to do it!"

"But if you did," he insisted, "would you?"

"No!" Her response was as instant and as instinctive as snatching a finger from the fire, and she saw in the small relaxation of his posture that he believed her.

"There is something horrible in the dream-sea," she whispered. "I saw it last night. I normally cannot dive without willing it. But it is the second time it happened recently that I was pulled into it the moment I closed my eyes. And I saw ... a second City."

"In the dream-sea?"

"Yes. It was abandoned or almost abandoned."

"There is only one City," Julian said. "First City. Our refuge. Built for us by the Ancestors."

"I saw another one."

"How does it look?"

"It is more beautiful than First City. Far more elaborate. I don't think we could build anything like it. But ... something terrible happened there. There are no people. Only cages."

"Cages?"

"Yes. The dream-sea is alive but not conscious, at least not in the way we are. But there are things there ... entities. They may have been asleep, but they are awakening. I think this stupid conspiracy has woken them, and the gate is being pushed open, one chink at a time. If you say that the Slaughtered Ones are still alive, then they are pushing it, while the Army of the Revealer is pulling from our side. But there are other entities that want to keep them there. I don't know what they are."

"So, they were caged?"

"Yes," Mara whispered, her eyes roaming across the room,

because she could not look into Julian's face, so unbearably close. Her gaze stopped on Rose Lion's smiling portrait, and she suddenly saw the resemblance between mother and son.

"At least one of the Four is imprisoned. And I ... I opened the cage."

~

Julian had to go to the office. He asked Mara repeatedly if she would be okay, and she reassured him that she could take care of herself. She did not tell him about the gun but its weight in her pocket gave her confidence.

Wandering the empty rooms of his palatial home, she was, again, amused by the contrast between what she thought of as "Elvira's parts" and "Julian's parts." Husband and wife had so little in common in terms of taste that some of the rooms looked like a frozen stylistic battlefield. She could point to a busily inlaid table on curving legs as Elvira's and to a streamlined chair next to it as Julian's. Would he toss out all of Elvira's frou-frou acquisitions now? But it had been more than a month since her death, and her bedroom remained intact. He must have loved her after all, albeit in his own strange fashion.

Thoughts of Julian Sparrow whirling in her head, Mara went back to the bedroom to see if the wardrobe contained any outerwear. She had changed into a long purple velvet dress with a built-in corselet like most of Elvira's clothes, and she was irritated by the way it chafed her midriff. She longed for her own simpler and more convenient attire, but her clothes were still damp. She did not want to go back to her apartment, apprehensive of Mr. Seal and any other fanatic he could have sent her way. But she could go shopping. Her purse still contained more than a hundred florins: enough for a modest shopping spree. She was not sure what would happen with her funds afterward; she did not know whether she could, or should, access Ronald's accounts. But she decided to postpone this decision until later.

She paused by the bed that she had made to the best of her ability by piling up most of the decorative cushions in the corner. She picked up the icon of the Four that Elvira Sparrow had kept by her bed and that, she suspected, had been given to her by her killer. It was nothing like the horrible statues on the Animal House and in the Temple. Framed in glitter and painted against the pastoral green background, the four Slaughtered Ones stared benevolently at her, their features shamelessly humanized by the artist and with only subtle hints of their animal nature. The Lion was draped in a golden mantle and had a crown on his yellow mane, his broad-nosed face regal and heroic. The Tiger was slender and tall, his skin patterned by orange stripes. He was wearing a farmer's broadcloth and holding a hoe in his clawed hand. Mara remembered that in lean times, the Tiger was the one people appealed to. The Seal was a jolly, portly, smiling gentleman with exaggerated whiskers, clutching a glass bowl with goldfish in it. He was the patron of children, and remembering Mr. Seal's deformity, Mara smiled thinly, with no mirth. But her eyes lingered on the fourth member of the Quartet.

The Bear was depicted in a way that left its gender uncertain. It—or she—was a veiled figure, swathed in a voluminous blue-and-gray cloak. The artist clearly tried to convey the sense of majesty and repose, but all they succeeded in doing was making the Bear into a cloudy absence, a gaping hole in the middle of the devotional icon, giving the lie to the sugary reassurance of the portrayed faith.

Mara dropped the icon back on the stand, opened the wardrobe, and rooted among the clothes. She knew she was avoiding big decisions. She knew she was being childish, evasive, cowardly. But the focus on the here and now, on the details of everyday—the feel of fabrics, the creak of the parquet, the patter of rain outside—was her only defense against the horror that lurked in the depths of her own mind, and in the depths of the dream-sea. Was there any difference between the two? Mara did not know anymore.

She pulled out a shawl-collared jacket and an umbrella and marched downstairs. As she was dressing in the hall, she saw a phone on a decorative stand in the corner. It was the same model that she had: an elegant brass column with the speaker on top and the earpiece attached by a flexible cord and slotted into a holder.

Of course, Julian had a phone; after all, she had talked to him before they met. But this gave her an idea.

The thought of her mother had been nagging at her since she ran out of Mr. Seal's apartment. What if he went after her? What if he went *to* her, trying to find out Mara's whereabouts? Louisa Ferret adored her daughter's mentor who had saved them from grinding poverty. She saw him as a substitute father or perhaps faux husband to Mara—in her mind, these two functions were somewhat interchangeable. She did not know where Mara was, but what if Mr. Seal disbelieved her? Having seen the madness of conviction in his eyes and his mutilated body, Mara knew he was capable of anything. Not for the first time, she regretted not shooting him when she had the opportunity.

She dialed her mother's number. Shrill rings followed one another, beating down her hope of hearing her mother's voice until it died.

CHAPTER 21. MOTHER AND DAUGHTER

Mrs. Louisa Ferret fidgeted in her armchair, putting her swollen feet onto the velvet footstool and pushing them off fretfully, straightening the antimacassar that kept bunching up, sipping cold tea, and rustling the pages of the *Voice of the City*. The phone, that black alien machine with the round teeth-filled mouth of the dial, glowered at her from its carved wooden stand in the corner. Like everything else in her snug cottage, it was here thanks to the generosity of her son-in-law. Recently she had started adding the adjective *late* to his title, but only in the privacy of her mind and always accompanied by the instant recoil of guilt. She had loved Ronald or rather, had been in awe of him, hardly able to believe her daughter's incredible luck. But his prolonged absence was taking its toll on Mara, and Mrs. Ferret suffered in silence as the brooding darkness settled again upon her only child.

Louisa only occasionally talked about it with her closest friend, Mrs. Frieda Owl. She did not like to recall what was the most terrible experience of her life: her daughter's birth. And it was not because of the heavy bleeding that the midwife had been unable to staunch and that had cost her the ability to bear more children. The bleeding had been almost pleasurable, a gentle ebb, so soothing after the racking spasms of labor that she had been tempted to give in, to let herself slip away into sweet oblivion. But the panicking midwife, thoroughly unnerved by the fact that the baby, though big, well-formed, and breathing, refused to cry, thrust the newborn roughly at her, screaming that she should pull herself together for the sake of this creature that nobody but mother could love. She was jolted out of her surrender by the horror of having given birth to a monster. She clutched the baby and saw a beautiful little girl with tiny pink fingers and silky hair drying into a perfect blond aureole. And then the baby opened its eyes and fixed her with a remote, dark gaze, her eyes the color of rainwater, and clouds, and something else Louisa had no name for.

Louisa sighed and pushed away her tea. How could a mother be afraid of her daughter? And it's not like Mara had ever been a bad or ungrateful child. She had never done any of those horrid things that break a mother's heart. She had not run with a wild crowd; she had not messed with boys; she had always been studious, elegant, and smart. So, she was a bit standoffish, a bit cold, a bit solitary. So what? She conducted a perfect marriage, and even the strange nightmares that had plagued her childhood turned out to be a respectable Power and brought her the protection and affection of Mr. Seal. No, Louisa had no justification for the apprehension that seeped into her devotion to Mara. No justification, except the obvious one. She knew, even though she would never admit it aloud, that Mara did not love her. She also knew, especially in the small hours of her sleepless nights, that Mara did not love anybody. And still another piece of knowledge, buried so deep that she was only dimly aware of it.

She was relieved that Mara had no children and wanted none.

Louisa stood wincing at her creaking joints and strode to the window to stare into the muddy gloom outside. The windowpane reflected back her own face. The irony of her alienation from Mara was that they looked uncannily alike. True, Mara, tall and lithe, was more striking than Louisa had ever been, but they shared the same regular features, pale skin, and strong bones under the thin covering of flesh, which in Louisa was turning worn and stringy with age.

She would call, just to hear a human voice. Frieda Owl had gone away to visit her married son and Louisa felt lonely and exposed. Her night had been troubled by nightmares. She could not remember any details except the sense of overwhelming dread.

She hooked her index finger in a hole of the dial when a piercing peal went through the house. It took her a couple of heartbeats to realize the phone was not forestalling her intention. The sound was of her newfangled electric doorbell.

Louisa hesitated. She did not expect anybody. Perhaps Mara decided to drop by for an unscheduled visit. It would be out of character, but nice.

"Coming!" she yelled, and padded toward the front door, which she threw open. A silhouette was outlined against the inflamed sky.

~

Mara was about to get into the cab she had called when Julian's car pulled by, sending water spray into the air. Mara tensed. She hated explaining her actions but knew, from her experience with Ronald, that she would have to do it.

However, Julian confounded her expectations. He opened the passenger door and poked his head out.

"I'll be your driver," he said. "A penny saved, and all of that. Hop in!"

She dismissed the cab and got into Julian's car. She realized she wanted him with her; a nebulous apprehension wriggled in her mind. She was impatient to check on her mother but fearful of what she might find.

He waited, his hands on the steering wheel, without asking any questions. She gave him Louisa's address.

"I want to check on my mother," she said.

"Do you have any siblings?" he asked as he navigated the narrow side streets.

"No. I am an only child. Do you?"

"Same. My parents died when I was young. Typhus."

Mara knew that there had been a bad epidemic of typhus before she was born.

"All my cousins, uncles, and aunts prayed to the Seal in addition to their normal devotions to their own totem," Julian continued, "and attributed my parents' demise to their impiety. I knew even then it was bullshit."

"The Seal? Oh yes, he is the patron of disease, isn't he?"

"And children, for some reason. And all kinds of other things. But it is a story, isn't it? And there is another story beneath it, which is darker. And perhaps another one beneath that one."

"And beneath all of them, the truth," Mara said.

He glanced at her, but at that moment, the car plunged into a puddle so deep that its chassis was submerged. Julian swore, and the engine whined.

He did something that caused the car to rock back and forth, trying to get out of the puddle. The street had been deserted until now, but then a cab drew in behind them and honked at Julian who gave the driver the finger. The man jumped out of the cab but instead of attacking them, as Mara half feared, engaged in an animated conversation with Julian, peppered with technical terms she did not understand. Meanwhile, the shivery apprehension was growing inside her until she felt like walking all the way to Louisa's house. The problem, however, was that she did not know where they were. Mara was normally a pedestrian and when seen from the window of a moving car, the City looked unfamiliar.

The cab driver went back to his car and pulled out of the alley.

"He is bringing chains," Julian explained.

They sat in silence until Julian spoke:

"Your mother is fine. Don't worry."

She did not believe it, but his kindness in gauging her frame of mind and trying to offer reassurance touched her. Obeying some obscure impulse, she put her hand on his knee. He covered it with his hand. She could feel every tiny skinfold on his palm, warm and dry, his long, slim fingers pressing down on hers. In the wavering dashboard light, their hands lay together like bodies washed out on the beach.

The cab driver reappeared with chains that he fixed to the back of their vehicle and the front of his. Julian pushed the ignition, as Mara sat in a daze, the car rocking around her like a boat on choppy water.

They were pulled out of the puddle, and Julian thanked the cab driver, while Mara clung to each precious moment of that between time, before the reality of what had happened to her mother could no longer be held at bay. Because with every second, she knew, with growing certainty, that something bad had indeed happened.

Julian climbed back into the car, but instead of driving on, he pulled her to him and kissed her. Though he parted her lips with his tongue, it was she who invited him in. And then something strange happened: She tasted salt, blood, and then she was so gloriously impossibly alive, so present, in that moment, that it felt like dying. It lasted maybe a couple of heartbeats, but she knew that those were joined heartbeats, his and hers. And then it was as if a glass wall came down, separating them, and she tasted her husband's kisses instead, honey and wormwood.

She broke away.

"Take me to my mother," she said.

They drove into the street and Mara saw that her mother's tiny house was brightly lit. And also, that the front door was ajar.

She was out and running toward that glittering trap, despite Julian's cry to wait. Her brain was feverishly and in great detail picturing the confrontation with her mother, the sharp words she would use to berate her for carelessness in not locking the front door.

She plunged through the door and into her mother's fussy living room. And saw Louisa huddled on the chair, her arms tied to its back. A man was standing behind her, holding a knife to her throat. The man was Mr. Seal.

"Mara!" His lardy face lit up with joy, so terrible that she felt nausea bubbling up in her throat. "I knew you'd come, my dear! Now we can be together again!"

Louisa lifted her head, tossing back her graying hair, and looked at her daughter with clear eyes.

"Run, Mara!" she said.

The knife touched the pale skin, drawing a delicate line that swelled with ruby drops.

The gun leaped into Mara's hand, seemingly of its own volition, and she fired into the face of the man who had been her mentor for seven years and who she hated now with the blazing and pure intensity that seemed to set the drenched night on fire.

There was a deafening retort, and she thought, *I did not know it would be so loud!*

Then she saw her mother slump on the chair, her face obliterated.

~

Julian burst into the room as the deafening retort of the gun reverberated in the small space. He stopped short as if running into an invisible wall when he saw Louisa, or rather, what Louisa had become in the single moment it took the bullet to go off course.

He was snapped out of his trauma stupor when a large body pushed past him, almost landing him on the floor, as the other man ran out. He rushed to Mara who dropped the gun and was on her knees, cradling her mother's faceless corpse. The hem of Louisa's housedress rode up disclosing the pale legs dappled with varicose veins. Her long, graying hair was trailing in the glistening puddle that surrounded the head like a halo.

"Mara!"

He shook her shoulder, but she was as unyielding as a piece of wood.

The gun was half submerged in the puddle of blood, and he wanted to pick it up, but the thick metallic stench was too much, and he had to stagger away and throw up. When he turned back, the mess of blood, bone, and brain cupped in Mara's hands was moving.

Something poked from Louisa's shattered skull, something growing and alive, a grayish shoot that rose from the liquefying tissue. The body slumped, dissolving, losing definition, kept together only by the flimsy restraints of its clothing. A stream of viscous water crawled toward Julian.

A black flower shaped like a double butterfly bloomed above the body, growing out of its decay. Mara snapped it up. It stood tall and proud in her hands, its thick velvety petals giving off a sickroom stench. She kept it raised for a couple of seconds, as if offering it to Julian who made no move to take it. She blew into the black mouth of its crown. The flower expanded into a stain of darkness that punched a hole in the light of the room. There was a glimmer of color, but then the blackness rushed back, creating a tunnel of night, a vortex that tore through the room as if it were a flimsy stage set. A gust of salty breeze lifted Julian's hair.

Mara stepped into the vortex. It dwindled to a small hole

suspended in the air and then disappeared. The blood-splattered room was again the only reality.

PART TWO

THE LAND OF SICK SUNSHINE

CHAPTER 1. MR. DOG

She is standing ankle-deep in the dirty water as warm as blood. The water ripples in long brown slicks over the mudflats. It is a shallow sheet stretching in every direction as far as the eye can see. There is no land.

She looks around. The air is foggy, humid, and laden with the overripe smells of rotting flowers and soft, bloated flesh. Her feet sink into the fine silt of the bottom, and she feels tickling, as if hair-thin antennae are probing her soles.

Two parallel rows of stakes lead away from her, creating a path through the vapors.

She walks along the path, her feet plopping every time she lifts them from the greedy mush crawling with innumerable half-seen bodies the colors of decay, all eating and being eaten, tasting her bare flesh even as they die crushed by her steps.

A misty humpback emerges from the mist, a small island.

The island is surrounded by mangroves. An inverted forest of their shaggy air roots bars her way, alive with wet smacking, groaning, chirping, and an occasional splash.

She stops in consternation. She cannot go there.

But go there, she must. She has to reach the island, there is *nothing else to do, and through the mangroves is the only way. Cautiously, she parts the beards of hanging roots. Her body shudders in protest as the slimy tendrils drag along the skin raising red welts.*

The water between the trees is peat-colored and it stinks. The sharp medicinal odor indicates that there are dead plants and animals rotting in it. Gritting her teeth, she steps into it. The water reaches up to her knees, and her ankles sink into the mud.

There are slim reddish shapes like restless punctuation marks darting in the water. There are dragonflies as big as her palm clinging to the slimy, horsetail-like plants. An iridescent beetle the size of her fist is slowly and ponderously devouring a tiny frog.

She forges on, shuddering in disgust, praying that the water does not rise higher. But it does.

Suddenly there is a mighty splash ahead of her in the green murk of interlacing boughs and air roots.

Something the size of a cab tire pushes through the vegetation. It is a snail shell, streaked with dirty brown and green. It is supported on the surface of the water by the pale slimy foot, whose corrugated edge is paddling in rhythmic ripples.

Just a snail, she tells herself, big but harmless. *But then the shell tips over and a peevish human face peers from under its edge.*

Another splash on her left and another shell carried on the expanse of rippling flesh approaches the clearing. This one is off-white and slightly bigger. Its face is female, with a pug nose and pouting, thick lips. The lips part with a hiss and a long black tongue shaped like an arrowhead shoots out and spits something at the first snail. The gob of mucus lands with a wet smack in the middle of its forehead and eats through the skin like acid. Black cracks appear on the foot-paddle. The attacked snail cries out in a shrill human voice and tears its mouth into a large hole, from which a wet scarlet rag emerges, detaches itself from the snail's body, and flops like a skinned bird toward its adversary.

Sobbing and slipping, stung by insects, splattered by mud, she is running through the grove. And then her feet hit the firm ground and she collapses.

She hauls herself upright and looks around. She is on a white-sand beach, similar to the one she used to come to before.

Is she back? Was that slough of disgust an aberration, a tiny, corrupted corner of the dream-sea, and the rest is as it used to be: the ocean of stories where even horrors are sublime?

She lets herself hope, walking away from the sea. Her body feels itchy and unclean. The beach is fenced in by thorny shrubs but there is a narrow trail ahead, the shrubs bent and broken as if a large animal has dragged itself through.

She finds herself in a large clearing overgrown with flowers. The air is thick with the mingled stench of rust and salt.

The clearing is velvety black. Large flowers shaped like double butterflies stare at her mockingly with their invisible eyes. There are so many of them that the ground beneath is invisible.

"No!" she screams, overwhelmed by disgust so profound that it feels like dying. Something snaps inside her, and the veneer of herself cracks and splinters. She tugs at the juice-swollen stems and pulls them out. The flowers shrivel and fall apart where her hand touches them. Leaves and petals flutter to the ground in a rain of cinders. A wave of scorched earth follows in her footsteps.

But when she looks back, the clearing is black once again. Double-butterfly blooms rise from the ashes of her passing.

The grainy surface under her left cheek rasped as she restlessly moved her head, trying to find a position in which the brightness of the bedside lamp would not be so overwhelming. She was stifled by the bedclothes, soaking with sweat.

Mara tried to kick the blanket off and then realized there was no blanket. She opened her eyes, and they were flooded by sunlight, so pitilessly bright that she inhaled in shock and swallowed a mouthful of sand.

Mara scrambled to her feet. *Back at the beach, finally!*

But is it my *beach?*

The texture of her experience was all wrong. In the dream-sea, there was no space or time. She was never quite *there* and yet while there, she could not remember having been anywhere else. And she was never quite *now*, but always one heartbeat ahead or behind of herself.

But here, the brute physicality of her body and her surroundings could not be denied. Time was passing, seconds bleeding away. The rays of the sun beat on her head like a hammer. She was perspiring, and her mouth was parched. Her body, conditioned by the damp chill of First City, rebelled against the heat.

She was on a long white-sand beach ridged with low dunes, a curving headland to her right. In front of her was the sea, a gleaming surface, rocking restlessly in the harsh sunlight. The sun, naked and furious, hung above the horizon.

The sea shocked her. It was so like the dream-sea and yet unlike. Its steely glare and the splayed sun above made it seem hostile and yet she had seen the dream-sea in moods of hostility that had made her cower. No, it was not that. This sea was not hostile, but neither was it benign. It was indifferent to her. It neither knew nor cared about her presence. It was an unimaginably huge mass of water, magnificent and mindless. It had no need of worship or admiration, or fear, or any other human reaction. It was there, and if she went away or had never been born, it would still be there.

She was wearing a padded jacket over a purple velvet dress, and it felt like she was being oven-cooked. She took off her stifling clothes and walked into the surf, instinctively bracing herself for the overwhelming thrill of the dream-sea. But instead, she got chills: The water was unexpectedly cold. She washed herself. Dark brown stains on her hands dissolved and were taken away by the waves.

She came out and stood in the sun until she was dry. Her reddening skin was sprinkled with the powdery residue of salt.

She put on her knickers, petticoat, and the jacket that was cut out in the front, so it barely covered her breasts. Mara decided that a heatstroke was too high a price for being decent. So, she left the dress on the beach. She did not like this dress ... besides being too heavy, it did not sit right, and there was something about it ... She tried to pinpoint the elusive memory, but it scampered away.

She studied the terrain. The beach rose gently and terminated in a sort of earthen wall dotted with thick-leaved, purple-flowered plants. To the left shimmered the headland. But to the right ...

She had never seen anything like that. Folded formations of yellow and pink stone shone in the liquid glare of the sun. Ridged and lined like stacks of paper, the eroded cliffs blocked the view of the land beyond. Birds wheeled and dipped above them. And there was something else that drew her like a magnet.

Mara trudged toward the cliffs, her feet raising little plumes of sand. She had to climb some rocks to gain access to the shelf of stone that sloped up to the cliffs. Yes, indeed, she had not been mistaken. There was a large black hole right in front of her.

She had never seen a real cave in her life, but she had read about them in the travelers' breathless depictions of the South Continent. She peered in; grayish twilight greeted her rather than the pitch blackness she'd expected. Something flapped past her; a fat bird like a dark-colored dove that landed and waddled on the beach. A random memory popped up: She had once known a girl named Lucy Dove.

Mara edged into the cave. It was cooler here but not cold. The reason for the light was several large openings in the cave's ceiling. There were more brown doves flapping in and out.

As she went deeper, she realized that the entire cliff must be honeycombed with caves. The floor was very slick, and she had to walk carefully. The walls were festooned with calcium deposits like petrified ballroom ornaments.

The passage narrowed to a bumpy tunnel, but Mara pressed on, toward the pinpoint of green light. The tunnel expanded once again, and she exited into an even bigger cave that was open to the sea. The emerald water splashed below, dappling the walls with dancing reflections. The setting sun shone straight into the cave, filling it with gentle glow, but the part where she stood was draped in shadows. It was almost as beautiful as the dream-sea.

She contemplated the scene, trying to lose herself in it and not succeeding. Something struggled to crawl out from under the security blanket of the present moment.

Where am I?

I cannot stay here. Night is coming. I'm hungry. I have to find a way back.

Back where?

Suddenly a new sound insinuated itself into the soothing monotony of the surf. Footsteps.

She ran back before she considered whether it was wise. It was not so much loneliness that drove her as the need for distraction. The more eventful the present, the easier it would be to erase the past.

She burst out of the tunnel and into the first cave, filled with the ruby light of the sunset. A man was down on his knees, slapping his hands on the stone, as if looking for something small. He leaped to his feet, a stubby shotgun smoothly pointing at her. His eyes widened when he saw her.

But if he was shocked by her appearance, Mara was equally shocked by his.

He was gaunt and tall, thin to the point of emaciation, his bald pate covered with a funny cap that slipped sideways and disclosed an angry red sore on his forehead. His skin was leathery and dark, even though his eyes were so pale they seemed transparent. He wore dirty but solid overalls with multiple pockets. Ordinarily, she could classify people by their social standing, but the man baffled her.

He cocked his head and regarded her with an unreadable expression.

"And what have we here?" he inquired, addressing the air above Mara's left ear. He had a lower-class accent that reminded her of Bunny and, for some reason, reassured her.

"Where are we?" Mara asked. "And who are you?"

"A remnant?" he murmured, talking to himself like a man used to solitude. "No! A worker? No, no, no! A whore?"

"Look," Mara said, "I've lost my memory. I don't know where I am or how far we are from the City. But I know *who* I am, and I'm definitely not a whore!"

"From the City?" he said. "You don't know how far we are from the City? Well, the width of the sea, I would say!"

She felt such a sudden onrush of weakness that she had to sit. Something hard and round like a pebble cut into her buttock and she reached down and clasped it in her hand. The man's shotgun followed her movement but he stayed put.

So, it was the South Continent, the fabulous land of deserts, mountains, and coffee! The land innocent of people, the putative cradle of humanity, where animals lived unmolested but still estranged from men by the curse of the Ancestors! She could not believe she was there and yet it seemed somehow inevitable. Was the dream-sea a gateway? Could it devour distance in the real world as it disdained measurements within itself? When she had entered ... And then her mind flinched away like a probing finger from an open wound.

"So, you're from the City?" continued the man with an undertone of either surprise or mockery, she could not decide which. "Well, well, well! Is this the latest City fashion?"

He was referring to her partial clothing. Mara got angry again.

"I told you," she snapped, "I don't remember anything! I must have been sick! I found myself on the beach. It was too hot, so I took off most of my clothes. I'm hungry and thirsty, and my head hurts. Couldn't you offer me some water at least?"

The man unclipped a canteen from his belt and threw it at her. Mara unscrewed the top and drank greedily, spilling water all over herself. The man watched her impassively.

"Look, City girl," he said. "You can't stay here. It'll be dark soon. Remnants are coming."

"Remnants?" she repeated. "What are they?"

"Never mind. Come with me."

He made her walk before him. She walked stiffly; the thing she had found hidden in her pocket where she had managed to slip it as the man fumbled with the canteen.

They came out onto the beach. The ruby sun was falling through the web of rosy clouds into the sea of molten bronze.

"You said you found yourself on the beach?" the man asked.

"Yes."

"Show me where."

She retraced her steps. Her discarded dress was lying close to the line of the surf. The man lifted it, examined it, and then looked around.

"There are no footprints leading here. Did you walk in the water?"

"I don't remember!" she screamed in frustration.

"There is blood on this dress," he said. "Are you wounded?"

"Wounded? No!"

He dropped the dress and strode away, Mara hurrying to keep up with him.

"What's your name, City girl?"

"Mara Raven."

He stumbled over a piece of driftwood.

"What's yours?" she asked.

The man smirked.

"Dog," he said.

"Dog? What kind of name is it? It's not a human name. It's not a totem."

"It's my name. Anyway, never seen a dog? You will."

When they surmounted the ridge that separated the beach from the scrubland above, only a red fingernail of the sun showed on the horizon. The twilight was intense, purple, and brief. Dog walked a narrow trail through the dense growth of bushes and dwarf trees, the balmy air filled with an array of tart, green, earthy smells. They came out into a clearing where a larger tree with leathery leaves and white cuplike flowers loomed above a cabin. Small and whitewashed, it was very plain, with a flat roof and two tiny unglazed windows. Dog pushed the unlocked door. Mara followed.

Inside was dark and cluttered. Dog lit a lamp that transported her back to her early impoverished childhood: a kerosene-filled container with a wick and a glass mantle. In the wavering light, she could make out the furnishings. There was a plank table loaded with crockery, some open shelves containing a quantity of boxes and jars, and a narrow pallet along one wall with a blanket thrown over it. And there were animal skins piled up along one wall.

She studied them. She could not tell what creatures these skins came from except that they must have been rather small, with orange, brown, and white fur. Though treated in some way, they still preserved the anatomical outlines of their former owners: small paws, pointed muzzles, bushy tails. Mara knew that animals were hunted on the Plains and, of course, cows and sheep were butchered in the countryside, but she had never seen such a blatant display of animal remains, screaming their affinity with humans.

"Sit down, City girl!" Dog commanded. Freeing space on the

cluttered table, he placed there a plate with flat bread and some smelly cheese. Mara was no longer hungry: The skins destroyed her appetite. But she ate to keep up her strength. Dog, who had removed his cap but made no further concessions to domesticity, noisily munched on a piece of cheese.

"So," he said, "what's new in the Big Whore?"

"What?"

"The City, girl. The City! What's new? Have the Ancestors come back?"

"Stop calling me 'girl,'" Mara said. "I have a name."

"And is it yours? Not stolen from the Ancestors?"

"I don't believe in the Ancestors!"

"A Humanist, huh? Not many of those here. Not much of anybody here, except the remnants and the coffee-slaves."

"And what are you?"

"Neither. A trader. A hunter."

"I can see," she said nodding at the skins in the corner. "What do you do with these?"

"Sell them, of course."

"I didn't know there was much demand for animal skins in the City today."

"Never heard of fur parties?"

Seeing incomprehension on Mara's face he laughed.

"You're an innocent! Anyway, there are ships that come every month or so to pick up coffee berries and deliver supplies. They buy my skins."

"Is there a port here?"

"Down the coast, where the trading station is. Closer to the plantations. Bear Haven, they call it."

Mara shuddered.

"Not much love lost between you and the Ancestors," said Dog. "Perhaps this is why they dumped you here."

"Nobody dumped me! I transported myself, I think. I have a Power ..."

Mara stopped, realizing that it was imprudent to reveal her link to the dream-sea, but in any case, Dog was not impressed.

"Don't know about Powers," he remarked. "Not much use for them here. This land sucks them from you along with everything else. Anyway, City girl, it's time to turn in. Tomorrow is a long day."

Mara wanted to ask for elucidation but suddenly realized how exhausted she was. It was as if her entire body emptied of energy in one rush. Dog threw a blanket in the opposite corner from the pallet, and she barely had the strength to totter over and lie down.

Before closing her eyes, she looked at the round thing she had found in the cave. It was a ring.

CHAPTER 2. OTHER DOGS

She woke with the sun on her face and dust in her nostrils. Her heart was pounding. Something terrible was dissolving in her brain, being washed away by the onrush of consciousness.

She sat up. She was alone in the cabin; the door was thrown open; a choir of perky chirping and musical thrilling was coming through. Birds here sounded different from the sulky pigeons and dispirited sparrows of the City.

The thought of the City brought back the same flinching from a memory wound as before. Mara quickly went outside.

Dog was pissing against a bush. Embarrassed, she ducked back in, but he was unfazed.

"Rise and shine, City girl!" he cried. "Do your business, get ready! We have to go soon!"

He shook himself off and went over to the water trough under the tree. He scooped water in the pitcher and poured it over his bare upper body. Mara stared, fascinated and appalled. His skeleton was so sharply outlined that it seemed to try to elbow its way out of the flesh. His stomach was a concave hollow below the aggressive ridges of the rib cage. But worst of all were the suppurating lesions and scabs that dotted his leathery skin.

There were enough of them to make her recoil in disgust, yet not so many as to create the impression that he was in the throes of a violent contagion. Whatever ailed him seemed more like a slow wasting.

"Go ahead!" he shouted at her.

Collecting her wits, Mara went into the shrub. While she looked for a secluded spot, she was absorbing the strange ambience of the South Continent, so different from the Plains: the sun, hot even though it was early morning; the leathery leaves of the thorny bushes; the spicy smells of invisible flowers; the small, aggressive butterflies that fluttered before her face.

She came back and following Dog's example washed herself with the cold water from the trough. He appeared, wearing—to her surprise—a clean shirt.

"Take off these rags, girl!" he commanded. "Here are some real clothes!"

They were a man's clothes and too big for her, but clean. Mara felt profound relief when she discarded the jacket and petticoat, polluted by the residue of unremembered horror. The pants were made of some rough fabric, the red flannel shirt had long sleeves that protected her sunburnt arms, and a floppy hat sat crookedly on her tangled hair.

She put the ring she had found in the caves on a thong and hid it under her shirt.

Dog came back down the track followed by two large beasts. Mara started to back off but then recognized the animals and chided herself for being a fool. They were horses.

"This one is yours!" declared Dog.

"What?"

"We have to go to Bear Haven. Do you want to walk? Or can your Powers move you there?"

Mara shook her head.

"So, you'll have to ride."

"But I've never ridden in my life!"

"There is a first time for everything."

True enough, she thought, approaching the beast, which he assured her was a tame and gentle mare. It looked anything but gentle and tame to Mara. She could see muscles rolling under its glossy dark coat, and the rock-heavy hooves stomping in the dust. The acrid smell of it made her gag.

Dog pitched her up into the hideously uncomfortable saddle. But after some minutes of helpless confusion, Mara realized that nothing was required of her. The horse started moving, and its rolling gait was not unpleasant. The animal seemed to know the way. Mara relaxed.

The dusty track led through the scrubland, flat at first but then beginning to rise in folds and gentle undulations. On her left Mara could see a deep ravine, choked with a fragrant tangle of greenery that looked as if it were trying to escape the dusty bareness of the slopes above.

"There is a creek down there," said Dog.

"Does it ever rain here?" she asked.

"Yes, in winter."

As they rounded the shoulder of the hill and another stretch of the scrubland shimmered in the sunlight, she considered whether the congestion of the City could be eased by emigration to the South Continent. The land did not appear to be inhospitable. Despite the relentless heat, she was beginning to like the cloudless azure sky, the yellow hills, and the nearness of the sea. If First City was indeed about to be destroyed by the Army of the Revealer, could not the sane part of the population simply relocate here, build another, human, City, untainted by memory and guilt?

"Can anything be grown in this land?" she asked Dog.

"Coffee."

Of course. Her favorite drink came from here. Then, surely, other crops could be grown, too.

Dog passed her a canteen.

"Drink!" he commanded. "You'll dry up if you don't. Drink even if you're not thirsty."

She obediently gulped the tepid water. Her thighs felt raw.

"I want to rest," she said.

"Later. No shade here."

Further on, as the land rose in yellow folds, she could see some scattered trees, dark green parasols in the field of stubble. They rode on.

How did I get here? The question caused her physical pain, like tearing the scab off a half-healed wound. She remembered her latest dream-sea visit but before that, there was a blank space, bordered by waking up in Julian Sparrow's house. She knew something had happened after that, but she could not—or would not—remember what.

"You ride well, City girl!" shouted Dog.

"What?"

She had forgotten where she was, forgotten about her mare; carried away by a stream of dark thoughts and inchoate images that seemed to be forcing their way into her like an infection. She came to with a start and realized that Dog had dismounted and was holding the reins of her horse. Nearby a parasol-shaped tree with a gnarled, thorny trunk threw a patchy shadow onto the dry grass.

As they ate and drank, she marveled at his resilience. She was wiped out, but he seemed unaffected. Was he as sick as he appeared?

"Do they still have the Guardians' procession every full moon?" asked Dog.

"Well—" stammered Mara, taken aback, "no, not for the last four years or so, they stopped it because of the disturbances."

"What disturbances?"

"I don't quite remember. I was at school. I think some devotees wanted to join the procession, the constabulary tried to keep them back, people were trampled ... That kind of thing."

"When I was a kid," said Dog, "Ma and Pa would take us to Victory Boulevard every full moon. It was our treat. Sometimes, when one of us misbehaved, they would leave us home alone. Mostly it was me, I have to say. Once they went—Ma and Pa, and my two sisters and my little brother—and I was so pissed I climbed out the window and ran there all on my own. It was a beautiful night, the moon so round and big. It's often this way here but not in the City. And then I saw the Fish, Fowl, and Fur Guardians at the head of that long winding line of creatures, all of them so grand and so big and strong ... I promised myself I would be a Guardian when I grew up. Pa gave me a good hiding when I returned, and I thought I would pay the old bastard back when I had fur on my back and claws on my fingers."

"You wanted to be a Guardian?" asked Mara. "Don't you know what they do to the children who are pledged to the Temple?"

"Cut off their balls and their titties," said Dog. "Most people would be better off without them anyway. And it's not like I have much use for my little friend here, in this place."

Mortified at the turn the conversation was taking, Mara tried to think of a clever way to deflect it from the topic of sex, but it was done for her by the circumstances. One of the horses neighed and then a strange yelping sound carried over the ridge of the nearest hill, an abrupt rise and fall of shrill inarticulate voices. Dog swore and jumped to his feet, bringing up his shotgun that had rested against the trunk of the tree.

"What's that?" asked Mara, unsure whether to be afraid. Dog listened with his head cocked and then relaxed and grinned at her, without relinquishing the shotgun.

"You wanted to know what my name means?" he asked. "Now you'll see."

A wave of small bodies the color of sand and mud tumbled over the crest of the hill and raced toward them. The tethered horses tossed their manes but did not panic.

At a distance of about fifteen meters from the tree, the creatures slowed down. The first wave of them hung back, the latecomers tumbled over the vanguard, snarling and snapping, but finally they all settled in the dust.

Mara had never seen anything like these creatures. They were no bigger than a raccoon but of amazingly varied body shapes. Some were compact and sleek, with short hair, long fox-like muzzles, and curving, muscular tails. Some resembled a walking bolster, with disproportionately short legs and long floppy ears. Some were covered in tangled wool like miniature sheep, full of burrs and thorns. And yet they were all mixed together with no apparent rhyme or reason, a beetle-like black creature resting its short muzzle on the broad back of one of the woolly ones, or a living sausage sniffing the back quarters of something that looked like a tiny coyote. But what they all had in common was the intense, purposeful gaze with which they regarded the humans.

This gaze gave Mara the shivers. There was dumb longing in this gaze but also a strange accusatory quality that was at the same time unconscious of itself. The creatures wanted something from her but neither she nor they knew what it was.

It seemed to go on forever. Finally, some animals at the outer edge got up and trotted away. The rest followed until they were all gone. And only then did Mara realize what their gaze reminded her of.

It was like the vast, wordless, unselfconscious presence of the dream-sea.

"Wow!" laughed Dog. "We were lucky! No black hounds, small fry, and they're harmless!"

"What are they?" whispered Mara, spellbound.

"Dogs."

"What kind of animals are they? What do they want?"

"Nothing, I guess. This is what they do, the small ones, at least. They stare. They live in these big bands but occasionally hunt alone. Sometimes a solitary one will follow you around a whole day. If you shoo it off, it'll go away and then come back. I tried to feed them, but they won't take any food. Foxes will if you leave it for them, and coyotes and others, but not these. And the big ones are dangerous. People hereabout call them the black hounds, and some are as big as a calf. They band together and attack the plantations. Tear your throat out, they will. But not the small ones."

"So how do you know that the black hounds and these small creatures are the same species?" asked Mara.

Dog shrugged.

"Because they are. Something in their eyes. The way they look at you. The Guardians may blab about the Ancestors, but really, animals don't give a snort for us. Or birds. Sure, they'll peck your eyes out if you're dead or steal your grain if they can get away with it. But they won't approach you. Animals run away from the stink of man. Not even big ones, like wolves or panthers, attack unless the body is wounded and bleeding. But dogs—they will. They have a score to settle with us."

"So why do you call yourself Dog?" asked Mara.

He started packing the food and water back into his saddlebag.

"Maybe I also have a score to settle," he said.

CHAPTER 3. FINDING MARA

Jeremy Seal stayed in the bathtub till the water got cold. He heaved his bulk out and grimaced when he saw the maroon stains left on the porcelain. The clothes he had worn in Louisa Ferret's house had already been discarded in the dumpster. Mr. Seal was not afraid of the constabulary looking for evidence, but he was fastidious.

He was not sorry about Louisa Ferret's death. This stupid bitch was unworthy of her daughter, and despite her devotion to Mr. Seal, she was no longer of any use in connecting the two. In fact, this accident of Mara's unwillingly causing her mother's death was the best thing that could have happened under the circumstances. It removed another unnecessary obstacle between Mara and himself. She would have nobody to turn to but her mentor.

Of course, there remained that annoying and inexplicable fact that she had shown up in the company of Julian Sparrow ...

Mr. Seal waddled into the living room—he would have to cut down on food—and poured a glass of brandy. He wanted to focus on the final proof of his rightness—Mara's ability to open up a gate between the City and the dream-sea and to step physically through it—but the thought of Julian Sparrow niggled him like an annoying insect. Against his will, his memories turned to Ronald Raven, his erstwhile friend and Mara's husband.

He had hated the man. That hate had grown to almost pathological proportions after his whirlwind of courting and marrying Mara. The fact that he had set up the marriage only inflamed the feeling. For Ronald, having everything that Jeremy lacked, was a shallow, boring, and one-dimensional human being, whose only distinguishing characteristic was greed. Jeremy had decided on him as a perfect husband for Mara: handsome enough to keep her out of mischief, empty-headed enough not to interfere with their work. He had been wrong on both counts.

He had not predicted Mara's passionate love for her husband that seemed to stir some corresponding feeling in Ronald's well-regulated heart. The fact that this feeling seemed to be compounded of desire and dread in equal measure only under-scored the strange transformation that Ronald underwent after their marriage. According to Mara, he never asked her directly about her experiences in the dream-sea. And yet he also pumped Jeremy Seal endlessly for information on the Ancestors and even requested to see some secret archival material; the request that to Jeremy's chagrin was granted by the Chief Guardians in view of the Raven family's substantial contributions to the Temple. He became moody and pensive; he hired some dubious people to do some dubious digging.

Mr. Seal remembered their last conversation well. Ronald had dropped in on him unexpectedly. It was late in the evening and Jeremy was astonished by how tense the man looked, his fingers twitching, as if he was trying to grab something invisible. He started with no preamble:

"I want to go to the South Continent."

Jeremy was flabbergasted. He knew that the Raven family had business interests in the coffee plantations there but could not imagine any emergency that required Ronald's presence. His next words confirmed that he was not planning a business trip.

"I believe that the key is there."

"What key?"

"To the gate."

Jeremy Seal could not believe his ears.

"Since when are you interested in the Abode of the Ancestors?" he exclaimed.

"Since you set me up with Mara," Ronald replied, forcing Mr. Seal to reevaluate his estimation of his friend's intelligence. "I know what she is."

Jeremy Seal paled. He had never told Ronald anything about his belief that Mara was the Revealer. The notion that this moneybag had somehow stumbled upon the truth that had taken Jeremy the best part of his life to uncover was intolerable.

"Why do you think it's in the South?" he asked.

"Because of what happens to my workers there."

Jeremy bit his lip. The fate of the indentured workers was an open secret in the City, but he did not expect Ronald Raven to make the connection.

"It also happens in the countryside," he said, stalling.

"Yes, but not to such an extent. I know the South is where the gate is."

It made Mr. Seal breathe easier. Clearly, Ronald was not as shrewd or well-informed as he had suspected. He did not realize that the gate was a condition, not a place. And while violated bodies could create cracks in the gate, there was only one key that could unlock it permanently, and the key was Mara. Still, there was something in Ronald's guesses and his determination that did not sit well with him.

"Are you taking Mara with you?" he asked, deciding to arrange an assassination on the next day if Ronald said yes.

"No." Ronald shook his head. "No way! In fact ..." He hesitated. Jeremy's heart skipped a beat. Was he going to say he was divorcing

Mara? This would be wonderful—until he realized that if Mara was free, she would probably start dating, and that was something he could not face again. But what Ronald said next was unexpected.

"I feel like I have known her for a long time. Too long. And I need to find out why."

Mr. Seal frowned. He had had the same sensation sometimes, but it was understandable in his case. He spent almost all of his waking hours thinking about her.

"What do you mean?"

"Look, you and I have known each other for ten years. But I sometimes have this weird sensation that it's been longer than that. The same with Mara. It's not that I know her well, you understand? I don't know what makes her tick. She spooks people. Sometimes, she spooks me."

"Don't you love her?"

Ronald grinned crookedly.

"Had I not known it was impossible, I would have said you're in love with her yourself," he said with an unerring, casual cruelty, causing an almost physical spike of hatred in Mr. Seal. "Yes, I do love her. And because of that, I want to understand what she is and what her Power is. I want to help her control it."

Mr. Seal was speechless. He understood only too well what the unspoken part of Ronald's statement was.

I want to help her control it.

I want to control it.

Ronald Raven was a rich businessman. But if he somehow got hold of Mara's Power, he would be the ruler of First City—and beyond. The role that Mr. Seal knew he was destined to play.

He could not kill Ronald there and then—the man was twenty years younger and in better shape. But Mr. Seal had agents who could do it for him, even though justifying it to the Guardians would take some finesse. But Ronald's next words threw his plans into disarray.

"I'm telling you, the South Continent is where the answers are. And I'm going there. Mara is not to know. I mean it. I'll fake my disappearance. Let her go to the constabulary if she wants to, but you're not to drop a hint of where I am, or something bad will happen. Really bad. Mara is never to set foot on the South Continent."

And that was that.

Ronald had been missing for thirteen months. Halfway through this period, Mr. Seal had become convinced that something bad had happened, but to Ronald himself. He felt relieved to be alone with Mara again. And yet ...

If Mara found out where her husband had gone and somehow followed him, it was imperative to bring her back as soon as possible. Before whatever had happened to him happened to her, too.

～

They reached Bear Haven in mid-afternoon.

The place hardly merited a name, Mara thought, let alone a name such as it had. It was a scatter of whitewashed one-story houses with flat roofs and shuttered windows. The only street roughly followed the contours of the crescent-shaped bay protected by a breakwater. Some fishing boats were moored at the jetty.

The place appeared deserted, placidly basking in the dazzling heat. Mara was drenched in sweat and sore from the riding. Nevertheless, her mood had improved. She was in a new place that seemed equally remote from the City and the dream-sea, the two destinations that were now tinged with different kinds of horror in her mind.

"Where is everybody?" she asked Dog.

"Resting." He spurred his horse on as they descended the

steep hillside toward the bay. "Everybody sleeps in the afternoon."

Mara thought that was a peculiar custom.

"How many people live here?" she asked.

"Depends on what you call living," answered Dog.

They were now on the rubble-strewn track that led to the backyards of the houses. Their horses' hooves produced an indecently loud clatter in the stillness.

Suddenly a door was flung open, and a man appeared, blinking in the light. He was wearing what Mara first thought was a dress—a long, bleached robe that reached to his ankles. But there was no mistaking his sex: The lower half of his face was masked by an unkempt beard that blended with the mussed-up long hair.

"Holy mouse!" he yelled, spotting Mara, and stared at her with his mouth hanging open. She could have counted all of his teeth on the fingers of one hand.

"Let me introduce Mara Raven," said Dog, "fresh from the Great Whore. Mara, this is my friend Dan Fox."

At least he has a human name, thought Mara.

"How d'you do, Mr. Fox," she said in her best dinner-party manner.

Fox blinked several times, closed his mouth, opened it again, and produced some inarticulate sounds. It would have been funny but for the fact that the man was as sick as Dog or rather, more so. She could see nothing of his body beneath the robe, but he appeared to be crooked in some way, standing with a kind of posture that she associated with hunchbacks. His plentiful facial hair, ginger red shot with gray, could not hide the fact that his skin was unnaturally dry and dotted with broken capillaries. His eyes were bleary, and not because of his interrupted afternoon doze.

"Haven't seen such a pretty face in some time, have you, Foxy?" Dog continued in the same bantering tone. "Well, stop gawking! Help the lady down. We both could use some food and drink."

Fox's house was unlike any Mara had ever been to. The whole space under the flat roof was a giant undivided room, with white-washed walls hung with a variety of strange objects: animal skins stretched on wooden frames, pictures (very amateurish, Mara thought), crudely painted decorative trays. There were a number of splotchy rag rugs scattered on the tiled floor, some cushions, and a couple of low tables. In one corner there was a pallet covered with a bright green blanket. Apart from a stove and some shelves stacked with crockery, this was the extent of the furnishing. The room was cool, shadowed, and unexpectedly clean, so that when Mara and Dog settled on the rugs, she could not find a speck of dust on them.

Fox bustled at the stove, casting curious glances at Mara. Eventually he served them with coffee in disappointingly tiny cups. Mara sipped the tar-like liquid and choked. Dog burst out laughing.

"That's not the muck they serve in the City!" he said. "This is the real thing!"

Indeed, it was, and Mara felt the jolt of caffeine travel straight to her brain and sweep away the cobwebs of fatigue.

"Do you live here alone, Mr. Fox?" she asked.

"Who else?"

"Your wife if you were married."

Fox stared at her as if she suggested some obscene arrangement.

"Not many women here," chimed in Dog, "and you wouldn't want to meet those who are."

"Well, what do people do here? Work in the coffee plantations?"

"No, no workers here. They live by the plantations. The supervisors also, but they rotate. A couple of them are here now, waiting for the ship from the City."

"The ship?" asked Mara. "When is it due?"

Dog shrugged.

"A couple of weeks from now, I think. Right, Foxy?"

Fox nodded. He kept stealing furtive glances at Mara.

"How did she come here?" he asked, addressing Dog. Mara flushed.

"I'm capable of speaking for myself, Mr. Fox," she said.

"I'm sorry," muttered Fox. "I'm not used to outside company. Especially ladies. Sorry."

"It's all right," Mara said, mollified.

Fox rubbed his hands together.

"Mara Raven," he said. "Are you here to inspect the plantations?"

Mara stared at him speechless and then something clicked. Of course! She never thought about it because she never thought about Ronald's business. It was part of the pretense that he was still alive, still taking care of things as he used to, keeping his child bride away from the dirty world of moneymaking. But in fact, she had known it all along.

Raven and Co owned extensive coffee plantations on the South Continent.

"No," she said trying to keep her excitement down. "I'm here accidentally. It's difficult to explain. But I would like to meet the person who is currently supervising the Raven plantations."

Dog and Fox exchanged glances.

"This can be arranged," said Dog casually. "Can't it, Foxy?"

"I suppose," Fox muttered, still sounding uncomfortable.

"Where is he?" asked Mara.

"Wolf? Where he always is. Up at the mansion. Having fun."

As opposed to Fox, Wolf was not a common name.

"When can we go there?" asked Mara.

Again, the dumb pantomime of exchanging glances. Mara was getting tired of it.

"We need to let the horses rest," replied Dog. "Tomorrow morning."

Mara reluctantly agreed.

The rest of the day dragged on in a half-hearted fashion. After declaring he had "some business" to attend to, Dog disappeared, leaving Mara alone with Dan Fox who crouched in the corner, eyeing her. Mara tried to engage him in a conversation but gave up, since he replied only in monosyllables. Eventually she declared she wanted to go out and take a look at the settlement.

Outside the air was as balmy and as relaxing as a hot bath. The chilly, drizzly, drenched days in the First City seemed remote and unreal. She probed the blankness in her memory gingerly, like a freshly missing tooth, and flinched away with a stab of pain and a taste of fresh blood on her tongue.

She walked toward the quay. The golden ball of the sun hung above the dazzling expanse of the sea.

The quay was deserted but Mara heard steps behind her back. She turned around to see a woman approaching. *So, there are women here*, she thought.

In the honey light of the late afternoon her blunt features had a kind of strong earthy presence, but she was by no means beautiful: a stocky middle-aged woman wearing sensible clothes, her thick graying hair braided and wound around her head.

She paused in surprise and then approached quickly, scanning Mara's face.

"What are you doing here?" the woman asked. "Why are you standing in broad daylight?"

"Why not?" responded Mara.

The woman frowned.

"They'll be after you soon enough," she said. "What are you, dumb?"

"Who are 'they'?" asked Mara.

For the first time, the woman's stolid face showed surprise.

"You are not from the plantations," she said slowly, as if digesting an astounding revelation. "You are ... Who are you?"

Mara was getting tired of introducing herself.

"Who are 'they'?" she repeated.

"Wolf's boys," said the woman. "Hunting remnants. They'll hunt you down too, no matter who you are. Come with me."

She walked back into the settlement and Mara followed, glad to be distracted from the dark thoughts that were beginning to gather on her mental horizon like storm clouds.

The woman stopped before one of the larger houses adorned with a striped blue-and-white awning, and her identity became clear. The house bore a sign: *Alice D. Bobcat. Grocery and Dry Goods.* The single shop window displayed a jar of dusty sweets and a large wooden mallet.

The woman—Mara presumed it was Alice D. Bobcat herself —opened the padlock and pushed Mara into the murky heat of the shop. It smelled of coffee and spices.

Her hands on her hips, Mrs. Bobcat (Mara noticed a gold band on her finger) surveyed Mara from head to toe and slowly shook her head.

"When did you get here?" she demanded. "How come I haven't seen you until now?"

She made it sound like an accusation. Mara sighed and repeated the gist of her story. She did not identify herself by her family name.

"A Power?" said Mrs. Bobcat. "The Ancestors must indeed be returning if a chit of a girl like you has this kind of Power. You are not a Temple get, are you? You look normal enough to me."

Mara winced.

"I'm not a Guardian, no," she said. "And I have had this Power since childhood. Only now it's getting stronger. And yes, most people in the City believe the Ancestors are returning, and a lot of them are only too eager to help."

"Help? How?"

"By killing other people," said Mara.

An ambiguous expression crossed Mrs. Bobcat's face. She sat down in the single chair behind the counter, still staring hard at Mara.

"So, it has come to this," she said. "Does it mean there will be nowhere for me to go back to?"

"How long have you been here?"

"Long enough. Five years. I have to go back soon."

"Are you sick?" asked Mara.

"Not yet. Women hold out better than men. But ten years is the limit for everybody."

"Aren't workers indentured for longer?"

"For life. As long as life lasts, which is not very long."

"What happens to them? They die?"

"No, they become remnants ... You really have no idea, do you?"

"No. And not many people in the City do either. But you are not indentured, are you?"

"Nobody who lives in the settlement is. We're here of our own free will. If a poor man has will."

Mara winced under the force of the implicit accusation in Mrs. Bobcat's words.

"People have a rather romantic idea of the South Continent," she said. "Intrepid explorers, this sort of thing."

Alice Bobcat gave a short, explosive laugh.

"Explorers? I've never been beyond the plantations, and I never wanted to. I grew up in Lonelyhearts, you know? When I go back, with the money I've saved I'll buy a cottage in the suburbs. Not too far from the heart of the City, of course, but not too close either. I'll take my niece to live with me."

"Lonelyhearts ..." began Mara.

"What?"

Mara shook her head. How could she tell this woman that Lonelyhearts was destroyed, and her niece was likely dead?

"What are you doing here, then?" she asked instead.

"The shop. The workers don't need it, at least not those who are too far gone, but there are supervisors, hunters, hermits, plain nuts. That's enough customers, especially since there is no competition."

"Are there other women here?" asked Mara.

"In the settlement? No." And noting Mara's gaze, Mrs. Bobcat gave another of her explosive braying laughs. "You think I could get more money by selling myself? I wouldn't have any customers, lady. And not because of my age. You don't know what this place does to a body."

Mara frowned, remembering Fox's obvious malaise.

"But you thought I'd escaped from the plantations. So are there women there?"

Alice's face closed like a trap.

"There are rumors," she said. "I don't go there myself. Wolf does as Wolf pleases, and the owners let him."

"The owners?" asked Mara. "Do you ever see any of them?"

Mrs. Bobcat's eyes shifted.

"They are not for the likes of me," she said. "One of them came here a year ago but he went up to the plantations."

Mara's heart leaped.

The dry staccato of the horses' hooves outside startled both of them. Alice ran to the window, peered out.

"Wolf and his boys!" she whispered. "Get behind the counter and get down, quick!"

Mara did as she was told but she managed to sneak a peek through the dusty pane. In the gathering twilight all she could see was a group of mounted men passing by. They did not pause and gradually the sound died down.

"Are they immune to whatever ails you here?" she whispered to Alice.

"Who said that?"

CHAPTER 4. REMNANTS

"He's in here," a low-level Guardian told Mr. Seal. He was covered with grayish down, and his hands were fleshless and crooked like a chicken's legs.

Mr. Seal nodded and looked through a spy hole into the interrogation cell where a man dressed in a decadent black satin shirt was pacing back and forth.

He had gotten only a brief glimpse of him in Louisa Ferret's house before Mara's shot went so disastrously awry. He had to run away because he realized she would shoot him if he stayed. But he had noticed a fancy private car outside, and it took little time to find out the name of the owner.

Julian Sparrow.

What had Mara been doing in his company? Were he and Mara ...?

Mr. Seal forbade himself from thinking in that direction. Ronald had been enough. Nobody else should come between him and Mara again. In any case, Julian could not be Mara's choice. He was older than Mr. Seal had expected and had little in common with handsome Ronald Raven. Mr. Seal studied the man's face, his crow's feet accentuated by the harsh light of a bare bulb. Somehow, he looked more familiar than that single glimpse could account for, even though Mr. Seal knew he had never seen him before Louisa's death.

His lips pursed, he gestured at the Guardian to unlock the door.

Julian whirled around, and again Mr. Seal felt a brush of some bad association, like the faint whiff of a familiar stench.

"I demand my attorney," Julian said. "Now!"

Mr. Seal motioned at him to sit on the chair across the desk from his own and stared him down until Julian obeyed. This was a good beginning.

"No attorneys, Mr. Sparrow," he said. "In the light of the situation in the City, President Otter signed the Emergency Order allowing us to hold people without charges for up to two weeks. In your case, though, charges will be forthcoming. And they are serious."

He expected Julian to ask what charges, but the man remained silent, and Mr. Seal clarified.

"Double murder and terrorism."

"You are not from the constabulary," Julian said. "Who are you?"

"Aren't you interested in hearing the details of your indictment?"

"I am not interested in hearing the details of a patently false accusation. Not until I know who I am talking to."

In his undercover work, Mr. Seal almost never had the opportunity to use his full title, which he was proud of. Surely, it would do no harm to cut Julian Sparrow down to size by telling him exactly who he was dealing with.

"I'm deputy chief of the Temple Security Bureau, Jeremy Seal," he said. And realized his mistake when he saw the slight widening of Julian's eyes.

Had Mara told him about their relationship?

"I thought the Temple Security Bureau only dealt with matters related to religious observance."

"According to the Emergency Order, the Temple has been given extraordinary powers to deal with the current outbreak of religious extremism and terrorist activities."

"Oh yes, the Army of the Revealer! What does it have to do with me? My wife was one of their victims."

"You are accused of her murder. And of the murder of Louisa Ferret. Both done to use their bodies for terrorist acts."

Julian laughed.

That was unexpected, and Mr. Seal bristled.

"You know what happened in Louisa Ferret's house," Julian said. "You were there. You were holding a knife to the woman's throat. As for my wife, I know who killed her, and so do you. You have to come up with something better."

"I don't think you understand your situation, Mr. Sparrow," Mr. Seal retorted. "First City is on edge. Do you know how many people died in recent attacks? Courts would be less interested in legal wranglings than in giving the people someone to hate. The fact that you are rich helps. In the Dark Years, the rich were hanged."

"In other words, due process is out the window, mob justice is in. But you forget that the Temple is not as popular as it used to be. That wimp Otter may have caved in to political pressure, but he has no love for the Guardians. He will be less than enthusiastic about putting a Lion on trial on trumped-up charges."

Mr. Seal bit his lip. He knew Julian was a member of the powerful Lion family. He also knew there was more truth to his statement about the tensions between the Temple and the secular bureaucracy of the Animal House than he may have been aware of.

"You are not a Lion, Mr. Sparrow," he said. "You gave up your totem."

"You know that this is not how it works. Totem lines have

been twisted and tangled throughout the City's history. But each of us has a special connection to one of the Ancestors, whether it is reflected in our name or not."

"I thought you did not believe in the Ancestors," Mr. Seal retorted.

"It's not a question of belief but of knowledge. I know more than you think, Mr. Seal. And so do you. So, let's cut the crap, shall we? Tell me what you want from me."

"I want Mara," Mr. Seal said.

~

Mara and Dog rode up, into the hills that rose over Bear Haven.

Mara had wanted Mrs. Bobcat to come with them, but the latter flatly refused, adding an enigmatic warning: "Don't let Wolf stare at you with those big ugly shiners of his. He'll eat you alive!"

The weather today was indistinguishable from yesterday: dry heat, the cloudless turquoise sky, and the glittering sea below. Dog was silent and moody.

"Who is this Wolf?" Mara asked to break the silence that was getting oppressive. "Alice Bobcat told me he's dangerous."

"Alice Bobcat is a gossip and a fool," Dog retorted.

"So, he's not dangerous?"

"I did not say that."

Mara gave up.

The dusty track wound about the flank of the hill covered with desiccated scrub. But as they rode into the uplands, the scenery changed. Green patches appeared in the scrub and on the plateau above Mara could see a thicket of low trees with large, floppy leaves.

"The plantations," said Dog.

"There?"

"Yes. Coffee bushes have to be protected by shade, so they plant banana trees."

Mara was not sure what a banana tree was but forgot to ask because her attention was drawn to something that heaved and thrashed in the thorny shrubs by the side of the track. For a moment, she thought it was a large bird with broken wings. Then that it was an animal unknown to her, perhaps one of those bigger dogs Dog had talked about. Then that it was a wounded man.

Dog reined in his horse. The creature in the bushes gave a particularly violent spasm and rolled clear onto the track. Mara gasped.

It did indeed look like a large bird, the size of a man. But its thin, grubby body was human-shaped, though terribly emaciated. It was barely more than an articulated skeleton covered with thick, lifeless pinkish skin and clumps of feathers, black and dusty like the feathers of a crow. Its bald head, which it wrenched at an impossible angle toward Mara, had no face. It was only a giant beak of the same color as the rest of its body, snapping open and shut. She could see no eyes.

"What is this?" she whispered in horror, and then cried, "What is this?"

Dog dismounted and, lifting the creature as easily as if it were a handful of twigs, threw it back into the scrub where it flailed one last time and lay still.

"It's a remnant," he said. "I don't know what it's doing here. Another of Wolf's follies, I bet."

"But *what* is this?" Mara insisted.

Dog shrugged.

"This is what's left of a worker after seven or eight years of indenture. Well, some last longer."

"This?" whispered Mara. "Why?"

"Ask the Temple. They should know."

Mara's head was spinning as they rode toward the plantation, and there was a sour taste in her mouth. Another enigma was added to her list but this one came with a particularly horrendous question mark attached.

Did Ronald know what happened to the workers in the coffee plantations of Raven and Co?

And the pitiless answer: How could he not know?

When they crested the hill, a different panorama opened before them. The upland valley was divided into plots; each plot planted with straight rows of dark green bushes with oval leaves and shallow spreading roots. Clusters of red berries adorned the bushes. Around each plot and between the rows grew the floppy-leaved trees Mara had seen from below. It all looked orderly and innocent. And deserted.

"Where is the coffee?" she asked, trying to keep her mind off the horror she had just witnessed.

"This is. These are coffee plants."

"Those berries?"

"There are beans inside them. These are called cherries. See, that's where they dry them."

He gestured toward long rows of matting raised on trestles. They were covered by thick layers of straw-colored pebbles.

"They dry them and then they hull them in the mill. The beans are removed, cleaned, and sorted. And then ground. This is what coffee is made of."

Mara nodded, scanning the deserted plantation in search of workers. Remnants.

The Book of the Remnant.

Something moved. A man emerged from the trees and walked along the matting, raking the spread berries with his hands, turning them over in the sun. He was indeed a man, Mara was relieved to see, scraggly and stooped, dressed in nondescript overalls but undoubtedly human.

"What is he doing?" she whispered.

"Turning them over so they dry evenly."

Dog was speaking in a loud voice, but the man gave no sign

of hearing him, shambling along the matting and mechanically raking the coffee cherries.

"Is he deaf?" Mara asked.

"Probably. Deaf and maybe blind. He's one of the old ones; he's been here a while. That's how they start changing."

"This is horrible! How does the government allow this?"

Dog smirked.

"Coffee makers pay high taxes."

The worker came to the end of the row, turned around, and shambled back. Mara glimpsed his face, pale and puffy, the eyes almost lost in folds of swollen tissue.

CHAPTER 5. WOLF

Their horses cantered on along the edge of the plantation until they came to a well-beaten track leading up into the hills again. Eventually the track ended at a whitewashed wall pierced by a solid-looking but open gate. Through the gate they could see the lush emerald lawn dotted with puffy thorny balls like vegetable hedgehogs. There was another white wall inside.

"Leaving the gate open?" muttered Dog. "He's getting careless. And where is Weasel?"

As in response, a man ran across the lawn to the gate. Mara braced for the sight of another monstrosity, but the man was quite unremarkable, young and freckled. Like Dog the first time she had seen him, the man was holding a shotgun.

"Hello, Franz!" cried Dog. "Alone holding the fort? Where is Lark and his fellows? Larking about?"

"You!" exclaimed the man. "What are you doing here? And who ..."

He did not finish the sentence and gaped at Mara.

"I have a guest and I want to introduce her to the boss," replied Dog. "And put this peashooter down, will you? You'll shoot off your little friend before it's time for the both of you to part."

Weasel flushed an angry red but lowered the weapon.

"I have to tell the master," he said. "Wait here!"

He glared at Mara.

"What shall I say her name is?" he asked, addressing Dog.

"You'd better ask me what my name is!" Mara cut in.

"Wolf's boys are rather deficient in social graces, ma'am," said Dog, grinning. "You'll have to forgive them." And to Weasel, "Her name is Mrs. Raven. Make sure you don't shake it out of your head as you run back to the boss. Mrs. Raven."

A strange expression—half incredulity, half consternation—crossed Weasel's face. He jerked his head, as if wanting to offer homage but then thought better of it, turned around, and loped toward the house within the compound. As Dog and Mara slowly rode past the gate and up the graveled drive, the house came into full view. It was similar to the ones in Bear Haven but more elaborate, with an open veranda and ironwork grills on the windows. The front lawn ended rather abruptly as if whoever had laid it lost interest and the rest of the compound was dusty, beaten earth with some bedraggled fowls of an unknown variety lethargically pecking at it. There were sheds and huts clustering behind the house.

Weasel reappeared, told them to dismount, and led their horses away. Dog had wanted to keep his shotgun, but Weasel had objected in the most unambiguous manner with his own weapon aimed at them. However, he also added a sort of explanation.

"The master is in a good mood," he said. "He wants to speak to the lady. If you know what's good for you, Dog, you'll wait outside."

"And have you for company? No, thankee. I'll take my chances with his good mood."

"Suit yourself," said Weasel, shrugging.

"Hey, Franz," shouted Dog at his retreating back, "who's making his coffee nowadays?"

This innocuous query made the young man's shoulder twitch like a sting but he neither replied nor looked back.

It was cool and shadowy inside. There was no anteroom or hall; the front door opened into a large, irregularly shaped living room with several low sofas, rugs, and coffee tables scattered on the tiled floor. It was like Fox's house but grander. However, while Fox had some primitive daubs of pictures for decoration, the master of this house possessed a more eccentric, if not more refined, taste. At first, Mara thought that the heads mounted on the walls were plaster casts, though she was not sure of what. But as her eyes adjusted to the soothing dusk created by the lowered blinds, she realized that those were stuffed and mounted heads of game.

While totem animals were routinely stuffed and displayed in local temples and in the Temple itself, taxidermy as a frivolous hobby was frowned upon. In the past, before the Dark Years, it had been a crime. Mara knew that nowadays some rich folk in the City had private collections of animal heads. However, she was sure nobody had a collection like this.

Each of the creatures had a shadow of humanity remaining in its features. There was something that looked like a goat, with fluted horns, but its mouth was small, pursed, and soft-lipped like the mouth of a pouting teenage girl. Another head belonged to a large bald bird with long lashes flirtatiously lowered over blue eyes. Yet another was of a raccoon with human teeth.

"What is this?"

"Wolf's collection," Dog replied. "He goes to hunt remnants with his boys and then brings them to an old man down in the settlement who is taxo ... whatever you call them who stuff corpses ..."

"A taxidermist."

"Right. So, the old man stuffs them for Wolf who boasts he'll publish a study that will shake the City worse than Charles Finch's kooky theory. Only his heart hasn't been in his study recently."

They were interrupted by a strange noise, like something heavy being dragged on the floor.

The huge room was linked to the rest of the house by several curtained archways. It was from behind one of them that the strange sound emanated. The curtain stirred.

A large four-legged body pushed itself into the room, lifting the curtain and pulling it behind like a billowing cloak. Mara's mind went into overdrive trying to make sense of the creature. A crippled cow? A giant snake? An overgrown rat?

It was a man.

He entered by crawling on all fours, a big, skeletally thin man; his bald head gleaming as if oiled. He was clad in a white linen suit.

"Hello, Wolf," Dog said. "Let me introduce Mrs. Mara Raven."

"How do you do," Mara said.

The man got up slowly, unwinding himself like a rusty spring. His face was gaunt, sharp as a hatchet, with restless, roving eyes surrounded by the skin worn and wrinkled like old crepe paper. He reminded Mara of somebody, but she was not sure who.

"Pleased to meet you," he said in a deep, beautifully modulated voice, and gallantly kissed Mara's hand. She noticed the dusty stains on his sleeves and trousers left by crawling.

"Are you the manager of this plantation?" she asked.

"Yes. Theobald Wolf at your service. And I am pleased to meet finally the charming owner of Raven Fine Coffee Company. You will see, dear madam, how faithfully we have been guarding your interests."

"My interests," said Mara. "Oh yes, of course."

She felt punch-drunk. But she should have known. She had

only herself to blame. She let Ronald's lawyers and his snotty family appropriate the reins of power because she wanted it this way, because it was comfortable for her to mope and sulk and bask in romantic grief and go for a dip in the dream-sea from time to time. Far more comfortable than to face the reality that she was now the legal owner of Ronald's company and thus responsible for everything that was done under its auspices. Responsible for the aromatic drink that sharpened the senses of the City's inhabitants and kept their minds off the growing chaos. Responsible for Bear Haven, which prospered on the crumbs dropped from the company's table. Responsible for the crawling Mr. Wolf and his collection. Responsible for the remnants.

"Is everybody here sick?" she asked.

Mr. Wolf winced as if she had committed a faux pas.

"No, no," he said. "In fact, the rate of those affected by what I call the Southern Malady, colloquially known as changeover, has been dropping steadily due to the progressive hygienic measures we have been promulgating. But must we start with those regrettable incidents that no matter how sensational are still only a footnote to the giant work we are undertaking here? The work of civilization, of expansion, of freeing Man from the constraints of his own superstition! And of course, we must not forget the commercial aspect of our enterprise, which, as I have said, looks bright indeed. Perhaps you'll do me the honor of joining me for a cup of coffee and letting me present our latest yield figures?"

"Yes," Mara said, dazed. "Yes, let's have coffee."

Wolf gestured at a low coffee table made of beaten bronze and surrounded by cushions for seating. Mara remembered having seen such tables in some avant-garde coffee shops in the City.

"Are those tables made here?" she asked.

Wolf beamed.

"Yes!" he replied. "There are some fine craftsmen down in the settlement. Mr. Fox for example. They are developing a new style that can conquer the City. The economic possibilities here are unlimited, Mrs. Raven, practically unlimited."

Throughout this exchange Dog remained leaning against the wall, his arms crossed. Wolf never even glanced at him and addressed only Mara.

"You don't mind my companion joining us, Mr. Wolf, do you?" asked Mara. "Mr. ... Dog is acting as my guide."

"No," said Wolf, "of course all your companions are welcome. Please join us."

Still, he did not look at Dog and the latter flopping onto a cushion opposite to Mara showed no appreciation of his hospitality. Wolf clapped twice.

The curtain at another archway was drawn aside and a uniformed maid emerged bearing a large tray with a cone-shaped bronze vessel, spreading the intoxicating aroma of freshly brewed coffee. She put tiny cups in front of each of the guests and deftly poured foaming coffee into each. Next, she placed on the table a sugar pot, a plate of sliced cake, and distributed spoons and napkins.

Mara strove to keep her expression blank. Nevertheless, she could not stop staring at the maid.

She was indubitably female, as indicated by her small, perky breasts (four of them) that lifted the front of her black dress. She walked upright. But there was a sinuosity to her body that was of a small, slinky mammal rather than of a human. Her face was a shallow muzzle with tiny needle-sharp teeth, the nose and mouth fused together. There was a dark patch between her eyes and two bands of the same color curved on the sides of her head, framing small, incongruously human, pink ears. Her forearms revealed by the three-quarters sleeves of her dress were dusted here and there with sparse orange fur.

A Guardian? No.

The Guardians Mara had seen in the City, including the Fur Guardian, had been the results of surgery. Even those whose scars were barely visible had something awkward and artificial about them. This woman had none. As horrifying as she looked, all her parts fit together with the naturalness of an organic body.

"Isn't it wonderful?" enthused Wolf. "The coffee is a new blend, which I have developed recently. If it meets with your approval, we can start producing it locally, which will cut the manufacturing costs. Of course, we will need to import more workers."

"Just grab them off the streets," Dog butted in. "The City's too small for all the people anyway. Ain't it so, ma'am?"

Wolf shot him a venomous look.

"We can offer better conditions here than in the City's factories," he said. "A slum inhabitant can be restored in body and spirit by engaging in healthy agricultural labor here. A new man on a new land."

Dog broke into raucous laughter.

"If you were not under the protection of our gracious owner ..." Wolf began with a growl in his throat. Mara decided it was time to assert some authority.

"I'm interested in your projects, Mr. Wolf," she said. "Please tell me more about them. You're right that the economic and social situation in the City is regrettable and anything that can ameliorate it should be considered. But are you indeed suggesting moving part of the City's population to the South Continent?"

"Yes, I am," said Wolf. "I am speaking of colonization."

"The Temple would call it blasphemy."

"The Temple's power is based on empty superstition!"

"Indeed? I have to confess that I'm in agreement with you on this issue, Mr. Wolf. But Humanist views are increasingly in the minority in the City nowadays."

"This is why it is imperative that the South Continent, humanity's new home, be developed as soon as possible. This will break the religious authorities' chokehold."

Mara swirled the coffee in her cup and finished it in one swallow. The bitter grounds settled on her palate.

"Help yourself to some cake," Wolf suggested. Mara took a bite out of politeness. The cake was dry and almost inedible.

"Matilda's bake?" asked Dog, crumbling his portion between his calloused fingers. "She used to do better, didn't she?"

Wolf disregarded the remark and went on talking about the increased harvest of coffee berries in the last year. He had a beautiful voice, smooth like egg cream, and an exaggeratedly refined accent that sounded to Mara like a caricature of those of Ronald's friends who boasted of having been born within walking distance from the Animal House. But he had a natural eloquence that tugged her along, making even the meaningless statistics he was quoting seem important and fascinating. And yet sometimes there was a slight hitch, a sudden pause, an intonation shift that seemed like the vocal equivalent of the dusty stains on his clothes left by crawling.

"The land is fertile!" he was saying. "Coffee is only one of the crops that can be grown here. Wheat and rye are also a possibility, and especially corn. And there are native fruits and vegetables here, quite delicious. We're only beginning to develop a market for those. Think how many people we can deliver from the misery and congestion of urban life! Eventually we can sustain a population twice or three times the population of the City!"

Was he insane to deny the evidence before his eyes? Chills traveled up and down Mara's back as she contemplated the madness so sublime, and yet so obviously dangerous.

"Did you talk to my husband about your plans?" she asked.

It was a gamble, but it paid off.

"Mrs. Raven," said Wolf, fixing her with his glassy stare, "when your husband visited a year ago, we talked about you, about your visionary capacity that, as he was eventually obligated to recognize, transcends his own. My arguments in favor of colonization made little headway with him, but I'm convinced that you and I can find a common language that will enable us to deliver the people of the City from their captivity and open a new age of prosperity and enlightenment. He saw the enormous potential of my colonization program. But I'm sorry to say, he was too preoccupied with his own fantastic suspicions and illogical investigations to pay proper attention to reality. Didn't he talk to you about his visit?" continued Wolf.

It either meant that he did not know Ronald had not come back from the South Continent or that he wanted her to believe he did not know.

"My husband and I have not spoken for a long time," she said.

Wolf's smile was meant to be sympathetic and understanding.

"It does not surprise me, Mrs. Raven," he said. "Forgive my saying so, but he seemed hardly worthy of you. You are obviously a woman of great vision ... and astounding beauty."

Mara felt like laughing. Wolf was unquestionably dangerous, but he was too consumed by his visions to be interested in her in a creepy way. He was seeing somebody who could help him further his mad plan.

"Thank you," she said.

But now she had to consider how to extricate herself from this situation. She could not rely on Dog. He seemed to have his own agenda, and Mara did not know what it might be. Was he trying to show her that a madman was running the Raven plantations? Or was there something even more sinister at play? The ring she had picked up in the cave lay against her chest.

She had nobody to rely on but herself.

Has it ever been different?

Hoping to gain time, she lifted the coffee cup to her lips and realized it was empty. Wolf noticed it.

"Matilda!" He clapped. "More coffee for our guest!"

The maid reappeared with another tray. Mara could not keep

her eyes off her. Her every movement was natural and even graceful but grotesquely inhuman. Her small, glittering eyes were positioned to the sides of her muzzled head and had no whites.

Mara could not help herself.

"What is she?" she asked Wolf.

"She is a sorely afflicted creature whom I keep and support in exchange for the services rendered in the past," Wolf said. "I do it out of kindness."

"So you don't screw her anymore?" Dog inquired.

Wolf lunged at him, upsetting the table.

CHAPTER 6. MEETING IN THE DARK

Julian Sparrow nudged the door and to his surprise, it swung open. He expected the constabulary to lock up the scene of a violent crime. But they had their hands full with other things.

He stepped into the dark hallway, letting his eyes adjust. There was an acrid stench of stale violence in the air. He imagined the splashes of blood drying on the walls and the floor, adhering to the picture frames, splattered on the coats hanging from the coat-tree. Would these specks grow in the darkness with the blind persistence of moss and lichen, spreading over the flowery wallpaper, blending with the design, evolving into a lush tapestry of death?

If they did, it would be in tune with everything else happening in the City.

He had not been afraid in the interrogation room of the Temple Security Service. The arrogance of old money and old connections was an emotional cushion that protected him from panic, even though he realized that with the City in turmoil, it may no longer shield him as it once had. Even the shock of seeing that his interrogator was the man who had held Louisa Ferret hostage did not bring his defenses down. And he was proven right. One call from Laura Lion, his distant cousin, an occasional lover, and the owner of a majority stock in the family's shipping firm, had set him free. He had not been afraid in the Temple Security wing. But he became afraid when the gates of the Temple compound locked behind him and he was told to walk several miles to the City center—the last petty spasm of Seal's malice.

What he had seen on his walk haunted him still. But here, in this dark and empty house smelling of blood and defiled family life, his fear was magnified to the point that he had to take several deep breaths to calm down. Was Louisa Ferret's body and face still obliterated, still slumped on the rug in the living room? No, it could not be. The constabulary would have taken it to the morgue. At least, Julian hoped so.

Taking another deep breath, he reached for the light switch on the wall and clicked it. Nothing happened.

This was not too surprising: First City had been experiencing rolling blackouts for the last couple of days. Old-timers who still had candles and kerosene lamps at home looked in smug superiority at their electricity-addicted offspring. He had come prepared for this eventuality. His chrome-plated flashlight was big and hefty enough to provide not only illumination but also protection in case he was attacked. Remembering what had happened here, he could not bring himself to acquire a gun.

Details of the house emerged in the moving light like pieces of a jigsaw: a patch of fussy wallpaper here, a picture made of dry flowers there. Julian tried to imagine Mara's life as a child in this home that seemed to him suffering from split personality: a rather large and expensive standalone house furnished with the frugality of genteel poverty. Then he realized that Mara could not have grown up here. The house was undoubtedly bought for her mother by her husband, Ronald Raven.

Julian had met Raven a couple of times at some social event

or another where previously the secular elite of First City used to mingle and congratulate themselves on their successful emergence from the Dark Years of superstition and strife into the light of reason and progress. He remembered little of Mara's husband except that everybody considered him an empty-headed bully who owed his money to his mother's Tiger connection. Why did she marry him?

Julian reminded himself that he was the last person to judge other people's marriages. But he *had* loved Elvira in his own fashion and missed her laughter and easy chatter. Had Mara loved her husband? And where was he now?

More importantly, where was Mara?

He steeled himself as he entered the living room. To his relief, it was empty. Louisa's corpse had been removed, though large dark stains on the floor and the sofa indicated that not much cleaning had been done.

He shone his flashlight onto the floor. It was here that Mara had picked up that horrifying black flower that grew out of her mother's death and used it to ...

To open the gate.

There was no sign of it now, but the floorboards were warped as if this portion of the room had been flooded. The water was gone. But blood and pieces of brain stuck to the parquet, deposited here by the splash of the dream-sea.

Julian shuddered and moved the light around the room. He paused it on a large silver print of Mara on the mantelpiece. It was a good likeness, made by employing the latest technique of photography, but it was not a studio portrait. Mara was unsmiling, her hair carelessly falling onto her shoulders, her eyes and lips free of makeup. She was wearing a black high-collar dress and seated against a dark background, so her white face stood out like a scream. Julian could not bear looking at her for more than a couple of heartbeats. He shifted the flashlight but in doing so, something in the background of the print drew his attention.

He came closer and examined it in the direct light. At first, it seemed that the background was of a pleated dark fabric like a curtain. But as he shifted it, he could make out pale splotches against the darkness. They slowly resolved themselves into piles of what looked like bodies, all thrown together in abandon, heaped upon each other, an outflung arm against a bare leg, one slack face below another ...

No, it could not be! His eyes were playing tricks on him, or a residue of his nightmares was seeping into his waking brain, contaminating it.

But was it not what was happening to the City at large?

Julian was so intent on studying the picture that he did not hear the creak of a floorboard behind him.

Mara had never witnessed a fight like this before.

Well, that wasn't exactly true; she had seen an occasional street brawl. But such events seemed unreal, somehow disconnected from the ordinary flow of life, over so quickly that she was never able to grasp what exactly happened. There would be two huffing, ill-dressed workingmen in unseemly closeness to each other and then one or both of them would be wiping blood off their faces, and Mara's mother or husband or friend would hurry her along, averting their eyes, speaking in an unnaturally loud voice, pretending nothing happened.

But this was different, Dog and Wolf grappling so close to her that their flailing limbs delivered glancing blows. The sweat on their faces. The sharp animal odor of fear and rage.

She edged closer, disregarding the danger. There was something about this spectacle of naked, mindless violence that made her feel more alive than she had ever been. Something stirred inside, some heavy, wordless presence, and the real Mara felt like a thin skin stretched over it, like a balloon about to burst.

Wolf started the brawl. Dog responded by head-butting him, while Wolf delivered a knee blow to his adversary's crotch that failed to elicit the expected reaction. They seemed to be evenly matched: Wolf taller and heavier but Dog wiry and nimbler.

Mara's personality trembled and strained: a soap bubble about to burst. She tried to hold the presence back but could not.

Then she heard whimpering, and the presence retreated.

The whimpering was coming from Matilda, who crouched in the archway. It was clear she did not understand what was going on. Pity for her brought Mara back to herself. She patted the creature's head.

"There, there," she whispered.

Dog, having wrestled free from his enemy, hit his throat with the edge of his palm. As Wolf grunted in pain, Dog grasped his protruding ears and savagely banged his head on the wall, once, twice. On the third time the larger man's eyes rolled up and he slid into a heap on the floor. Matilda rushed to her master, hissing in distress. Dog kicked her aside with casual brutality.

"Stop it!" Mara cried.

Dog turned around. His face was glistening, a fresh scarlet scratch oozing on the forehead.

"She's an animal," he said, "as he is."

He prodded Wolf with his foot.

"Are you also beginning to turn, Mrs. Raven? A little too early. Or have you been here longer than you make out?"

"They may be animals," Mara said, "but so are you, Mr. Dog."

Dog grinned and she saw how many of his teeth were missing.

"I may be sick," he said, "but I'll die a man."

"How can you be sure?" Mara asked.

"I changed my name."

"From what?"

"I forgot. I made myself forget or it wouldn't be a real change, would it?"

Mara looked at him and then at the unconscious man on the floor.

"He's your brother," she said, "isn't he? You are a Wolf, too. Those creatures, those dogs we saw, some of them looked like wolves or jackals. This is why you chose this name."

"True," Dog said, and spat at the unconscious form on the floor. "He is my brother, though not much love lost between us. Always destined for great things, Theo was. He had meat when everybody else in the family chewed dry bread. He had education when I was pulled out of school to earn a living, and my sisters went to work in factories or worse. So, when he came here as manager of the Raven plantations, he started having plans. Money was not enough for him. Other managers drank themselves to death or took the money and ran away before their years were up but not Theo. He was convinced he could cheat the free land, even though he bore the name of the beast. He was not happy to find me already living here. And he was even less happy when he started changing and I remained the same."

Mara dropped to her knees. Wolf's eyes rolled up in their sockets, but his chest rose and fell. Blood dribbled down the side of his neck. Mara undid the buttons of his linen suit.

The same transformation that had melted and reshaped the body of Matilda had begun to work its inexorable magic on Wolf. His torso was lean and corded with inhuman ropy muscles, thickly covered with fur—not hair.

She looked at Dog.

"He is becoming his totem," she said.

"Exactly, Mrs. Raven."

"And my husband knew about it."

"Of course, he did."

"Did you kill him?"

"Why would I? I'm not a killer like Wolf and his boys."

"Who are his boys?"

"Yokels from Lonelyhearts who are hired to hunt remnants, get drunk, and chew coffee-berries to get as high as a kite. They think they have the best deal in the world until they discover they're changing and by the time it penetrates their thick heads, they find themselves being gunned down by their buddies. We'd better leave before they come back."

Wolf moaned, still unconscious, blood dribbling from his wound. Totem or not, it was inhuman to leave an injured man, but Matilda could take care of him ...

Where was Matilda?

She was not there anymore. Somehow, she had crept away.

"Ancestors' bones!" swore Dog. "She went to fetch her son!"

"Her son?"

"The guy who let us in! He's a Weasel like her but not changed yet! Quick, we have to get to the stables. I was a fool to leave my shotgun there!"

After grasping Mara's hand, he dragged her to the door. She looked back at the body lying in an untidy heap on the floor. Perhaps it would be kind to extinguish the seductive words swarming like maggots in the disintegrating, but still human, brain.

~

Julian whirled back, swinging his flashlight at the intruder, hoping to blind him. Instead, he was blinded as the reflection from a wall mirror leaped into his eyes. But the intruder did not attack, and as Julian lowered the flashlight, he saw why.

He was holding a gun in his pale, pudgy hand.

"We should stop meeting like this," Julian said.

Mr. Seal shrugged.

"It's easy. Unless you tell me the truth, you end up with a

bullet in your brain, and our next meeting will be in the Abode of the Ancestors."

"What truth?"

"Where is Mara?"

"I don't know."

Seal's finger shifted on the trigger.

"You have five seconds to live. Where is she?"

"I don't know. When I walked out of this house, she was not with me."

He saw a flicker of hesitation on Seal's face. He must have watched the house after running out. He must have seen that when Julian staggered back and was violently sick in the gutter, he was alone.

"Did you kill her and hide her body?"

"Don't be an idiot! Didn't your goons search the house? There is no room here to hide a dead mouse."

"Watch your mouth!" Seal hissed. "I would not mind shooting you for the fun of it. The City is better off without the likes of you!"

"That's debatable." Julian relaxed. It was as if he had been in this situation before and had survived, even though he knew for sure that he had never faced a gun held by an unstable and trigger-happy man. "I think the City is better off without the Temple, and the clowns bred there."

"Where is Mara? How did you manage to smuggle her out?"

"She walked out on her own."

"She did not. I watched the door. There is no other exit."

"Not through the door. Through the gate."

"Hush!" whispered Dog.

They were hiding behind a shed halfway to the stables. The shed was constructed of warped, unpainted boards, some of them broken and lying on the ground. There was a nauseating smell wafting from its dark interior.

As they had rushed out from the house, they heard Weasel's exclamation of dismay accompanied by soft gabble, apparently Matilda's attempt to communicate with her son. Weasel would be armed, which was the reason Dog had been unwilling to tackle him until he got his shotgun from his saddlebag. But now they were cut off from their horses. As they were running through the maze of sheds and outhouses, they glimpsed a group of mounted men passing through a side gate into the compound and heading for the stables.

Dog swore.

Mara's heart was beating wildly but she was not frightened. What was happening to her seemed more like a sped-up convalescence from a chronic, draining illness. Now, suddenly, the colors were piercingly bright; the rough touch of the wall thrilling; the warm air alive.

Dog craned his neck, listening to the hubbub of voices.

"Five of them," he whispered. "Almost everybody's here. Shit!"

"Perhaps we should hide," suggested Mara.

Dog shook his head.

"Useless. We need our horses and my gun. They'll track us down if we try to hide in the scrub."

"How?"

Dog opened his mouth to answer but at that moment there was a movement inside the shed, the rotten stink came in on a wave, and a long, dark, sinuous body crawled around the corner and into plain sight.

"This is how," said Dog, pushing Mara to the wall and positioning himself between her and the creature.

It was another remnant, and it stank so badly Mara's eyes watered. She squinted at the creature's matted, filthy pelt, its narrow snout, and tiny piglike eyes. It looked like a hybrid of a fox and a caterpillar, covered in unwashed human hair. It lifted its snout and wrinkled its large, moist, dribbling nose as it swiftly crawled toward them.

Dog picked up a piece of broken, nail-studded board. The creature snorted and reared, and Dog brought the board forcefully upon the remnant's head. It screamed, "Help!", an articulate human sound, and then keeled over and lay still, a trickle of dark blood worming its way through the dust.

"Run!" cried Dog.

But it was too late. The creature's cry was heard, and Wolf's boys came running from the stables, their shotguns drawn.

CHAPTER 7. REVELATIONS

"She did it!" Seal whispered. The gun wavered, and Julian tackled him.

He did not have the time to consider that he was committing suicide. Something else took over; something quick and predatory that until now only poked its head through the veil of nightmares. And the predatory thing saved him.

Julian threw himself at Seal, his head lowered, aiming for his chest. Seal was so taken by surprise, and Julian's action was so quick, that he staggered back when they connected and let go of the gun that slid on the floor to the corner. Julian delivered a blow with the edge of his hand to Seal's neck. The other man wheezed, gasping for air. He was taller and heavier than Julian but in bad shape, and the blow bought his attacker the second he needed to pick up the gun.

While Seal gasped for air, trying to get his wind back, Julian opened the chamber and emptied it of bullets that he threw into the fireplace. The gun, heavy and blunt-nosed, was a revolver, and though Julian did not own one—until recently, they were illegal in First City—he knew how to handle it. He was not sure where this knowledge came from.

Seal lowered himself onto the sofa, watching Julian with his small, glassy eyes. The man looked sick.

"That was reckless," he said.

"I'm not a murderer like you."

"I only kill people who deserve it."

The cynical phrase reverberated in Julian's head as if he had heard it before. Seal must have noted the shadow of déjà vu pass over Julian's face because his mouth twitched in a knowing smile. A drop of blood oozed from a crack in his dry lips.

Julian felt confused and unsure. He loathed the man standing before him, but there had been that moment of unwanted familiarity, almost recognition, when he had first seen him. And now this feeling came back but without any memory attached to it. It was more a curdled nostalgia tinted with bitterness, as if he and Seal had been together in some forgotten battle and emerged out of it, the only survivors, bound by camaraderie of violence, and yet hating each other for the burden they shared.

"Sit down," Seal said. "We need to talk."

"Talk? You were about to shoot me!"

"The gun was to jog your memory. I would not shoot you. We have too much history together."

"We have no history together!" Julian snarled. "It's the third time I'm seeing you, and I'd be happy never to see you again."

"It's the third time you, Julian Lion, or Sparrow, whatever you call yourself, have seen me, Jeremy Seal. But what about our totems?"

～

Time slowed down for Mara. A group of ragged youths floated toward her through viscous air, their shotguns and zits equally bathed in a piercingly clear light, made almost beautiful by its impartial serenity. The ribbons of their fantastic clothes undulated gracefully, strips of fur and leather sewn to their jackets. The one at the head of the group had a black widow's peak; his mouth gaping as if he suffered from a stuffed nose. They all appeared pitifully young to Mara, even though they were probably her age or older.

By her side, Dog stirred, coming forward with the same leisurely slowness, lifting his hand, mouthing something unintelligible. But Mara paid him no attention. She felt as if something huge was tearing her apart, trying to emerge, and with the last effort of will she tried to keep together the tattered remnants of herself, to prevent the birth of darkness into this clear light. She knew the sensation of almost-birth; it was the same one she had experienced in the dream-sea when the land mermaids had delivered her of that terrible entity that was about to gobble the living islands one by one ... In desperation, she silently cried out for her dream-sea allies to come again, to protect her and themselves ...

But the mermaids could not reach here, into the heart of the sunny land where men became beasts. With one mighty shove, the presence inside her broke out.

"What do you mean?" Julian asked.

"A man named David Mole wrote comments on the *Book of the Remnant* two hundred years ago. His writings were mostly destroyed during the Dark Years, but some excerpts survived. I read them."

"So?"

"You know the *Book of the Remnant*, don't you?"

"I went to school like everybody else," Julian responded. "Humans lived in the Abode of the Ancestors in harmony with animals, presided over by the Four: Lion, Tiger, Seal, and Bear. And then humans rebelled, killed the Four who were then named the Slaughtered Ones, and were exiled into First City as punishment. The gate was locked behind us, and here we are, mucking along without our benevolent totems, and trying to expiate our sin. Nobody believes in this nonsense anymore except the crazies in the Army of the Revealer."

"People don't believe in it because the story doesn't make sense, right? If the Abode of the Ancestors was so wonderful, why the Rebellion? If the Slaughtered Ones were killed, why do we still worship them? If our totems were powerful and benevolent deities, why are the animals living on the Plains dumb beasts?"

"I don't know," Julian spat. "More to the point: Why are we discussing theology?"

"Because if Mara opened the gate, then understanding the Book is vital to following her."

"Following her where?"

"Mara has gone into the Abode of the Ancestors."

"The Abode? She told me she was swimming in the sea of dreams every night!"

"They are the same."

"What?"

"Yes. That was Mole's theory. What the Temple calls the Abode of the Ancestors is the ocean of collective memory and imagination. Everything we believe in, every story, every hope and every fear, nightmares and delusions, visions and exaltations. They are all real. It is us who are a pale reflection of humanity's dreams."

"You are quite a poet," Julian said, impressed in spite of himself. "But you said that Mara opened the gate. How? What was that black flower?"

"Another of Mole's insights. Our physical bodies are the lock and chain that keep us imprisoned in this dismal City on the dismal Plains. Open the body and you open the gate."

"Open the body?" Julian exclaimed. "How?"

"By violence. Violence is the key that unlocks the gate. The black flower that grows out of the victim and blooms for a short while contains the imprint of their personality that is drawn back into the dream-sea. People had known about them for a long time and tried to use them to enter the dream-sea in their physical form. Some hoped to meet their totems; others believed it was possible to use the dream-sea as a shortcut to other places in this world. But nobody succeeded until Mara. She had broken down the barrier that kept First City isolated from the dream-sea."

"Why her?"

"Because she is the Revealer."

"She does not want to be the Revealer!"

"Mara does not, but her totem does."

"Who is her totem?"

"Don't you know?"

There was salt on her lips, like the salt of the sea, the South Sea, the harsh, beautiful water sparkling like steel, not the mild shimmering medium of her dreams ... And something gummed her eyes, as if she woke up from a fever sleep.

She curled her body around the absence at its core, around the hole where the baby used to lie. And then she remembered that there had never been any baby.

But she still felt so light that a gust of wind could blow her away, hollow and desiccated. The only thing that kept her down was the stickiness of her limbs that glued her to the hard, grainy surface ...

She uncurled herself, propped herself up on her gunk-covered hands, staggered to her feet. The first thing that she saw was the orange ball of the sun hanging at the horizon and she thought, Why didn't it set already?

And then she remembered that the sunset of her arrival in the South Continent had been two days ago.

She looked around at the slaughter.

Wolf's boys were scattered around on the hard, barren ground that was not so hard anymore, having soaked so much blood that it was now almost squishy. *Scattered* was the right word because there were many more lumps of dead flesh than there had been living bodies. They had not been shot or stabbed or battered. They had been torn apart.

Black petals soaked in puddles of blood, surrounded by clouds of blowflies whose restless swarms brought the only movement into the stillness of the tableau. She picked one flower, but it was wilted, its loose crown falling apart. Useless. Not like the flower that grew out of her mother's dead body.

She remembered it all now. And with the memory came a pitiless and welcome clarity.

She wanted to cry, but there were no tears left. There was no sorrow or remorse. Only dry stony rage.

The sun dropped below the wavy line of the hills; there was a young moon, soft and innocent in the mauve sky. The lemony fragrance of flowering shrubs mingled with the metallic stench of blood.

She methodically went through the torn, mutilated bodies. Dog was not there.

Her hands were sticky; her clothes crusty, chafing against her skin.

The dark was thickening; she forgot how short the twilight here was. She turned around and retraced her way to the house, stumbling over scraps of litter and frightening a pair of fowls who ran away from her with an indignant clucking that seemed obscene in the stillness.

The house was dark and quiet. She walked into the huge living room, her hand futilely fumbling on the wall for the electric switch until she realized there was no electricity. She remembered seeing a kerosene lamp on one of the tables. When a homely flame flared up, she saw a heap at the opposite wall. It was Wolf, his head blown away with a shotgun blast. His flower had wilted as well.

Mara made her way into the kitchen and washed her hands and face in the stone sink. She considered washing the blood and brain matter from her clothes but then shrugged and went back out.

Outside, the stars were clear and huge. She remembered that there were neither stars nor the sun in the dream-sea, and she thought: *They are not needed.*

Suddenly, she heard whimpering. Turning back, she saw a moving shadow by the door. Matilda was crouching at the base of the stairs, rocking and faintly moaning to herself.

She stood still.

This creature, so useless, so deformed, so ugly. What right did it have to live when her mother and baby were dead?

She could kill it with one blow. Even if her true self did not come back, there were rocks on the ground and shotguns among the dead.

She hesitated.

Matilda lifted her head and looked at her with those dumb, glittering animal eyes, filled with wordless pain.

She took one step toward the remnant. Then another. Matilda moaned and stretched a hand toward her. In the moonlight, the dusting of fur was almost invisible.

She took Matilda's hand. Matilda calmed down and stopped moaning. She made another sound: an almost-articulate one. She listened and there it was again.

Maatildaa.

A human name.

"I am ..." she said, and stopped. Did she want it all back: the pain and the guilt and the horror? Was it not better to be a force of destruction, as pure and dry as the dust and the stones under her feet?

"I am Mara," she said. "Come on, come with me. You cannot stay here."

She helped Matilda to her feet and together they started down the track.

~

"And the four of them stood at the gate. And one had stripes like cinders and ashes. And one had a face like a leper. And one had a body that crushed rocks and made the earth bleed as it crawled. And of the last one nothing can be said because its claws tore off the skins of the living and made it a garment thereof."

Julian sat in his car, his forehead resting on the cold windshield.

Seal had gone. Julian regretted disabling the gun. He should have put a bullet through Seal's head. Maybe he should have put a bullet through his own head.

Not that it would change anything. Somebody else would be born, bearing the imprint of his totem, carrying the burden of a forgotten and repudiated nightmare. Nothing ever died in the dream-sea where stories mutated and multiplied like worms in the grave, breeding monsters.

"Each of us is a copy of our totem," Seal had said. "You know how woodprints are made? You have a carved block, and then you can print off as many copies of the design as you like. Only some are better, sharper, and some are worse. It is the same with people. We are smudged prints of whatever Ancestor was used to make us."

"Used by who?"

"The Four. They are different from the rest. They are the creators, the rulers of the dream-sea. They took control of it after ..."

"After what?"

"I don't know. I read David Mole's writings, but a lot of it seemed like the ravings of a madman. He claimed that we are not really human, for example."

"What does it mean?"

"I don't know. I also don't know what disaster had placed the Four in control of the dream-sea. But control it they did; and they created the rest of humanity, and built First City as a refuge, for humans to start anew."

"But they are called the Slaughtered Ones! Who killed them? What was the Rebellion?"

"They cannot be killed. Dreams and stories do not die. But the Rebellion did happen. Two of the Four rebelled against their leader and imprisoned her. The third one stood on the sidelines, unsure what to do."

"How do you know?"

"Because there are still people in the City who carry personalities of the Slaughtered Ones, their totems. As you should know."

Nausea rose in Julian's throat as he remembered the rest of the conversation, and he rolled down the window and leaned out. The spasm passed quickly; the cold patter of the rain cooled off his forehead.

"Are you saying that I am an imprint of one of the Four?"

"Yes."

"The Lion. You are the Seal, I assume."

"Correct again."

"Who is the Tiger?"

"I know who he is. He does not matter now."

"But there is no family named Bear."

"Because she was imprisoned by her fellow deities who rebelled against her rule."

"Who are the ones who rebelled?"

"I'm sure you can figure it out by now. The Lion and the Tiger."

"And the Seal tried to play both sides ... I see you live up to your totem."

"We all do. The Lion is reckless and violent. The Tiger is hungry and greedy for power and possessions. The Seal is ... calculating and uses subtle means of control. And the Bear is ..."

"The Bear is Mara's totem. Is that what you were going to say?"

"Yes. The Bear is filled with negativity so profound and so relentless that nothing can stand in her way. She cannot love. She cannot even hate. She takes because everything has been taken from her. She kills because she was killed. She has the power to shape worlds, but she uses it to smash them to pieces."

"This is not Mara!"

"None of us is our totem, Mr. Lion. But none of us can escape the story that has made us what we are. Mara is the Bear's imprint; the only one to be born in the City for centuries, if not forever. Her presence weakens the barrier, the gate, that protects the City from the rest of the dream-sea. She is the Revealer because she reveals the truth: We are phantoms, dreams, delusions; echoes of lost stories. First City is part of the dream-sea, and it is time we all went back, to our origin."

"I don't believe you!"

"It is the truth, and you know it. Mara is the pivot. And if she has gone into the dream-sea, chances are she has also released her totem from her cage. The Bear is coming, Mr. Lion. The only question is where you will be when she comes. The City is doomed. We can either embrace its destruction and hope our totems will save us when it dissolves in the flood of dreams, or ..."

"Or resist."

"It did not work the last time. It won't work now."

"I am not my fucking totem! I am Julian Sparrow, a human!"

"You only dream you are."

He turned the key in the ignition. He was so cold that his fingers went numb, and he had to try twice to steer the car into the empty street where broken glass and loose cobblestones lay submerged in the puddles.

~

Alice D. Bobcat had finally settled into her nice warm bed when there was a wild knocking on the door. She sat up in bed and listened. She was fairly confident in the sturdiness of her locks and chains, but one could never let one's guard down in the South. Being the only grocer in the tiny settlement protected her from the wildness of Wolf's boys, while her friends Dog and Foxy kept the remnants away. But she was all too conscious of the precariousness of her situation. With the Southern Malady softly chewing upon her body and reshaping it in unmistakable ways, and with Wolf, the undisputable master of their community, going bonkers, each minute was like a grenade you had to toss away before it exploded in your hands.

The knocking did not subside, so Alice fetched her shotgun, lit a candle, and went to the door. She opened it a crack but kept the chain on. Her eyes widened when she saw her visitors.

The strange girl Dog had brought to the settlement, the one with disquieting color-shifting eyes, stood there, her clothes all wet and stained. And next to her ...

"No way!" Alice barked. "No remnant in my house!"

"She is with me," the girl said but with a forcefulness that felt almost palpable to Alice. "If I come in, so does she."

Alice hesitated. She could have locked the door and gone back to sleep ...

But Mara—yes, that was her name—was among the handful of women in the South. Whatever had happened to her, or whatever had been done to her, Alice would not be able to live with herself if she turned her away.

And moreover, Alice was curious. The few drops of information doled out by Fox were so startling that she could not stop thinking about them. Mara was the key to what was happening in Bear Haven, and Alice was not going to let herself be kept out of the loop.

She pursed her lips, unlocked the door, and waved the two of them in, glancing along the empty track to make sure they had not been followed.

Inside, her suspicions were confirmed. Mara's clothes were

stained with blood, though she did not appear wounded. Alice commanded her to undress and shoved a dry petticoat at her. Mara's companion found a corner and tried to make herself disappear. Alice ostentatiously pretended the remnant was not there. The sight of this creature, an animal still walking upright and decked out in human clothes, made her blood run cold.

"Did Wolf's boys get to you?" Alice asked.

"Wolf's boys are dead," Mara replied. There was something in her flat tone that put an end to Alice's questioning, though not before she asked about Dog.

"He is alive," the girl said, and fell silent.

Not sure what else to do, Alice lit a small woodstove and set about making coffee, which she diluted with milk and loaded with sugar. She cut slices from a loaf of home-baked bread, and then sat across the table and stared at Mara who ate as daintily as if she were in some fancy restaurant in First City. Without asking Alice, she gave some bread and coffee to her remnant companion.

Mrs. Bobcat knew who this strange girl was, having been told by Foxy who had gotten the information from Dog. Alice had only partly believed it, considering that Foxy was in the first stages of his changeover and more than slightly befuddled. The old fool was overdue to board the first ship home, which she doubted he would do, knowing the strange spell that this land cast over its guests. But now, looking at the vertical crease that cut Mara's smooth forehead, Alice was unaccountably persuaded that this was indeed the current owner of the Raven plantations, Wolf's owner. Moreover, she did not doubt that Wolf's ruffians were all dead and perhaps Wolf as well. And on top of that, she suspected that she did not want to know how it happened.

But she had to find out, for Wolf had been the undisputable master of their small community, and his death and/or removal would create such an upheaval that the hidden forces under the surface of their feigned normalcy would burst out and destroy her tidy shop, her flannel petticoats, and her stash of money hidden in an old kettle.

While Mara was eating, Mrs. Bobcat tried to make sense of her reaction. Mara was the age that Alice's unborn daughter would have been had she not slid out of her womb on a tide of blood. She should have called up the unspent maternal feelings locked up in Alice's childless breast. Instead, she was shivering, as if the girl were not the daughter Alice might have had but the daughter's ghost.

Mara did not look traumatized. She looked as self-contained as a lizard, poised and unblinking.

"Did Wolf do something to you?" Alice asked, still trying to figure out if the girl was in shock.

"I did something to him."

"Is he dead?"

"Yes."

Alice exhaled.

"Who is in charge now?"

"I am."

"Are you really Mr. Raven's wife?"

"I am his heir, so I am the owner of his plantations."

"Are you sure he is dead?" Alice asked. It was the question she had asked herself many times.

Mara's inhuman eyes finally focused on Alice's face.

"Did you meet him when he came here?"

"Yes," Alice said. "A very handsome man. He talked to some of us here in Bear Haven. He wanted to know how we live. But mostly he wanted to know ..." She hesitated; her eyes unwillingly drawn to the corner where Matilda huddled.

"How the land changes you?"

"Yes. We don't talk about it much among ourselves, you know. Bad luck. It starts happening sooner with some, later with others, never for the few lucky ones, like Dog. When it does, you have to get the hell out of here. But if the ship is delayed, or you don't have money for return passage, or you're an indentured worker, well then ..."

"I don't understand," Mara said, "if you know that it'll happen, why do you stay here?"

"This is what Mr. Raven asked me. And I told him: I don't know. It is the land itself. It cradles you, and soothes you, and you like it so much that you tell yourself: one more day ... And then the changeover starts. And you don't want to go at all."

"Is it happening to you?" Mara asked.

"Perhaps," Alice responded. "I'm a woman; we last longer. But not forever."

Both of them looked at Matilda.

"Do you know that First City is being destroyed?" Mara asked. "There is nowhere for you to go back to."

"What?" Alice reeled. "The City? How can it be? Is nobody defending it? The Temple, the Animal House, the Guardians? People in charge!"

"I told you," Mara said. "I'm in charge now."

CHAPTER 8. SOUTHWARD

He had known it since he was a child: a sense of difference, so subtle that it was like a faint whiff of stale sweat still clinging to washed-out clothes. He had known it when his Temple-bred companions snuck sweets and naughty pictures into the dorm, but he would refuse to pollute himself and would lie stiffly in his bed, dreaming of the glory, for which he had neither words nor images. He had known it when the worst bullies left him alone, put off not so much by the hulking strength of his body as by the sharpness of his mind. He had known it when his teachers lowered their voices and averted their eyes, as he passed in the corridor wrapped in the cloak of his misfortune, which they were obliged to call his purity.

Mr. Seal paced his dark living room. It was the middle of the night but through the huge uncurtained plate-glass window that was his only luxury the lights of the City still blazed, a scatter of pearls, rubies, and diamonds dwarfed by the dull dome of the night that arched over man's petty dominion. Mr. Seal paused and his gaze traveled upward, into the cloudy darkness, disdaining the City's pathetic lights. It was there, beyond the clouds, beyond this gaudy backdrop of humanity's monotonous self-exhibition: the answer. The solution.

The end.

The problem was that he could not access his totem's memories or Power. He had tried. Oh yes, he had tried so many times that he had lost count. As a child. As a young man. As a failed Guardian. As a Temple Security agent, clawing his way up the slippery ladder of success. And every time, he encountered a blank wall.

Seal was not his father's totem. He discarded his birth name, Crow, having cut all ties with his family and only recalling it with a flash of schadenfreude when he had read his elder brother's obituary. Not that it mattered: Totem lines were notoriously slippery and tangled, and he was convinced there must have been a Seal somewhere in his lineage.

But what about the rest of them? His fellow gods. His rivals, friends, or lovers, he could not tell which because he did not remember their shared past. The Slaughtered Ones.

He regretted telling Julian the truth, but he had been alone in his knowledge for so long that he could not bear the burden any longer. He had hoped to share it with Mara one day, but things had gone so horribly, disastrously wrong that he had to face the possibility that she would try to kill him when they met. She had, after all, aimed for him when she and Julian had walked into Louisa's living room, where he had been trying to convince her to tell him the whereabouts of her daughter. It was her unfamiliarity with firearms that saved his life—and indirectly, revealed to Mara who she truly was.

So here he was, alone again. An imprint of the Seal but with no way to access his totem's Power. And opposed by the woman he had dedicated his life to, an imprint of the most feared of the Four whose face was veiled because it was too terrible to see. What had their relationship been in the dream-sea? Had he sided with her against the Tiger and the Lion? He must have, though all his guesses were defeated by the blankness of his memory.

But the pain that tore through him had little to do with the Bear, and everything to do with Mara. She had rejected him. She had chosen another. He had lived with her love for Ronald because he knew it to be a schoolgirl's infatuation. But Julian was something else, and he could not bear thinking of them together. It did not matter that he knew how ridiculous, shameful, impossible his love for her was. It did not make the pain any less.

In First City, locked in the prison of human flesh, they could never be together. So, First City had to be destroyed, drowned in the dream-sea where it had originated. They had to go back, start from the beginning.

But first, he had to get rid of his rivals, or rather, of the only one left; the only one who could oppose his plans. The Tiger was gone. Seal did not know what happened to Ronald in the South Continent, but assumed he was dead. Ronald had never known what he was, though some of the Power of the Tiger, the unstoppable and fiery greed that burnt every obstacle in its way, had percolated into his business success. But he was too stupid to question himself, which shored up Seal's contempt for him and enabled him to accept his marriage to Mara. In any case, Ronald was out of the picture. Another imprint could be born, or perhaps it already existed. The obscure writings of David Mole indicated that sometimes multiple imprints of the Four had simultaneously been loose in the City, especially during the Dark Years. But Mr. Seal was confident that First City would be destroyed before this could become a problem.

No, the only one to take care of was Julian Lion.

Again, Seal regretted having been so frank with him. He had hoped to sway him to his side. At least, the gnawing loneliness of being who he was could abate somewhat.

He had been a fool. Even if Julian did not have access to his totem's Power, he had money and connections. He was a hindrance.

And he was in love with Mara.

He thought of the way her ash-blond hair tumbled down her forehead when she read and of the flutter of her eyelids as she was falling asleep and beginning to dream. He thought of the way her waist and hips acquired the sleek curvature of a vase after she had lost her baby fat at the age of sixteen. A familiar pressure was beginning to build somewhere in the region of his stomach, spreading above and below.

He squashed it. It did not matter anymore.

He lowered himself into the armchair that squeaked in protest. He was gaining weight. It did not matter either.

The City was falling away from him just like the garment of his heavy, unwanted, mutilated flesh. It was happening because he was making it happen.

He thought of the pathetic suicides, the fanatical Army of the Revealer he had trained and egged on in the hopes of mastering the lore of black flowers through them. Edna Lynx. George Hare. Thomas Hawk. William Hart. Except for Hawk who still had his uses, they were all dead, and Mr. Seal tamped down a flare of anger at their failure. They had accomplished nothing. Mara's presence alone was enough to weaken the gate that kept First City intact and to bring about the seepage of the water from the dream-sea, the endless rain that was washing away hateful humanity.

He did not need the puppet Army of the Revealer anymore. But he still had the influence that its creation had given him.

Mr. Seal's finger hovered over the phone's dial. It was not that he hesitated; he knew exactly what had to be done. But there was something that stopped him, a shadow of a forgotten dream.

He dialed the unlisted number.

On the third ring, a familiar voice answered, sounding

peevish and somehow diminished by the naked immediacy of a phone conversation.

"Yes?"

"Mr. President," said Mr. Seal. "Jeremy Seal, deputy chief of the Temple Security Bureau, speaking. I have found out who finances the terrorist Army of the Revealer. I ask your authorization for his immediate arrest and interrogation. And this time, I ask that any pressure from the Lion family be resisted. The fate of First City depends on his elimination."

Laura Lion stood in the garden and let the cold rain sluice down her body, drenching her silk dress, soaking her blond hair, sloshing in her dainty shoes. She experienced a peculiar sense of satisfaction in seeing herself from the outside: a scarecrow woman, her beauty washed away, dissolved by the insolent beat of the water falling from the sky. It had been falling for so long that the weather's pretense to strangeness, charming exoticism, even the uniqueness of disaster, had long ago dissipated.

She pivoted slowly, observing her garden through the wet lashes. The black boughs of cherry and apple trees made a fine tracery against the gray sky. It shuddered under the rain. The empty flower beds were precise rectangles and squares of black mulch, almost as beautiful, she thought, in their own spare, dismal way as they had been when filled with a garish riot of color. The garden statues of the Four (not the monstrosities one could see atop the Animal House, of course, but modern versions that were sleek, stylized, elegantly indifferent) seemed to shiver and hunch. She patted the head of the Lion in a comradely gesture.

"Laura!"

A sudden flash of anger spiked through her sweet melancholy.

She had told them that she did not want to be disturbed! She wanted to prepare, and so should they.

"Laura!"

She blinked the water away and the dark male shape was upon her, propelling her toward the terrace and the open glass door.

"Are you crazy? You'll catch your death of a cold!"

Julian Sparrow! She had not seen him in some time, and he was already fading, together with the rest of her loves and hates. His presence was disconcerting, almost insulting, because it brought her back to where she did not want to be. Back in her shivering, cold, pitiful body.

He dragged her into the sitting room where the fire was burning. She did not want to feel the warmth, but it forced itself upon her.

"Go up and change your clothes, for Ancestors' sake!" he ordered her. "What is it with you people? Is everybody insane in this bloody City?"

She clamped her lips. How dare he speak to her so. Julian so-called Sparrow, a minor branch of the family, a mediocre money-maker, her third cousin, her occasional lover ... But the anger did exactly the opposite of what she wanted: It broke the mood and made her aware of the ridiculous figure she cut with her hair plastered to her head, and her nose dripping.

With all the dignity she could muster, Laura Lion shrugged and went upstairs to her bedroom, leaving puddles in her wake.

When she came down, she was back in a tailored wool dress and in her human body. Julian was pacing back and forth, looking gaunt and older than she remembered him to be.

"What do you know about the Raven plantations on the South Continent?" he asked with no preamble.

Laura blinked.

"The Raven plantations? What in the Ancestors' name ... Wait! It's about that woman, right? Mara Raven?"

Julian nodded. Laura laughed; the apocalyptic mood sloughing off.

"You've got cheek! You come to me to ask about some woman you want to bed! But what do you care about her plantations?"

"Are they really hers?"

"Yes, even though Ronald Raven's younger brother pretends they are not. Raven will have to be declared legally dead soon and the will be unsealed. It all goes to her."

Julian did not ask how she knew. The Lion family prided itself on having a finger in every pie.

"Did you know Ronald Raven well?"

She shrugged.

"I don't think anybody did. He was a pain to do business with. Too single-minded, unstoppable, and greedy. No finesse to him but a lot of push."

Julian bit his lip.

"Do you think he had a Power?"

"What?" Laura snorted. "A Power? No way! We all know how Guardians acquire their Powers! Ronald would be the last man in the world to let his little friend down!"

Her double entendre amused her into a better mood, and she smiled at Julian.

"Did he cheat on Mara?"

"Not that I know of. No gossip to that effect, surprisingly. But why do you care? Are you planning to marry her for her plantations? It would work out pretty well: She is a widow; you are a widower. The holdings in the South would double in size for the family. You are still a Lion, after all."

"I have no such plans," Julian said. "In fact, I am considering selling my stock in the coffee production."

Laura's eyes opened wide.

"Why?"

"Because of what's happening to the indentured workers. I

tried to recruit contracted workers for a set period but it's not helpful. The same sickness happens to them."

"They are not the only ones."

"What do you mean?"

"The City is dying," Laura said. "And once the City is gone, the entire world will be like the South."

"You don't seem upset about it," Julian retorted. "Are you like those crazies in the Army of the Revealer, trying to hasten the end of humanity?"

"Humanity," Laura said, "is nothing to rejoice. It's a heavy burden, cousin. Far too heavy. We did not ask for it. And it's time to return the unwanted gift."

Julian snapped his suitcase shut. Laura had arranged for a berth for him on her company's ship, the *South Queen*, leaving in two days from the White Harbor on the ocean edge of the Plains. His own company owned a coffee hauler too, but it was in the dock, undergoing repairs. His company was not doing well. It was the least of his worries right now.

The sailing took only three days, the improved steam engines devouring the distance. Julian admired the advances of technology; he had dreamed of being an explorer as a child, and it was only the death of his parents that forced him into taking over his father's business. Now his career choice felt simultaneously ironic and propitious. Who needed steam power when you had your totem's Power?

Except he did not.

If his Power was anything like Mara's, he wanted none of it. He cringed with disgust remembering the glassy inhuman sheen in her eyes and the black flower cupped in her blood-smeared hands. If it took the death of a human being to unlock a gate into the dream-sea, he was better off using the slow mechanical transit across the real sea.

But what was real?

Julian walked back to the mantelpiece, picked up Elvira's picture, and looked into the pretty, insipid face of his dead wife.

That was real. The strange quasi-paternal affection he had had for Elvira was real. The grief he had felt when he learned about the murder was real. The sorrow, the regrets, and the nostalgia for that first bloom of love, so quickly wilted ...

And then there was Mara.

He shuddered as he thought of her. An imprint of the deity so fearsome that even her associates could not abide the sight of her.

And at the same time, her image stood before him with unbearable vividness, her wide-set eyes with their strange shifting colors, the paleness of her skin, the heavy fall of her hair ... He did not know whether he found her desirable; she was there, so unquestionably real that it seemed more possible—more fitting, in fact—to erase reality than to end her existence.

He walked to the window and pressed his aching forehead against the weeping opacity of the glass that returned his reflection without any indication of what—if anything—lay outside. It seemed to him that there were no more days in the First City, only the endless succession of nights of all descriptions: drizzly, pouring, stormy, gloomy, dejected, chilly, cold ... Where was all this water coming from? From the dream-sea? Was First City drowning in liquefied nightmares?

Enough!

Julian knew what he had to do. Find Mara, confront her with the truth, and then ...

Then do what needed to be done to save the City.

He could not follow her with the help of a black flower: The image filled him with revulsion. So, assuming she ended up on the South Continent, he was going to use human means of transportation: his car first, then the ship. There was a railway connecting First City to the White Harbor, but he loved his car. It was custom-fit to navigate rough terrain at the cost of a small fortune, and he was going to make good use of it.

He picked up his suitcase and froze. There was a sound from outside. He raced to the door leading into the kitchen. Just as he fumbled with the latch of the back door, the front door came crashing down. He heard heavy boots trampling all over his slick parquet floor that Dana Mouse, his housekeeper, had waxed just this morning. She had done too good a job, as always, as one of the intruders skidded on the slick surface and brought down a spindly console. That slowed down the rest of them enough to gain Julian a couple of seconds. He slipped into the dark back garden and made for the gate. Unfortunately, he always kept it locked: with the breakdown of civil order, robberies and home invasions were becoming more frequent. The key was in the kitchen, together with the key to the garage.

The noises coming from the house made it clear they were smashing things looking for him. Julian crouched in the shrubbery. When they came out, he would try to rush back into the house and into the garage to get his car. Once he was in, he would be able to get away, as the Temple vehicles were no match for his. It was not much of a plan, but it was the best he could do.

One of the intruders came out into the backyard.

There was no illumination. The new moon had not risen yet, and the stars were few. Julian remembered how, as a child, he used to stare into the night sky, feeling that there should have been more. Flattened to the ground among the dense decorative shrubs, Julian had a fair chance to be unnoticed.

Except that the Guardian who came out had a special Power.

He was thin and gaunt, his face covered with scraggly down, and his limbs as devoid of articulation as matchsticks. But his huge, round eyes, yellow and slit-pupiled, glowed with their own intense light. His beak clacked.

Julian barreled into him before he had a chance to alert others, his fingers locking around the Guardian's scrawny windpipe, cutting off the airflow.

The Guardian was stronger than his fragile build indicated. His pungent chicken-like smell suffocated Julian, and his talon-like fingers scoured his face, drawing blood. Julian concentrated on making sure he didn't call for help. The sounds of their scuffle were drowned in the noise coming from the house where the rest of the Guardians sent to rearrest him were apparently delighting in trashing his obscene secular wealth.

The owl-like Guardian freed one skeletal limb and tried to go for Julian's eyes. In desperation, Julian squeezed and twisted his neck. A horrible cracking sound—and the Guardian subsided into a feathery heap.

Julian rose to his feet, looking down at the man he had killed with his bare hands. A man? A creature? He did not care. A euphoric flush, as potent as an orgasm, made him shiver.

The heap twitched. The head, resting at an unnatural angle, rose and fell, hammering on the soaked ground.

The back door slammed as more Guardians came out.

A meaty black flower rose from the corpse, the double-butterfly bloom opening up above the huddled remains.

"Here he is!" somebody yelled.

Julian grasped the flower and lifted it. The darkness retreated like a frightened animal. A tear in the night bled yellow light onto the wet grass.

"Stop him!" another voice commanded, accompanied by the crack of a gunshot.

Julian stepped through.

CHAPTER 9. THE CITY ON THE BRINK

James Otter, the constitutional president of First City, paced in his luxurious study—all dark wood and bright hand-woven wall hangings—without sparing a glance for the heavy bulk of the man who sat before him, his back straight, his hands folded in his lap. Mr. Seal's pale, fleshy face was as impassive as usual, but inside he was brimming with contempt for the president. James Otter was nothing but a puppet, a nonentity that served as the meeting point for the delicately balanced interests of the rich merchant families and the Temple.

"How can that be?" Otter demanded for the fifth time, stopping in front of Mr. Seal. "You sent ... how many Guardians?"

"Fifteen."

"Fifteen Guardians to arrest one man you had already had in your custody and then stupidly released for whatever reason ..."

"The magistrate let him go on bail," pointed out Mr. Seal. "Not without some external pressure, if I may add."

"Whatever. But now you are telling me he escaped from fifteen Guardians who encircled his house, killing one of them in the process. How?"

"By using a black flower."

James Otter bit his thumbnail; his sleek head lowered and the famous smile that was largely responsible for his election was supplanted by an ugly grimace.

"Listen," he said. "I may sound like a nincompoop, but I don't understand this business with black flowers. I mean, I was given a briefing by the Fowl Guardian, but it was too mystical for my taste, so I can't say I paid too much attention. I'm a practical man."

Mr. Seal barely repressed a contemptuous smile; *In this case*, he thought, *a practical man is a synonym for a fool.*

"The lore of black flowers is ancient," he said, adopting his best academic tone, "and it is even mentioned in the *Book of the Remnant.* When a person dies by violence, a black flower blooms for a short while out of their body. This flower is a nexus between our world and the Abode of the Ancestors."

Otter snorted. "A fairy tale!"

"It is not, and we have proof. I don't need to tell you ..."

"No, you don't," said Otter. "The Lynx woman was a security fuckup to end all fuckups. But I thought that the crazies of the Army of the Revealer used their bodies to wreak havoc. Floods or rains or twisters are produced, not black flowers."

"After a flood or a twister, nothing much remains. And black flowers only appear for a short while. An esoteric Temple tradition teaches that the black flowers are symbols of the human soul, the gift of the Ancestors to house the spiritual essence of humanity separate from the physical body."

"Metaphysical nonsense!" James Otter scoffed.

"We did some experiments with black flowers," said Mr. Seal, "and were able to confirm that they possess some unusual properties. Unfortunately, one must have a Power to control them."

He had no intention of revealing to the president that these experiments had been conducted with unwanted children snatched out of Lonelyhearts, and that he had personally presided over a little farm situated outside the City, in one of those circular ruins that were reputed to predate the Rebellion. Unfortunately, he could not force the flowers to do anything useful, and due to pressure from some bleeding hearts—supported, Mr. Seal was sure, by the Fish Guardian herself—the experiment was discontinued. It rankled him to admit, even to himself, that Julian had been more successful.

"Are you saying that Julian Sparrow somehow crossed into the Abode of the Ancestors?" Otter asked.

"Yes," Mr. Seal said.

The president collapsed into the armchair, staring at Mr. Seal. *So much for freethinking*, thought Mr. Seal, *so much for your so-called Humanism. Just mention the Slaughtered Ones and you wet your pants!*

"What do you want the City to do?" James Otter asked.

To disappear!

"The situation is serious," Mr. Seal went on. "We need to apprehend Julian Sparrow."

"In the Abode? This is insane!"

"No, not in the Abode, of course. Nobody can stay there for long."

Except Mara.

"People who do have the Power to control black flowers use them for crossing vast distances in the blink of an eye by creating a shortcut through the Abode. We have records of this dating back to the Dark Years. I believe Julian Sparrow used a black flower to escape outside the City."

"There is nothing outside of the City."

Mr. Seal stared at him. Otter gave a nervous laugh.

"The South? Why?"

"Nobody would look for him there."

There were other reasons, of course, that Mr. Seal did not intend to share with the president.

"We know he communicated with Laura Lion, his relative,"

he continued, pressing his advantage. "She arranged for a berth on the *South Queen*, a coffee hauler. I have a hunch he won't show up for the departure."

"Then he won't get to the South Continent, will be forced to return to the City, and we'll pick him up here," Otter responded.

"No. He does not need to sail to the South Continent because he is already there. This is why, sir, I ask your authorization to sail on the *South Queen* myself."

"This is insane!" the president of First City moaned, and Mr. Seal gritted his teeth.

"Look outside, sir!" he commanded, and James Otter looked into the murk between the half-drawn curtains. The square in front of the Animal House looked like a slate-colored lake and the houses beyond, shrouded in vapors, loomed in the dusk like a line of broken cliffs. The City appeared deserted, sinking back into nature, shedding signs of human endeavor.

"If nothing is done," said Mr. Seal, "the City will drown in nightmares."

And not a moment too soon, he added to himself.

Viola Marmot slept on the stairs.

She had brought an old mattress with her, dragging it through the chilly mud of the flooded streets, until it was soaked through and through and smelled of rot. But she had no heart to throw it away. Somehow clinging to it gave her a sense of importance. As long as she had something to own, she was still a citizen, a person, a human being.

There were fires burning in Foxes Square, but she avoided them, despite her body's insistent clamor for warmth. Previously, she had heard a thin screaming coming from that direction and a roar of men's voices. In running away from the flood that had claimed her tiny first-floor apartment, she stumbled upon a ragged figure on the curb. At first, she thought it was one of the sacrifices. But then she realized that the girl was alive and that the blood on her clothes was not from a mortal wound.

"Do you need help?" Viola asked, but the girl fled. Too bad: She could have used companionship. The girl in no way resembled her dead sister, Carla, but she was a female and this counted for something. But then, Viola reminded herself, she would be with Carla soon. This thought had kept her moving as she trudged through the water-veiled, twilit streets, first surrounded by bewildered refugees and eventually alone. She was not sorry about the loss of her rented apartment. After Carla's death, she was not able to stand its hollow emptiness, haunted by the suspicion that it had all been for nothing; that the Army of the Revealer was a fraud perpetrated by the rich traitors in the Temple and the Animal House; and that she would live out the rest of her life like her mother, stranded on the shoals of dismal drudgery and never reaching the sea of liberation. But now things were starting to change. She was on the move. She was active. And she had her mattress to remind her that even though the City had been cruel to her, she was a worker, not a charity case. The little she owned she had gained with her labor.

Eventually, wet and tired, she found herself in the area of funky apartment complexes, fashionably ugly tall buildings whose black marble cladding, sleek windows, and metal doorframes gleamed in the fluorescent-lit rain. It was a rich area. Viola had only been here a couple of times before when the late Edna Lynx had taken her to worship in the Lynx temple nearby. Edna was not from this area; her family had old money and lived in one of the stately brick residences along the Bird River. But Viola remembered that the strange girl who had come to one of their meetings, the last meeting in fact before Carla's death, had lived around here. Viola tried to recall the girl's name, but it slipped away, dissolved in the lapping waves of fatigue. Nevertheless, the girl's shifting gray-green-blue eyes rose up in her memory with a dim sensation of clotted grief and fear. She had argued with George Buzzard ... but Viola's mind shied away from the thought of George.

Viola surveyed the empty street. The streetlamps were on but there were no lights in any of the windows, except a wavering flicker that might have been a candle. On the lower floors the jagged edges of the broken panes chewed at the rain.

She walked to the first building and pushed the door open. The entryway was cluttered with broken eggs, the slimy mess of yolks and whites, spilling into the darkness of a small side apartment whose door was ajar. It must have been the concierge's place. Viola peered inside but saw only the murk fretted with darker shapes of the furniture. Still, there seemed to her to be some movement inside, like the tendrils of seaweed floating in the water. She decided against going in.

The light bulbs on the landings of the staircase were mostly gone. She climbed one flight of stairs and tried the door of the nearest apartment. It was locked. The building shuddered and swayed, as if rocked by an invisible current. Viola dropped her mattress onto the landing, curled up on it, and was instantly asleep.

The cold woke her. Gray light seeped into the stairwell from above. She was soaked and miserable. And hungry. It occurred to her that even with the Return of the Ancestors so close, one still had to eat, drink, and keep warm. Her thin, worn-out flesh had a mind of its own, stubbornly clinging to the minutiae of survival. Of course, Viola could do what Edna had done ... and again, the physical shrinking away from the thought of suicide was so powerful that she jumped to her feet and looked around, as if an Ancestor was standing behind her, urging her to slice her own body open. And she would not, could not, do it. Her faith was strong. Her survival instinct was stronger.

A soft, slippery noise from below made her totter toward the edge of the landing. Her body seemed to consist of sodden, mismatched parts that refused to come together. Looking down, she discovered a thick spongy tongue of grayish flesh issuing from the concierge's doorway. The tongue was fastidiously licking the remnants of broken eggs from the tiles of the foyer. Having cleaned the tiles, the tongue withdrew, and Viola dashed down the stairs and out of the building, leaving her mattress behind.

Outside she discovered a gray rainy day, no different from the innumerable gray rainy days that had preceded it. There were even some passersby around. Nobody paid attention to her bedraggled condition, and disappointed at the apparent postponement of the apocalypse, she started walking aimlessly toward the City center.

On her way, she saw some strange sights. The main thoroughfares were barricaded with burnt-out cabs or broken furniture. Most barricades seemed to be deserted but some were manned by shivering boys and girls with green ribbons tied around their wrists and foreheads like bandannas. In a small municipal garden with denuded trees, several green-beribboned youths were stomping on the ground, waving their hands in unison. In a square, a few green ribbons got hold of a well-dressed woman and were washing the makeup off her face in a puddle. She hung limply in their hands like a rag doll. In a street temple a gaggle of women, young and old, prostrated themselves on the mud-splattered floor, while at the entrance several baby carriages were parked askew with their wailing cargoes. A man was walking in the middle of the road, carrying a hefty statue of the veiled Bear that looked like it had been swiped from a public park. From another, bigger temple, pungent smoke billowed out. It seemed that somebody had lit the entire stock of incense at once.

Somebody bumped into Viola. The man's forehead was badly gashed, and his clothes smelled of wet ashes, but she recognized him. It was Thomas Hawk, the erstwhile leader of their secret cell.

"Viola?" he said. "Where is your sister?"

"My sister is dead," she said, and was perked by the realization of her superiority over him. He was bedraggled, faded, badly confused. And she was centered and poised, ready for the end of the City and all its injustices. She remembered her envy of Hawk's easy polish, her resentment of his expensive clothes and impeccable manners, even her firmly squelched but self-renewing lust. But this was all in the past. The Return of the Ancestors was underway. The last would be the first.

"Carla is dead?" He rubbed his forehead, flinched when he saw blood on his fingers. "Yes, of course, that bastard ... I told him to wait. Sorry, accept my condolences."

"Where are you going?" she interrupted.

"To the Animal House. There is a meeting. Going to be. The Provisional Government ... Otter is going to make a speech."

"Otter?"

"Yes. He's on our side, you know? He's formed the Provisional Government until the Revealer comes ... To reign in her name. The Fur, Fish, and Fowl Guardians have been arrested. Or maybe they'll be."

Politics! It did not matter, not anymore. But the numbness that protected her from the world cracked, letting in the here and now. And instead of the familiar dull despair that she had tried to keep in check with prayers, fasting, and binge eating, Viola felt a surge of determination.

"Don't you have a place nearby?" she asked. "I need to change clothes. I'm cold. My apartment has been flooded."

Hawk blinked. He seemed to have trouble focusing.

"Clothes?" he mumbled.

"Fresh clothes, food," she repeated. "We are going to the Animal House. And from there we will march to the Temple. It has not been purified, has it? The false Guardians need to be expelled. We need to wait there."

"Wait?" repeated Hawk.

"What's wrong with you, man?" cried Viola. "This is what you taught us to prepare for! Now it's here! We are going to call upon the Revealer to come now! D'you think she'll come for the corrupt elitists like Otter? We're her people and she'll come for us. And until she does, we'll be the Guardians!"

CHAPTER 10. THE GATHERING

Mara rode first; this was how she wanted it, even though Alice Bobcat remonstrated with her. *"You don't know the way,"* she had said, *"let Foxy or me lead."*

"But the horse remembers the way back," Mara had replied, and Alice gave in. She did not object even when Mara insisted that Matilda the remnant ride pillion with her. The horse shied a little at this burden—domestic animals could not stand remnants—but Alice calmed it down.

It was another glorious day. The sea was soft turquoise under a veil of mist. The sky was clear, and the sun poured its gold upon the pink rock. The air smelled of sage and rosemary.

Mara, dressed in a man's overall provided by Alice, too large for her and sagging at the chest, surveyed the terrain with cold, unblinking eyes. For the last hour she had said not a word.

Alice rode second, and Fox followed, slouching in the saddle of his gray gelding. His presence should have been reassuring to Alice but was not. She knew she had only herself to rely on.

Alice tried to question Foxy discreetly before they left, but the old fool only muttered something and shook his head. His changeover must have advanced more than she suspected; there was already something shifty and vulpine about his face and he stank to high heaven. Soon enough his humanity would rot away, and a dumb creature would be left behind like the horrible puppet that rode with the City girl. Alice was honest enough to recognize that her fear and loathing stemmed largely from the fact that the creature was female.

At least, the remnant was a known quantity. But the City girl —the name Mara Raven did not suit her somehow—was something else. Just looking at that fresh young face set in a mask of implacable determination, her eyes as empty as the sea, gave Alice the shivers.

Lulled by the rhythm of riding, Alice fell into a not unpleasant self-pity. What was she doing here, surrounded by thugs, monsters, and strangers? All she had wanted was some adventure, some chance to break away from the grinding poverty of Lonelyhearts. She heard about the South Continent by chance, when she got a job in one of those new-fangled coffee places that were springing up throughout the City. It was her first lucky break: The coffee shop's owner preferred wits and reliability to a pretty face. And when she learned where coffee was coming from, when she heard that there was a small settlement out there with nothing in the way of creature comforts, not even a grocery store, she thought it was the second one. She just knew, felt it in her bones, that here was the chance of a lifetime. The owner who liked her tried to warn her off with rumors of strange diseases, but she was undaunted. Lonelyhearts was full of sickness anyway. Its shaky platforms, erected to prevent the diseases of the countryside, were nevertheless home to rickety children and ailing adults, the casualties of poverty. Alice was determined to find a way out.

And now what? True, she had made some money; not as much as she had hoped for but more than she had expected. She also had her stash of coffee, which in the City was worth ten times what she'd paid for it. She had not begun her changeover, though there were some worrying signs, but she was determined to leave before they developed into full-blown symptoms.

But what was the place she was going back to? The City, the home that she painted in such glowing colors in her imagination —the dreamed-of suburban cottage, far from the stinking confusion of Lonelyhearts; the cozy network of friends and relations; the balmy evenings on the promenade along the Bird River; the excitement of the Temple parades—all this was now tinged with horror. It was as if whatever was brooding under the sunny surface of the South Continent, the darkness that reached for you and ate away your humanity, had now touched the City itself, and it was melting, reshaping itself into an abode of beasts. Or something worse than beasts, if Mara Raven was a sample.

Alice stole a furtive glance at Mara who rode as if born to it —and yet Dog claimed that the girl just about wet herself when she saw a horse. Dog! Here was another sore point. Was Dog dead, too? Did whatever happened at his brother's mansion destroy him? Was his body lying under the golden sun that bred maggots in it? The girl claimed Dog was alive, but Alice was not willing to bet on anything she said. A stab of grief went through her. Dog was a friend. If they were in the City instead of this land that smilingly stole away your desire, she would admit, at least to herself, that she hoped he would become more than a friend. And now he was missing. Something terrible had happened in Wolf's mansion, and the girl who was, in whatever incomprehensible fashion, responsible for all this, calmly insisted on riding back to the source of all evil, the Hollow Cliffs where remnants congregated. And the worst thing was that she, Alice, could not disobey. The girl looked at you with these strange, inhuman eyes of hers and you felt as if you had been turned into a remnant already, without speech, mind, or will of your own.

They rode on for two hours until Alice screwed up her courage to address Mara.

"We need a break," she said. "Food, drink, pee. It'll take at least another hour to get to the Cliffs."

Mara nodded. They found the nearest parasol tree, dismounted, watered the horses, and set up a picnic cloth. It was a gloomy affair. Fox fidgeted and kept his eyes on the ground. Mara drank water and ate nothing. Alice had to force herself to chew and swallow a slice of bread and butter. Matilda had disappeared into the scrub and then came out again and crouched in the shade of the tree, gazing at Alice fearfully and—she thought—hungrily. Overcoming her distaste, Alice offered her bread, only to discover stains of blood and some feathers around the creature's thin-lipped mouth. She turned away with disgust.

"She has to eat," Mara said with a cold smile. "Life feeds on life."

"She's an animal!" spat Alice. "She should have been put out of her misery long ago!"

"But she's still wearing her clothes," Mara pointed out.

This silenced Alice. In fact, the remnant was properly dressed, and the clothes were in good order, all things considered.

"She still wants to be human," continued Mara. "Doesn't this desire make her one?"

"There is more to humanity than clothes!" Alice retorted.

"What, for example?"

Alice screwed up her courage and looked straight into these strange, shifting eyes, which she now knew without a doubt were more inhuman than Matilda's weaselly muzzle.

"Love, kindness, loyalty," she said. "Nothing you would know about."

She expected Mara to get angry and braced herself for an outburst, but it did not happen. Instead, Mara looked at her with pity.

"The people in the City are destroying it because they want to become animals. To merge with their totems. Here, on the South

Continent, it happens naturally. The remnants are the future, Alice. The future of humanity."

"Never!" Alice snapped, unnerved by Mara's icy tone and mirthless smile. "This is nonsense! People get sick if they stay away from the City too long. This is all there is to it! Even your husband knew it!"

"Did you talk to my husband a lot?" asked Mara.

Alice shrugged.

"He talked to just about everybody in Bear Haven. He wanted to know what we thought of the changeover. He ordered Wolf to round up as many remnants as he could find. Wolf wasn't that crazy at the time ... I mean, he hadn't started his collection yet. It was your husband who put him to it."

Mara did not seem surprised or shocked.

"Where did my husband go afterwards?" she asked.

Alice glanced at Fox in search of support, but the old fool had dozed off.

"I don't know," she muttered. "But Dog ..."

"Dog knew?"

"Yes. Your husband hired him as a guide to the Hollow Cliffs. They were gone for a week. Dog came back alone."

"Didn't you ask him?"

"Of course, I did! But there is no arguing with him when he decides to keep his mouth shut. Wolf questioned him too, but it did not go well."

The conversation petered out after that. Alice's body crawled with gooseflesh.

They mounted the horses again and rode toward the sea. They passed the almost invisible path that branched off the main track, leading, Alice knew, to Dog's cabin. She had to suppress the desire to go there and take a peek. If Dog were alive, and if he were hiding from the City girl, Alice had no desire to give him away.

Finally, they saw the Hollow Cliffs, eroded ramparts of limestone in pastel tints of yellow and pink. The sea beat in their caves like the heart of a sleeper.

"We have to leave the horses here," said Fox, breaking his self-imposed vow of silence for the first time since their departure from Bear Haven. "It's too steep for them to go down."

Mara nodded and stood by as Fox hobbled the horses and tethered them to a wind-bent gnarly tree. This accomplished, the four of them scrambled down the rocky slope toward the beach.

Mr. Seal shifted in the too-narrow seat. The train rumbled hypnotically through the flatness of the Plains, mirrored in the flatness of the gray sky. Everything seemed tired, run-down, and washed-out: stubble-covered fields, interspersed with the occasional huddle of seemingly abandoned farmhouses and studded with clumps of bare trees like an unfinished sketch of woods.

He had been persuaded that the fastest way to get to the White Harbor was by regular train but now he was beginning to regret that he had not insisted on a car. The other passengers' presence, no matter how hard he tried to shut it out, felt like the annoying buzzing of a fly. Who were they? Sailors? Tax collectors? Idle tourists? (Hardly the latter; there was no mood for sight-seeing in the City now.) There were five other men in his car and perhaps as many in the next one. The rest of the train consisted of freight cars.

Mr. Seal tried to convince himself that the next couple of days would pass quickly. But he knew better. While he was stuck in this rattling box with human trash, only to transfer later to a sailing box with another collection of accidental humans, things were happening on the South Continent. He felt it in his bones: that Mara, having discovered the extent of her Power, was making things happen.

He shifted again and muttered imprecations under his breath, earning a curious glance from the man in the opposite seat who was kitted out in a serge jacket with too many buckles, fancying himself an intrepid explorer, no doubt. Mr. Seal stared him down, and the man returned to perusing the *Voice of the City*.

How could it be that both Mara and Julian discovered the Power to use black flowers and he did not?

The question rankled so much that it felt like a physical pain in his abdomen, like a flaming ulcer. He knew without a doubt that he was an imprint of his true totem, the Seal, as Julian was of the Lion, and Mara of the Bear. So why could they do what all his experimentation with the stolen kids of Lonelyhearts failed to teach him? Was it because the balance of power among the Four was not what he believed it to be? Or because he, Jeremy, was somehow inferior, flawed, imperfect? Just as he had been in his family, the runt of litter, easily dispensed with by his parents who kept the other four brothers but dedicated him to the Temple? Just as he had been in the Temple when the grafts to make him into a Guardian failed?

Mr. Seal ground his teeth.

"Did you say something?" the man in the opposite seat inquired.

"No!" Mr. Seal barked, returning to the drenched landscape outside. Even that far from the City the rain continued, but it was lighter, more of a drizzle, really, and the weather forecast said that it was sunny on the coast. Mr. Seal was not looking forward to it. The sun always burnt his sensitive skin.

The sliding doors at the end of the car banged open and a man walked through. Mr. Seal cast a baleful glance upon him. What was the fool doing here? The two passenger cars were marked as first and second class, and second-class passengers were not supposed to invade the precincts of their social betters.

The man hurried to the other end of the car and exited into the vestibule. Was he looking for the washroom? Mr. Seal decided to complain to the conductor.

The doors slid open again, and the man reappeared. He walked to the middle of the car and stopped. The train swayed and the man caught the back of a seat to balance himself. He was a boy, a gangly teenager with blooming zits. Nobody paid any attention.

Something was wrong! Mr. Seal did not like the look on the boy's face. He had seen this look before when he spied on the Army of the Revealer. He rose from his seat.

"The Ancestors are coming!" the boy cried. "Welcome the Ancestors!"

Several passengers jumped up but before they could reach him, the boy whipped out a homely-looking knife, probably stolen from his mom's kitchen, and plunged it into the side of his own neck. Bright arterial blood spurted out, pattering on the newspaper spread in the lap of the nearest passenger who grabbed it with both hands like a shield.

Time slowed as Mr. Seal looked in the slack-jawed face of his death.

Over the screams of the passengers the pattering of blood intensified until there was an uninterrupted rush, the waterfall of blood that doused the man with the newspaper who scrambled away over the back of his seat, emitting high-pitched squeals like a wounded rabbit. The others were trying to get out of the car, as the second-class passengers, attracted by the commotion, crowded at the doors. The tight knot of people jostled and cursed; somebody crashed into the well of the connecting platform.

The boy crumpled, his body deflating like a pricked balloon. But the stream of blood intensified. A crimson river that issued from this insignificant source lapped at the seats, floated the luggage, swallowed the feet of the passengers who climbed on the seats to escape it. A heavy smell of the abattoir blew along the car.

The car was beginning to disintegrate, the blood eating holes in the floor, exposing the busy metal parts working underneath like the mandibles of a giant insect. The blood dripped onto the tracks, and there was a tang of electricity and the smell of burnt flesh.

A velvety black orchid bloomed from the collapsing remains, more beautiful than the boy had ever been in his short and pitiful life. Mr. Seal reached out for it, but the flower swayed away from him, cringing like a living being.

The flower grew at a precipitous rate, its cup gaping like a hungry mouth. It towered over Mr. Seal who was irresistibly drawn to it. No, he was drawn *into* it.

The flower was now a hole in reality, a vortex punching through the disintegrating car filled with panicking passengers. It was as if the world was merely a painting on a cheap curtain, and the curtain was being torn asunder. Through the hole Mr. Seal saw what lay on the other side: the roiling sea. The water was not blue or gray but of a somber scarlet color.

He felt dragged into the sea and though at the last moment he tried to backpedal, to cling to the dissolving dream that had been his life and his identity, he could not. He was gulped by the maw of the black flower that had now expanded to fill the car.

He was thrashing in the viscous liquid of the sea with black hairy tendrils floating through it. He tried to draw a breath, but the liquid rushed into his lungs, choking him. It embraced him with its acid bite, dissolving his skin, eating away his eyes, burning into his liquefying flesh.

And with an inaudible scream, Mr. Seal exploded.

Julian spat blood into the dust threaded with tiny twigs and desiccated needles. There was an ant busily scampering among them, and the blob of bloody mucus landed upon it like a flood. The ant made desperate swimming motions but eventually succumbed and went down.

He was lying on his side, his cheek tickled by racing shadows. He was out in the open air and instead of being cold and soaked, he was hot.

This made no sense. He attempted to stand and succeeded on the third try.

Blue and green swam in his eyes. Another ant scurried on the back of his hand until Julian shook it off. The colors finally stabilized and resolved into a landscape so garish that Julian was convinced for a moment it was a fever dream. His eyes, used to the somber autumnal hues of First City, could barely cope with the onslaught of brightness. The sky was vibrating with intense azure; the tree leaves gleamed like emeralds; and the hills above him glittered with gold and pink like a confection. The air smelled of Elvira's flowery perfume.

He tried to make out the unfamiliar configuration of this noncity space. He was in a narrow ravine choked with vegetation. There was a stream hidden by its tangle; he could hear water purling.

Julian stood there. There was a smooth feeling in his head, as if he could push his mind and it would roll on effortlessly, like a skater. He contemplated giving this push, seeing his mind disappear into a bright, frictionless gulf.

Something interfered: an unpleasant salty taste. He brought his hand up to his face.

His lips were swollen and tender, his chin caked with dry blood. He coughed and spat out a tooth.

And this white nugget drew his mind back from its free fall like an anchor, bringing it down with a thump onto the hard bedrock of memory.

"Ancestors!" Julian cried, and hated himself for it.

He staggered to his feet and inspected himself. His clothes were torn and stained. His neck was tender, his joints hurt, his rib cage felt bruised, but nothing seemed broken.

He looked around again, taking in his surroundings. Now the

raw immediacy of noncomprehension was muted by knowledge. He could name the place.

He was in the South Continent.

A soft chuckle escaped him and frightened him into renewed silence by its sly quality. Now that he had his mind firmly planted within the here and now, madness appeared as a frightening abyss rather than a glide into freedom.

He had used a black flower to enter the dream-sea. And then he had exited hundreds of miles away, in the sunny wilderness of the South. Just as Mara must have done. He had a Power, as she did. Seal had been right, after all. His totem, rejected so firmly when he had taken Elvira's name, had come through for him. Julian Lion. Jeremy Seal. Mara ... No! He could not bring himself to name her totem.

But there was a difference. Julian tried to remember his sojourn in the dream-sea but while his brain swarmed with hallucinatory images, they eluded his grasp like fish in an aquarium. Every time he tried to focus on one, it fell apart. It must have taken Mara years to train herself to remember clearly. But he knew that he had traversed the gray expanse where baby corpses were stuffed into suitcases and bodies smoldered in ditches. He could not remember anything else.

Oh ... no, wait! There was a mass on the horizon, towering into the sunless sky, spires and rooftops ...

He had seen it from afar. The City Mara had told him about. The nameless City submerged in the dream-sea.

Julian took a deep breath. He wanted to be here, after all, and whatever Power the fight with the Guardian had awakened in him, he was going to use it. He had to find Mara. He had to figure out where the fourth imprint was. Seal had not named him, but Julian had a pretty good idea of the man's identity. They revolved around Mara. The Bear, the veiled queen of the Slaughtered Ones. Why? He did not know but suspected that the answer lay in the occluded depth of his own memory. Or maybe it hid in that nameless City in the dream-sea.

Or maybe they were one and the same.

He decided to follow the course of the ravine. He was too weak to try to climb its steep slopes. Here at least he had shade and water, while the hills were scorched by the sun. He was sure he would eventually come across a human presence. The South Continent was huge and there was only one tiny settlement surrounded by coffee plantations. He could be anywhere. But he had to rely on his Power. It would lead him to where he was meant to be.

To Mara.

"The Bear is filled with negativity so profound and so relentless that nothing can stand in her way. She cannot love. She cannot even hate. She takes because everything has been taken from her. She kills because she was killed. She has the power to shape worlds, but she uses it to smash them to pieces."

"This is not Mara!"

"None of us is our totem, Mr. Lion. But none of us can escape the story that has made us what we are. Mara is the Bear's imprint; the only one to be born in the City for centuries, if not forever. Her presence weakens the barrier, the gate, that protects the City from the rest of the dream-sea. She is the Revealer because she reveals the truth: We are phantoms, dreams, delusions; echoes of lost stories."

This is what Seal had told him, and as much as Julian loathed the man and his totem, he knew in his bones that it was the truth.

But of course, there was another side to it.

None of us is our totem.

Julian could draw upon his totem's Power. Perhaps in time he could access his memories. But he was not him.

He was Julian Sparrow, husband of the late Elvira Sparrow, a merchant and a citizen. A human.

First City was the only place in the world where human

beings could live. It was built with human hands and human ingenuity. It was humanity's last stronghold.

It was not perfect; Julian knew it better than most. It had poverty and wealth. It had violence and inequality. It had fanaticism that was destroying it from within.

But it was a human City.

He would find Mara. He would talk to her. He would convince her to join him in defending First City against their totems.

And if he could not? If she was as consumed by her totem as Jeremy Seal was by his?

Then he would kill her.

He went down to the stream to refresh his parched mouth.

I'm going to kill all four of them. I'm going to make sure that the Slaughtered Ones are indeed slaughtered. They have harried us for millennia, and now they are about to invade our last refuge. Our City. I'm going to kill the Four and then the fools, and the fanatics, and the madmen who find their humanity too hard to bear will be defeated. And the City will stand and will endure.

As Julian set out down the ravine, it occurred to him that this megalomaniac thinking was a symptom of his own insanity.

But so what? He had killed the Guardian and plucked the black corpse-glower from his body, treating the man as a tool, reducing his dreams and aspirations to bits and pieces of mangled flesh. This was an event of such colossal meaninglessness that the only way to redeem it in the human universe was by seeing it as an act of war. And he understood war. He was ready to fight.

CHAPTER 11. REUNIONS

By the time Mara, Alice, Fox, and Matilda negotiated the sandy beach and approached the caves, the sun was dipping below the horizon. Mara paused, the peach and gold of the sunset illuminating her suddenly gaunt face. Alice shuddered and looked away: It was as if she could simultaneously see Mara's beauty and the rotten corpse that would one day become superimposed upon each other.

They lit their lanterns, but when they walked into the cave, it was not totally dark. Sunlight dribbled through the openings in the roof, sliding off the slick limestone-molded walls. As they went down toward the sea inlet, it grew lighter, the water glowing and its radiance diffusing through the moisture-laden air. Alice had never been here before. Everybody knew that remnants gathered here. But her fear of these former humans was abating. She glanced at Matilda who followed, timidly grasping Fox's arm as if for protection. The creature, ugly as it was, was harmless; why would others of its ilk be any different?

A tittering noise came from a side tunnel.

Alice froze. Bats were beginning to glide through the hole above her, but these were silent.

The sound came closer, accompanied by shuffling. Something crawled out of the tunnel.

"Ancestors!" whispered Alice.

The creature was a giant rat, gaunt and sickly but still retaining enough human features to be recognized as a remnant. The pink, naked paws did not simply resemble human palms but *were* human palms; the eyes were inflamed and hungry, but their bloodshot whites and murky irises once belonged to a man; and the overbite of yellow teeth looked as if it had ruined more than one blind date in the past. But the rib-protruding body, creeping close to the ground and dragging a naked tail, was that of a rodent.

Alice hesitated, bewildered by a clash of recognition, one part of her screaming, *It's a beast!* while another, *It's human!* The hesitation cost them dearly.

Fox carried the shotgun, but he backed off, blinking foolishly, and the ratman attacked, aiming for his throat. Fox managed to deflect it, but the ratman sank its teeth into his arm, gnawing at it. Matilda threw herself at the creature. She clawed at its eyes, battered its head with her paws. The creature snapped at her, letting go of Fox who staggered backward. Alice snatched up his shotgun but was afraid to shoot into the shadowy scramble of flailing limbs. There was a thin scream and Matilda's body flew off the ratman and hit the wall. She lay there like a crumpled doll, blood spreading in a shiny circle around her. Her throat was torn out. Mara rushed to her and cradled her body.

Alice fired.

The bullet took the ratman in the face. Brain and gore splattered the cave walls. A lantern left unattended on the floor rocked, sending a flurry of panicky shadows into the darkness, but did not go out. The retort of the gun echoed in the tunnels, over the endless monotony of the sea.

Smaller shadows, the size of Alice's pinky, raced over the floor toward her. One of them bit into her foot through the sturdy leather of her walking shoes. She tore the creature away, felt it squirming in her hand. It was an insect with a bumpy carapace and multiple legs.

It had a human face, a scaled-down version of the ratman's, with unblinking, idiotic eyes and a tiny overbite.

Alice screamed and flung the creature away. More of its fellows milled on the floor, falling out of the dead ratman's smelly fur.

And now other remnants started appearing out of the tunnels, in all sizes, from a tiny birdlike man with his lips grown into a sharp, horny beak to a fat, yellow-eyed, furry woman. Mr. Finch, Mrs. Raccoon, and others, indentured plantation slaves, or hired goons, or adventurous prostitutes, all stripped to their primal animal essence but retaining enough human features to carry a faint imprint of the faraway City. John Tick, Stan Crow, Elsa Coyote, Isaac Fly. They swarmed toward Alice, Fox, and Mara.

Fox hesitated, glanced at the two women, and then dropped to all fours and crawled toward the approaching tide of remnants, desperate to shed the remains of his humanity, to be accepted into the animal commonwealth. Stan Crow, an emaciated creature with a skeleton head and scruffy black feathers, poked him with his beak. Elsa Coyote yapped and nipped at his flank. Their ranks parted and closed behind him.

Alice picked up the lantern, held it aloft. Light and the smell of gunpowder and sweat, human odors, held the creatures in check. They stopped: an uneasy crowd of shifting, grotesque forms. Above, in the dark reaches of the cave, Elisha Bat screamed inaudibly, unfolding his leathery wings and grasping at the stalactites with his clawed fingers. In the blackness of the sea, from which all light had leached away, Maria Walrus flapped her vestigial arms.

"Go away!" Alice commanded. "How dare you! You bring shame upon the City!"

Luminous eyes stared at her as if they indeed understood and were ashamed, for even the criminals among them had been aware of the human law. But now they were animals innocent of the law, or so they were willing themselves to be. They started advancing again.

"Stop!" said a booming voice, distorted by the cave echo. "Beat it, all of you! Shoo!"

The shotgun in Alice's hands drooped; she jerked it up, still unable to believe what she was hearing, but relief was already flooding her body.

"Dog?" she whispered.

He strolled through the massed remnants, kicking them aside with the ease of a farmer making his way through a flock of sheep. They scuttled away, disappearing in the darkness of the side tunnels. Fox went with them.

He looked even gaunter than before, his ridiculous cap askew on his bald head, the thin hatchet-like face split by a crooked smile. But it was Dog, unquestionably himself, unquestionably human.

"Dog!" Alice rushed toward him. "You are alive!"

"No thanks to her!" Dog jerked his head toward Mara. "Do you know what she is?"

"Do you know what you are, Mr. Dog?" Mara responded, and the chill in her voice sent shivers down Alice's spine. Instead of answering, Dog turned to Alice.

"When Wolf's boys attacked us," he said, "I thought I would divert them, let her escape. A girl like her versus an old fool like me, no contest. But I needn't have bothered. She called up ... something. It was as if she opened herself like a dress, and something came through. I saw Guardians, I saw statues in the Temple. I live with remnants. But that thing ... That was ... I could not stay. I could not look. I ran away. I hoped she would be killed by the thing inside her but no such luck. Well, we can remedy this. She cannot be allowed to live!"

Alice realized that Dog had a shotgun as well, and that it was rising slowly, pointing at Mara. Almost without volition, her own shotgun jerked up.

"Drop it, old friend!" she said. "You can't shoot her. She's a chit of a girl!"

"She is not! She is one of the Slaughtered Ones. Right, Mrs. Raven?"

Mara's eyes shifted from Alice to Dog and back again, huge in her paper-white face. The mix of emotions in them was as shifting as their color—fear, defiance, and something else that Alice had no name for: a profound, soul-shattering regret.

"I am both," she said. "As are you, Alice. As are you, Mr. Dog. We are human masks over our totems' animal faces."

Dog spat on the ground.

"I am a man," he said. "I'll die a man. Not like my brother."

"I am trying to do the right thing," Mara went on, her voice so low that Alice had trouble making it out over the susurrus of the sea. "Yes, I let her out. She was locked in a cage in Second City, and I let her out. She has got her hooks inside of me now, but I am not her. I am Mara, daughter of Louisa who I killed, student of Jeremy who betrayed me, wife of Ronald who left me. I could let her take me over. It would be so easy. But I can't. I won't. She is nothing but anger and revenge. She hates the City. And the City is the only thing that is left to me. I'll defend it— against myself."

"What are you talking about?" Alice cried. "Dog, what's going on? Are you saying that her totem is ..."

"Yes," Mara said. "My real totem is the one that nobody dares to claim for themselves. And I am going to confront her."

"How? The Slaughtered Ones are in the Abode of the Ancestors, and since the Rebellion, we cannot enter there."

"Are you so blind?" Mara said. "Look around! Look at the remnants. Look at yourself. This world is separated from the Abode by the thinnest of membranes, and it has already been punctured so many times that it barely holds. And it does not hold here, in the Hollow Cliffs. Why do you think remnants congregate in these caves? The sea that is lapping at them is the dream-sea. The Hollow Cliffs are an interface between the dream-sea and the tiny world of men."

"She is right," Dog said. "I figured it out. This is why the remnants are gathering here in the sea caves. They are trying to get back to where they belong. Whatever you call that place, the Abode of the Ancestors or something else."

"I call it the dream-sea," Mara continued. "Our world is like a foam bubble floating on the sea of dreams. And at the center of the bubble is First City. It is the only human stronghold carved out from the dream-sea, and the further we are from it, the less human we become."

"Even if it's true," Alice said, "what has it got to do with us?"

Instead of answering her, Mara turned to Dog again.

"My husband was here," she said. "Did you kill him?"

Dog smirked.

"I would not blame you if you did," Mara continued. "I know what he was. But I need to know the truth."

"Why do you think he was here?"

Mara tugged a thong out of her shirt collar. Threaded on it was a golden ring, flashing ruby highlights.

"It's his wedding band. I found it in the cave on the first evening I came here. You were looking for it, weren't you, Dog? You lost it. Ronald would have never parted with his wedding ring. You'd taken it from his dead body. Where is it?"

Alice expected anything—remorse, denial, or even a shot. Her hands tightened on her shotgun. But Dog only shrugged.

"I have no idea where your husband is, ma'am," he said. "But I did not kill him. Why would I? He hired me to do a job, which I did to the best of my ability. He paid me, fair and square, and left that ring in my safekeeping when he went for a swim in one of those sea caves. You are right that this place is the border. And though it is not in any Temple teaching that I know of, the Abode is the sea too, or maybe *a* sea. And your husband went fishing in it."

As the sun slid below the rim of the ravine, Julian took off his shoes and sat with his sweaty, chafed feet in the cool water of the stream, twirling his toes and observing with wonder the rapid darting of elegant, long-bodied insects. He did not know what they were, and their complicated dance appeared to him deeply soothing in its indifference to him.

He was hungry. As he started walking again, he saw that the land was flattening out, the slopes falling away, and soon he found himself on a sort of plateau. There were some squat, short trees with deeply fissured bark and oval green fruit that looked familiar. Olives! They were the latest rage in the City, served in exclusive restaurants. Julian had spent a considerable amount of money on an olive-tasting with Elvira. He picked up an olive, bit into it, and spat it out. The fruit was hard, bitter, and oily. He realized that in its natural state, it was inedible and had to be prepared in some way to become part of civilized living. Somehow this realization seemed significant to him.

He limped on through the landscape of rolling hills dotted with parasol-shaped trees and shrubs. The evening air was balmy, perfumed with the mingled scents of wild sage, mint, and rosemary. And ahead, beyond a low ridge, lay his goal. He had heard the rhythmic beat some time ago, and at first, it seemed to him like the breathing of some giant sleeping beast. He climbed the ridge, and the beast was there, heaving, golden-scaled, and so big as to make everything else seem blissfully insignificant.

Julian went down to the beach and dipped his hands in the dancing waves. His scratches burned. A silvery path led to the flaming ball of the sun suspended in the pink sky.

Julian splashed some water onto his sweaty face and winced at its bitter taste. The sun was reddening like a wound, bleeding spectacular colors across the sea and the sky. Julian could not remember when he had last seen the sunset in the City.

A snorting sound came from above. He looked up.

On the ridge, several silhouettes milled around.

They were horses. Julian was old enough to remember the time when they had been the chief mode of transportation in the City. He never liked the big, clumsy animals and was only too happy to exchange his father's carriage for his own boxy, gleaming car.

He approached them carefully. There were three of them and they were tethered to the tree. There was a backpack hanging from its branches. One of the horses whinnied and he felt its warm, reeking breath on his cheek.

So where were the riders?

He looked around and suddenly saw what he had been missing: a magnificent pile of yellow-pink rock, fretted with dark openings like an unfinished palace that was disintegrating into ruins without ever having been a complete structure. Large birds, black against the luminous sky, circled over it.

There were several lines of footprints in the sand leading toward it. Julian was no hunter, so he could not figure out how many people had walked there but he decided to follow. His goal was to find Mara, and he could not do it without getting some information. It would be good to see a human face in this emptiness.

His hunger was getting worse. He rooted in the backpack and discovered some flat bread, which he inhaled in several bites, promising himself to pay the owner back. If of course, his money was of any use so far from First City.

He swung the backpack over his shoulder and headed toward the cliffs. The horses neighed and strained their tethers, trying to follow.

They walked toward the sea cave where Dog said he had left Ronald Raven to take his midnight swim in the dream-sea. Alice objected at first. She wanted them to go back to Dog's place, rest, and recuperate. But Dog pointed out that struggling back through the dark tunnels infested with remnants would be as dangerous. They had water and some food and could camp out on the underground shore.

"There is light down there," he said.

Pumped with adrenaline, Alice followed Mara. She did not let go of her shotgun, though she was not sure what use, if any, it would be in the Abode of the Ancestors.

She was to enter the Abode? She could not wrap her head around it. So she concentrated on the here and now: the slick flowstone where the tunnel angled down; the scurry of shadows on the walls from the bobbing lantern Mara carried; and Dog's voice.

"Mr. Raven wanted to know everything about the remnants. How many of them were there, how long they survived after the changeover, what they ate, where they went ... He pestered Theo—Wolf, I mean—but at the time he could not care less about the remnants. He had his grand projects, Theo did, and he was trying to talk the company owner into bringing in more people, enlarging the settlement, enlisting women and families ... They had a falling-out, I think, maybe Theo got beat up or something ... Your husband is a strong man, Mrs. Raven."

"Call me Mara, please."

"So, he started questioning everybody in Bear Haven, Fox, me ... He even talked to you, Aly, didn't he?"

"He did," said Alice. "I had nothing to tell him."

"Of course, we don't talk about remnants among ourselves. Bad luck, or so they say. Some endure longer, some begin to change after a couple of years ... Make your money and run away, that's the motto. Isn't it, Aly, old girl?"

"Speak for yourself," Alice muttered.

"I didn't think about the changeover much," Dog went on, navigating a sharp turn. "What's the use? But your husband, Mara, he said something that stuck with me. He said: 'Remnants are the totems.' And he was right. Guardians go under the knife to look like their totems, so they can have their Powers. I had a buddy named Jamie Owl when I was little. He became a Guardian and I remember seeing him afterwards in a procession, those big yellow eyes and gray feathers ... Anyway, they have to go under the knife, but here it happens naturally. This is what remnants are. Natural Guardians. That's it."

"And you wanted to be a Guardian," Mara said. "So why are you resisting the change?"

Dog scoffed.

"Did you see the crowd back there?" he asked. "That's your answer."

"You want to be human," Mara whispered. "I do, too. Even poor Matilda clung to her humanity. Not like ..."

"Like whom?" Alice asked.

"What happened to Ronald, Mr. Dog?"

"Just Dog. He suggested it to me, you know? Your husband. He saw dogs running around and told me to adopt them as my totem. I was plain old Frannie Wolf until then. He said it would stop the changeover or slow it down. He needed me to hunt remnants for him."

"Did you kill them?"

"Some. Some he wanted alive. To see if they retained language, this sort of thing. He lived up at the manse with Theo, and after a while Theo came around and got interested too. So, they started the collection. Theo was beginning to change himself and some of them get crazy before it happens ... Not that he wasn't crazy to begin with ..."

The tunnel's ceiling dipped so much that Alice's hair got snagged on stalactites jutting from above. Dog had to hunch down, and Mara tucked her head onto her chest. It occurred to Alice that it would be easier to navigate if they crawled on all fours like infants. Of course, that was a ridiculous idea. Going on all fours was for remnants, not humans.

Fortunately, after a couple of meters the ceiling rose again, and the tunnel expanded. Shiny flowstone on the walls magnified the light of their lanterns, breaking it into slivers of diamonds. A fresh draft caressed Alice's face, bringing with it a strange medley of odors: salt, and night flowers, and rust.

Dog stopped, lifting his hand. Alice heard it, too: the echo of footsteps reverberating in the hollows of the cliffs. Somebody was following them.

Julian stood in a huge, dim chamber with a flock of birds wheeling and flapping above his head. There was a rhythmic boom of waves somewhere to his left and the last glow of the sun dappled the damp limestone walls. He could see several openings in the cavern's walls leading deeper into the cliffs. But there was no trace of the riders of the horses left on the headland. Had they even gone here? And how was he to follow with no light? He hesitated, all but prepared to retrace his steps and go back when a faint scream came from one of the tunnels, followed by a series of bumps.

Julian scrambled through the opening of the tunnel, hitting his head on the dripping stalactites. He navigated the narrow stone gullet, drops of water landing on his face.

He burst into another cave that was magically illuminated with an emerald glow reflected from the pounding waves of the sea that flowed into it. It was empty, or so he thought, until he saw two crumpled objects by the wall. He approached slowly, his nostrils twitching with the odor of fresh blood. And then he stood, gazing down at them in amazement.

They were Guardians; two Guardians recently—very recently—dead, one, a female with her neck broken, her head lolling at an unnatural angle, and the second, a male, with his brain blown out. But what were Guardians doing here? He had never heard of any being sent to the South Continent.

He knelt and examined them more closely. The blood and the wounds did not bother him. He was unaffected by such sights. It was only in his dreams that the sight of dead children filled him with enormous and impotent pity.

He realized that those must have been high-ranking Guardians because their alterations were so extensive. The male's face was obliterated but it was obvious that he had been a quadruped in life. Julian had never seen anybody so thoroughly modified. The woman's face was a slack animal muzzle.

Julian was getting to his feet when something heavy careened into him, throwing him against the wall. Claws raked his neck and got stuck in his shirt. Needle-sharp teeth pierced his forearm.

He managed to dislodge his assailant and the two of them rolled on the floor in a frenzy of flailing limbs. They collided with one of the dead Guardians and the body slowed their roll, allowing Julian to utilize his heavier weight to get a purchase on the creature's throat and pin it down to the ground.

It was yet another Guardian, a smaller one, naked as a baby, his back flattened into a hard oval shield, his face lipless, noseless, and goggle-eyed, his skinny hands clawed. There were four of them, an additional pair of limbs having been grafted below his natural armpits.

"Ancestors!" muttered Julian. The creature was small; had they converted a child? There were reputedly insect Guardians but until now, Julian had never seen one.

"What the fuck are you doing here?" he demanded. "Who sent you? Who killed those two?"

The Guardian continued his senseless grasping and twitching, as mechanical as the burrowing of a tick. Julian shook him to make his point; the creature did not react.

"Who sent you?" he bellowed. "Where are the rest of you?"

There was no reaction, and looking into the protruding eyes surrounded by a rim of smaller, glittering eyelets Julian was suddenly struck by the conviction that the Guardian did not understand the question. Not that he did not want to answer; he did not know that he was being asked.

"Who are you?"

No answer: only the terrible automatic clenching and unclenching of the tiny hands. The Guardian did not understand human language. Whatever had been done to him had not only changed his form into a semblance of an insect; it had also reduced his mind to that of a tick.

Julian released the creature and it scuttled away into the darkness.

He stood in the cave, shivering. The Guardians' minds were not tampered with; the Temple's propaganda claimed, to the contrary, that reshaping them in the image of the Ancestors gave them special Powers without taking away any of the human accomplishments of speech and reason. If this creature was a Guardian, it was of a kind Julian was unfamiliar with.

He looked around. There were several tunnels leading away from the cave. He did not know which to choose.

The light was dying, but Julian saw a glimmer in the tunnel before him. He squinted; the glimmer disappeared. But there was something wrapped around a stalactite at the entrance.

He unwound it: a strand of ash-blond hair.

Julian stared at it for a second and then dove into the tunnel.

~

Whoever was following them was making a lot of noise, bumping into the walls and dislodging clattering pieces of rock. Alice did not think it was a remnant; they seemed to navigate the caves much better. Just in case, she raised her shotgun, and so did Dog. Mara seemed oblivious, impatiently tapping her foot on the rocky floor, eager to get going.

The body that emerged into the uncertain light of their lanterns was big enough for Alice's finger to tighten on the trigger. But two things happened at once: The man—now she could see it was a man, not a remnant—raised his hands and Mara cried, "Julian!"

The man lowered his hands and took a step forward, but Dog made a growling sound and waved him back. Alice could see him better now. He was a handsome fellow, closer to her age than to Mara's, trim and broad-shouldered. And despite his dirty clothes, Alice instantly knew he was one of Them: somebody rich and powerful. A merchant, a politician, or a Temple bureaucrat. One of the lords and masters. No surprise that people in the City were calling upon the Ancestors to come back and cut them down to size!

But would you rather have a human master or an inhuman one?

"Julian!" Mara repeated, shaken. "How did you get here?"

"The same way you did."

"The corpse-flower? But how ... You are not ..."

"Yes, I am. An imprint, like you. A shadow of my totem. One of the Slaughtered Ones."

CHAPTER 12. VIOLA'S ARMY

Almost dragging Hawk by the hand, Viola Marmot marched toward the Animal House. They had been to his apartment where the naked body of a young man, his face purplish and swollen, drooped over the side of the unmade bed. Viola decided not to inquire. She forced Hawk to wash up and change clothes and raided his wardrobe for something suitable for herself. She was surprised to find a whole section of frilly dresses but eventually settled for pants and a man's shirt that hung loosely on her wasted body.

Rain-whipped, the streets of First City were deserted but not empty. Behind each window people were watching the streets in hope and fear, and the cold, wet air was thick with their stares. They had to negotiate several barricades manned by green-beribboned boys and girls armed with constabulary-issue handguns and hunting rifles, their faces shining with a light she recognized. They might have been stopped if Hawk, shocked into sanity by the sight of the guns, had not produced a card with the words *Free Pass* printed against a smudged image of the Fur, Fish, and Fowl trio and signed by the "Provisional Government." Looking closely, Viola realized that there were four figures, not three, on the card: a murky silhouette was added to change the Temple sigil into an impromptu image of the Slaughtered Ones.

The streets were filling up as trickles of people—youth with green ribbons, working men in dirty overalls, women with and without babies, families keeping together in apprehensive clusters —flowed in the same direction, toward the Animal House.

Viola heard a dry patter like hail and realized it was gunfire. It happened again. The crowds were mostly silent but some of the green ribbons sang discordantly, old Temple hymns or the latest pop tunes. There were fires being lit under the eaves of smaller houses and in doorways; their sultry light was refracted by raindrops that hissed and evaporated when they touched the flames. Somebody was screaming in an alley.

The streetlights were coming on, but the houses remained dark as more and more people poured out to join the march. For the first time she saw uniforms. A constable threw away his gun and fell down on his knees, sobbing. A knot of people gathered around him; he was lifted to his feet and drawn into the current of bodies. Something churned ahead as if some wreck was pushed out by a whirlpool and indeed, a heavy shape floated above the moving heads, jutting into the velvety sky. It was a large effigy of the Lion dragged from some temple and hoisted on the people's shoulders. Somebody had tried to crown it with a clumsy wreath, but it slipped off and was trampled by marching feet.

The silence of the crowd was unnerving, and Viola was relieved when a chant born somewhere in the moving mass quickly spread onward in concentric circles, and a surf of human voices beat against her with one irresistible demand: "We want Ancestors now!" Viola joined in. Hawk did not.

They came to the Animal House. The square was black with people and red with firelight. Makeshift torches were lit as people surged toward the entrance where a chain of armed constables was holding them back. Viola was buffeted and pushed around by the throng.

"We have to get inside," she told Hawk.

He nodded. On his own he probably would have slunk away, but in the muddle that his world had become he clung to Viola because he could obey her. He led her around the square on the margins of the crowd and slipped into the doorway of an inconspicuous brick structure.

Inside was a long corridor illuminated by glaring electric lights and lined with glass-fronted doors. Hawk led her through. Again, she heard gunshots outside and a mighty roar like the swell of a river in flood.

"Fools!" Hawk muttered.

"They're firing on people!" Viola cried. "Wait till the Revealer comes; she'll avenge innocent blood!"

Hawk pushed one of the doors, indistinguishable from the rest. Inside was a maze of cubicles; drifts of papers spilling off the desks. He strode through. Viola followed but not before swiping some files off the table, delighting in the impotence of the paperwork that used to mean power.

There was another door at the back of the room, but it was locked. Hawk stared at it stupidly. Viola pushed him aside, lifted a chair, and smashed it into the plywood. She ordered Hawk to help her, and together, they forced it open.

She was about to push through when an enormous wave of sound reached them from the outside, the exhalation of a giant, as the hydra of the crowd gave voice to its fear through its innumerable mouths. And on top of that, another sound: the crash of stone above their heads.

～

The draft was blowing stronger, and the medley of scents was more pungent. Alice wrinkled her nose. She knew the sweetish stink intertwined with the brine and jasmine. Carrion bloom.

The light coming from beyond the bend in the tunnel was

enough for Dog to turn down his lantern. It was strange: a somber red glow like the light of the sunset filtered through stormy clouds. But the sun must have set a long time ago.

"Is it far?" she asked Dog.

"Almost there."

Alice looked back where Mara and Julian walked together, her hand in his.

They rounded the sharp bend, and Alice drew in her breath.

The cave was enormous, its domed ceiling glowing with sullen scarlet light. It merged with the red sunless sky, the seam line between them invisible. The cave was open to the sea—but not the same sea that they had left behind.

The scarlet water was viscous and jellylike, languidly licking the pebbly beach. It was shot through with dark hairy tendrils, and it glowed like the sky dimming and brightening rhythmically like the beat of a human heart. The surface of the bloody sea extended as far as Alice could see, merging into the curtain of carmine vapors that intermittently veiled some rocky shapes in the distance. The stink of rot was stronger but so was the smell of night jasmine and white flowers.

"The dream-sea!" Mara exclaimed.

Something pattered behind their backs. Alice whirled around.

A remnant came out of the tunnel and padded toward the sea. It walked on all fours; its awkwardly hunched back was studded with stubbly quills. Its bald head glistened in the feverish glow. Without paying them any attention, it plunged into the sea and swam away. Alice remembered Joe Porcupine, who had bought some fishing tackle from her about a year ago—an older, quieter man, an ex-constable who had succumbed to the lure of adventure.

"They are going home," Mara whispered.

Not all of them. Alice saw several bodies in various stages of decay against the cave wall. Some of them were hardly more than skeletons, and with those, human features were still discernible: a bulging cranium, a narrow pelvic girdle. Others were anonymous carrion.

She turned to Mara.

"Here we are!" she yelled, her patience at the end of its tether. "What the fuck are we doing now?"

Mara never had the chance to answer.

~

Viola Marmot squeezed Hawk's hand as the two of them ducked. The electric lights flickered and went out. The building shook and they were peppered by the plaster falling from the ceiling.

"What?" Hawk gasped.

It was as if thunder was walking on the roof above them.

Viola dragged Hawk through the door. Choking on dust, bombarded with flying splinters, they staggered into another empty corridor, its floor littered with dirty paper and broken glass. Waves of noise washed over them, spilling through the broken skylights together with the rainy light. The crowd was screaming outside.

"Earthquake!" Hawk whimpered.

"Don't be daft!" Viola hissed. "It's coming from above! Help me up, I want to get a peek!"

Hawk was shaking but Viola pushed him to the wall and tried to use his yielding body as a ladder to get to a skylight. But before this could be accomplished, another splintering roar threw her to the floor. At the end of the corridor the ceiling caved in and something big, dark, and sinuous emerged from the hole, a thick, restless tentacle that lashed back and forth before withdrawing. The air filled with an acrid animal stench.

"Run!" she screamed and bolted forward where the corridor ended in another door, badly warped, and hanging off the hinges. The building shook and boomed. Glancing back, she saw Hawk's inert body caught in the coils of the dark thing as it was lifted and thrown with a wet smack against the wall.

She emerged into a gloomy foyer, skidded upon the marble floor, and went flying, eventually colliding with a deserted reception desk. Winded by the fall, Viola rolled onto her back and lifted her eyes to the flapping thing that screamed and cawed as it perched precariously on the unlit chandelier.

It was a Crow, an ordinary scavenger she had seen many times in the rubbish dumps of the City. But this one was the size of an eagle. It was so big that its wings brushed the walls of the foyer.

The Crow released a stream of evil-smelling excrement. Viola scrambled aside. The Crow cocked its head, staring at her with a round, glassy eye. The chandelier shook off a drizzle of crystals.

The double door that led outside groaned and suddenly gave way, torn off its hinges and slamming flat into the marble floor, as a torrent of people poured through the opening. In the gray light Viola could barely make out their faces, as smudged and dirty as their clothes. A wave of shouting washed over her.

The Crow lifted off its perch and flew at the crowd, heavy and ungainly, a blacker shadow in the chaos. People screamed and tried to get away but there was nowhere to go as the crowd outside the building pressed in. Some bodies were borne on the surging mass of people, as those in the front, slashed and bloodied by the giant bird's sharp talons, tried to run back, stumbled, and were lifted by the mighty waves of the mindless human sea. Viola fought to stay upright, knowing that if she fell under the feet of the mob, she would never stand up again.

Suddenly a sharp crack could be heard above the hubbub of voices. The Crow's wings beat one last, frantic tattoo and then the bird crashed into the floor and lay still.

The crowd froze; even the people outside got an inkling of something extraordinary happening inside and stopped pushing. For a moment, there was stunned silence, and then the human sea heaved again and disgorged a pale young man in a constable's uniform. He was holding a smoking gun.

The man looked as incredulous as the people who surrounded him. He glanced at his gun, then at the mass of feathers at his feet, and then back again, as if refusing to believe he had brought down an Ancestor.

"String him up!" somebody shouted.

"Blasphemer!"

"Murderer!"

"Ancestor-killer!"

The constable's mouth was working but whatever he was trying to say was drowned by the rising roar of the mob. Rough hands seized him; fingers digging into his clothes and flesh.

"Stop!"

Viola jumped onto a desk to stand above the sea of people. Until she was facing the multitude, she had no idea what she was going to say. But now, buoyed by their anger and fear, she suddenly felt more alive than she had ever felt in her life. She had always been the one on the margins, the one listening and not speaking, obeying and not commanding, eclipsed by her pretty sister, her charismatic leader, her condescending friends. They were gone. She was in the center now.

"Are we like the Humanist killers or the corrupt Temple lackeys?" she shouted into the lacuna of stunned silence created by her unexpected appearance. "Are we not the children of the Revealer? Would she approve of our starting her reign with shedding of innocent blood?"

"He killed the sacred bird!" somebody shouted, and the low, menacing growl of the crowd started again, the beast awakening and slipping out of her control.

"Fools!" Viola shouted back. "Don't you see that the Crow appeared here to show us the way? The Revealer is not here yet! The Crow has sacrificed himself to ease our tribulations and you are profaning his sacrifice!"

She jumped off the desk, bent over the dead bird, and reverently touched its ruffled feathers stained with blood. The pungent smell of oily feathers made her eyes water.

Viola dipped her fingers into the bird's blood and drew a square on her forehead.

"The sign of the Four!" she said. She had never heard of such a thing before, but now it felt right and proper. She jerked up the constable who almost collapsed at her feet and drew another square on his forehead.

"Now you are consecrated to the Revealer!" she declared. "And until she comes, you are consecrated to me as her prophetess and humble servant. Do you swear loyalty to the Army of the Revealer?"

"Yes," he whispered.

The human sea heaved and surged, and then one by one, people approached the dead Crow, knelt reverently by the totem's side, dipped their fingers in its blood, and drew squares on their foreheads.

"We are marching on the Temple!" Viola declared, marveling at how her squeaky voice suddenly acquired that ringing, irresistible volume. "We are marching on the Temple, to purify it for the Revealer when she comes! We are marching on the Temple to punish those who defiled our faith, profited from our toil, and stole our children. The Ancestors don't need mutilations to bestow their Powers! They freely grant their boon to those who love them! We are marching on the Temple and the spirit of the Crow who has given his life to enlighten us will lead us on! Who of you are coming with me? Who of you are worthy to join the Army of the Revealer?"

And as the crowd roared its assent, Viola Marmot surveyed her Army and knew it was invincible.

~

At first, Alice thought that it was another remnant. And then she realized it was something else.

The shadow that came out of the tunnel seemed to grow in stature as it advanced upon them. It drank the crimson light, plunging the cave into a fever-tinged twilight. The stench of wet ashes emanating from it overrode the stink of death.

Alice lifted her lantern.

And now she could see it clearly—or clearly enough to regret seeing it at all—its skull-like head with empty eyes in the deep bony sockets, its parchment-like skin dotted with purple lesions stretched around a flattened muzzle, its yellow fangs set in inflamed, swollen gums. The head swayed from side to side as the rest of the body became visible: the body of a four-legged animal, skeletal and famished, with protruding ribs and a restless twitching tail. The body was bare of fur, but the dry, yellow hide was singed and streaked with soot, creating the impression of faint stripes.

Alice screamed as the Tiger crept toward them on its sack-like belly, its eyes as unseeing as the eyes of a starvation victim.

"Ronald's totem," Mara whispered behind her back. "But where is Ronald?"

"Dead," another voice said.

It issued from the creature who had crawled out of the sea while they were distracted by the Tiger.

The monster that was flopping toward them, red liquid oozing down his swollen, pallid bulk, was not a man but he spoke as one, and the incongruity only added to the horror of his appearance. The hairless folds of his huge body drooped in baroque festoons, layers of subcutaneous fat draping his spindle-like frame. His glistening skin was sallow and thick, covered by weeping lesions; his face, pale and disproportionately small, was awkwardly perched on top of his pointed head, tacked on like an afterthought. His flipper-like legs were crooked and small, with a stretch of inflamed skin between them.

"Mr. Seal!" Mara cried.

"You did it, Mara!" the creature said, and Alice cringed at hearing the cultured, confident voice of a scholar emerging from this abomination. "I knew you would, my dear! You opened the gate. You brought down the barrier. You set us free!"

"It wasn't me! It was all those people in the City who killed in the name of the Ancestors! The fools and the fanatics who tried to shake off their humanity as if it was a heavy burden!"

"And it is," the Seal said, smirking. "We made a mistake, didn't we? Imposing humanity upon animals was a blunder. But we can make it right, can't we? You and I, my dear. The other two ... Let's say that now I'm firmly on your side, and they won't be able to stand in your way."

The Tiger growled.

"What do you mean, 'imposing humanity upon animals'?" Mara demanded.

"I see you don't have access to the memories of your totem yet," the Seal responded. "You will when you are one with her, as I am with my totem, as Ronald is with his. Only in the case of your husband, my dear, I am afraid his totem was a bit ... hungry, which is not unusual. The Ronald you knew is gone, fully dissolved into the Tiger. I would suggest that you hurry to be reunited with your totem if you don't want it to happen to you. She may condescend to keep a nook of her mind for your use."

"I know what my totem is," Mara said, "and I'll kill myself before I become part of her. But you did not answer my question. What did you mean by 'imposing humanity'?"

"Humans are dead," the Seal said.

"Then how does the dream-sea exist? Isn't it fed by humanity's imagination, stories, and memories?"

"It was. But humans killed themselves long ago, leaving the ocean of stories behind."

"How?"

"I don't know. But we were left, the four of us. In First City they call us the Tiger, the Lion, the Seal, and the Bear, but we're known by other names as well. We decided to recreate our creators. Animals were left behind after humanity extinguished itself, and we used them. We made men and women out of the beasts of the field, though part of their animal nature persisted, hence totems. We imprinted these new humans with memories and personalities of the dead that still floated in the dream-sea, left behind after the dissolution of the bodies. We set aside part of the dream-sea for them, making a simulacrum of the world of the past, building a City where they could hold their human shape and human personalities. So, a new humanity was made. But it was a mistake. What we have made, we can unmake."

Alice finally found her voice.

"I am no bloody animal!" she yelled.

"But you are," the Seal said. "Do you think that you are a woman, Alice D. Bobcat? Or should I say, bobcat? Just a bobcat, pretending to be human. An animal, that's all you are. Don't you feel it already, the bobcat stretching its tail, unsheathing its claws, awakened by the wilderness of the South Continent, begging to be free? Just a couple of years out of the City and your humanity is falling away from you, and the animal is emerging. You call the transformed ones remnants but it is you who are real remnants; pretend humans are flimsy imitations branded with the name of the animal that you are."

CHAPTER 13. THE SACKING OF THE TEMPLE

The Temple loomed before them, and some of Viola's Army hung back, intimidated by its magnificence. The Temple had been built with the City, or perhaps it predated the City. The *Book of the Remnant* was vague on this point. But it had been rebuilt many times. Almost reduced to rubble during the Dark Years, it had been recently renovated yet again in a style that some disgruntled purists called the Wedding-Cake Modern. But no matter their elitist jibes, the majority of ordinary citizens, and Viola among them, were enchanted by the brightly gilded cupola topped with symbolic images of the Four (not the horrible gargoyles of the Animal House but smooth and welcoming effigies radiating the bounty of Nature); by the capacious portico lined by marble columns with leafy pilasters; by the stylized mosaics of frolicking animals decorating the triangular pediment above the beaten-bronze doors. Inside the Temple, as Viola remembered, were more statues and paintings, and an altar always decorated with fresh flowers, and rows of devout Guardians ranged along the nave.

She turned to her Army and waved her hands, urging them on. But she saw her own hesitation mirrored in their faces and instantly learned the first lesson of leadership. There is no faking it. You must believe wholeheartedly in every word that comes out of your mouth even if deep inside, you know it to be a made-up story.

She took a deep breath. She was Chosen by the Revealer. She had come to purify the Temple and purify it, she would.

She strode up the marble stairs and pushed the doors twice her height. The doors did not budge. Frustrated, she threw herself against the unyielding bronze.

Somebody joined her. It was the constable who had killed the Crow and who she had saved from lynching by the crowd. He put his weight into the push, and the doors creaked open.

Except for her dead sister, Viola had never loved anyone in her life. But now a surge of love, hot and impersonal, rushed through her body as she heard the crowd surge behind her. She smiled at the constable and saw the moist devotion in his eyes.

She expected a line of armed Guardians inside but there was none. At first it seemed that the Temple was deserted. The enormous soaring space was lit with the multicolored lights streaming through the lofty stained glass windows.

But then she saw the three figures, tiny and lost in the gargantuan nave. The Fur, Fish, and Fowl Guardians.

They stood facing Viola and her Army. They were not dressed, of course, but they also lacked the regalia of their office, which Viola remembered from the processions of her childhood. There was nothing to indicate their status except their bodies.

The Fur Guardian's sad, animal eyes stared straight into hers from beneath his overhanging pelt-covered brow. The Fish and Fowl Guardian stood a little behind him, as if to indicate their secondary status. The Fowl Guardian was as Viola remembered him: an obese creature covered with sparse, grayish down whose folds of flabby flesh hung down to his gristly, skeletal knees. His spurred feet scrabbled at the floor like a rooster's. The Fish Guardian had once been female: Below her thin waist, her scale-covered hips flared. Her legs had been fused together up to her ankles in an approximation of a fish tail and she stood upright with some difficulty, supporting herself with a stick. Her face was silvery gray, with bulging eyes.

Viola looked at them and saw them for what they were: pathetic frauds.

She strode to stand nose-to-nose with the Fur Guardian.

"Out of the way!" she said. "You will pollute the people's Temple no more. We have come to take what's ours. We have come to bring back the Ancestors."

"Young woman—" the Fur Guardian started.

"Shut up, you freak!" Viola said, and her voice, suddenly strong, echoed and swirled in the vast spaces of the Temple. "Your lies are over. You won't stand between us and the Ancestors anymore!"

"You don't know what you're doing!" the Fish Guardian gargled.

"Shut up!"

She turned to her constable.

"Arrest them!"

He pulled out his gun.

"Don't!" the Fur Guardian cried. "You don't understand! We are your Guardians! We have been guarding you from the horrors that lurk outside First City, knocking on the gates, trying to get in. We have been mutilating ourselves, so you'll be whole; letting them feed on our minds, so they won't feed on you! We tell you sweet stories because you can't handle the truth. You think these statues are real? You are trying to let in the Four whose faces no one can see without going mad and whose names are—"

After snatching the gun from the constable's hand, Viola fired.

She had never held a gun before, but it fit snugly into her hand and when she pulled the trigger, she knew that the weapon approved. It was not she who had to silence this blasphemy; it was the gun, and the Army, and the ruins of Lonelyhearts, and her dead sister.

The Fur Guardian looked with infinite surprise at the red blossom on his chest and crumpled, still trying to say something that she did not want to hear.

The Fowl Guardian gabbled in distress. The Fish Guardian rushed toward her fellow, only to slip in his blood and flounder on the floor. A number of lesser Guardians poured from the side aisles and the chancel. But they stood no chance against Viola's Army.

People fought with their bare hands, some grabbing smaller devotional statues and using them as cudgels; some breaking off the backs of the pews and laying them into the mass of animal-human bodies; some smashing effigies and breaking glass, trampling down rich embroidered hangings; overturning vases; shattering icons; even tearing mosaics off the wall in an orgy of gleeful, liberating violence.

The Guardians turned and tried to flee, leaving Viola's Army to demolish the false Temple.

And Viola, their leader, their general, watched the destruction and knew it was good.

Several of her lieutenants, bloody and dusty, surrounded her and cleared the path to the High Altar. She walked toward the dais surrounded by statues of the Four. But first, she turned around and shot the Fish and Fowl Guardians.

Caught between the Tiger and the Seal, Julian realized that they were going to die.

He, Mara, the stocky woman named Alice, and the strange, gaunt man with no human name at all. For some reason, it made him angry. If he had to choose a company to depart his life with, it would not be these strangers. And probably not Mara who looked as if she was about to faint, her face so pale it reflected the red glow of the sea like a mirror. She sidled up to him, and he put his arm around her.

The man—Dog, yes, Dog—raised his shotgun, and Alice did the same with hers. Julian revised his opinion. If he had to go down fighting, maybe they would not be a drag, after all.

"Stop!" Mara stepped forward, shaking off her near-collapse. "You can't kill them with bullets. We are in the dream-sea now. Human weapons don't work here."

"I don't think I'll take your word for it," Alice grunted. "Nobody calls me a beast!"

"She is right," the Seal tittered. "Your pathetic inventions are useless here, Bobcat!"

Alice pulled the trigger. Nothing happened. Dog did the same. His shotgun sagged and melted as if it were made of toffee, dripping onto the ground in slimy slicks of metal and wood.

Julian tensed, ready to pounce. He needed the Seal distracted and then he would go for the creature's eyes, trying to claw them out. The rest of his anatomy was so inhuman that he doubted he could do much damage.

"Now," the Seal continued, "Mara, my dear, you are coming with me. Your totem still needs you. And of course, I need you. I always have. As for the rest, I think we can dispense with Dog, and Cat, and yes, Mr. Sparrow. You have repudiated your totem, and he repudiates you!"

Is it true?

Julian started creeping toward the pallid bulk on the shore when the Tiger made his move.

Almost forgotten in the conversation with the Seal, the Tiger had been lurking by the wall, his striped bulk expanding and contracting like a puff of acrid smoke. But now he leaped forward, a hollowed lightning, the stench of wet ashes so overpowering that Julian was momentarily unable to breathe, his eyes watering. He blinked away the tears, stunned that he was still alive.

The Tiger stood between them and the Seal, his threadbare tail swishing back and forth, his fangs bared in his skeletal face.

"What ...?" the Seal gargled. The Tiger hissed and advanced upon him.

A conversation with the man named Jeremy Seal flashed through Julian's mind.

"Who are the ones who rebelled?"

"I'm sure you can figure it out by now. The Lion and the Tiger."

"And the Seal tried to play both sides."

"Ronald!" Mara cried. She tried to run toward the Tiger, but Julian caught her arm and restrained her.

"He may not even remember you!" he whispered.

The Tiger and the Seal faced off against each other. It was the Seal who backed off.

"You fool!" he spat. "She is more powerful than ever, and she won't forget this betrayal. Your imprint Ronald Raven was more reasonable than you. I almost brought him over to my side. Too bad you have not absorbed his rationality. Well, have it your way! You'll regret it!"

After turning around, the Seal flopped toward the margin of the sea and dove under the incarnadine water that closed over him with a jellylike slowness.

Mara, wrenching herself free from Julian, ran to the Tiger and put a hand on his emaciated flank. He towered above her, growing again, becoming a cloud of sulfurous hunger that seemed to fill the entire cave, leaving no room for anything else.

"Ronald!" Mara called her husband again.

The Tiger turned his head and looked back. His hollow eyes met Julian's. There was no humanity there. But there was still something familiar.

Regret.

The Tiger contracted, becoming a large animal again, and

padded toward the shore. The heavy red swell grew agitated, and an evil-smelling draft blew into the cave as the Tiger launched himself into the sea and swam away.

The four people left on the shore collapsed in relief like marionettes with cut strings. Alice sat; Dog prodded his melted weapon as if unable to believe it was useless, and Julian came closer to the water, straining to see into the distance. The somber luminescence of the sea lightened and the bleeding sky above it— if it was the sky—was like an open wound bandaged with black rags of clouds. Mara stood apart.

"Well, well, well," Dog said, finally breaking the silence. "I guess it's time to head home."

"No," Mara said. She turned around to face them. "We are not going home. We are going into the dream-sea. We are going to find the Second City where my totem was imprisoned. And we are going to put her back in her cage."

PART THREE

ISLANDS OF MEMORY

CHAPTER 1. MRS. CAT

She is being rocked in a cradle, smothered by a scratchy blanket smelling of smoke and lard. A voice is whispering into her ear, and she understands it without understanding a word.

Little baby, don't you cry ...

Mama! She reaches out to touch something slippery and warm ...

A dream.

Mara woke in the dream-sea.

She was lying on the shingle beach in the lee of a large rocky pillar shaped like a struggling man trying to emerge from a strait-jacket. The rock was slick and white but where the man's face would be pressing to the fabric, it was red.

The sky was the same as before: a uniform dome lit by the sullen orange glow, darkening at the horizon into burnt sienna. Random sparks flickered above the horizon as if another confla-gration was about to start. There was no sun. No moon or stars.

She got up and walked to the water margin where red viscous waves lapped lazily against the scatter of pebbles and bones. Black rags of clouds drifted above the sea, dimming the harsh scarlet light. It was as if in permanent setting, the sun had broken, smearing its blood and guts across the sky.

Her back hurt. Her mouth was parched. Her stomach rumbled.

She had never been hungry or thirsty in the dream-sea before.

This was what having a body meant: hunger, and thirst, and pain, and slow dying. A human body. An animal body.

Julian appeared from behind the white rock.

"I found something," he said.

Mara followed him. He still would not look at her.

On the other side of the rock, the beach continued, rising to a line of cliffs that towered above them. After the confrontation with the Seal, the layout of the land had shifted so imperceptibly that it had not registered at the time. Only later did they realize that they were not in a cave anymore but on a rocky island jutting out of the blood-red sea. There were other islands in the distance, but the visibility was so poor that they could not make out how far they were.

The cliff face was pitted and fretted with erosion. But as opposed to the beach where only polished bones testified to past life, the rock crawled with organic presence. Giant meaty valves clung to it like cockles without shells, spasmodically contracting and relaxing; yellow and purple anemones waved their stinging tentacles; pink creatures that looked like salamanders or fish with tiny legs sprawled on the ledges. Clumps of hairy growth choked the cracks.

Mara stared at it in consternation. That was so much like what she used to witness in her dreamfishing but whereas before such displays had glowed with inexpressible magic, now it appeared raw and disgusting. The rock face stank of spoiled meat.

"What do you want me to do?" she asked Julian.

"We need to eat," he responded. "We need water. Unless you want to drink that red stuff."

"Eat? We can't eat this!"

"We may have no choice."

Mara felt tears gathering in her eyes and fought so hard to beat them back that she missed Julian's next sentence.

"What did you say?"

"I said that maybe you can produce a fire. Then we can cook this shellfish."

She rounded up on him.

"Produce a fire? How? What do you think I am?"

He was staring at her coldly and she realized what she had said.

Mara sank to the ground.

"I know what you think," she said. "But repeat after me—*I am not her.* I am not my totem. I have no Power to command the dream-sea."

He towered above her, and she hoped that he would sit, bring himself to her level. But he did not.

"But you used to be able to, right?"

"No, not really. How can I explain? When I went dreamfishing, it was like a dream. Maybe more vivid, more controlled. My mentor ... I read about what people call lucid dreaming. That was what it was like. And my body remained in the City. Now we are all here, and I have no more Power than any of you."

Finally, Julian lowered himself to the pebbles, though he still kept his distance. Mara stopped herself from reaching out to him and touching his hand.

"But you still want to confront the Bear?"

"What choice do we have?"

"Return to the City," he said, but she heard hesitation in his voice.

She looked at him. "Does the City still stand? And for how long?"

Footsteps stopped his answer. Dog and Alice appeared from behind the white rock. To Mara's surprise, they looked chipper. Alice was carrying her shotgun, Dog's having melted away.

Instead, he was toting a canteen and what appeared to be a bunch of bones but turned out to be bleached sticks.

"I found a spring," he declared. "Water's fresh. And some driftwood. We can make fire."

Julian jumped to his feet, and Mara repressed a pang of jealousy when she saw how his face lit up.

"What can I do?" he asked Dog who snorted.

"I doubt you ever made a fire, Mr. ... Sparrow? I bet you had servants do it for you. No, let Aly and me take care of that."

"My name is Julian," he said. "And no, I never made a fire or cooked my meals. But it's a good time to learn, isn't it?"

They stared each other down like fighting cocks in the barnyard, which Mara found both amusing and appalling. Then Dog grunted.

"The spring is that way." He jerked his head to the left. "I saw some big things like shells lying around. See if you can get some more water. We could all use a drink and a washup."

Julian went away, and Dog started building a driftwood fire. Mara noticed that both he and Alice who was collecting some dry weeds avoided looking at her.

The anger and bitterness washed over her like a drowning tide.

Who do they think they are?

I don't need them. I don't need anybody.

I don't need my mother. She is dead anyway.

I don't need my daughter. I killed her.

I never had a daughter ...

She fought to put it down with an almost physical effort that left her weak and shaken.

It's her thoughts and memories, not mine.

I am not her. I am not!

She went to Alice.

"Tell me what to do," she said, and Alice pointed to the juicy shellfish on the rock and told her to pull some off so they could cook them on sticks.

After they ate, they had a war council.

"Does it ever get dark here?" Dog grumbled. In fact, it was getting lighter as the sky scintillated with washes of fuchsia and pink, painting the water in the colors of a candy store instead of an abattoir.

"There is no sun or moon in the dream-sea," Mara replied. "Time is flexible. It's story time, not celestial time."

"Whatever that means," Alice scoffed.

"What it means," Mara said, "is that we are now in the world shaped by the imagination, hopes, dreams, and nightmares of people long gone. And we are caught in their whirlpool, playing roles not meant for us, wearing faces and bodies of the dead."

"So, it's true what he said? That we are animals made into humans?"

"It is true."

"Then why should we try to do anything?" Dog asked, adding a branch to the fire even though with the pinking of the sky, the temperature rose to the balminess of the South Continent. "Let's follow the remnants."

"No way!" Alice cried, indignant.

"Why not, Aly? You and I never amounted to much, did we? We were ridden over roughshod by every snotty clerk in the Animal House, every rich moneybag in the City, every corrupt Temple wheeler-dealer. Making Guardian was the only chance for us. And what are Guardians? And remnants? Indentured workers are not snatched off the streets, you know? At least not all of them. Most of us who came here knew what to expect, didn't we? You think Foxy didn't know what he was turning into? Be honest with yourself, old girl. We are animals, and what's so bad about it? Animals are free."

Julian suddenly spoke up. "Is this why you changed your name, Mr. Dog?"

Dog grinned.

"You got me here," he said. "One look at my dear departed brother, and I didn't want to end up like him."

"I changed my name, too," Julian said. "For the same reason you did: to weaken my connection to my totem. But you did one better. There is no totem named the Dog. I read in one of those old books that survived the Dark Years that dogs and cats refused to serve the Ancestors. I didn't know what dogs and cats were, but I assumed they were domestic animals, like cows and sheep, but they no longer wanted to obey the fake humans, so they were killed off. But they survived on the South Continent, didn't they?"

"True," Dog said. "Never heard this story, but it makes sense. If we are animals made into human shapes, why should other animals obey us?"

"Whatever," Alice snorted. She turned to Julian. She was beginning to like him more than she liked Mara. She tried to tell herself that it had nothing to do with his green eyes, pleasant smile, and posh manners but she knew better.

"Is your totem really the Lion?" she asked.

He nodded.

"Listen," he said, leaning in. "I understand how you and Mr. Dog feel. But you have seen the other two. We have no other choice. Mara is right. We need to go deeper into the dream-sea. We need to find the Second City. And we need to lock her ... her totem up. It was done once; it can be done again."

Mara lifted her eyes to him, but he paid her no attention, addressing Dog and Alice.

"We are not our totems. Who cares what we are made of? We are humans with our own thoughts, aspirations, and desires. We are not beholden to the Ancestors or the Slaughtered Ones. We have our City, the only human City in the world. How can we let it be destroyed by fools and fanatics?"

"The City never did anything for me," Dog retorted. "You gentlefolk got us into this mess, you clean it up ... if you can!"

"Speak for yourself, Dog!" Alice interrupted.

"Aly ..."

"No! I'm tired of cowering, skulking, running away! Tired of being cooped up with a bunch of morons and crazies! The ship was late, don't you know this? I have nowhere to go back to! I might as well go with them, see for myself, and find out the truth!"

"How can you trust them, Aly?"

"How can I trust you?" she parried. "I don't trust anybody but myself; life in Lonelyhearts taught me that."

"Lonelyhearts has been leveled," Mara whispered.

"And good riddance, too. Should I cry for the slums where I had the choice of fucking against the wall or going to bed hungry at the age of twelve! No, if I help you to save the City, I'll want my cut. And not only for myself! If the City was a cage for you, it was a double cage for me, and the likes of me. Things are going to change now!"

"They will," Julian said. "I promise."

Alice shrugged.

"All right," she said. "We will come with you, Dog and me. But all this talk about names made me think of something. That creature, the Seal, he really bad-mouthed my totem, didn't he? Well, he is nothing to write home about himself but if a name-change protects you against shedding your humanity, I want a new name too."

Dog and Julian stared at her with mingled expressions of surprise and what looked like admiration. Mara nodded.

"Dogs and cats," she said. "The animals who refused."

"That's right. I'll be Mrs. Cat now," Alice Deborah Cat said, stretching by the fire.

~

Viola Marmot sank into the soft bed. Above her arched the decadent painted ceiling with its unbecomingly lush pictures of dancing animals, and she thought: *Tomorrow I'll order to have it whitewashed. We don't need Temple luxury.*

Her belly was pleasantly full; even overfull, as it was beginning to ache. She tossed around in bed, petulantly. Used as she was to the scant diet of uncooked greens, perhaps it had been unwise to dine on the contents of the Guardians' larder. But she could not resist the sumptuous nut-and-fruit concoctions. And after all, her warriors deserved a reward, a victory celebration. They had gathered around the huge table in the Guardians' quarters: her lieutenants, the backbone of the new world. She had not really appointed them; it was destiny's doing but she was pleased with destiny's choices. Especially with Greg Coyote, the young constable who had shot the Crow. He had been at her side all the time, faithful and attentive, with his crisp manners, clean-cut face, and gleaming blond hair. Viola felt a soft loosening in her insides thinking about him. It was he who had found some cured meat hidden at the bottom of the Guardians' larder and shown it to the massed Army outside, denouncing the executed traitors' hypocrisy: They who were supposed to protect the holy animals, secretly gorged themselves on their charges' flesh! The Army was so outraged by it that they forgot their own hunger and discomfort, camping as they were in the forecourt of the gutted Temple, with nothing to eat and no shelter from the ever-present drizzle. Viola thought that tomorrow something should be done to feed and house them.

But she could not lower herself to such mundane concerns. Not after the glory of this day. Even Greg Coyote was nothing compared to the blinding light of the revelation that seemed to gather around her. She could feel it, the halo of chosenness.

"It's not for me!" she muttered. "It's for you!"

The Four, the Slaughtered Ones, seemed to smile benignly at her from their secret paradise. She had already noted, disapprovingly, that there were no effigies of them in the Guardians' quarters. Traitors and hypocrites!

She tossed in bed, unable to sleep. The thought of inviting Greg Coyote in to stand guard occurred to her but she dismissed it: Such a step would be open to misinterpretation and as the messenger of the Revealer, she should be above suspicion.

The warmth, the golden candlelight, finally lulled her to sleep and her last thought was that tomorrow she would order the highest-ranking officials in the City, including that traitor, the so-called President James Otter, to be brought before her.

Outside, the Crow Army huddled in the intensifying rain, heavy drops splattering on the bare heads and torn clothing of the street boys and girls, unemployed workers, whores, peddlers, and an occasional middle-class straggler. The rain was too heavy, and the water stank of more than the City's pollution. One man who miraculously had a functioning lantern raised his hand to the feeble light and swore to see it stained red.

"It's a rain of blood!" he yelled.

This was not the first time this meteorological phenomenon occurred in the City, but the Crow Army had had enough blood for one day. Even though they had been told to stay in the square outside the gutted Temple where the corpses of Guardians still littered the aisles and those few who had been taken prisoner were locked in the vestry, the Army decided, as one man, that their need for shelter outweighed the orders given by some stuck-up bunch of self-appointed bullies. Viola would have slept less soundly had she realized how thin was the pall of enchantment she had thrown over her followers and how quickly worn out by privation they were. Several burly stevedores started smashing the already splintered doors of the Temple and their efforts were redoubled when somebody spied glowing motes dancing among the heavy butcher drops. It started raining fire.

People, already bone-tired and cranky, rushed into the shelter of the Temple. The glowing motes were alighting on their soaked clothes and hair and setting them aflame. The victims danced frenziedly, trying to put the fire out, and in the process spreading it to their neighbors. An ex-Lonelyhearts mother of two who had come to the Animal House to demand food for her children and then joined the Army, swept in by general enthusiasm, fell and was trampled.

Finally, the bronze doors gave way and the Army poured inside, their clothes bloodied and singed. In the vestry the locked-up Guardians started a ruckus.

At least the soaring dome of the Temple protected them from the rain of blood and fire and once the corpses were piled aside and votive candles lit, the Army felt almost comfortable. Some were openly grumbling that their so-called leader, that upstart chit of a girl, did not let them bivouac in the Temple from the beginning. Others, their appetite wakened by danger, rummaged in the vestry for something edible.

It was then that a train worker, older than most of the Army and with a family in the City, poked his head into the portico. Outside it was almost as bright as day but the light had a feverish, flickering quality. The rain of mixed fire and blood had become sheets of flame. The few trampled bodies left in the square had burned into crisps.

"The City!" the train worker howled. "The City is on fire!"

Their glory forgotten, the soldiers spilled into the portico. First City was shielded from view by the rugged flanks of the Hill. Nevertheless, they could see the brighter glow through the ragged curtains of fire dancing in the square. Down below the Hill, their City was burning.

CHAPTER 2. THE LAST RAIN

Julian picked up a stick of driftwood and tossed it away with a curse. It was not driftwood at all but a bleached oar-shaped rib bone of some enormous and deformed creature.

They were stuck on the island. Mara's stories of the dream-sea made it out to be a place where thought was action, where one could glide underwater with no need for air and traverse huge distances on the strength of a wish.

Nothing could be further from the truth.

The scarlet viscous water burned like hell. Mara had tried to swim in it and ended up with an unsightly rash. And there were creatures in it that deterred Julian's attempts to build a raft—assuming he could even find enough driftwood to do so.

The other islands were close enough—Julian could see them from the beach and did not like what he saw. One rock seemed to be covered with a twitching hide. Another one had a number of caves from which long, glistening tentacles emerged to wave in the air. And the biggest of them was dotted with what appeared to be ruins of strange fortifications. Looking at them made Julian's flesh crawl.

Mara came over. Julian felt her presence like an invisible fire burning by his side.

"I had a dream," she said in a low whisper that had somehow become her new voice.

"We are in the dream-sea, right? What else would you be having?"

"The dreams we are surrounded with are those of the dead. This one was mine."

Julian did not want to acknowledge that when he did manage to doze off in the perpetual light, he was also having vivid dreams. He was not entirely sure they were his own.

"I dreamed of my mother," Mara went on.

Julian started. He did not want to be reminded of what he had seen in Louisa Ferret's blood-splattered living room.

"I killed her."

"You did not mean to," Julian objected.

"No. But I should have known better than to use a firearm I had no experience with, right? So, maybe I did intend to kill her, after all."

"Don't be morbid, Mara."

"I also killed my daughter," Mara went on, staring fixedly into the crimson vapors dancing at the horizon.

"Your what?"

"I was pregnant—or thought I was. And then, I aborted it."

"Just stop it, Mara, will you?" Julian yelled. "You can't abort an imaginary pregnancy, and even if you did, that's not infanticide! Elvira had an illegal abortion, okay? Neither she nor I were bothered by it."

Mara's eyes were enormous in her gaunt face, and Julian realized that their color had changed. Instead of the shifting blues, greens, and grays, the irises were tinged with burnt sienna and black ruby as if the bloodied waters of the dream-sea were seeping into them.

"Aren't you dreaming, too?" she asked.

Julian stormed away rather than answer.

The open suitcase with a dead infant inside. The black smoke. The stench of hot metal and burning flesh. And the heaviness of the gun in his hands.

They are not my memories. Then whose?

Viola Marmot was woken from a dream of her sister by shouting and the smell of burning. After pulling on her worn jacket and trousers, she rushed to the window.

What she saw was a confused melee of people veiled by smoke. The acrid stink made her eyes water, and the sky seemed to her unnaturally red like peeling skin. She blinked the tears away: It *was* unnaturally red. The inflamed sun swam above the horizon.

She ran out of the bedroom and almost collided with Greg Coyote.

"Revealer!" He caught her hand. "Don't go outside! It's dangerous!"

I'm not the Revealer, she wanted to scream, shocked by this blasphemy. *I'm only her messenger!*

But what if I am?

"I have to be with my Army," she said. But then she hesitated. "What happened?"

"Rain of blood, rain of fire," he answered. "They say the City is burning."

She rushed into the courtyard. The bronze door of the Temple, which she had ordered to keep locked, was breached. A dead Guardian was lying half in, half out on the threshold.

At first, the crying, screaming, and bewildered people in the courtyard did not even notice her. She tried to yell, but nobody heard her. Coyote fired several rounds into the air and the pandemonium died down as they turned toward her.

Viola looked back into the red-rimmed, maddened eyes of the people and tried to rekindle the inner conviction that she needed to reassure them. But the fire of righteousness that had burnt so bright yesterday was smoldering weakly, outshone by the real fires outside. Nevertheless, she forced out words that felt flat even to herself.

"The signs and portents are speaking!" she shouted. "The Revealer is at hand! The Temple is ours now; it has been purified! We shall march onto the City, to take the Animal House!"

The crowd stared at her with hundreds of blank eyes, and the wave of enthusiasm that she expected failed to rise.

"We came from the City!" a solitary voice sounded from the back.

Viola hesitated.

"But now we go back as victors! We shall bring the Temple lackeys in the Animal House to justice!" Greg Coyote stepped forward to stand beside her. "And we shall come back to the City with the riches that the false Guardians have robbed from us!"

"What are you saying!" she whispered, furious. "They will loot the Temple!"

"They need it!" he whispered back.

And judging by the gleeful energy of their destruction, they needed it.

She tried to convince herself that it was just and proper for the poor of the City to take back their blood, sweat, and tears in the form of gilded screens, silver vessels, silk vestments, and gaudy icons. She looked on, silently, as two men fought over a bejeweled painting of cooing doves. But she turned away, sickened, when they dragged out the remaining Guardians and executed them.

Feeling tired and superfluous, she walked away to observe the swirls of oily smoke drifting from beyond the shoulder of the

Hill. The sun was low, fat, and red like a pomegranate. Shouldn't it be higher, climbing its daily path?

Coyote materialized by her side, his eyes bright and eager in his soot-smudged face. He seemed, somehow, more substantial than the pale, frightened boy about to be torn apart by the mob for killing the Crow. Was it only yesterday? The square she had drawn on his forehead was fresh and dripping; renewed—she did not want to know with whose blood.

"We are ready!" He snapped his constable's salute at her.

She nodded and returned to the courtyard, where the looters were urged into formation by the curses and blows of the thugs who she had thought of as her lieutenants. By the time she got to the outer gate, her boots were soaked in blood.

There was blood on the road as Viola led the way down to First City. The Army was behind her, slowed down by the booty they were carrying. One man was lugging a heavy gilded statue of the Fur Guardian.

"It must have rained blood all the way down to the City," Coyote opined. "We'll need to boil water when we set camp."

"There will be no need for this," Viola said. "The Revealer must have come. She will provide."

Coyote winked at her and she turned away in disgust.

The first houses appeared; the Army was entering the City from the side of Victory Boulevard, and there were no poor suburbs here. The houses were old and substantial: granite-clad four-story buildings with sloping roofs, columns at the entrance, and decorative balconets. Normally there would be nurses with their charges taking a morning stroll or sitting on the benches along the boulevard.

But now the tree-lined avenue was deserted; the houses frowned at the intruders. There was no sign of the conflagration; except for some dark stains on the pavement, this area of the City seemed untouched by any disaster.

Viola should have felt relieved. But instead, she came to an abrupt stop and the entire Army shuffled to a standstill behind her. The people looked around uneasily.

In a moment, she realized what had stopped her. The City was silent. And it had never been so; even in the depth of the night, the City had breathed, and cried, and moaned in its sleep; there had been laughter, and drunken song, and the shriek of tires. But now, at noon—or was it noon?—the City was as still as the countryside.

"Let's move!" Coyote cried. "On, to the Animal House!"

They resumed walking; Viola scanning the windows. There was nothing out of place; even the curtains were immaculately drawn. It was as if the series of recent catastrophes had never happened.

But there was not a single person peeking from a doorway; not a single curtain twitched to reveal the presence of an observer.

Something moved! A quick, low-slung shadow crossed the empty road a block ahead of her. Viola paused.

"Don't stop!" Coyote hissed into her ear. "They need you to be confident!"

The trees on the boulevard were mostly bare except for some pines and firs. But somebody must have done quite a bit of gardening to prettify the lives of the rich. There were lushly blooming flowers in the winter flower beds. In the crimson light they appeared black. They looked disturbingly familiar to Viola, but she could not spare them any attention; she was scanning the street in the desperate hope of seeing a pedestrian, a refugee, even a corpse.

There was a private car by the curb. The door was hanging open. Viola peered inside.

Something scuttled across the back seat, jumped out. Viola started violently and then almost laughed at herself. It was a mouse! Just a mouse!

The mouse disappeared into a doorway. Viola looked back: The Army was staring accusingly at her with its many eyes.

As they advanced deeper into the heart of the City, they could see more signs of fire but it did not seem to have done as much damage as they had expected. Some ruins still smoked but mostly the fire had been put out by rain. Whole blocks appeared untouched. Instead of celebrating, however, the people were subdued. The eerie silence and emptiness of the City were worse than any devastation they could imagine.

"They must have left," Viola whispered. "When the fire and blood came, they must have left."

"Left the City?" Coyote asked.

It seemed impossible but what other explanation was there?

But the City was not totally deserted. More and more urban wildlife was out in the streets. There were swift flocks of sparrows and pigeons rising suddenly from the roofs; crows cackled in the trees; mice and rats scurried on the sidewalks, unafraid. It was as if the desertion of the humans had empowered the animals; Viola, who had so often lamented the scarcity of animal life in the City, was now thoroughly spooked by its abundance.

Indeed, some of the animals she was beginning to see did not belong in the City at all. A buck deer and a couple of does scampered across the boulevard. A fat hamster strode unhurriedly ahead. A swift dun-colored creature pounced upon it; it was a lynx, such as Viola had only seen in street temples before. She was reminded of Edna Lynx who had sacrificed herself for the Return of the Ancestors.

Was this what she had gutted herself for?

"All those animals ..." Coyote mumbled. He sounded spooked.

A vulture rose into the air from a flower bed. A fox sniffed at a memorial.

Victory Boulevard widened, opening out onto the Animal House square. Or should have. For a wild moment, Viola thought that she, who had lived in the City her entire life and knew it like the back of her hand, had lost her way.

The sweep of the square was familiar, even though the wide expanse was empty, deserted by the constables who normally patrolled it. But it could not have been the right place because the Animal House was gone. A dirty, peeling building poked from the opposite corner of the square, a shabby ruin.

Behind her, the Army gave a collective moan; they accepted the evidence of their eyes before she allowed herself to.

The Animal House was still there but the carved animals were gone, leaving behind sores of raw plaster and scuffed stone.

Viola walked toward the building.

When she and Carla were little, their mother had given them a box of painted wooden animals. They had fought over it and the box had fallen and broken. She thought of its splintered lid and of her sister, murdered. Hot tears pricked her eyes, and the walls, once so grand and now pitiful, shorn of their decorations, blurred.

She came close, touched the mutilated stonework.

There were heavy footsteps behind her. She turned around.

The Ancestors had escaped their stone imprisonment, but they were not gone.

Pouring into the square from the side streets, the Ancestors came: not the wary, small animals she had seen before but their archetypes, magnified by the human imagination into gods.

The Deer's mighty hooves made the cobblestones ring; his giant head with its branching antlers was borne above the panicking crowd.

The Fox's bushy tail swept the human trash aside.

The Eagle rained darkness from his spreading wings.

The Snake squeezed the life out of a man and broke his body.

The Raven pecked out the corpse's eyes.

Squeezing against the crumbling wall, Viola saw her Army decimated and wanted to beg their forgiveness, but her voice was lost in the din made by the monsters. Somebody smashed into her, buffeted by the stampede; she saw it was Greg Coyote and was glad he was still alive. They held hands.

Something else penetrated her shock: a surprise that the Four, the Slaughtered Ones, were not here, and then a relief that they were not.

Suddenly the Ancestors paused in their onslaught, looking apprehensive. The Fox's nose twitched; the Deer let out a bellow. In the streets, the ordinary animals ran away in fear.

The pavement shook and buckled. Viola's legs folded and she slid to the ground, dragging Coyote with her. Those soldiers of her Army who were still standing fell to their knees, believing an earthquake was about to finish them off.

But this was not an earthquake; the tremors subsided. The unrelenting pressure from beneath the pavement, however, continued. The paving stones gave way, shot into the air, and rained back down upon the thick crop of velvety-black flowers shaped like double butterflies that forced their way from the ground.

"What is this?" Coyote sobbed.

But now Viola knew; she had seen such a flower some time ago when the Return of the Ancestors had been something to dream of, and hope, and kill for. George Buzzard had shown her one and told her how they were obtained. So, there must be a lot of dead bodies now in the City, she thought, for so many of them to pop up like a flower show. Enough to satisfy any Buzzard.

The Ancestors seemed to be perturbed by the sickly sweet-smelling flowers. They fidgeted as the thick carpet of velvety black grew under their hooves and paws. The Eagle flapped his wings and flew away. The Deer galloped down the boulevard, scattering lesser animals like pins. The Fox hissed and backed off.

For a moment, there was silence and quiet, as the Ancestors retreated, and the lesser animals crouched and hid in the shadows. The black flowers grew as tall as a five-year-old and stopped growing; their butterfly crowns swaying in the brightening light. Stranded among them, the men and women of the Army moved slowly, reverently, touching the petals.

And as each of them found his or her flower, their borrowed forms were shed. Rick Raccoon, a factory worker whose beloved wife had left him for his best friend, shrank into a black-and-white creature and scampered away. Maria Marten who had worked her hands to the bone for her two sickly sons, puffed her orange fur and snapped up a mouse. Lola Kite swooped in upon Dick Rabbit whose engagement ring she had worn. Roger Squirrel hopped away from his best buddy, Tom Rat.

Pressed to the crumbling wall of the Animal House, Viola and Greg observed the transformations until there were no more humans left in the square. The animals, predators and prey alike, had slunk away or run on their errands to eat or be eaten according to their nature. They looked at each other. Then Greg tugged away the hand Viola was clutching and touched the flower that had grown in front of him.

The coyote dropped on its haunches, and she looked into its dirty-brown eyes and thought: *Do they kill quickly?* But the coyote did not attack; it bared its dirty yellow fangs, one of which, she noticed, was broken, cocked its head, turned around, and disappeared among the black flowers. She remembered that she had read somewhere that animals could not stand direct eye contact with humans. At the time she thought it was typical human arrogance.

A black flower pushed up in front of her. Its nodding crown was turned toward her, and its smell was not sickly but sweet and irresistible like the smell of jasmine. But before she touched the beckoning petals, she straightened up and looked around at the deserted square now carpeted with velvety black. She was the tallest creature here, towering above the flowers, whose crowns swayed as quadrupeds crept close to the ground.

I'm the last one! she thought.

She was glad that the light had changed; no longer the sullen red dusk that had greeted her eyes when she woke up, seemingly so long ago. It was bright and golden, but she could not tell what hour it was.

She looked up. The sun was above her but even as she watched, it swelled, smearing itself across the sky, until the entire heaven was one uniform brassy dome.

Viola smiled and touched the flower.

～

Dog and Cat sat across the dying fire from each other.

They only needed the fire for cooking raw shellfish, as it was uniformly warm on the beach. That was the only good thing about it.

Dog was staring at the piece of wood he had started whittling and gave up. Cat was staring at him.

Alice realized how bad their situation was but strangely, she felt better than her companions. Dog was sulking; Julian roamed the beach trying to find something useful that could take them off the island, and Mara stood at the water margin. When she did come over, Alice was shocked by the change in her appearance. Her once-pretty face looked skeletal and decades older; her ash-blond hair was tangled; and her eyes were reddish-brown, as if the reflection of the crimson water permanently stained the irises. She must have been feeling guilty for stranding them here, Alice assumed, but she never asked. Now that she knew who Mara's totem really was, her previous fear of her was tinged with disgust. But for herself, Alice Debora Cat had finally come into her own. She did not know what a cat looked like, though it stood to reason that it was not very different from a bobcat, but somehow, she felt that being Mrs. Cat was more genteel, more powerful, and—somehow—younger than the plain, old Bobcat.

"I think I'm going for a swim," Dog said.

"What?" Alice sat up. "This water is like acid; it will take the flesh off your bones."

"Maybe that's what I want," Dog growled.

Alice pursed her lips. She remembered the remnants going into the dream-sea, and the Seal and the Tiger disappearing into it. She knew what Dog was saying.

"No, you don't."

"What else is there, Aly? Rotting on this fucking beach forever? We can't go back to the Hollow Cliffs, and even if we did, what's the difference? We will become animals anyway; it will just take longer."

"She says—" Alice started.

"She? She promised to confront the Four and to take on the Bear, and she can't even get us off this island. I don't trust a word she says!"

"You are right," Mara said.

She had approached them so quietly that Alice was startled to see her. The light started curdling into dirty maroon once again, and the dark circles around Mara's eyes stood out like a scream.

"I failed," she went on in a low voice. "I thought I had the Power over the dream-sea, but I don't. It was her all along. My totem. The Bear. She used me to break out of her cage. She used me to bring together the imprints of the Seal, the Tiger, and the Lion, so that the rest of the Four could be swayed to be back under her command. I am sorry, Mr. Dog, Mrs. Cat. I failed you. I failed First City. I came to ask for your forgiveness before I go into the sea."

"Before you kill yourself and leave us here to rot," another voice interrupted.

It was Julian. He looked as gaunt as Mara, but Alice noted that he had made some effort to clean up his tattered clothing. His face was like a thundercloud.

"It was always your problem," he went on. "You give up. You despair. And in your despair, you become dangerous. Spiteful. People who care nothing for themselves care nothing for others."

Mara whirled around, color rising in her sallow cheeks.

"You speak as if you knew me, Julian! May I remind you that we only met three times after I examined your wife's dead body?"

"Leave Elvira out of it. And yes, I know you, Mara. Do you think you are the only one who has access to your totem's memories?"

"So, are we to be graced by a visit from the Lion?" Dog interrupted. "Sorry to be rude, Julian, but after meeting the Tiger and the Seal, I think I'd rather not. I've had enough deities to last me a lifetime."

Julian smiled.

"No fear. The Lion has no interest in taking me over. He is back where he belongs—with her."

"So, no more Rebellion?" Mara asked.

"It failed. The Four are unified once again, and the experiment of recreating humanity is over."

"So, what will happen to First City?" Alice asked.

Julian shrugged.

"I think the Army of the Revealer will demolish it. They don't know what they are doing, of course, but when they find out, it will be too late."

"And who is defeatist now?" Mara exclaimed. "No, I refuse to let the City be destroyed. I am going into the sea. I will confront my totem ..."

"And be dead or worse," Julian countered. "Your husband and your mentor have been absorbed. Do you want it to happen to you?"

"Do you have a better idea?"

"Maybe. We are stuck on this island. But there is a way to traverse distances. Remember, both you and I came to the South Continent without the benefit of a ship by taking a shortcut. If we had a black flower, we could do it again."

Alice had no idea what they were talking about, but she was struck by a change in Mara's expression—dejection mutating into horror.

"Do you know what the flowers are?" she exclaimed. "How could you suggest such a thing?"

"We have no choice."

"I don't understand," Alice interrupted. "What are black flowers?"

Mara and Julian glanced at each other, but he pursed his lips and shook his head, leaving her to explain.

"Black flowers bloom when somebody dies by violence," she said. "Remember—we are in the dream-sea and have always been, living out the nightmares of humans who are long gone. When the Four created a new humanity, they used animals to mold their bodies, and memories of men and women to shape their personalities. Black flowers are souls of the dead, growing at the bottom of the dream-sea."

"Hold on, hold on!" interrupted Dog, to Alice's relief. "I'm a simple Dog, ma'am, not learned in gentlefolks' ways. Would you consent to explain again in words fit for such as Aly and me?"

Julian snorted.

"I think you understand," he said. "Our bodies are simulacra, held in their human form by the City. Our souls are borrowed from the souls of the dead. And once you kill somebody, their soul wants to go back to the depths of the dream-sea, and if you have a Power, you can use it to hitch a ride, so to speak. In short, violence is a solution when you are stuck."

"But ..." Mara exclaimed.

Dog grinned.

"I get it," he said. "We could get off this rock before we finish off all the shellfish if we kill somebody. My dad taught me a similar lesson a long time ago. But there are only four of us. And since neither Aly nor I have the Power you are talking about, one of us has to go. Did I get it right?"

"Yes," Julian said.

"No!" Mara exclaimed. "No way! We are not going to start killing each other or ourselves. The fanatics in the City did it and look where it got us!"

"We have no choice," Julian said. "It is war."

"What war? How do you know anything about it? The last war in First City was during the Dark Years, centuries ago. It's your totem speaking, right? Don't let him into your head!"

"Too late for both of us," Julian responded.

Alice finally shook off her consternation.

"Nobody is getting killed," she said, putting as much authority into her voice as she used to when boisterous customers came into her grocery shop asking for home brew. "We'll find another way!"

The scarlet dome of the sky suddenly went black. In the thick darkness, shot through with the smell of blood and rust, their small fire was the only spark of light.

"What ...?" Mara exclaimed.

The light came back.

But not the dismal red glow or even the inflamed pink fire in the sky they had gotten used to. The light was silver and cool, deepening to gold at the zenith. There was still no sun or moon, but the illumination seemed closer to daylight than anything Alice had experienced since coming to the Hollow Cliffs. And the sea ... The sea was different, too. It was mint-colored with silver highlights, the waves glittering and sparkling, as if the nonexistent celestial bodies had dissolved in the water, the sun and the moon and the stars gleaming from beneath the waves. Alice looked around in wonder. The sand on the beach was now as white as sugar, and when she glanced back, instead of mollusk-infested cliffs, she saw the curving crescent of bushes with bright green leathery leaves.

Mara leaped to her feet.

"It's my beach!" she exclaimed. "It's where I used to go dreamfishing!"

Julian's gloom was dissolving in wonder.

"What does it mean?" he whispered.

Mara turned to him, the hope and excitement in her face dying.

"It means that First City is no more," she said. "The dream-sea is all that is left. We are on our own."

CHAPTER 3. THE FIRST OF THE FOUR

There were four islands arranged in a rough semicircle. They were not equidistant, though; the largest one was the farthest away and the most ordinary looking. It was covered with dense bushes and trees that seemed to Julian to be the same ones as grew on the Plains—birch, plane, and ash—rather than the tropical vegetation of the South. There was a shallow ravine running through its middle.

The closer islands, though, were far from ordinary.

The smallest of them was pinnacles of black lava rock bordered by foaming white surf that broke on the jutting fangs of stone.

The second one was the opposite—low-lying hillocks of sand and a wide beach littered with some dark shapes that looked like waterlogged tree trunks but occasionally stirred.

And the third one, which Julian found himself being drawn to, was crowded with ruined gray structures like windowless barns. Somehow, he knew these were fortifications, though he had never seen anything like them.

Mara came over. The change in the dream-sea brought her back to the woman he had—almost—fallen in love with, but with a difference. It was as if her emaciated flesh was falling from whatever hid inside her like a worn-out scabbard falling away from the sword. But he did not know what the steel of the weapon inside was: determination or despair.

She looked at him. Her eyes were green-blue-gray again, like the dream-sea.

"We will have to swim," she said.

He nodded. The islands were close enough and the water no longer burned like acid, though it was bitter and salty like tears. He was not a great swimmer, but he thought he could manage.

It turned out he did not have to.

The sluggish surf in front of them boiled with movement as a glassy dome broke the surface of the water. Something emerged from the sea and strode toward them.

It was a slender transparent creature, its body shaped like a woman's to its shoulders and its upper part fishlike. There were scattered luminous concretions in her flesh, glowing like cheerful holiday candle lights. She seemed too fragile to be dangerous, but she looked so bizarre that Julian's mind froze, unable to decide whether to attack or not. Mara ran toward the creature.

"It's a land mermaid!" she cried. "They helped me before."

The mermaid's fish face was incapable of showing emotions, but she lifted her translucent hand and beckoned them to follow. She turned around and walked back—but not *into* the water, rather *on* the water. Where her feet touched the waves, they stilled, forming an invisible walkway. Mara followed.

Julian called for Dog and Cat, and they ran after the land mermaid. The surface under their feet was firm and slippery like glass.

The mermaid led them to the rocky island but instead of trying to climb the toothy cliffs, she went around the curving shoreline. The four of them followed. Julian noticed that the sea was crinkling in gentle waves all around them except for the glassy walkway left in the mermaid's wake.

On the other side of the island, there was a small black lava beach. The mermaid gestured toward it and then dove into the water so smoothly there was hardly a splash. The walkway disintegrated under their feet, but the sea was so shallow here that they waded through to the shore with no difficulty. As they stood on the black pebbles, Julian saw that there was a gap in the rocks leading to the island's interior.

He looked around. Black stone, blue sea, the shiny silver dome of the sky. The landscape was spare and stark but not monstrous as it had been on the mollusk island or inside the Hollow Cliffs. And yet Julian felt nausea rising in his throat. And something else, something tickling the foundations of his mind like a nightmare crawling out of its lair in daytime.

A nightmare, or a memory.

Mara bent down and lifted a white object from the beach. She showed it to Julian. A handful of finger bones, smooth and shiny. Except for rough scratches on their ivory surface as if somebody had tried to cut the flesh off with a knife.

"You know where we are," she whispered.

Julian shook his head, but the tickling grew stronger, the antenna of some misshapen crustacean rising out of the dark water of his unconscious.

"I am not my totem," he said.

"No. But you are his imprint. Just as he is the imprint of somebody else."

"What do you mean?"

"We are animals remade in the shape of humans, living off the residue of dead men's stories. The Four who made us are the rulers of the dream-sea. But where do they come from? Why are they called the Slaughtered Ones?"

"The *Book of the Remnant* says—"

"The *Book of the Remnant* is a lie. No, Julian, they are monsters, but they were humans once. And you and I, and the man who was my husband, and the man who was my mentor, the four of us, we can pierce the sludge of myths and stories and touch the bedrock of reality. We can remember."

"Even if we can, so what? What good does it do? First City is gone. We are alone, drowning in the sea of nightmares."

"So why are you here?" Mara challenged, looking him in the eyes, and for a moment, it was as if they were just two people, a man and a woman, a widower and a widow, the air between them brimming with the future. And then it was gone, and they were being drawn away from each other, crushed under the weight of history that was not even their own.

Julian snorted.

"I am here because I want to meet my totem. And I want to kill him. I want to make him a Slaughtered One for sure this time. And I don't care what happens next. If humanity is never to rise again, so be it."

"You are talking like a soldier, Julian. But you are just a merchant. It's not your memories that speak through you."

"Maybe so," Julian sneered. "But what about you, Mara? Who are you?"

Mara looked away, and he saw tears glistening on her cheeks. Instead of pity, he felt anger.

"I am a daughter," she whispered. "And a mother. And a victim."

"A victim? Your totem is responsible for all that!"

Glimmers of red were rising in her blue-green-gray eyes.

"If I am robbed of my life, why should anybody else live?"

"Hello, gentlefolk!" a familiar voice cut through their conversation. "It was nice of that jellyfish to bring us here, but I don't see how this place is much of an improvement. I don't see no shellfish here, and I'm getting peckish."

Julian had almost forgotten about Dog and Cat, but here they were. Cat was rooting in the pebbles, unearthing more bones but not even a strand of seaweed.

"First City is no more," Mara said, "but there is Second City in the dream-sea. The answer to all the riddles is there. If we reach it, we can bring humanity back."

"Is it true?" Alice D. Cat asked, and the hope in her voice made Julian's heart beat faster. He suspected that this hope was false, but so what? Every soldier goes into the battle believing he will survive, while knowing that he probably won't.

It's not your memories that speak through you.

"Yes," he said. "But we need to overcome the Slaughtered Ones first."

"And then the City will rise again?" she insisted.

"Yes," Mara said. "The human City will rise again."

"Then what are we waiting for?" Cat asked. "There is nothing on this beach but bones and hunger. Let's go!"

Julian walked toward the crack in the rocks, and Mara, Cat, and Dog followed. The air was getting chillier as they approached the heart of the island.

The island of Hunger.

As they passed through the narrow defile, Julian glanced up and saw clouds scud across the uniform glow of the sky. Thin and gauzy, they coalesced into recognizable shapes: sketchy human profiles, erased by the wind and reforming again, becoming more bestial, mutating into long muzzles, filled with broken teeth.

Behind the rocks, the interior of the island was a desolate stretch of barren sand and thin soil. There was a rickety weather-beaten cabin, surrounded by shallow excavations as if somebody had tried to dig graves and given up. The single window was broken, and the discolored door hung off the hinges. To Julian, the place looked familiar.

Inside, the cabin was almost bare. Some sticks of crude furniture, scattered clothes on the floor and a battered cooking pan on the table. An unpleasant smell pervaded the stale air. Dog sniffed and muttered something.

Mara lifted the lid off the pan and dropped it, its clatter obscenely loud in the hush.

There was a cooked human head in the pan.

Bloated and scalped, it stared through Julian with its egg-white eyes. He clapped a hand to his mouth, fighting nausea. Mara retched.

The daylight dimmed and a shadow fell onto the floor. A sinuous shape squeezed through the doorway, shoving Cat and Dog aside, scattering them like bowling pins.

The Tiger stood in the middle of the cabin, his striped bulk filling it, his breath stinking of wet ashes, his long tail swishing around, striking Julian's thighs like a lash. His empty sockets sought Mara.

"Ronald!" she cried. But there was nothing human left in the Tiger, nothing but insatiable hunger and blind greed. The totem advanced toward her, the tongue like a dry rag hanging out of his maw.

"You bastard!"

Julian launched himself at the Tiger, all his fury with Mara, with Mara's husband, with himself, boiling over. The Tiger swung his giant head around, his broken fangs closing upon Julian's arm. The pain was blinding, and Julian realized that the dream-sea did not transform the body away from mortality. You still had to eat, and sleep, and void in the dream-sea. You could still feel pain. You could still die.

He battered the beast's muzzle with his free hand. The Tiger shook his head and tossed Julian into a corner. He crashed into a shelf, his head ringing. His feet shot from under him as he tangled in the clothes on the floor and his head hit the wall. Everything went dark before his eyes, but there was a crimson fire somewhere in his head that made him grind his teeth and stagger to his feet again.

"You ...!"

The name evaded him.

Mara backed off, the Tiger advancing upon her, his fangs bared, his stinking breath forcing air out of the room. Mara bumped into the wall, her face blank and slack, tears running freely down her cheeks. The face of a frightened girl.

Julian groped for a weapon. His fist closed around the handle of the pan. The cooked head in it fell out. The Tiger's muzzle dipped, and he crunched the head and gulped it down. Mara cried out. Julian reversed the pan and drove the handle into the beast's eye, some detached part of him wondering where he had learned to fight so dirty.

The beast roared, an almost human cry of outrage, and his immense claws raked Julian. He managed to duck but the second swipe tore his clothes and plowed through his chest, leaving ragged wounds that quickly filled with blood. The pain was even worse than before.

Julian felt a cold, overwhelming rage rise from the base of his spine. He was going to die; it did not matter. He had to kill the beast first. The pan had been bent and was now useless as a weapon. Julian slid down onto the floor, faking unconscious, calculating that when the Tiger loomed over him, he would try to tear the beast's throat out. But it did not come to this. An eager feline shape launched itself onto the Tiger.

Rolling on the floor under the clawing paws, choking on the ammoniac stench, Julian did not know what was happening. His eyes were blinded by dust and blood; his ears deafened by snarls and growls but somewhere, distantly, he could hear a man's voice crying, "Aly!"

And then it was over. Something heavy fell onto him, burying him under the mound of stinking, lice-ridden fur. He crawled from under the Tiger's carcass, his torn arm and the deep furrows on his chest dripping blood. Stepping over the Tiger, his throat torn out far more efficiently than he could have ever done with his weak human hands, Julian staggered toward Mara and Dog who were huddled together in a corner.

A shape was lying on the floor between them, Dog's calloused hands cradling its head. Julian looked down.

Mrs. Alice Debora Cat was still mostly cat, her tortoiseshell fur bristling along her flexible spine, her white belly torn and stained by the Tiger's mauling, her claws retracting. But her face was feebly trying to regain its human contours, the pink button twitching and reshaping itself into a no-nonsense nose; the toothy mouth contracting into severely pursed lips; the spindle-shaped pupils rounding out.

"Aly, you old fool!" Dog cried. Tears and snot ran down his face.

"I'm sorry!" Mara whispered. "Oh, I'm so sorry!"

She laid her hand on Cat's head. But Cat shook her off and turned her slackening face toward Dog. She wanted to say something, but her half-transformed mouth could not produce articulate words. And then she was dead.

Julian tried to get up and lay back with a groan. The lacerations on his chest were tender and throbbing. Strangely, even though the wound on his arm was more serious, it did not bother him so much. Mara had managed to clean it out and bandaged it with the clothes from the cabin. But the Tiger's claws had brought an infection into his chest and now it pounded in the rhythm of his heart. Finally, he managed to drag himself upright and go behind the cabin to relieve himself.

Dog was still sitting by Alice's corpse, which he had covered with some of her own clothes. Torn by her metamorphosis into Cat, they no longer fit her expanded body. The Tiger's carcass was not around; Mara and Dog had pushed it off the island and it sank.

Julian staggered toward the water's edge, glancing irritably at the unchanging silvery sky. The endless light seemed to drive nails into his dry eyes.

Mara materialized by his side.

"The first one to go," she said.

"He was your husband." Julian did not know why he felt he needed to say that. Perhaps he wanted her to bury Ronald, so he could finally bury Elvira.

"Not really." Mara shook her head. "I mean ... yes, Ronald Raven was my husband, an imprint of the Tiger, the totem of hunger and famine. But the man who created the Tiger so long ago ... I don't remember who he was. Not yet. But I will."

"These are the islands of memory," Julian said.

"Yes. But whose memory?"

"The Four's."

"No. The Four are just names that humans had given to their fears a long time ago, and who became real in the dream-sea. But ... you know, Julian, once my ... my husband, he gave me a pearl necklace. And he explained how pearls grow. There is an ordinary sand grain, a commonplace, like millions of other grains. But somehow it is lodged in the right place and a pearl accretes around it, layers and layers. But there is still an ordinary grain of sand deep inside."

"So?"

"What if we are like that? The dream-sea grows pearls of stories. Layers of fears, loves, hates ... And you have a monster, like the Lion or the Bear. And then another layer, and here we are, Julian Sparrow and Mara Raven, ordinary people, with our own stories. You said it yourself: They may be inside us, but we are not them."

"And ..."

"So maybe there is still another layer. A grain of sand inside the black pearl of the Four. Something that happened to ordinary people, people like us, deep in time before the dream-sea rose and flooded the world. A story. And we are remembering it."

Julian was silent.

"The story of the four of us?" he finally asked.

"Yes."

"Do I want to remember it?"

Mara smiled.

"Probably not. But can you help it?"

Julian turned away and went back into the cabin where Dog was holding his solitary vigil. His wounds throbbed. He did not know how much time had passed; the light never changed, there was no day or night, and somehow it seemed a worse deprivation than hunger or thirst.

A man must not be robbed of time.

Dog was asleep, and Julian envied him. But he jumped up the moment Julian crossed the threshold, positioning himself between him and the body. For a moment, Julian stared into his red-rimmed eyes.

"We must bury her, Mr. Dog," he said.

"How? There is no shovel here and the ground is flinty."

"Sea burial, then."

"No way! Toss here into ... this ..."

"There is no other way." And because Dog was still staring at him, growling in his throat, Julian decided to be ruthless.

"You know what happened here," he said. "We are marooned. Do you want to risk it happening again?"

Dog dropped his eyes.

"All right," he said. "But how do we get off this island?"

"Mara will show us the way," Julian said with more conviction than he felt.

Dog spat into the dust.

"Aly loved her," he muttered. "She would never say, the old fool, but she did. Reminded her of her niece or something. She killed herself for her. Took on my old employer, and she was no match for him. But she fought well, she did. We fight well, us, the free animals. Cats and Dogs."

"She killed him," Julian said. "She killed the Tiger, one of the Four. His real name, you know, was Famine."

Dog smiled.

"Then why are we so hungry?" he asked. "Never mind, mister. You're right. We have to bury her."

They carried the body to the water's edge, Julian staggering under its modest weight. Mara came out from behind the cabin and walked toward them, as if offering help, but Dog snapped at her and she hung back, her face hidden by her loosened hair. They walked through the shallow water toward the depth. Julian felt something sinuous brush his leg.

When the water came up to their chests, they let the body go. It sank like a stone, the dream-sea once again showing its capricious nature. But as they started plowing back toward the island, Dog caught Julian's hand. Turning back, he saw the water churn and boil where the body had sunk as if invisible fish fought over it. Dog made to go back but Julian restrained him.

A big fish surfaced, jumped into the air, and paddled there in defiance of gravity. It was about the size of Julian, the color of glass faintly flushed with rose; hard to see against the leaden background of the sea and the sky. From its nose projected two tentacles, almost twice as long as itself, weaving in the air. The fish dipped and suddenly its fins unfolded into membranous wings. Now it resembled a bizarre bat.

Mara gave a strangled cry and ran, splashing, into the sea. The batfish glided toward her. More fish of the same kind jumped out of the churning water, unfolded their wings, and flew toward Mara.

Julian ducked under the water, squinted into the liquid grayness. He could make out the place where they had deposited Cat's body. There was a neat oblong hillock on the sandy seafloor. The fish had buried her.

He surfaced, the brine burning every wound and scratch, to see Mara laughing, standing up to her waist in the sea, and surrounded by batfish. They were no longer transparent. Nosing her like eager puppies, they were acquiring color from this contact, each touch making them more solid. Some were bright fire-engine red, some sky blue, some grass green, the bright primary colors of childhood.

"I thought they were bottom-feeders!" Mara cried. "But they feed on the deepest dreams!"

Julian did not know what she meant but he did not care, seeing what the batfish were up to. Their long feelers were busy weaving and intertwining, creating a sort of net or hammock. They dipped to the surface of the water, the net composed of multicolored living strands, borne between their fluttering bodies. They were clearly offering Mara a lift.

"Come on!" she cried, waving to him and Dog. "Move! They're taking us out of here!"

The net will never carry the three of us, he thought, as he ran clumsily, raising plumes of water, toward the school of the flying creatures. But it did. He, Mara, and Dog ended up in an undignified pile, like nursery kids squeezed into a shaky playpen. The living hammock stretched but did not break as the school rose higher and slowly flapped toward the low-lying island surrounded by mudflats in the middle of the sea.

CHAPTER 4. THE SECOND OF THE FOUR

At the end, they were deposited down safely, though rather casually. The net unraveled and they tumbled down into soft mud, Julian grunting in pain as Dog's boots pinned down his wounded arm. Mara scrambled away from under both of them, and finally disentangled, they surveyed their new island.

Or was it even an island? Julian was not sure. They were on a mudflat covered by a thin film of dirty water. The mud, which liberally smeared every exposed inch of their bodies and stuck to their clothes, smelled like a sewer and was of a sickly brownish-black color. The water was foul. The rest of the landscape was veiled from sight, mercifully perhaps, by sulfurous yellow fog that made their eyes water like the vapors from one of the City's chemical works. The fog parted momentarily to reveal the sky that had curdled into an inflamed pinkish-red glow.

"Where do you reckon we are, sir?" Dog asked.

Julian smiled at being promoted from "mister" to "sir." But it was Mara who answered.

"We are in a place I know, Mr. Dog," she said. "There is an island here; we need to reach it. I think we'll find what we are seeking there."

"And how do you propose we reach your island?" Dog growled. "The fog is dirtier than a bog-house."

"Just follow the sticks," she said, and pointed to a double row of canes poking up from the viscous mud that formed a sort of path. But they were not poles but rather engorged tubes of writhing tissue like vertical worms.

They staggered through the mud that gulped at their shoes with obscene intestinal sounds. Something loomed ahead, and the closer they approached it, the worse the stench became, sticking to the back of the throat like tar. Mixed with the acrid chemical vapor was the sweetish stink of rotting flesh.

"Something's dead up there!" Dog growled.

"More than you know," Mara responded, covering her nose and mouth with her shirt.

Julian followed suit. This island sickened him. He was used to the smell of death. (*Used? How?*) But there was something particularly foul about this place.

This is not clean death.

What death is ever clean?

His wounds were getting worse; he could feel infection eating through his swollen, pus-leaking flesh. He was racked by bouts of shivering; his temperature must have been rising. At least, his hunger and thirst receded. Who could possibly think of food in this charnel house?

The convoluted shapes ahead resolved into a forest. Short, gnarly trees festooned with beards of air roots poked from the peat-colored water. But this forest was dead. The trees were rotting carcasses struck by some plant blight, their branches bare, their aerial roots dusty and brittle. The only thing that survived was the thick yellow lichen that dangled from the canopy like vomit. And even worse, there were decomposing corpses floating in the filthy water they had to wade through. Julian tried not to look too closely but he could not help noticing that though most were fish, some were glassy mermaids like the one that had led them to the island of Hunger. He plowed on and breathed through the mouth. Eventually, the plopping mulch of the bottom felt firmer and then the ground rose. They were out of the swamp.

For a moment, what lay before him looked serene and beautiful in a melancholy way—a long, narrow tidal plane hemmed in by a bare ridge; brown sand and green algae-infested pools under the red sky. But then he saw great slick logs scattered here and there twitching feebly and realized they were dying animals.

One of the logs crept toward them. It was a blubber-swollen, smooth creature with a tiny, toothy head. The animal looked like an enormous slug. But it was too obviously sick to be threatening. Its slick skin was covered with pustules. There was a gash in its side, and yellow froth was seeping from the wound. The animal made strange coughing sounds. Julian turned away, nauseated.

More marine animals stirred on the beach but seemed too weak to pose any danger. Julian saw a smaller, cuter creature— probably a baby—nuzzle its mother's bloated corpse. Some of the dead and the dying were feasted upon by swarms of hopping sand fleas and flies the size of canaries.

"Nice place you brought us to, ma'am!" Dog addressed Mara.

"It is his island," she said, more to herself than to him. "The island of Pestilence and Betrayal. But we will make it to Second City, I promise."

Turning to the ridge, she screamed at the top of her voice, hoarsely and crudely, so uncharacteristic of the Mara he knew, that Julian jumped.

"Show up, you fucking bastard! You bag of filth! I know you're here! Afraid to look me in the eyes, are you! It's time for us to have a little chat!"

"Is that the way to talk to your mentor, Mara?" said a voice close behind them. Expecting their enemy to pop up on the ridge, Julian swiveled around, almost losing his balance.

One of the swollen carcasses on the beach, thickly swarming with flies and sand fleas, got up, shaking off but not dispersing his retinue.

Mr. Seal had changed since they last saw him, and not for the better. The fat-draped, sexless body remained the same but now it was covered in running sores. The spindly legs seemed to have shrunk and were little more than fleshless claws, unable to bear his weight. He could stand upright only by supporting himself on his companion: a cartwheel-sized snail with a splintered shell and a human face poking from under its overhang.

"You!" Mara spat. "You filthy coward! You traitor! What do you call a teacher who betrays his student? Who is worse than that?"

"A daughter who betrays her mother? A mother who betrays her daughter?"

"I did not ..." Mara began, and then a shadow of confusion passed over her face, and she shook her head as if trying to dislodge something.

Julian stepped forward.

"I would not waste a bullet on you!" he snarled. "Let us pass! We are going to Second City, and you can't stop us."

"Second City?" the Seal sneered. "Dead City. The City of the Dead. You killed the Tiger; now there are only three of us left, and let me tell you, your totem is not happy about it. You can't fight your totem, Julian Lion."

"I can and I will. He is not my totem anymore. Let us through!"

Mr. Seal focused his rheumy eyes on Julian and suddenly his wounds erupted in gouts of blood and black gangrenous matter. He doubled over, blinded by pain.

Mara hugged him, held him upright, oblivious of the blood and the smell. With Julian in her arms, she turned to the other inhabitants of the beach.

"He is killing you!" she cried. "You owe nothing to him; he is the enemy of all living! He promises survival but delivers only pain! Help me and I'll give you a clean and swift death!"

And the rotting animals heard.

They dragged themselves toward the Seal, the lord of Pestilence, who warded them off with swarms of flies and puffs of stench. They died as they were crawling, leaving pieces of themselves on the dirty sand. And still, they advanced. The Seal stomped his foot; his bulk wobbled. The advancing animals burst open, their flesh liquefying. Julian howled, feeling his bones poke through his skin.

The snail that supported the Seal's gross body suddenly stretched forth his human face on a long, raw neck. He opened his prissy mouth in a silent scream, and something flew out, the wet rag of a detachable tongue. It landed with a smack on his master's face and dripped acid that ate through the Seal's flesh.

With a convulsive blow of his crooked hands, the Seal split the snail's shell and the creature's slimy, pitifully thin but human body fell, dying, onto the sand. But with the last remainder of his strength, Julian lurched forward, butted into the Seal's flabby belly, toppled him, and stomped onto his acid-eaten face. Mara and Dog joined him. And then the dying animals came and fell upon the flopping hulk.

Covered in blood and slime, Mara lifted her arms and cried out, a hoarse, inarticulate plea for the cleansing waters. And the sea heard.

Over the dead mangrove, over the sick beach, a great wall of emerald-sparkling water rose, washing away the feverish color of the sky and revealing the bright golden dome. Its frothy crest curled above Julian's head, and he lifted his face and he felt only a glad welcome, as the pain ate into his bones.

The wave collapsed in a flood of mint-scented water that spun Julian like a toy, blinding him, rushing into his lungs; lifted him and rocked him and hurled him onto something hard. He knew he was drowning and was not afraid.

He drew water into his lungs and breathed.

He opened his eyes. In the golden-green liquid light, dark objects swooped and glided and hovered, playfully juggled about by the dream-sea. The water was sweet and cool in his lungs and upon his skin.

He started swimming, trailing clouds of blood, but as he swam, the clouds lightened and dispersed. A parrot-beaked fish poked him and disappointed that he did not want to play, swam away.

He breached the surface, sputtering. The air was fresh and sweet; the light like that of a summer noon, only the entire sky glowed with a warm golden sheen. He saw land ahead and half swam, half rode the waves toward it.

The waves deposited him on the beach of Pestilence's island. He recognized the ridge.

The sparkling sand was littered with white branches of drift-wood and bone. Dry skeletons snapped under his feet as he walked along the beach. Looking down at himself, he discovered he was naked and healed, his arms and chest scoured with old scars.

He found Dog first, and then Mara. Dog was busy impro-vising a loincloth from seaweed, his skinny body gleaming clean and whole in the golden light. Mara sat on the sand, staring out into the sea, and he averted his gaze from her nudity, suddenly afraid of something more complicated than simple desire.

They looked at each other shamefacedly. There seemed to be nothing to say. They went beachcombing, Dog stubbornly holding his disintegrating seaweed loincloth in place. After a while, they started coming upon objects tossed up by the dream-sea: an old sewing machine; a scatter of strange coins; a baby's rattle; a coffee mug with a broken-off handle. Eventually, they picked up miscellaneous clothes. Dog decked himself out in a worn pair of a worker's canvas pants, a too-small plaid shirt, and too-large boots. Instead of a hat, he wore a woman's gaudy scarf.

Julian resigned himself to patched-up breeches, a dinner jacket, and sandals. And Mara slipped into a long, old-fashioned gown made of faded brown silk. It fit her perfectly.

The ridge that hid the rest of the island from them dipped and flattened out. Beyond the beach, they could see a green meadow dotted with clumps of bright flowers. And there was a gray, squat building in the middle of it.

CHAPTER 5. THE THIRD OF THE FOUR

The structure in the meadow was not a house. It was a squat concrete shelter, a bunker, with an empty doorway and unglazed window slits, overgrown with vines and wildflowers. Inside it was dim and cool, offering a welcome shelter from the heat, which had increased considerably, despite the fact that there was no perceptible change in the golden dome of the sky.

Julian, Dog, and Mara ducked through the doorway. The bunker was empty except for the bunk beds along the walls, some rusty chicken wire, and a clutter of unidentifiable objects on the floor. They scattered with a metallic clang when she stumbled in. Mara lifted what she thought was a seashell, only to discover that it was a piece of metal. She showed it to Julian.

"It's a cartridge," he said. "Unused. For a Sig Sauer, maybe."

"For what?"

"It's a type of handgun," Julian muttered.

"Is it like the one I fired?"

"No." Julian scooped more ammo from the floor. "We did not have anything like this in the City. It's a weapon of war. Very advanced."

"A weapon of war ..." Mara repeated. "Is it here?"

"It should be, but I can't find it. Only ammo."

Dog, meanwhile, made himself at home, sweeping more ammo off the bunk beds and rooting in the debris on the floor.

"Look!" He lifted something up. "Chow!"

It was a battered tin.

"Meat loaf!" Julian sounded so enthusiastic that Mara gaped at him, only to discover that her stomach rumbled, too.

"And see this?" Dog was showing off his latest find, a small oblong cardboard box.

"Cigarettes!" Julian exclaimed. "Look for matches, buddy!"

"What are cigarettes?" Mara had never heard the word.

"They are ..." Julian started and trailed off, as if unsure. Meanwhile, Dog was opening tins with a rusty opener he had fished from under more boxes. Julian and Dog fell upon the preserved meat with a hearty appetite and Mara followed suit. After the meal, the mystery of cigarettes was solved. Julian and Dog lit slender paper cylinders, which instead of bursting into flame smoldered and released clouds of pungent smoke. The men breathed it in with delight. In the City, Mara had heard of people inhaling the fumes of narcotic substances, but it was a rare and exotic vice and she had never seen anybody doing it. The idea that Julian, let alone Dog, dabbled in it was news to her. She suspected it was news to them as well.

After the meal, Dog plunked down on one of the beds and soon started snoring softly. Julian glanced at Mara and by unspoken consent they got up together and wandered outside.

They walked to the edge of the meadow and sat in the soft grass that sloped down to the dunes of the beach. The sweet smell of the daisy-like flowers mingled with the bracing ocean breath. They sat with their backs to the beach, so they would not have to watch the sudden capricious shifts of the color of the water, from sparkling topaz to deep purple, and a giant square jellyfish that tried, laboriously, to mate with a long strand of bladder wrack. Facing into the meadow, it was almost possible to pretend they were still in the South Continent when it had been part of reborn humanity's precarious home. Even the uniform golden dome of the sky could, with some creative squinting, be reimagined as the sunset.

Julian stretched on his back on the grass and put his head in Mara's lap. She smelled the strange smoke he had been inhaling. Timidly, she rested her hand on his hair. He muttered something inaudible.

"What?" She bent closer.

"Little sister ..."

She snatched her hand away, terrified; she did not know of what.

"It's coming closer, Mara," he said in his Julian voice, a reassuring urbane drawl. "Only two more to go. You and me."

"What do you mean?"

But she knew, of course.

"We killed the Tiger and the Seal," he said. "Hunger and Pestilence. I know my totem is close. I can smell him."

"What does he smell like?"

"Gunpowder and dirty socks. Blood. Smoke."

"That thing you lit ..."

"Yes. This is a good smell. Men together, sharing a cigarette. Brothers in arms. He is trying to seduce me."

"But you won't be seduced?"

Julian shook his head.

"No, I know his other face too well. The Lion is mindless rage; filthy and stupid. I'll kill him. But it may mean that you'll have to face her alone. I'm sorry, Mara."

She wanted to strike at him, to cry out, *Don't you dare abandon me! Not again!* But she did not. Instead, she turned her head and looked at the dream-sea that flashed ruby red. A triple rainbow suddenly arced over the carnelian waves.

"Can they really be killed?" she asked.

He snuggled closer into her lap.

"We saw …"

"Yes. But what did we see? You're remembering, Julian, aren't you? Those are islands of memory. But whose memory?"

"Theirs."

"No. They are just … figures. Names that humans give their nightmares. Hunger, Pestilence, War. And … and her. The veiled one. Even if we kill the Tiger, the Seal, the Lion, and the Bear, they'll come back under different names."

"But you said we could restore First City! Bring it back!"

"I want to. I am not my totem. I am not the Revealer. I am Mara, a human being who made mistakes and who wants to atone for them. But is it enough to kill an abstraction?"

Julian sat up.

"A grain of sand inside a black pearl. This is what you are talking about, right?"

"Yes. Pearls of stories, accreting around one woman or one man. Layers of memories, traumas, loves, and hates. People like us deep in time before the dream-sea flooded the world. And then they became kernels of monsters. And these monsters created us, Mara and Julian. We are not them. We make our own choices. But can we escape their heritage?"

"Are we really people?" Julian whispered.

Mara looked away.

"Maybe not," she said. "But maybe it will be our salvation that we are not. The history locked in the black flowers … it is not our history. But to be free of it, we have to remember."

He was silent, staring into the dream-sea. The triple rainbow blazed in the colors of delirium, but the waters suddenly turned deep, soothing blue.

"You called me 'little sister,'" she pressed. "Why? We are not related, Julian. I have no brother and you have no sister."

He shook his head but did not look at her.

"Is this why you never dared to make love to me?"

He finally raised his eyes and smiled.

"Even if it's true," he said, "and there are other lives inside the Four, what difference does it make? We still have to confront them, to fight them, to avenge our murdered City. This is the only thing left to do."

"Yes. But remember, Julian, we are all made in the image of those lost humans. Black flowers are their memories, their stories, their souls. And yet we live our own lives and make our own choices. So, if we remember the original story of the Four, perhaps we can remake it. Perhaps there is more than vengeance left. Perhaps we can resurrect the City, and even better, remake it."

"It's a dangerous hope, Mara. A soldier must be ready to kill and to die. A soldier must never hope to come back alive."

"But you're not a soldier, Julian," she said. "You're a merchant. A City merchant, a ladies' man, Elvira's unfaithful but loving husband. These are somebody else's memories. You had your life in First City, and it was a good life too. And I'm not your sister."

He smiled. On the beach, the square jellyfish burst out in a bouquet of brilliant tentacles. Julian cradled Mara's face in his hands, and she thought, *Finally*. And as their lips met, she tasted only his flesh and a tang of smoke. They lay down in the soft grass and she closed her eyes to the golden sky and the blazing rainbow, feeling his stubble scratch her wind-roughened cheeks. Dog slept through it all or pretended to.

She fell asleep on the shore of the dream-sea. And within its ceaseless dreaming, she dreamed.

She is staring down at the tabletop covered with a dirty oilcloth. There are breadcrumbs scattered around the ring left from the supper plate and unthinkingly, she is beginning to sweep them into the palm of her hand. Bread should not be wasted.

But then she hears his steps in the anteroom, and she jumps up and the crumbs are flying onto the scrubbed wooden floor. She falls on her knees; he abhors dirty floors! Cockroaches will come, he says, looking at her meaningfully. You would like this, wouldn't you?

It's a joke, of course, but it is beginning to wear thin.

And as she is sweeping up the crumbs, the baby lets out a long, piercing wail. She has been doing this too much recently. Is she sick? Or is it her milk that is turning rotten in the baby's mouth? You're poison, he says, people like you.

But it is her own daughter! How can she poison her own child?

He walks in as she is frozen in her ridiculous position, kneeling with her head under the table, unable to decide whether to finish the cleaning or to attend to her daughter. So, she does neither, which of course, is the worst choice of all.

His tread is heavy; once upon a time, it used to sound solid, reassuring, and masculine.

He gives her bottom a sound kick.

"Shut her up, will you!" And a curse, one of the filthy words, which has become a source of amusement to him recently. He would use these words when they were making love. She would freeze and he would plow on.

She straightens up, goes to the cradle, where her daughter is yelling her lungs out, her tiny face beet red. She knows she should pick her up, but her arms hang uselessly by her sides. Suddenly she is pierced by a bolt of hate toward the baby.

"Shut the brat up!"

"Why don't you do it?" she snaps at him, without turning around. She does not want to see his jowly face, which, she knows, is flushed and stupid from the drink. "It's your child!"

"No, it's not! It's not my child! You think I don't know you've been screwing around? You whore!"

Outside, a dog is barking.

Mara sat up.

The triple rainbow still blazed above her. She could not have slept long.

"Shh!" Julian's arms tightened around her. They were naked

in the soft grass. His skin was smooth and white, muscles like steel. She buried her face in his chest.

"Let's go away!" she whispered.

"We can't. There is nowhere to go."

Dog appeared in the doorway of the bunker, cleared his throat, and shambled away. Julian and Mara burst out in giggles and raced to retrieve their clothes.

"You know," Mara said, "in that other life ..."

"Yes?"

"My husband betrayed me, and you were not there to save me."

Julian went into the bunker and started putting together intricately worked pieces of metal. It looked like a jigsaw puzzle to Mara, but he ended up with a black, oily gun. He squinted into the muzzle, spun the drum, and loaded it with cartridges.

"I know," he said.

Dog yelled from behind the ridge and popped up on the edge of the meadow. He slipped, went down on all fours, then righted himself and rushed toward Julian and Mara. Behind him, gray figures spilled into the meadow.

They were men, or so Mara thought, glad to see human likeness in this place, even if their clothes were in tatters and they carried weapons. But then she realized that though their filthy gray uniforms covered human bodies, they had no faces. A fat pulsing spider sat upon each man's face, obscuring it completely, its legs running under the man's dusty hair, its clustered eyes swiveling as it directed its steed.

Julian took aim and fired.

One gray man swayed and fell, a scarlet bloom unfolding on his chest. Another shot took his comrade in the face; his spider exploded into chunks of insect flesh and the man's denuded skull flashed briefly as he turned around and fled. Others lifted their guns.

"Down!" Julian snarled and pushed Mara so she fell into the

grass. Dog had ducked into the bunker and was frantically rummaging through the hardware.

The spider-soldiers fired, and Mara was deafened by the barking sound, beaten down by it, pressed into the dirt. But though the bullets swirled around Julian like angry wasps, they did not touch him. His body was beginning to exude a sickly yellow glow.

Julian fired again, and more spider-soldiers fell. Above the din, Mara could hear a rumbling growl.

I must do something! she thought desperately. *I have allies here! Mermaids, bottom-feeders, Light Puppies* ... But they felt like dusty, pathetic toys; odds and ends of impotence.

More spider-faced soldiers poured into the meadow, rushing over the bodies of their fallen comrades. The dead and wounded were piling up, creating a barricade. But the soldiers never stopped; oblivious to the angry stuttering of Julian's gun, oblivious to their deaths, they pressed forward. Mara crawled back into the doorway of the bunker and collided with Dog. They fell into a sprawling heap.

Suddenly the shooting stopped. Pushing Dog aside, Mara scrambled to her feet. The gray spider-faced tide was reaching Julian who desperately fumbled with his gun. One of the front-line soldiers lifted his own gun and aimed. In slowed-down time, Mara saw the bullet exiting the black hole, buzzing toward Julian. And still she was paralyzed.

The rumbling growl intensified and filled the meadow. A giant shadow, golden in the golden light, leaped into the massed ranks of the spider-faced soldiers, scattering them like bowling pins. His hide polished metal, his mane a plume of glory, the Lion savaged the enemy, and the enemy turned around and fled before his wrath. And Mara, her back to the concrete wall, her hands empty, momentarily rejoiced in his victory.

The Lion trod on the bodies, smashing them like grapes, his clawed feet being painted crimson. He ducked his massive head, his mane shining like a halo, brighter than the sky, and licked the bloody ground. Then he raised his face. His leprous lips stretched in a smile. The empty, ragged holes of his eyes focused on Julian who stood very still, his back to Dog and Mara.

The Lion growled again. Slowly, as if mesmerized, Julian stepped toward the beast. One step, then another.

"No!" Mara tried to scream but her voice was forced back into her throat. Julian stepped closer and the Lion roared.

Dog tossed something at the beast.

It was a piece of rusted junk, a bent, battered rifle. It somersaulted in the air and glanced harmlessly off the Lion's mighty back. He roared again, flattening the grass with his thunder, and jumped. He soared in the air above the heads of Julian and Mara, and came down upon Dog who tried to sneak behind the bunker. But the Lion's claws snagged him and pulled him back. The beast planted his paw on Dog's chest, as he squirmed and tried to break free.

Julian fired.

The Lion screamed in pain and outrage, a wordless but strangely human sound. The beast left Dog on the ground and in one huge bound launched himself at Julian. There was blood streaming down his flank.

Julian turned around to flee but the Lion was faster. He brought down the running man. And as his fanged muzzle dipped toward his prey, Mara acted.

She picked up one of the pieces of hardware littering the ground. She did not know what it was; it did not matter. Pointing it like a child's toy gun, she pulled the trigger. A spark exited from the barrel and flew toward the Lion, expanding into a ring of light, emerald with bright purple lining. The Light Puppy slipped around the Lion's head like a necklace and encircled his mane. The beast roared and rose on his hind legs, towering above the scatter of human bodies. Thick saliva streamed from his bloodied maw.

"Die!" Mara ordered.

The necklace of light tightened around the Lion's throat, suffocating the beast. He shook his head like a drunk, dropped back on all fours, tried to gallop away, but the stranglehold was inexorable, cutting into his armored hide. The Light Puppy blazed with a blinding brilliance, as if drawing sustenance from the Lion's fury. The beast's mangy fur started smoking. The reek of burnt flesh filled the air. The Lion strained to roar but only a puny whimper came from his blocked windpipe. He rolled around in a frenzy, crushing the bodies of spider-faced soldiers. He rolled over Julian. His mighty tail flailed around, pulverizing grass and flowers and raising fountains of dirt.

Mara rushed forward to drag Julian away, but Dog caught her, held her, oblivious of her frenzied kicking and thrashing.

The Light Puppy cut so deeply into the Lion's neck that it was no longer visible. The beast's head was collared by black, viscous blood and burning fur. The Lion twitched; his claws digging deep into the churned soil. And then he lay still. His collar of fire gave the last squeeze and the giant leprous head separated from the body and rolled away, followed by a rush of blood the color of tar and smoke.

Wriggling free of Dog, Mara stumbled toward Julian. He lay on his back, his breath wheezing in and out like the breath of an old man. His chest was crushed.

Mara dropped to her knees, smoothing his black hair away from his dirty face.

"Hang on, hang on," she whispered. "It's nothing, just a scratch ..."

Julian smiled.

"Little sister ..." he said. And then he died.

Mara did not know how long she sat by his body. It was a change in light that made her lift her head, look around with eyes that were as dry as sawdust. Was night coming?

There was no night on the shores of the dream-sea but the

darkness was coming, the golden light changing to deep gray dusk. The dome of the sky was colorless, shedding a pale glow that failed to illuminate the meadow where shadows were gathering, clustering thickly around the corpses of spider-soldiers, mantling the Lion's giant shapeless body and his separated head. The meadow smelled like a butcher's shop. For once, the dream-sea was in no hurry to clean up.

Against the white sky, Mara saw a black silhouette. Dog. He had been sitting on the grass across from her, sharing her vigil.

"I guess it's now only you and me, ma'am," he said.

Mara nodded, remembering his own vigil over the body of Cat and how Julian had helped him to bury her, while she herself had done nothing.

"Yes, Mr. Dog," she said. "It's only us now. Two against one; good odds."

She kissed Julian's mouth and closed his eyes. His face looked peaceful in the dimming light. His chest was a bloody mess.

She looked around. Even though there were many bodies of spider-soldiers lying around, she could see no black flowers. Were the soldiers creatures of the dream-sea rather than avatars of human beings? Somehow, she did not think so. It was rather as if their souls had been burnt to cinders a long time ago.

She swallowed and then reached down, placed her hands on Julian's temples. Her fingers sank into the flesh that was dissolving, first into blood and then into water, the streams lightening from red to pink to clear as they ran down the meadow toward the dream-sea, to rejoin their source.

She tugged upward. The black flower bloomed in her hands. Its butterfly crown trembled and turned toward her.

The vortex opened, piercing the dusk.

Mara kissed the petals, and they tasted like Julian's lips.

"We'll meet soon," she said, and turned to her waiting companion. "We're on our way, Mr. Dog."

CHAPTER 6. THE LIFTED VEIL

They cut inland. Previously when the dream-sea had been just that, the sea of dreams, Mara had thought of its small islands only as launching pads for exploration of its magical waters with their tangled currents and delightful—or dangerous—marine life. It had never occurred to her that islands were important in themselves. Now, she realized that the islands represented the aspects of the dream-sea that had become dominant. The dream-sea contained everything humans had ever imagined, dreamed of, or feared, but only in inchoate, unstable states. Whatever entities were in the ascendant, they emerged from the fluid chaos and established terra firma outposts for themselves. She assumed that the bigger the island, the more important the force that had claimed its possession. By this token, the island they were on belonged to an important force.

Of course, she thought, *it does. The most important force of all.*

But perhaps not. Again, she was struck with the conviction that there were other entities in the dream-sea beyond the Four; perhaps more powerful than them, but somehow paralyzed or barred from protecting humans. She thought that they may have had a hand in establishing the City. And if they did, then the defeat of the Four may enable them to resurrect the City, to bring back its inhabitants in their human form. After all, the black flowers still bloomed, containing the personalities and the memories of the dead.

In fact, they bloomed vigorously on this part of the island. Having stepped through the vortex, Dog and Mara climbed a rampart of eroded sandstone bluffs and were now walking on a gentle rise toward a range of hills. At least, this was what the terrain seemed to be as much as they could make it out in the dim twilight. Mara had never known the dream-sea illumination to be so bad; it was no better than the dusk after the sunset, before full darkness. The sky was of a weird white color, like curdled milk, and it reluctantly dribbled enough light for them not to stumble too badly. The narrow path they were on wound between masses of black flowers that fused into shadows in the distance. An occasional twisted tree clawed at the pale sky. The low hills hunched up morosely.

Dog strode ahead of Mara, unfazed by the gathering darkness. His confidence helped her to forget the icy knot of dread that lay, implacable and heavy, under her breastbone. Even her grief for Julian could not compete with its paralyzing weight.

He suddenly stopped, bent down, and lifted something from the ground.

"What's that?" Mara tried to peer over his shoulder. He showed her his find. Uncomprehendingly, she stared at the thin black disk, its edge broken off. There was a neat hole in its dead center. Elusive familiarity tugged at her.

"It's—" she stammered. And suddenly, she knew.

Taking the disk from Dog, she turned it over. There was a circular paper label, so faded that she could not read what was written on it, but it appeared to be in a script different from the City's.

"It's a gramophone record," she said. "Music. Like on the radio, only preserved. You need a contraption to play it."

Dog ran his calloused fingers across the disk's grooved surface. "Songs," he said. "A good big-band marching tune."

Mara sent the disk spinning into the thicket of black flowers.

"We'll hear these songs again, Mr. Dog," she said. "You'll see."

There had never been gramophone records in the City. Marvin Gazelle had experimented with wax disks to record sounds but that was all.

They slogged on.

We'll do better next time!

There will be no next time, Mara.

The voices in her head fell silent as they approached the foothills. The land had risen; the field of black flowers was left behind. They stood on a gravelly incline littered with an incredible profusion of broken objects. It was like the war junk in the bunker but magnified thousandfold and mixed with detritus of peace. Shattered dishes, bent cutlery, rusted pieces of machinery, useless tools, broken weapons, torn books, their pages spread out like enormous butterflies, open suitcases gaping their toothless mouths, more jagged gramophone records with lost labels ...

Mara took Dog's hand and together they navigated the field of lost things. She cut her foot on a sliver of glass. The light was getting progressively worse; it was now like a moonlit night, though of course there was no moon in the ashen sky. But as they approached the top of the hill, sickly yellow radiance spilled from the other side.

A doll with a baby face stared at them from the dusk, or was it a real baby? Mara did not pause to see; she needed to reach the top.

They crested it together and stood looking down into the valley, bereft of words.

There was a City cupped in the hills; for a wild moment, she thought it was First City. But it was not; even during the Dark Years the City had never been like this. And yet for all the horror it inspired this City looked familiar. She had been here before.

It was well-lit, its labyrinthine streets edged with glowing yellow pearls of electric lights. But it only showed the devastation more clearly.

Houses, taller and narrower than the houses in the First City, stared at the rubbish-strewn streets with the empty eyeholes of their shattered windows. Some were simply upright ruins, tottering before the final collapse, their obscenely revealed interiors spilling furniture like guts. Many roofs had caved in, tiles sticking out like rotten teeth, smokestacks tilting. Elaborate façades decorated with plasterwork and gilded scrolls were pock-marked by bullet holes. Ironwork fences had been wrenched apart by explosions. A pedestal bore a single leg, the rest of the statue littering the square in unrecognizable fragments. A small garden sprouted burnt bushes.

There were dark oblong shapes lying on the pavement along each street, each alley. They had been carefully placed at intervals, as if whoever had done it tried to pay respect through geometry. But there was no disguising what they were.

Mara swallowed. The cold nugget of dread expanded, filling her. She shivered in her thin silk dress.

And then she realized that the cold was coming from outside, wafting from the dead City. The unnatural brightness of its streets was caused by the reflections of streetlights off the thin drifts and wedges of snow that lined the pavement. The ruined building glittered with rime. The waters of the dream-sea that had covered this City were now frozen by the presence of its ruler. The ruler she had let out of her cage.

"We'll feel warmer as we walk," Dog said and started down the slope.

The cold hit them like a hammer. First City had a mild, wet climate; even in winter, snow was rare. Now Mara felt as if her body and brain alike were frozen. But as they crossed the boundary where the gravel gave way to the pavement, she realized that the cold was a blessing. They passed the first body bags but even though there was an unpleasant sweetish taint in the air, she knew it could have been worse if the temperature rose.

Or maybe not. In this wasteland of time, littered with the debris of history, would not the natural processes of decay and regeneration stop forever?

Prompted by sick curiosity, she unzipped one bag. A man's face dappled with livid spots of decomposition stared at her with cloudy eyes. There was a bullet hole in his forehead.

From the hill above they had seen the City's center: a large square surrounded by impressive colonnaded galleries. The two wings of the colonnade radiated from a long gray building with an imposing architrave above its rectangular portal. A row of statues glimmered on top of the building, indistinct white smudges against the gunmetal sky. The building and the colonnade appeared almost untouched by the devastation, though there were delicate twin towers poking from behind the building, and these were scorched.

As they walked, Mara realized how big the building was. Neither the Animal House nor the Temple could hold a candle to it.

Mara felt small and insignificant in the building's massive shadow. It did not care for her; she was just a number, to be disposed of, put in a body bag, and swept away ... And a hot wave of hatred rose in her, so palpable that it made her choke.

I'm not a number; I'm not a piece of garbage.

You treated me like an animal. But animals bite back.

You will pay, all of you.

You took my life. Why should anybody else live?

Dog grasped her hand, pointing to the statues.

She barely looked at them, mesmerized by the building. Used to the decorations of the Animal House, she half expected these to be the same. But now, squinting through the murk, she realized that the statues above the architrave were neither of human beings nor of Ancestors. They were of dogs.

She was reminded of her encounter with a pack of wild dogs in the South. These statues were so realistic that she could see the straining muscles in the dogs' flanks, their hanging tongues, and flattened ears. But as opposed to the South Continent pack that had been composed of different breeds, many of them small and harmless, the statues were uniform: big strapping animals with bared fangs and demented eyes.

She stopped, reminding herself that these were statues. But their stone gazes turned her to stone.

"They're supposed to be free!" Dog cried.

The statues stirred into life. With a creak of tortured masonry, the stone dogs stretched their legs and broke free of the restraining matrix. With a deafening clang of stone, one by one, they jumped down into the square. The ground shook and cobblestones cracked under their weight. The biggest one dropped down on its haunches and barked, and they all followed suit.

Mara fell to her knees, her hands clapped to her ears, but she could not keep out the pitiless hammering sound that drove through her courage and determination, reducing her to a help-less sobbing wreck.

Dogs straining against their leashes, barking at the men, women, and children, herding them as their masters share a laugh and a cigarette ...

"No!" Dog yelled. "Down, you beasties! Don't you make me ashamed of my name!"

He strode forward, arms akimbo, his eyes boring into the eyes of the advancing stone animals. And they stopped, uncertain; the smaller ones dropping their heads in confusion, whimpering. But the big leader of the pack, a giant granite creature, his stone hide the smoky color of the sky, growled. Its carved hackles rose.

Dog walked on at the same unhurried, self-confident pace. And as he advanced, he changed. The sharp, long-nosed face elongated even further, growing into a muzzle. The bald pate sprouted a covering of wiry hair and the prominent ears perked up and grew pointed tips. His tattered clothes split as canine muscles corded over his limbs and a feathery wagging tail fell down between his legs.

The stone dogs growled and barked, perplexed at this development. Some of them retreated, creeping back on their sculpted bellies that scraped the cobblestones and ignited sparks in the frozen air. But the granite leader did not. It barked, its tongue of red sandstone striking against the white marble fangs. And then it launched itself at Dog.

They collided; the stone dog's weight brought Dog down easily. But he was much more agile than the creature and rolled away, freeing himself from the crushing mass of stone. By now other dogs had followed their leader, advancing upon the leaping, dodging adversary, their blunt noses twitching, even though their nostrils were mere indentations in stone.

"Run!" Mr. Dog yelled.

Throwing off her paralysis, Mara sprinted through the melee toward the portal. On her way, she collided with a stone dog and went down. A heavy paw stomped inches away from her head; she inhaled the cold, dead smell of wet masonry and saw the marbles of eyes roll in their sockets.

With an impossible effort, Mr. Dog lifted one of the smaller creatures and hurled it at the dog attacking Mara. Both shattered in an avalanche of stone fragments. She was showered by sharp pieces of stone and felt the warmth of blood on her cut cheek. But it did not matter because she was up and running.

Mara gained shelter from the portal and looked back. The stone dogs gathered in a tight knot, their chiseled rumps wagging as they tore at something in their midst. One of them lifted its head and howled; its muzzle dripped red. And as if in response, the body bags that littered the streets stirred. Those closest to the square ripped open like giant cocoons and something was struggling to emerge from their darkness.

Mara's heart was empty. She looked again at the slavering knot of guard hounds.

"You saved me, after all," she said. "Good boy!"

After turning, she went through the portal into the building itself.

The building was deserted, dusty, and boring. She stood in a foyer lit by an institutional-looking electric chandelier. There were picture frames on the walls, but there were only canvas tatters in the elaborate gilded frames. There were papers strewn about on the floor. She lifted one but could not read it; the letters were unfamiliar. She shivered; the idea that the lost humanity had spoken different languages was strange and disturbing.

There was a grand staircase with carved railings leading to the upper floors. She climbed, her feet tangling in the moldy remnants of the red carpet.

Above was a long landing with a series of identical doors upholstered with imitation leather. She walked along, pushing them open. The offices were empty and dark.

She reached the last door in the row and stopped. It was identical to the rest: the brownish padding held in place by bronze nails; the silly gilded handle. But she knew that this was the end of her journey, the bottom of the dream-sea. There was nowhere to run, walk, or swim; nowhere to hide.

And yet she felt at peace. Here she was, Mara Raven. Everything else had been taken away from her: her lover, her mother, her City. Only she remained, and it would have to suffice.

She turned the handle and pushed the door open.

Instead of an office floor, she stepped out onto a balcony suspended above dizzying space. She remembered the scorched towers behind the gray building. And she realized that the Bear had retreated from the bastion of bureaucracy to establish herself in a temple.

The periphery of her vision swam with the ruined magnificence of this place, pointed arches high above her head, spacious ribbed vaults, graceful, slender pillars and stained-glass windows. The City had never developed an architectural style to rival this breathtaking vertical sweep. But now the vaults were riddled with holes, windows smashed, and pillars broken.

But Mara barely paid attention. She stared up, craning her head to take in the monstrous bulk that occupied most of the interior of this alien temple.

In her previous encounters with the Bear, she had been only slightly bigger than Mara. But now she had fed on the harvest reaped by her servants in the City and had swelled up, grown so big and fat that her head with its living veil of rugous skin was wedged into the high vault, while her naked, obscenely flabby, yellowish bulk spilled from the narrow nave into the side chapels. Her clawed paws were folded in her lap. She stirred when Mara appeared on the balcony, her lard shuddering like jelly. The stench of rot made Mara gag.

The head, longer than Mara was tall, bent toward her, and the veined skin-veil twitched. Mara staggered, buffeted by revulsion and horror, drowned in a wave of self-hatred.

My mother.

My daughter.

Myself.

And at that moment she knew that this abomination was not merely her totem, using her to weaken the barrier that had protected the City from the liquid nightmares of the dream-sea. She was more than that. The Bear had grown from the seed that she had planted. Something she had done; something she had felt in her previous life had been the grain of sand around which the leader of the Four had accreted like a pearl of pus and blood.

Impossible! She is Death, the destroyer of worlds! And I'm just a woman! What could I have done?

But Famine, Pestilence, War, and Death only come when humans call upon them. And she had called, and her call had been heard.

Slowly, the paw the size of a column lifted into the polluted air and Mara knew it was going to crush her. A wave of relief washed over her. If she died, she wouldn't have to see the Bear's face. She wouldn't have to remember.

Julian. Cat. Dog.

They died, so I could bring back the City.

"Show your face!" she screamed at the Bear's towering bulk. "Show your face!"

The paw paused above her.

"I have the right! I must see it!"

And still, the monster hesitated.

"Light Puppies!" Mara cried.

They slid off her outstretched arms like bracelets of light, spinning and growing bigger and brighter, illuminating the dusk. The Bear flinched, causing an avalanche of masonry, but she had nowhere to go. Wedged into the temple, she could only ineffectually wave her claws at the flock of emerald and purple frisky lights that buzzed around her. One of them touched the fleshy veil and it curled and smoldered, swirling tendrils of greasy smoke.

The Bear roared and Mara flinched. But this time there was nobody to shield her. She was alone, and free, and there was no other way but forward.

The Bear roared again. No, it was not a roar: a woman's scream; a cry of pain and despair.

The veil fell off in a cascade of ashes. And Mara looked up, into her own face.

CHAPTER 7. A SUMMER DAY

hey are coming. They have been coming for some time, after the Army retreated. After the dusty-faced boys in torn uniforms were followed, with wailing and sobbing, by the women of the City on their way back into the heartland. After the curt radio announcements. After the terse silence. After the hoarding of food.

And now they are here.

Their alien uniforms. Their guttural speech. Their loud, contemptuous laughter. And the decrees, appearing every day on the walls of the municipal hall.

She reads the decrees and so does her husband. She points out the terrible grammar and the spelling mistakes. See, *she says,* they despise us. They don't even take the trouble to find good translators. Or to speak our language properly. And look who they have appointed as mayor! That drunk, that never-do-well! The traitor!

But her husband only stares at her, and she can no longer read that jowly face. He has gained weight recently. How can that be when they have so little to eat? Her milk is drying out; the baby is screaming day and night.

Is he hoarding food? Is he starving his wife and daughter so he can survive?

She goes to see her mother.

She breathes in the familiar smell of books and suddenly bursts into tears, uncontrollably, frightening the baby who is squalling feebly and kicking against her swaddling clothes; frightening even her little dog who is whimpering and pressing himself against her feet. He does not know her mother's house; she got him after the wedding and because his fur was almost blond, she called him Light Puppy. Now it has darkened, as her own hair has darkened to deep honey since she was fifteen. But even though she is only twenty-two, she found a streak of gray in her hair this morning. It will be ashen soon, *she* thinks.

Her mother's tortoiseshell cat sniffs at the dog and slaps his face lightly with her paw, just to show him who is in charge.

Her mother is holding her, and she burrows into the arms that have comforted her since she was a baby. Neither she nor her brother knows their father—or maybe fathers. Their mother brought them up by working her fingers to the bone. Sometimes they had no money for food. But they always had money for books.

Yet even in her mother's arms, she is still feeling the barrier that has grown between them since her marriage. Her mother was opposed to it, even though her husband is richer than her impoverished family. She used to feel safe and secure under her husband's protec-tion, safe in the knowledge that he loves her and will provide for her. She wants to experience this sense of safety again. But it is gone. She only has herself to rely on. And this makes her resent her mother even more.

They sit at the scratched table and her mother feeds her weak tea and dry bread. The baby is quiet; there is a moment of peace. Until she sees, on the dresser, a picture of her brother. Wearing the uniform of the defeated Army.

"Mama!" she says.

Her mother flares up.

"I won't take it down!" she screams. "They may kill me but I'm

proud of my son! And you, you should be ashamed of yourself! What a coward you are!"

She runs out in tears, clutching the baby, Light Puppy following at her heels. The City where she has lived her entire life is alien; neighbors' eyes are hostile.

At home, she clings to her husband. She would do anything for his approval, protection, and love. But even in bed, she feels him drawing away from her, closing off, his head filled with impenetrable thoughts like gathering thunderclouds.

Next morning, there is a knock on the door. When she opens it, it is her old teacher. Her heart swells with gratitude. She was always his best, most favored student. He encouraged her marriage when her mother opposed it.

She ushers him in, and her husband greets the older man warmly. They sit at the table. But when she wants to join them, her teacher closes the door in her face, and she is left outside, clutching the squalling baby, who, she suddenly realizes, is the ball and chain holding her in this death trap. She could have run away. She could have joined the Army. But she could not abandon her daughter.

Could she?

Next morning, her husband rouses her early.

"Take the baby," he tells her.

She wants to ask him: Are they running away? Are they going to seek out the Army? Are they going to find her brother?

But she does not. She knows the answer.

Outside, she sees the heavy bulk of her teacher leaning against the wall. He does not look well; his heavy face is jaundiced; his hands are shaking.

He is sick, *she realizes.* He has always been sick. With cowardice, selfishness, and fear.

Who is worse than a teacher who betrays his student?

Only a husband who betrays his wife. A father who betrays his child.

She cradles the baby to her breast but there is no tenderness in her. There is nothing but icy hatred.

As they go down the street, Light Puppy runs after her. Her husband aims a kick at the dog but then stops.

"Let him come too, why not?" he says with a sickly smile.

They are out in the street, and she sees soldiers with spidery insignias on their black uniforms herding people. Their giant slavering dogs are barking. Light Puppy trembles and clings to her.

When they pass a narrow alleyway, she darts into it. She is fast; she can escape.

A heavy hand closes on her arm as her teacher drags her back into what has become a column of shambling, defeated men, women, and children.

She still refuses to believe they are going where she knows they are going until she sees the municipal square thronged with people. She tries to find familiar faces, but the City is big. And even if there are some of her former classmates or friends, they all look like strangers. She is going to die alone.

Her husband and her teacher push her toward the crowd of people, surrounded by black uniforms and barking dogs. And at this moment, everything that has been her is gone. Nothing remains but a hollow shell, slowly being filled with the black water of hatred.

She spits in her husband's face.

A spider-decorated officer steps forward.

"What's going on?" he asks. And when the man who was her husband explains, obsequiously, the officer looks at her. It is strange to realize that he is human. A young man. A beautiful young man. She stares at his face because she knows she will never see anything beautiful again.

The moment passes. The officer shrugs.

"Okay," he says not trying to disguise his contempt, "bring her in and sign there. You'll be rewarded."

The baby wrapped in her shawl wakes up and whimpers.

The officer pauses.

"Is there a child?" he asks her husband incredulously. "Your child?"

"No child of mine," he mutters. The officer shrugs and shoves some ration cards and a handful of banknotes into his hand. As her husband walks away, she sees him share the money with her teacher.

She joins the other people in the square. Soldiers with dogs shove and beat them into forming a column. The column slowly inches its way toward the gaping door of the municipality building. Beyond the door is darkness. She hears dull thuds and an occasional muffled cry.

She shambles forward, and she knows that her life is only as long as the walk to that door.

There are several men waiting by the door, laughing and smoking. They are City people, not invaders. She recognizes one of them: He was her classmate.

The soldiers tell the people to undress and fold their clothes by the door. Naked as the day they were born, men, women, and children walk into the dark maw. Nobody comes out.

And now it is her turn. The pavement is covered with piles of clothes and torn papers. She can see into the building.

Two men are standing by the door with heavy clubs in their hands. The clubs are rising and falling rhythmically like drumsticks, only pausing to shake off excessive blood and brain matter. Beyond them, there is a growing pile of worm-pale bodies, stained with dark streaks. A rivulet of blood crawls across the threshold. A couple of soldiers with their guns drawn are watching the procedure but do not interfere until one of them shoots into the squirming pile to finish off a struggling old man.

She is frozen. The man who was her classmate yells at her to start moving.

Light Puppy is still with her. The man's voice makes him bare his teeth and snap at him. The man crushes the small dog's head with his boot.

Whatever is left of her is dead and something else moves inside the cocoon of her body. Something born of fear, hatred, and betrayal.

She removes her clothes. The baby is naked at her breast. She thinks that she might try to hide her under the pile, so perhaps one of the soldiers will find her and take pity on her and give her to another family to raise. But there is no love for the child left in her. She is her husband's get. She deserves to die.

But there is still one last thing to do. She is wearing a locket with a picture of her family inside. Her mother, her brother, and herself. All smiling and happy. She takes it off, dips her finger in the blood pooling by her feet, and writes: Brother, avenge us! *And then she gives the locket to her classmate.*

"When they come back," she says, "give it to my brother. This is the only way to save your miserable hide when our Army is back."

He is staring at her with dread, and she hears in her voice the cold power of the thing that is stirring inside her, the power that no man can deny.

She walks toward the threshold. Ahead, she sees the back of an older woman, thin and stringy, cradling a cat in her thin arms. She recognizes her mother. But she makes no effort to catch up with her and watches coldly as a man clubs her on the head and shoves her down, upon the moving, bloodied pile.

And now it's her turn. But poised at the entrance to the death chamber, her perception suddenly flares up, encompassing the past, and the future, and what might have been, arching over time and dream-time.

She sees her brother come back, and her classmate who cannot forget the eyes of the woman brought to the killing ground by her husband gives him the locket. She sees her brother, maddened by fury and revenge, shoot at random at POWs and passersby until he is taken down.

She sees her teacher prosper and grow fat on the gains of his betrayal until, tormented by the memory of his student who he had been secretly in love with, he is felled by a stroke.

She sees her husband marry another woman, have another daughter, and kill both of them for their inheritance.

She sees history unfolding as a pageant of misery and terror. She sees the human imagination conjuring up the dreaded Four who hold sway over mankind: Hunger, Pestilence, War, and Death. And in the dream-sea where nightmares become flesh, the Four congeal around one of the countless stories of horror that seep into and contaminate the waters of creation.

She sees her husband, consumed with greed, become Hunger. She sees her teacher, infected with cowardice and dark desires, become Pestilence. She sees her avenging brother become War that starts for all the right reasons and then consumes everything in its path.

And she sees herself become Death whose face no one can see because there is nothing in that face but emptiness.

And then she sees humanity destroyed and the dream-sea resurrecting its creators by imposing their form upon animals. And these new humans are doomed to replay the stories of their prototypes, paying for old sins by committing new ones.

CHAPTER 8. A NEW STORY

Mara woke on the beach. Cool mint waves licked her toes. She opened her eyes into the sky the color of mother-of-pearl.

She twisted around, enjoying the feel of the clean white sand on her skin. Dense dark green shrubs formed a wall around the cove where she was lying. A rosy shellfish shaped like a flower burrowed into the sand.

Mara got to her feet, stretched the kinks out of her body. There were pale scars on her arms and legs, but they did not hurt anymore. The dream-sea had healed her.

It had also washed her clean; she smelled of brine, not blood, or rot, or smoke. Her tattered gown had disappeared.

She stood up to her ankles in the water, looking at the sharp horizon where the emerald of the sea met the iridescence of the sky. The last woman in the world.

For she knew, felt it in her bones, that First City was gone, absorbed back into the dream-sea, its inhabitants turned small furtive animals once again, unburdened by memory and sorrow.

"And this is how it should be," she said aloud, feeling the

weight of her words drop into the expectant hush of the beach. "Humans do not deserve to live."

But it was as if the sound of her words defied their meaning. What would the world be without speech? Without grief and guilt but also without stories? Would the dream-sea survive?

She addressed the invisible intelligences, beyond the malevolence of the Four, which she knew existed somewhere in the sea of dreams and memories, hidden from her.

"Bring back the City," she said. "Bring back humanity. We'll do better next time. I promise."

How hollow could a promise be? Humanity had been given so many chances and squandered them all.

But they had defeated the Four, hadn't they? Mr. Dog, and Alice D. Cat, and Julian Sparrow, and ...

But had they, really?

She had looked into the face of the Bear; she had learned her story, which was also her own story, and she had survived the knowledge of the abyss. Isn't this all it takes to defeat Death: survival?

She knew it was not.

Her friends had sacrificed themselves to rewrite the dismal story of the Four's origin. And she alone survived because she had done nothing. She had grieved and remembered but what use was that to the future? The future was created by action: Alice launching herself at a bigger adversary; Mr. Dog standing up to the stone canines; Julian mastering his own rage to fight the Lion. Who cared why they did it? They did it and it was all that mattered.

Mara launched herself into the sea.

The cold peppery water shot up her nostrils, burning her air passages, and washed into her eyes, blinding them. It flowed inside her and the sensation made her cringe. But she persevered, painfully imitating her former joyous freedom of swimming, and after a while, imitation became almost as good as the real thing.

She swam above the ribbed sand and was surprised and dismayed to see it empty. No gorgeous and nightmarish marine life; no eager dreamfish; not even the transparent bottom-feeders that had helped her before. It was as if this portion of the dream-sea had become a dead zone. Could it be that without the constant influx of the human imagination the sea was already being depleted?

She knew she had to have a bait but her memory of how she had done it before, while dreamfishing, was hazy. Swimming above the empty sand, as empty as her hands and her heart ...

And yet she pushed, rooting inside herself, dragging out useless scraps of memory and regret. And then she was clutching something in her hand. Something small.

She looked at it. It was a pendant, a cheap pewter oval with two stick figures holding hands. The symbol of the Humanist Party, worn by radical young things: students, and poets, and waitresses.

She smiled. The City, all that was left of the City, was now lying in her palm. She stretched her hand, offering the bait to the sea, asking the question.

How can I bring it back?

And the dreamfish was suddenly there, the same creature that had, so long ago, answered her inquiry into Elvira Sparrow's death. An eye-fish, with an enormous human eye in its face that blinked and swallowed the bait. And then the fish turned and raced through the darkening water and Mara gave chase, knowing in her heart that it was not going to end with the capture of her quarry. This time there would be no awakening unless she brought back the world she could awaken into.

The eye-fish suddenly stopped, floating above an abrupt fall in the seabed. Mara approached and peered into the abyss.

Below the water gathered into a giant convex lens. And through it, distorted and foreshortened, she could see a lit-up tableau like one of the dioramas in the City's Natural History

Museum. A knot of human figures gathered in a plaza before a building.

To go back there? Impossible!

The fish turned to stare at her, its single eye pitiless and inquisitive like the eye of a vivisectionist.

"No!" Mara cried. "I was there! I saw it! I confronted it!"

And did what?

Nothing.

The story was still there, the grain of sand preserved in the darkest pearl of the dream-sea. And as long as it was unchanged, the Bear still lived. Mara felt her presence in her own bones, like a subliminal ache growing stronger by the moment.

How long till she calls upon you?

"But what can I do? It happened. It was. I cannot change the past!"

But you can change the story.

Suspended in the green water, Mara and the fish floated together above the lens. And then Mara stretched her arms and dove into the abyss.

She is frozen. A man yells at her to move it. She recognizes him: They were in school together.

Light Puppy bares his teeth at the man. He lifts his club. She scoops up the small dog and hurls it away from her, away from the blood-splattered plaza. The puppy lands on his feet and stares at her uncertainly.

"Go!" she screams, and it lopes away, disappearing into an alley.

She looks her classmate in the face, and he looks away.

She takes off her clothing. The baby is whimpering at her breast. She squeezes the last drops of milk into her tiny mouth, and the baby falls silent. She kisses her and piles clothes loosely on top of her.

She takes off her locket and writes on her family photograph in blood, Brother, find and raise my daughter. I love you.

She meets her classmate's shamefaced gaze again.

"I didn't want to come," he mumbles. "They forced me."

She shoves the locket into his hand.

"When my brother comes back with our Army," she says, "give him this. This is the only chance you have to save your miserable hide."

He nods and puts the locket away. The pile of clothes moves slightly. He pretends not to notice and positions himself between it and the officer who has walked away from the slaughter to smoke a cigarette.

She sees the thin, stringy back of an older woman ahead. The woman releases a tortoiseshell cat who slinks away from the killing ground.

"Mama!" she cries and runs to her.

They embrace and walk to the threshold, mother and daughter together.

CHAPTER 9. THE THIRD CITY

She crawled from under the pile of corpses at night and crept through the blood-splattered streets. She drank water from the puddles and chewed leaves from the trees.

And then she pierced a thin membrane like a soap bubble and swam through the warm, dark water silvered with moonlight refractions.

Did it really happen? She could never know but she doubted it. The woman whose memory Mara inherited had probably died in that building. Perhaps her daughter had survived but it was by no means certain. The classmate might have had a moment of contrition, might have saved the baby, and even raised her as his own. Such things happened. But it was equally probable that she suffocated under the clothes or was discovered by one of the soldiers and killed, her head smashed with a club. Such things happened, too.

But the story had been changed. There was hope at the end, and love, and forgiveness. The brother might have lived; might have come back; might have found his niece. And the mother did not die alone.

The story had been changed and now the two of them,

brother and sister in one life, lovers in another, were free of it. She was no longer an avatar of Death; he had shed the burden of War. But the two others still swam in the liquid dreams of the sea. Hunger and Pestilence, still carrying, deep inside, the memories of treachery and cruelty. And since the story could not be erased but only changed, they would find each other again and attract others of their kind.

"I don't care," Mara said to the softly splashing water. "I fulfilled my part of the bargain. Now it's your turn."

The water was silent, warm and velvety-smooth. And only then did she realize that it was lit by the moon.

Mara surfaced, gulping the warm air, scented with a profusion of strange, intoxicating smells: flowers and spices. The moon was full and low; the sky pearled with the first light of false dawn. Against the horizon hunched the peaked silhouette of a large, mountainous island. And massed against its waterline, scattered around its peaks, were the tallest buildings Mara had ever seen; vertiginous and slender, festooned with bright, multicolored lights that reflected in the oily water of the bay. A graceful, suspended bridge, longer than her mind could accept, linked the big island with a smaller one, equally dotted with gaudy, sparkling, eager lights that outshone the moon.

A new City was waking up.

Cleaving the dark water, Mara swam toward it.

ABOUT THE AUTHOR

Born in Ukraine and currently residing in California, Elana Gomel is an academic with a long list of books and articles, an award-winning writer, and a professional nomad. She has taught and researched in Israel, Italy, and the US, and is known in the academy for her (purely theoretical) interest in serial killers, alien invasions, and rebellious AIs. She is the author of more than a hundred stories, several novellas, and six novels of dark fantasy and science fiction. Her latest fiction publications are the dark fairy tale *Nightwood* and *Girl of Light*, a historical fantasy.

JOIN OUR NEWSLETTER

If you enjoyed this book, keep up on all our upcoming releases from Elana Gomel and authors like her. Join the Epic News List at www.epic-publishing.com/subscribe.

EXCERPT FROM RABBIT IN THE MOON
BY FIONA MOORE

Chapter One: Rabbit Season

KEN USAGI, CROUCHED at the prow of the low flat boat in the mangrove swamps of upstate New York, saw it first. A flicker of something off-white between the twilight trees, not a bird, not one of the horrible oatmeal-coloured giant squirrels (they'd had to shoot another last night and it had fallen into the camp chirping and twitching; nobody had dared even suggest that they should do the sensible thing and skin it and cook it). An enemy sniper? Despite his lack of field experience, Ken knew better. He crouched lower, willing it to show itself. He knew he should feel afraid, yet the comforting familiarity of the swamps, evoking early childhood memories of riding the poling boats through the tropical Toronto causeways, kept the adrenaline from coursing.

The adrenaline had been coursing the night he ran all the way out to the tundra, the sound of his Gore-Tex trouser legs squeaking against each other as they scissored over snowy hills, thick tread boots crunching the Nunavut late-winter snow. He had come out there before, mostly to escape the bigger children who always seemed to find him, saying *swamp-boy, refugee*, and other things he couldn't repeat to his worn-looking parents, but he had never run so hard as when he had that *thing* after him.

~

"Storm coming," Al said idly to Ken, his right hand on the outboard in the stern, keeping the boat on course as he cradled a pistol with his left.

Captain Manders slowly turned his leathery face, with the remains of a slightly fey handsomeness, and slit his pale eyes meaningfully at the Black youth. Al raised an eyebrow at the rebuke.

"Come on, sir, if there were Reds in this neck of the woods we'd know by now," the young man protested. "Just trying to make conversation."

"Trouble can come from anywhere," Manders retorted. Again, Ken wondered at the peculiar accent. The Seaboard States, with their dwindling population, battling their neighbours on one front and the environment on the other, were more than happy to accept volunteers, mercenaries really, from Texas, West-coast, or even Europe, but it was unusual to see one in charge of native-born Seaboarders.

"Ah, you're seeing Reds under the bed again, sir," Al replied. Then again, perhaps Al wasn't a native-born Seaboarder himself. He sounded like one to Ken but come to think of it, he'd never told Ken exactly where he was from.

"Mind the tiller, private," Manders said with finality, and Al quieted down with a slight pout on his post-adolescent face.

~

That day he had gone out to the snow-heaps at the edge of the town, where the industrial-scale hydroponic agrotech plantations loomed, to be alone, hating the Inuit children with their funny language he could never learn. He missed the hot swamps of his hometown, the threadbare stuffed rabbit he'd lost in the rush out of the South, sinking beneath the waves in the wake of the over-crowded commandeered ferryboat, *never mind, Kennie, you're a big boy now*, brooding, conjuring up armies from the South, from the fierce Red States that kept threatening war with the Seaboard or Westcoast, drawing up battle plans with pebbles and discarded bottle bits. Something bigger than him, bigger than the Inuit boys, bigger even than the teachers who kept telling him it was up to him to stop complaining and fit in.

Looking up, he froze. He saw a rabbit, white for winter, hopping along urgently. Behind it was a raven, hopping in front of it was another raven. They were driving it on, herding it, chasing it with their wings every time it tried to break away. He did not think they meant that rabbit well. Ken ran at the group-ing, yelling, scattering ravens and rabbit alike, hoping the rabbit would understand later that he'd saved its life.

"Do you see something?" Manders joined Ken in the prow of the boat, moving in that silent way he had.

Ken indicated the jungle. "Not sure if it's an animal or a sniper."

"If it was a sniper, we'd know by now," Manders said. "What did it look like?"

"Just a bit of white, something following the boat through the jungle."

"Keep a lookout," Manders said. "We're due at the Detroit Front by tomorrow night, so I don't want to waste time chasing phantoms. But if it is something, I'd like to know about it."

~

Ken's parents, hearing his stammered-out story later, said it must have been old Nick Fivefingers, the local tramp, in a Hallowe'en mask. The police chief who took Ken's statement the next day put it down to a recent screening of the *Star Wars* prequels and an overactive imagination, and warned his parents gravely against too much General Grievous. But Ken knew what had chased him for three kilometres through the snow, bursting ptarmigan-like out of the drift in a flurry of black and white bones and ragged fur and feathers, bigger than a grownup, bigger than a bear, then running, running before he found himself falling, bright light and rush of stinking air and he was lying on his back in a heap of melted snow with nothing to prove to parents, police chief or, later on, worried school guidance counsellors, that it had ever been there.

~

Ken felt that animal being-watched instinct, before he even saw it again, flickering through the trees. A cold shiver started at the top of his scalp and ran down his neck (where his hair had been pulled back in a tight sweat-resistant ponytail; barbers were scarce in the swamplands, and he didn't have the courage to shave his head like Al did or hack it off raggedly like Manders).

"Did you see that, sir?" Al said, before Ken could even open his mouth.

"Yes, I did." Manders shifted position in the boat, adjusting to a kind of down-on-one-knee pose. But for the accent, the semiautomatic shotgun and the combat gear, he might have been Daniel Boone, all stubbly beard and farmer's tan, scouting through the primeval wilderness of America. "Get down, Usagi, last thing we need is another inquiry into the death of an idiot journo."

Ken obeyed, but dug in his bag for his binoculars. He had to see it, to know for sure that it was what he thought it was.

In a way, the spirit or imaginary monster or Nick Fivefingers with too much whiskey incident had some kind of cathartic effect. Although the local children still teased him, particularly Steve Tulugaq, the police chief's son, who knew how to jimmy the lock on the filing cabinet where his father kept transcripts and statements, it didn't seem as important anymore, and his lack of caring eventually caused them to start leaving him alone. As he began working out, joined the school hockey team and got grades good enough to mark him out as someone who could be asked for revision advice, though fortunately not good enough to mark him out as an incurable nerd, he began getting on with the others. Even if, occasionally, in moments of boredom, he would doodle the creature's bony, beaky, bucktoothed face on random pieces of paper, in school, at university as he drifted through a major in English and journalism followed by an interminable internship at globeandmail.com, and out into the adult world.

A few minutes later, Ken saw it for certain. Just for a minute, but he recognised that bony face, that skinny frame, which could, admittedly, have passed for scrawny old Nick Fivefingers (now long-dead of exposure) albeit in a Hallowe'en mask of a kind the general store never sold.

"Got it!" he hissed.

"Thought I told you to stay down," Manders said absently, holding out a hand for the binoculars. "Hm, yes," he said. "Funny-looking thing, isn't it?"

"Will-o'-the-wisp," Al remarked.

"What?" Ken said.

"Will-o'-the-wisp," the young man repeated. "Don't you know? A kind of spirit, you see it out in the swamps. It pulls people off course, out into the treacherous parts where you drown."

"Swamp gas," Manders said dismissively.

"Isn't," Ken heard himself saying. "Al's not entirely wrong, captain."

~

"Kennie, why?" his mother asked. "You can surely aim higher than Iqaluit Online News. The salary's less than *half* what that environment zine was offering you, and you *know* there's no future in online media…"

"I want to go South," Ken had said, resisting anger at her use of the nickname. It wasn't her fault, just too many memories of what had happened when the other kids found out what his mother called him. She was right about the online media—as pads became harder to get, fewer people read the dotcoms—but job security could wait.

"Let him go," his father said. "It's just nostalgia. Misplaced memories of Toronto. When he's done making his macho gesture and found out there's nothing South but fish and Americans, he'll come back."

"What if he takes a bullet before that happens?" his mother mourned. But Ken's father was wrong. He no longer wanted to go back to Toronto; he knew it would be nothing but swamp now, and he wanted the ethereal green place of his earliest memories to remain inviolate. But something was driving him South, to the place where armies fought over the bare remains of the increasingly scarce fertile land, and away from that godforsaken place of snow half the year and dust the other half, of decaying polar ice and ravens and rabbits and diminishing marine life statistics, slightly hysterical assertions that the hydroponic systems and the much shorter winters would make Nunavut the agricultural saviour of the world, the last of humanity fading out against the surging ecosystem. He thought, *Better to be eaten by bears than nibbled away by rabbits.*

[…]

To get your copy of *Rabbit in the Moon*, visit your favorite bookstore or visit Epic Publishing's book page (www.epic-publishing.com/books).

www.ingramcontent.com/pod-product-compliance
Lightning Source LLC
Chambersburg PA
CBHW010646100726
47901CB00009B/2457